MAVIS CHEEK

Amenable Women

faber and faber

First published in 2008
by Faber and Faber Limited
3 Queen Square London WC1N 3AU

Typeset by Faber and Faber Limited
Printed in England by Mackays of Chatham, plc

A CIP record for this book
is available from the British Library

ISBN 978-0-571-23894-1

2 4 6 8 10 9 7 5 3 1

For Kate and Rachel, Faber's finest

Everybody praises the lady's beauty, both of face and body. One said she excelled the Duchess as the golden sun did the silver moon . . .

Christopher Mount, English envoy to Cleves, 1539, describing Anne of Cleves

King Henry has sent a painter, who is very excellent in his art, to Germany, to take a portrait to the life, of the sister of the duke of Cleves . . . Today it arrived . . . The face of the young lady appeared sufficiently lovely to decide Henry on accepting her . . .

Charles de Marillac, French Ambassador to the Court of Henry VIII, 1539

My Lord, if it were not to satisfy the world, and my realm, I would not do that which I must do this day for none earthly thing.

Henry VIII on the morning of his wedding to Anne of Cleves, 6 January 1540

Her frame was large bony and masculine and her large, low-German features, deeply pitted with the ravages of smallpox were the very opposite of the type of beauty which would be likely to stimulate a gross, unwholesome voluptuary of nearly fifty . . .

M. Hume, *The Wives of Henry VIII*, 1905

PART ONE

If you're married your husband bosses you and if you aren't married people call you an Old Maid. Oh! To be a widow . . .

Lucy M. Montgomery, *Anne of the Island*, 1915

I

Death Duties

At Edward Chapman's funeral Flora thought that she might, after all, be made mad by the death of her husband. She did not feel mad. Indeed, she felt quite normal, quite sane, quite calm – and even a little hungry. All of which were quite wrong and could justifiably be considered unbalanced. She had not expected widowhood (if she had thought at all about it) to contain this sense of setting out on a new adventure. Clearly these were not appropriate thoughts for a new-made widow of some considerable marital longevity. But yet – there she stood – at the graveside – monstrous ice-queen – and found herself speculating – not about her husband so soon to lie there and her loss of him – but about the other ancient one-time occupant of the grave (for graveyard space was at a premium nowadays) – and even more inappropriately having a very terrible desire to laugh at the thought that it might be a bygone woman upon whom her husband was soon to be laid.

History always intrigued her but Edward claimed it as his show and in a way he was right. Once married she did nothing with her interest. Lazily, maybe obstinately, she let Edward tinker around with the mysteries of the past and tinker he did. But now she was free to speculate – to herself if not out loud – and know that whatever she thought, whatever she suggested, would not be scooped up and taken over by one who considered himself something between the new Gibbon and that lovely young man on the television who knew his history, brought the sparkle of imagination to his history, and wore extremely tight blue jeans.

Edward was many things but – quite frankly – and she could be frank even at his graveside – he was not imaginative – except where his own existence was concerned. Why, were he alive now and at her side and she were to turn to him and say, 'Edward, I wonder who was in the grave before you?' he would say, 'Hmm. I'll have a think about that. Leave it with me.' Some weeks later, if his research were successful, he would tell her the name, rank, number. If it was not it would go no further. She preferred to speculate. Without Edward to complain about her meanderings she freely indulged them.

A graceless world it was now. After the Thatcher years of eighties greed, the sleazy nineties, now in the 'noughties' it was the turn of expediency over sensitivity. Graves being doubled up. Who would have thought it? New bones laid on old. It was the modern, ecologically sound way, so the local newspaper said. In villages and towns all over the country, old bones were making space for new bones in the dearth of new space for graves, memorial stones cast aside, and people who were once loved and cherished were forgotten. To be forgotten must be the saddest of things, she thought. Edward never would be, that was one certainty. It would be his headstone that took precedence now and whoever shared the plot would be relegated. Edward's way. She wondered, yet again, what on earth she should write on the headstone when she ordered it – very unlike him to overlook any instructions. About the only thing in this whole funeral that he'd overlooked. Flora smiled at the possibility of choosing something that was a little – well – double-edged. Mad indeed, but an amusing thought.

At least he was not here to complain about sharing a plot with a stranger. Dashing, still-handsome-at-fifty-six Edward would just have to lump it. All she knew was that the present incumbent was interred at least forty years ago, for that was the Parish's rule. Given that the world of death was becoming too full for undisturbed rest, sooner or later you got a roommate and Flora felt really sorry for whoever was Edward's. He or she would enjoy their peace and solitude no longer with

Edward lying on top of them, or to the side of them, for the rest of eternity. He'd soon be measuring out the space and making sure that he had his correct portion. Very fair, Edward.

Flora knew she was smiling. Quite unacceptably. What Flora was thinking, even more guiltily, was that it would make things down there very lively if the other occupant turned out to be a deceased member of the Socialist Workers Party or an Animal Rights activist or any other kind of militant. She hoped whoever it was could give as good as they got. Edward was never one to listen to the other side of an argument and it would do him no harm at all to have to do so for the rest of eternity. He'd planted a salmon-pink rose up against a terra-cotta-coloured wall against her pleadings, and he had voted for a brick-orange-faced reactionary in the last election on the grounds, she knew, of the unspoken hope he would Keep The Countryside White. 'Why?' she wanted to know, to which he only said, 'But me no buts and pass the cheese. It's the British way of life that's at stake here.' She had quietly remembered shops shutting at midday on Saturdays and the only exotic restaurants available being the Spaghetti Houses – and said nothing. Edward loved a nice curry now and then and never seemed to see the anomaly.

Flora always butted him no buts and passed the cheese, and silently hoped that when the Dobsons of Duck Cottage went off to Canada for a year and let their home they would let it to a family of Caribbean or Indian or African descent who had – *en masse* for preference – been to Oxbridge, who rode to hounds and who drove a four-by-four in just as aggressive a way as the rest of the villagers while wearing the latest Barbour, and who liked a pint at the local. That'd liven the place up. She swallowed a laugh at the irony of it all when she remembered thinking that it might liven the place up but that it would probably kill Edward. Now she would never know how he would respond to having his prejudices confronted. His own hubris got him first. She clucked out loud and hoped

7

no one grouped around the graveside had noticed. With a bit of luck they would think it was the rising sob of grief.

Such thoughts came without warning and they stayed. She tried to pull herself together by telling herself severely that she deserved to fall right down into the hole beside him for the monstrosity of it. She was his widow, for heaven's sake. She should weep. What she was actually thinking, rather self-pityingly, was that when her time came and they were all grouped around the hole in the ground, about the only thing they would have to say of her was that she was once that gorgeous Edward Chapman's wife and she could do lovely sewing, or used to. Talk about damning with faint praise. Her funeral and its orations would be over very quickly. Contemplating that was enough to make her join Edward down in his funeral bunker right now. Stitchery and marriage and retirement from teaching hardly had a sense of dash about it. And whose fault was that but her own? She allowed her face to crumple into a suitably gloomy expression as she contemplated the virtues of featherstitch and French pleats over Edward's more exciting public pursuits. It was a long time since she had used her dressmaking skills. What was the point if you were background – and plain background at that?

To be on the safe side in case the urge to hurl herself into the hole became too strong, Flora moved back a little and trod on a mourner's toes. The mourner squeaked. Flora did not look because she thought she might – oh please no – giggle. Funerals, like no other gatherings, put you right on the edge of madness. Whenever a crowd is gathered together on best behaviour and in solemn contemplation of something or other, the urge to laugh becomes acute. Capricious devils were always in attendance trying to make the solemn skittish. Try as she might, and she tried, and she *had* tried, she could not concentrate on the proceedings in any mournful way. Thoughts of possibilities came gaily into her mind as she attempted to look

8

up (or down) soulfully and keep her hands clasped in proper bereaved Madonna fashion.

Unfortunately – apart from its inappropriateness now – Flora had a smiling kind of face anyway. Looking suitably solemn was well nigh impossible. Her usual jovial countenance had been called imbecilic in the days when schoolteachers could say such things and not be sued. Once, at school, a piece of chalk was thrown at her when the death of Buddy Holly was announced to the class in broken tones by Miss Appleby and seven-year-old Flora appeared to take it rather well. Smilingly well. At that age it was all confusion, anyway, since the Church of England told you all the time that, thanks to Jesus, you need have no fear about dying and you could positively welcome it. But then, when someone called Buddy Holly died, you were supposed to cry. Or get hit with a bit of chalk because Miss Appleby was crying. A real muddle. Even more of a muddle when she saw a picture of this sainted dead person because he wore glasses and strangely shaped jumpers and didn't look like anything special. And his songs, to Flora's unaccustomed ear, sounded as if he was coughing.

But the chalk incident taught her very early that her face was plain, cheerful at best and if she ever needed to be solemn she must work at it. Nevertheless, here, at her own husband's interment, when the eyes of their world were upon her, she had expected better of herself. It was quite unacceptable. It did not bear thinking about. And it certainly did not bear smiling about. Concentrate, concentrate, concentrate . . . Except she immediately remembered W. C. Fields's sour statement that you should 'Start off every day with a smile and get it over with . . .' Which only made the desire to beam out broadly at the world worse. And why was W. C. Fields of all people roaming around her head? A diverting thought and nothing to do with grief . . .

Others were behaving correctly. To her side she could feel the shaking of her daughter Hilary's shoulders as she sobbed properly and dutifully and truthfully into her handkerchief. It was right and seemly that one of them should be seen to grieve. She envied her daughter the simplicity of those tears and wished she could do the same. But Flora was in much too complicated a frame of mind – too full of oddly unconnected thoughts – too little sadness and too much detachment – to cry. Still, Hilary was making up for both of them. In a minute or two she'd be wringing out her handkerchief and making a puddle with it. One of her father's handkerchiefs, actually, Flora could see the embossed E in the corner. Handkerchiefs . . . That made her mind slip easily into the problem of Edward's possessions; of course these would have to be disposed of. Hilary had already taken what she wanted, which, despite the sobs and sorrowing, was not a lot – mostly trinkets and things she had bought him over the years (ah – his horn shoe trees, I'll have those back – and the ivory back scratcher). If only he had been an Anglo-Saxon King Flora could have put all that remained in the grave there with him. What a sensible idea that was. No lingering moments with his favourite jacket or his face flannel. In they could go with good conscience. Of course, this would mean that by now the entire British Isles would be one huge graveyard since even Edward – not a man of huge possessions (quality rather than quantity, Flora) – would, if you included his *Encyclopaedia Britannica*, and Flora most certainly would include it, have filled a hole the size of a small tank. Her eyes refocused on the hole in the ground. For a moment she was back where she should properly be – with the hole, the coffin and bereavement. Alas, not in the right spirit of the thing and not for long.

As soon as Giles Baldwin (their local wine merchant – or vintner as he and Edward referred to him – in whose village restaurant Edward had invested a considerable sum, and lost it) began speaking about her husband's many talents – magnificent friend, wonderful husband, marvellous father, brilliant raconteur (if you hadn't heard the raconteuring sixty times already), terrific countryman, could sniff a good claret at forty paces, could do the *Times* crossword in twenty minutes (he could not, he took days sometimes, with the back pages of the paper removed from its main body and tucked under a cushion – not to be consulted until the last square was filled – Flora was always rather touched that he never could bring himself to cheat and check the answers), could jive like a teenager (once and once only at the village fete when he went in for a competition, did not win, and lay moaning at home for two days afterwards), could paint like Turner (Edward would have a fit, he was crushingly dismissive of what he called 'those splodges and misty bits' and liked to see every leaf on every tree) and was the best chum a man could have (to the tune of all his marital savings) – her mind roved free again. For, in short, her husband was – had been – someone of simple prejudice, self-belief and immense focus, who saw himself as a great man of towering intellect and ineluctable truths – one who rode through life on a charger of princely accoutrement, who was loved by men, adored by women and who, though often wrong, was never in doubt. How could she possibly not grieve for all that? Easily. Apparently.

Edward even had the ear of the local aristocracy – from whom – as Edward liked to say – he drew his shilling. And it was scarcely more than that. There, right at the edge of the assembled mourners, stood Foot. Foot was, if asked, a gentleman's gentleman. He was gentleman's gentleman to Edward's boss, Sir Randolph Heron (whom Foot would call his Master) and proud to be so – though Flora enjoyed referring to him as the Odd-Job Man up at the Hall whenever she got the opportunity. Edward always corrected her. What she called obsequiousness he called having a respect for tradition. Personally she thought that the marriage of Edward's respect and tradition was the union that kept little boys up chimneys and little girls yellow with sulphur but she held her tongue. By then, sadly, Edward had stopped being able to laugh at his pomposities. Handsome men are seldom called to account. Much is forgiven beauty and good looks. As Edward said cheerfully as their daughter grew and blossomed: 'Thank God her looks came from me . . .'

It was Edward's accession to the post of Estate Manager to the Heron family that encouraged his view of himself as Renaissance Man, gave him the opportunity to indulge the idea in many peculiar forms, and changed their marriage for ever. Flora shuddered at the graveside even now to recall the moment he used the phrase of himself. When she commented that Sir Randolph Heron did some very odd things in the name of being anciently lineaged (not least attempting a touch of *droit de seigneur* on Mrs Graves's daughter, which was neatly hushed up by Foot with a small reduction in their rent and referred to by the village as Sir Randolph's little enthusiasms), Edward pointed out that for his employer, as for himself, the important thing was to question, to look for new inventions, to assert and emancipate the human intellect and to revive the brilliance of the past. 'In short,' he said, and he gave her a little bow as if he had, at any rate, revived the courtesies of a bygone age – '. . . in short, we must uphold the tenets of Renaissance Man – or in Sir Randolph's case, the tenets of Renaissance Princes . . .' At which she had barely stopped herself from curtsying and falling over with laughter, and said nothing.

Unfortunately Sir Randolph was that item peculiar and highly seductive to the British who prefer to ignore their more sober and wise blue-bloods – a wealthy, well-bred eccentric. He had spotted similar traits of eccentricity in Edward and he encouraged them. The snob in Edward surfaced and within a year of employment Flora's fairly ordinary husband took flight never to return. Such is the power of feudal ascendancy. Such is the power of tradition and respect. Such is the snob. It did not help that Edward enjoyed saying – or as he put it 'dined out on' the fact that Flora was the only woman over eighteen in the village that Sir Randolph had not propositioned. This might be out of respect for his estate manager, of course, but it was most likely to do with something much more prosaic:

Flora's appearance. How very amusing. Flora's sense of herself grew even duller. She could not even summon enough enthusiasm on the part of an ageing and half-blind nobleman to be goosed. Nor to smack her husband round the face for such cruel audacity. In short – Flora went with the flow. Flora – in short – was – at that point – still in love with him.

Edward admired Sir Randolph's experiments with unspeakably silly things and had a go. His first essay into sterling deeds was his attempt to break horses whereupon he nearly killed himself. Looking back now she realised this was good practice for the final outcome of his life. He then went on to attempt the elaborate chasing of expensive silver goblets with a coat of arms he had invented for himself. This comprised two partridges, a sprig of hawthorn and dog to denote his countryside connections. Flora – who was very quietly reading a book on country lore and related matters at the time – for the sheer pleasure of removing herself from the here and now – pointed out that partridges were part of Athena's rituals, that hawthorn served as the female phallic symbol surrounding the Maypole and that dogs – little innocent-seeming mutts – apart from their connection with goddesses and witches – were the mascot of the Dominican Order. Edward's view of Catholics was dark and rooted somewhere around 1555 and the Marian purges and Flora was rewarded with a very visual display of inner struggle suffusing his face.

Whether he would have continued despite his wife's irritating miscellany of information was immaterial as the silver, before any chasing, elaborate or otherwise, was all stolen from the garden shed because he talked about his new skills, and exactly where the silver was kept, over a pint in the Priory Arms. It was not insured because, while he would bang on to anyone at the bar about the quantity of silver lying around in his shed, he had not banged on to his insurance company about same. Alas – Renaissance Men in the shape of her husband were not blessed with a sense of remorse. 'You can be very vulgar, Flora,' he said, when she pointed out the cost of it all. She felt extremely sorry for the wives of genuine Renaissance Men. No sooner had these linkers twixt ancient and modern managed a small volume of poetry and gone back to eating and sleeping again, than they decided to go a-tilting to possible great harm, or opined in public that the sun went round the earth and accordingly had their heads chopped off. No wonder everyone sighed with relief when it was all over and Europe reached the Age of Enlightenment.

Flora, too, just sighed with relief and continued to love her husband – if exasperatedly – for a while – despite the growing absurdities – for she could still remember the shy, curly-haired graduate from Cirencester who first fell off his bicycle at her feet and who later took her to where the silent otters slid and who could pick for her twenty different kinds of mushrooms. When they met Flora was staying with her Aunt Helen in Kent for a bit of fresh country air. She would have liked to call herself an urban chick except that she was plain, had heard herself referred to at the school where she taught in London as 'Miss Bun Face' and knew, by dint of having a pretty older sister who knew all there was to know about everything, called Rosie, that she could never be either fashionable or attractive. Rosie was the urban chick, Flora was the urban sparrow. She was aware of this. Edward was handsome. Not in any fashionable, attractive film-star way, but definitely good-looking in a reassuring young doctor way – tall, with that fair curly hair and serious blue eyes and a generous mouth. Quite a catch, she kept thinking without hope. Quite a catch. In those days he was shy and had yet to develop his themes of tradition and knowing your place, and the English countryside for the English.

At the time Edward was helping with some part-time coppicing and clearing work on the riverbank and lodging with her aunt. He rode his bicycle up Aunt Helen's path and Flora – who had just arrived from London – stepped out from behind the big bay tree – and the rest was history. He was full of apology, which gave her the upper hand for once, she decided years later.

Flora bathed his grazes and probably looked at her cheerful best while kneeling at his feet. Girls who were plain did not have a sporting chance and needed to consolidate as soon as possible. Magazines told her so. If magazines had also explained what particular consolidations they had in mind, it would have been helpful. Presumably whatever they were they could not remove a snub nose, freckled cheeks and a wide jaw of the permanently amused. Omens for marriage were not good.

When Edward's day off came around, he asked Flora, most sweetly, if she were free and they agreed to go for a cycle ride together. This they did in the beautiful long summer light, stopping to take swigs of water and to eat their biscuits and apples. They laughed a little and talked a little and it became a regular event. She had never felt happier – here was the world and at last she belonged in it. She rose early and successfully studied the OS maps for their routes – an achievement driven by sheer determination. The fortunate thing in terms of their progress as a couple was that there were absolutely no other young women around of a suitable age.

One morning, before he left the house, Edward said, 'We can go to Hever today. I've been studying the map. If you think you'll be strong enough. It's a bit of a trek but the journey's pretty.'

'Yes,' she said, feeling a strange sense of loss that she was no longer the one to suggest a route.

He smiled, so nicely, a smile of encouragement and said, 'Right then – I'll be back around twelve.'

When she asked her aunt what Hever was, her aunt told her about the moated castle which had once been Anne Boleyn's home and how it later was given to Henry's fourth Queen, Anne of Cleves. 'A pay-off after her divorce from Henry VIII. He chopped off the head of the first Anne and couldn't stand the sight of the second, poor woman. Got rid of her as quickly as he could. Large, plain and stupid apparently. She never married again,' said Aunt Helen. 'Unsurprisingly. Still – at least he didn't cut her head off for it.'

'For what?' said Flora, only half listening.

'For being what he called his Flanders Mare'.

To a young woman who has been called Bun Face, this was less shocking than it might be. 'Flanders . . .' said Flora dreamily. Perhaps she and Edward could go to Flanders.

'Yes,' said her aunt, nodding significantly. 'German.' As if this explained everything.

They stopped their bikes to look out over the Kentish countryside and down upon the little castle in the distance. Flushed with confidence, and the ride which had been hard, Flora said, 'This is where Anne Boleyn was born – Henry VIII's wife.'

'Really,' he said. 'I always liked history. I've a head for dates.' And she thought he looked impressed. He then cited the dates of various significant battles and the reinstatement of royalty. Flora looked equally impressed.

'Gracious,' she said.

'Yes,' he said. 'History's my thing.'

'He cut off Anne Boleyn's head, Henry did. And then they gave the place to Anne of Cleves. She was his fourth wife.'

'That's a lot of wives,' he said thoughtfully, 'called Anne.'

'Yes,' she said, 'I expect kings can do that sort of thing – chop and change –'

He looked at her with an air of surprise – and then threw back his head and laughed.

She suddenly realised that she had made quite a witticism. Witticisms were not her usual forte and it gave her a sudden jolt of confidence. She threw back her head and laughed, too, not caring that it was probably her least attractive condition.

They stood there, close together, bikes resting on the old wall and Flora thought it was beautiful. The sun gleamed on the water of the moat bathing the delicate crenellations in its lemony light, and swans floated elegantly around looking at the world from superior eyes. As she watched the birds gliding on the water she was still panting a little and her cheeks were pulsating with heat. It was not, she remembered thinking, the way to look when you were out with a new boyfriend. Horses sweat, gentlemen perspire and ladies glow. She was as shiny and damp as a well exercised mare and considerably more freckly than when she first arrived in Hurcott Ducis. Nevertheless, she had made him laugh and that must be a good thing and she enjoyed the feeling of intimacy it brought. So she said a little thank-you to the Flemish Mare, whoever she was, and thought no more about her.

Edward, still laughing, leaned his bicycle against the fence and stared at the clear blue yonder and became the very picture of a man with a serious question on his mind. He was absent-mindedly caressing one of her hands. 'I wonder if we should . . .' he began.

'Yes,' she said, as soon as the words were out of his mouth. She startled him with her fierceness. 'Yes,' she said again. 'I would like to marry you very much. And as soon as possible.' She then kissed him very, very hard on the lips which he seemed to find pleasing and his hand was under her jumper quick as ninepence. Unchartered territory. That, she presumed, was what they meant by consolidating. She was teaching at a primary school on the other side of London and she did not see it as a career.

After they were married and had moved to a village not far from her aunt's and she was still commuting to London and beginning to find she rather liked the job – he told her that he had never intended to ask her to marry him that evening. What he had actually been going to say was, 'I wonder if we should get a tandem?'

'Oh, she said. 'Well – never mind.' And she didn't. Nor, it seemed, did he. Later she came to think that he probably sub-consciously knew she would make a very good foil to the man he was about to become.

The world always questioned the how and the why of her and Edward. After he joined the Heron estate and was just beginning to show signs of ambition the wives of the Estate workers looked at him with open admiration and at Flora with increasing amazement. For the Estate's second summer party which the two of them attended, Edward wore a blazer with the Heron crest on its pocket, which pleased Sir Randolph tremendously. Flora could not believe that it was anything other than a joke. It was not a joke. After that it was only a matter of time. Edward was on his way. And Flora trailed behind, somewhat aghast but loyal, very loyal. Only in her head did she curl her lip and think sceptically about it all, which seemed prudent. She was a married woman and that counted for much. She would hold her tongue and put up with it – turn a blind eye, lie fallow, bide her time. Which she did until, suddenly, it was too late. There she was, Mrs Edward Chapman, mother of a beautiful daughter (now there's another surprise for you), and dull and unattractive wife of the Estate's dashing, handsome, be-blazered and adored wild card. Sadly there was little comfort in the child Hilary for the child Hilary was entirely her father's little girl and Edward displayed her proudly as if he alone had engendered her. 'She's so pretty,' he said, over and over again, as if he just could not believe it. Flora took a back seat. She could never get away now, even if she had the backbone.

Later, much later in their marriage, and thinking it over, Flora decided that if she had waited, she would never have married Edward. She would not have been blinded by his good looks and his interest in nature and the outdoors, neither of which, to be truthful, ever contributed much to the success of a marriage. She would have waited for someone more appropriate to come along – or – perhaps – remained single. Those urgers in print of a plain woman's consolation had much to answer for. As did she for not having more sense. But then – had she remained single she would never have had her daughter . . . And that, she thought, as she looked again at those sobbing, grief-bent shoulders, was unthinkable. Even if Hilary had not, so far, been the most rewarding of daughters. To Hilary Edward was a wonderful father – and if confidence in the world was anything to go by they both had more than their fair share of it. You'd never catch Hilary doing a Flora and mistaking a suggestion about a double bike for a marriage proposal. Hilary was strong-minded, utterly confident and her father's physical double. They admired each other enormously. The wholly inappropriate thought crept into Flora's willing mind – that with Edward out of the way there just might be a little room in Hilary's heart for her. Time would tell.

The sudden understanding, some years ago, of what her life had become came to Flora as she wandered through John Lewis's stationery department one day and found a greetings postcard of one woman talking to another and saying, 'I thought I'd married Mr Right instead of which I married Mr Always Right'. She bought the card because it was relevant and amusing and when, later, forgetting all about it, she emptied her handbag on the kitchen table looking for something else entirely, and the card fell out, Edward picked it up, chuckled, and handed it back to her saying, 'Who did you buy that for?' Which said it all, really.

The English cricket team, so Flora had read, were coached to look in their mirrors each day and quote a poem that told them to believe that they were their own universe, they were their own man, that they ruled the world – which – if it were to be believed – made them win the Ashes. In the same way, Edward looked in his mirror every day and saw a supreme being, loved and admired, at the centre of his own universe. If she looked in the mirror every day, not her favourite occupation and she tried to avoid it, she saw only a latterday Katharina to Edward's Petruchio (in her pre-Edward days she was keen on Shakespeare). She knew how Edward would love her to say to any of his absurder claims, '. . . And be it moon, or sun, or what you please; /And if you please to call it a rush-candle/Henceforth I vow it shall be so for me . . .' She had single-handedly proved that all it needed was for one good woman to remain silent. Since she allowed it she must accept it and so she did.

All that tree-hugger stuff, as he came to call it, went away once he drank his port with the noble baronet and learned to nod graciously at Foot, as ever in attendance. The appointment of the somewhat under-born Edward to such a big and ancient estate was seen as a remarkable achievement though the more truthful explanation of it was that many men who might have been appointed did not choose to have their heads blown off in any strange experiments or to eat the unmentionable parts of a pig's anatomy at the Annual Garden Party.

Later, when Hilary was old enough, Flora taught French and needlework three full days a week in gloriously liberating London. She had hoped to teach art and needlework – and rekindle her love of paintings (Edward was not one for visiting exhibitions) – or English literature but neither was on offer. Teaching was justifiable because they needed the money, thank God, and her job became the barrier to all Edward's excesses. Once her bottom hit the train seat and her newspaper was unfolded and the carriage pulled away from the neat little station at Hurcott Ducis, Edward's current pursuits and her own inadequacies were put to the back of her mind. After school Hilary sat and did her homework in the Estate office, Flora was back home with supper on the table by seven. Everything worked cleanly and calmly, and privately Flora congratulated herself. Even if Edward – and in later stages, Hilary – thought she should really be at home in a pinny. Neither of them approved of her other life, probably because it excluded them. They asked her about it little and she told them even less. That was a liberation of sorts.

But then Flora took early retirement. *Very early* retirement she said to anyone who asked. Charts, goals, mission statement all left her feeling weak and out of her depth. The days of turning up, teaching a subject and getting your students through an exam or two exploded into the educational version of the Spanish Inquisition: school turned into an academic dog's breakfast of tests and skills over education and imagination and although she rather dreaded the end she was quite relieved to go when it came. Yoof was the thing and new young teaching staff came in wearing jeans and trainers – a hurt child could no longer be cuddled and somehow, though she tried to look nonchalant about it all, it was time to go. She picked up her pension and walked. That it meant a much closer proximity (Hilary was long gone to her own home and life) to her husband made her grit her teeth and – no doubt – increased the imbecility of her expression.

'*Early retirement*,' she reiterated to people in the village, few of whom she knew well since Hurcott Ducis had expanded remarkably over the twenty years they had lived there. A new estate was built where the old Manor once sat and it lent an almost small-town-like quality to the place but it was well enough hidden behind shrubbery and an old, stone wall. Nevertheless, gossip was gossip and her news was everybody's. '*Very early retirement*'. Too many came up to her and said how young she looked for her age. She was only fifty-four for heaven's sake. One thing you could say about being plain in youth was that you remained at that level, approximately, well into your middle age. Suddenly you were ahead of the frightened beauties who began to crumble since you never had anything to boast about in the first place. Or that was the theory. Mentally, she guessed, you were stronger. What you've never had you don't miss. In some respects you gained because of attributes that were perhaps overlooked in younger days – in Flora's case, a good skin with none of those lines and wrinkles that look so sad on regretful erstwhile beauties, and a decent head of hair that was still mostly brown and undamaged by either lack of hormones or too many chemical helpmates. And a cheerful face when many around her of similar age looked either haggard (from anxiety and dieting she guessed), down in the mouth and disappointed, or bland from too many surgeon's scalpels. Her mouth would never turn down, even if she wanted it to. Small victories, her physical stabilities, but ones she rather cherished.

Edward, of course, was still firing on all guns – literally and metaphorically – and now that Giles's nephew ran most of his uncle's wine business (since the demise of the restaurant young Julian Baldwin held the reins very tightly) the two of them cooked up more hare-brained schemes than a pair of silly schoolboys. Sir Randolph had passed the point of any meaningful experimentation – meaningful anything really – and Edward was his own man on the Estate. Meanwhile Flora just felt older and older with a sense that part of her had been lost – the part she owned – the private life outside the village – the part that was not long-suffering wife nor heavily criticised mother.

Daughter Hilary made no bones about it – all that working in London when she was small was not what her mother should have been doing – she should have been in the kitchen, in that famous pinny, waiting to dish out the post-school buns and milk. The fact that Hilary loved the Estate office with its open fire in winter and its toasting fork put to good use and its big table where she could draw or write or doze – and its outdoor surroundings in warmer months where she could flop and play after her homework, was forgotten. Remembered were the few occasions, very few, when Hilary was sick, or the village school's heating failed. Then Edward was called in, and Flora would return home to find two pairs of eyes looking at her balefully from sofa-based telly watching. Oh Maither, Maither what hae ye done. . .?

It was scant consolation for Flora to think to herself that once she popped her clogs and (she liked to think, though she was not a believer) ascended heavenwards – Hilary would suddenly realise what she missed and how careless she was of Flora's kindness and affection. You are a long time dead, Flora would nod and say to herself. Hilary will find herself regretting so much once I have passed on. Fond thought . . . It got her through a great many of the worst of Hilary's dismissals. Mary Dobson, Flora's one soul-mate in the village, had a son who was equally critical. Mary and she sat and drank wine together and commiserated with each other and said one day, one day . . . Part of their shared life cycle of motherhood seemed to be One Day. It went with A Mother's Place is in the Wrong.

Flora thought long and hard about her retirement before deciding that she would have to do something. Something big. 'I'd like to find out the history of this village,' she said to Edward. 'Particularly this house.' To which he said, 'Good idea.' And commenced to do so himself. She was so fed up that she refused to be amanuensis to the project but Edward, being Edward and adored by all, soon got a typing helpmeet in the shape of one of the leaders of the local Brownie Pack, little Miss Pauline Pike. And that was that. In future, she told herself, save your breath to cool your porridge and keep your good ideas to yourself.

At least The History took Edward away from painting which he executed less with the High Renaissance grandeur of Michelangelo and Tintoretto and more in the flaccid well-bred mode of Winston Churchill and Charles Windsor. He even tried to paint a portrait of his wife but, after many and bitter exchanges, he abandoned it saying she was impossible to transmit to canvas. To which Flora, with a dim memory of Rembrandt's sketches, said that she thought artists rather liked grotesques. It fell on deaf ears. How little respect they ended up having for each other. When Edward once walked the land and knew and cared about the call of the kite, the silhouette of a deer, the shape of a moss, she felt differently. Now he was so immured in self-betterment and vainglory that she thought him an object of ridicule. She kept this to herself as wives should be loyal – and anyway no one would have believed her. *She* was the twerp, not he.

So she smiled, hid what she could of his daubings on the backs of doors, and lived with the results. She tried to have tender thoughts about him – she missed having tender thoughts about him – but the more crazy his ideas, the less she could think anything at all beyond frustration and sometimes downright fury. Whenever she read an article that said people who bottled up anger were prone to cancer she would sit for half a day sadly convinced that so it would be for her. But if she let it all out – well then it could be much worse – Krakatoa would be as nothing and the reverberations would continue for eternity.

Eventually boredom overcame resolution. Flora capitulated and offered to help with the History. Both the house and Hurcott Ducis were old and should hold enough secrets to keep the two of them occupied for the rest of their lives. But alas – Edward did not want a partner – he wanted a handmaid and in the person from the Brownie Pack it seemed he had found one. It wasn't intentionally cruel but to Flora's offer of help he waved a dismissive hand. 'No thanks,' he said, 'you'd be too critical.' He meant, of course, that she might correct him – and be proved right. You could do a lot of reading and learning on trains to and from London over the years, a lot.

Hilary, by now living in Cambridge and In Retail, never wavered in her support for Edward. This was wholly noble, Flora acknowledged, and unspeakably bloody irritating. When her father took up the piano it was at Hilary's sugges-tion, thank you, Hilary. Flora just smiled and wore earplugs. When he decided that he was a poet, Flora just smiled and wore earplugs. She found involvement where she could – read-ing aloud in the Home for the Elderly in the nearby market town, mending some of the old and rotting bits of embroidered stuff in the village church under the critical eye of Mrs Vicar, who could have shown God a thing or two in the art of acknowledging perfection – and occasionally giving a little extra French tuition. Nothing to shake the Universe – but then – when had she ever done anything to even shake this little cor-ner of it? Flora knew perfectly well that the people of the vil-lage, apart from Mary and one or two others, thought of her as quiet and dull and unadventurous. It was never far away, that unspoken question of How on *earth* did she get a man as exciting and handsome as Edward to marry her?

Gradually, as Flora settled into her comfortable rut she began to think that the next twenty or thirty years might be tolerable – her new role in life – her final job – the most skilful of all – Coping. She almost believed she had reached a plateau of calm with a comfortable emotional distance from Edward. Peace in her heart and mind at last. And then, Oh capricious perversity, he blooming well went and *died*. Initially she felt cross and cheated. He'd gone to glory and she was left holding thin, thin air. Only gradually, gradually, in the days between Edward's death, and the funeral today, this new sensation had stolen over her – a wicked sense of possibility . . . She was smiling again. She must stop. But it was quite hard – despite the horror of it – to be woebegone when she remembered the manner of his going. How *typical*. You could not, as she said to herself, make it up.

Vainglorious in the manner of his living, vainglorious in the manner of his death, Edward was in futile pursuit of yet another Grand Skill. He set off to float around the skies above Hurcott Ducis in the style of Phineas Fogg and with a brain positively bursting with the topographical possibilities of Ptolemy and Mercato and the wide-hatted John Speed (bloody *Encyclopaedia Britannica*). He was caught up with the History and went off at a tangent. Having abandoned his own attempt at a picaresque novel some years previously he now resurrected the idea of combining it with his History to produce the perfect book. Which, obviously, initially required a practical bit of showmanship first. Hence the balloon. Map it, feel it, draw it and then write it. 'The lie of the land will reveal much,' he told Flora. And when she, quite reasonably, suggested getting a professional to do the ballooning he was outraged. He had taken lessons, he knew what to do. Up he went, up and away, higher and gloriously higher – and then, with a truly Renaissance swagger he pumped up the gas – and – hardly surprisingly – set fire to his balloon. Edward's Inferno.

As if that were not enough – the charred basket landed smack in the middle of the River Hurst so that he not only plummeted to death, and burned to death, he managed to drown to death as well. The triple death. Quite horrible – yet also the death designated for the greatest heroes, suffered by the most mystically mythological of grandees, magicked by Merlin on to a would-be king. A fittingly spectacular ending, the stuff of legend, and worthy, at least, of a little corner of the Sistine chapel . . . Why, oh why couldn't he simply drop down dead in the street if he was going to do it? There was not a great deal of him left at the end but Flora still had to identify what there was. Even in death he was demanding. It was, perhaps, the nastiest experience of her life.

The whole thing was filmed which made it even more bizarre. Pauline Pike, Grey Owl to the Brownies, the too-too sweet young woman who wore powder-pink lipstick and a quantity of Nuits d'Or by La Russe – which Flora now knew because whenever Pauline Pike brought something to the house for Edward the entire ground floor smelled of it. Pauline Pike, apart from being a serial scent wearer, was a dab little hand with the video camera and something of a camp follower of Edward's exploits. Her little legs must have carried her over hill and down dale in pursuit of the grand journey for she and her machine apparently never lost sight of him. Flora was offered a viewing of her husband's final moments but declined. Not yet, was what she said. Not ever, thank you, was what she thought. And let the world think of her as a coward. It was better than the world thinking of her as a hard-bitten fishwife for she was quite likely to put her foot through the television screen in her disgusted fury. She told little Miss Pike that on no account was she to make the same offer to Hilary. A dash of maternal protectiveness for her distraught daughter who was fortunately so genuinely distraught that she seemed not to notice her mother's somewhat cooler view of things. Miss Pauline Pike patted her on the arm and gave her a copy of the video to tuck away somewhere for the future. Flora tucked it in the back of a drawer, not quite able to throw it away, nowhere near able to watch the thing.

Flora was in London when The Event happened, which everyone seemed to think was a blessing. Unfathomable platitude. Flora had kept one or two connections up in town – a dentist, a hairdresser, a department store account, a couple of friendly ex-colleagues – which proved very sensible and meant she could do all sorts of other things like visit art exhibitions, browse in bookshops and even – occasionally – see the odd matinee. Good reasons to take the train and have a whole day to herself. Never before had Flora had any sympathy with Virginia Woolf's wetly privileged Mrs Dalloway, the heroine who seemed to think that opening the French windows and going out to buy her own flowers was a huge lark – but now she could see her point. Stone walls may not a prison make, nor iron bars a cage, but a domestic setting with a Renaissance Man can certainly make you want to run naked down the road screaming from time to time unless you can get on a train and go. So Flora was At The Dentist's when all this was going on. Or actually somewhere between The Dentist's and Selfridges, her favourite shop in all the world, where she intended to celebrate the fact that she needed no fillings by having at least two cakes with plenty of them. Probably she was just emerging from Marble Arch tube when it happened. Later the thought would not go away that at the hour of her husband's death she was stepping forth from darkness into the light.

The Event, for so it was talked of in whispers, was referred to, in all seriousness, as Not a Pretty Sight. Giles had been with him at the time but wisely not *in* the basket, obviously, and Giles said it had been 'grim'. Like Pauline, Giles followed the smoking descent o'er hill and dale and riverbank and saw it all. Still, apparently, holding the bottle of celebratory old claret which they were due to drink to mark the success of the venture. Real men, apparently, drank claret whenever they celebrated – Flora's suggestion now and then of champagne was considered a deeply flimsy notion. The bottle, a Médoc 1996, was still there, with the cork thrust back into it, on the dresser in the kitchen. Providing Mrs Graves hadn't added it to the funereal crab spread.

The messengers of death met her train at the station. No one had told daughter Hilary and no one knew Flora's mobile number. This latter mattered not as Flora deliberately left the wretched thing behind when she went off on one of her jaunts. It was the only way to feel free. Thus, quite unprepared, and with a spring in her step from the double chocolate muffin and the substantial piece of carrot cake so recently consumed, she stepped down to be met like visiting, doomed royalty, by the official legation. And there, in the middle of a pair of startlingly bright Busy Lizzie beds (Hurcott Ducis went in for Prettiest Station in the South East – never won – sensitivity and imagination was not Wally Binder's forte) she was told the dreadful news. Edward was dead. To which she said the first thing to come into her head because it had to be a joke, which was 'If only –'. Which naturally enough did not go down very well with Giles (who, to be fair, had been through quite enough shocks and appeared very pale and close to passing out – as – it crossed Flora's mind – she should look and did not). Pauline, Wallace and Roger Tucker (who was a lay reader from the next village and one of the Parish councillors and presumably brought along because he was the closest thing they could find to God, the Reverend Arthur and Mrs Vicar being absent) were equally shocked. They soon put Flora right.

Pauline was sobbing loudly into an enormous white handkerchief and looked as if she had been doing so for some considerable time and intended to continue for even longer. Giles was shaking and stuttering. Flora felt irritated. She was tired, she had been in London all day, she had eaten cakes and chosen a new foundation for ageing summer skin, and she just wanted a cup of tea, removal of shoes, and a sit-down at home. Instead she was faced with the last Great Mystery to deal with. Her response, Flora thought, had therefore been quite understandable. 'If only . . .' She had not meant it literally. It was just something to say to alleviate her exhaustion at the prospect of dealing with death while her shoes hurt. Please could she deal with it all in a day or two? Or even – hell – an hour or two?

No chance.

Edward was tiring alive, and he was tiring dead. And if they were looking for a beaten breast, a trickling tear or a vengeful wail then they went away empty for she was quite, quite numb when they told her and still was several hours later. She remembered thinking that it was thoughtful of Edward to require a funeral when the April weather was good – which was a weird but true thought – and that she still wanted to put her feet up on the sofa and snooze. But she was newly widowed and you were not expected to be able to do anything of a restful nature. So they had stayed with her, they had watched over her, they had poured her stiff gins – what they had not done was to give her time to herself. She was yawning what might have sounded – very bad form – contentedly, when they finally left. Again, this was unsurprising given the stiff gins, but it probably looked hard as granite. Pauline, as she guessed, had continued to weep spasmodically, when not saying what a wonderful, wonderful man Edward is. Even more irritated, at the third time of the statement being made, Flora could not stop herself from adding '*Was,* Pauline, *was.* He's dead. Deceased.' Which set Pauline off again and had Flora wondering if it wouldn't be better just to give her one of the spare-room sheets rather than a handkerchief of Edward's.

Flora spent the following days making cocoa for her daughter, who arrived crying and who stayed and wept and lay around on the sofa clutching a photograph of her father so that Flora continued to feel an inappropriate rising irritation. The guilt of the inappropriateness making her more irritated. 'There, there Hil,' she said, holding her close and rocking her.

Even more inappropriately she wished her daughter would pull herself together a bit. When Hilary's tortoise died she wept on and off for a fortnight. How much longer would it take for a father? Mothers were required to go on being stoical for the rest of their days even when in pain themselves. Once, after Flora had two wisdom teeth removed and Hilary came to visit and Flora was in pain and said so, Hilary looked at the offending jaw, propped up on a pillow and said with thoughtful accusation, 'Well – I expect I'll follow in your footsteps at some point – you'll have passed on the wisdom tooth gene to me . . .' And Flora, weakened by suffering, forbore to point out that the likelihood of there being a tooth gene was fairly remote not to say bloody ridiculous. Those baleful stares over the years had stopped Flora's courage where her daughter was concerned.

Hilary needed to grieve and she would do it with her customary gusto. Flora must grin and bear it, or rather, *not* grin and bear it, she must just do her best, keep her head; comforting phrases, these, smoothed and polished over the years like the beach stones of Brighton. 'Mother is being very brave,' she heard Hilary on the phone telling her live-in partner Robin. Flora had never heard herself referred to as Mother before. It made her feel very old. Hilary had a way of making her feel old – and rather thick – like no other. Flora wondered if now that Father was dead this view of Mother might change, but she was not very optimistic.

They were choosing the music for the funeral when Robin rang and Hilary told him that she wanted some of her father's favourite piano pieces. She said it as if Edward was Paderewski incarnate. Flora winced. Not least because Hilary used to go home quite a bit earlier when his playing was at its height – sometimes right in the middle of her father's rendition of a Scott Joplin rag. Or was it Bach? Flora learned to look for small mercies and never forgot how her blood ran cold when Edward was found, on his knees, surrounded by the contents of the junk cupboard, desperately trying to find Hilary's old recorder. Fortunately Flora had the hindsight to put the thing in the bottom of the dustbin when Hilary finally finished junior school. It was unlikely, in her mother's opinion, that even one so magically gifted as Apollo could make the recorder produce a bearable sound. When the note on a recorder goes wrong, it really goes wrong. And when it goes right it is extremely hard to tell.

How many times had she heard 'Oh Mum – go with it. Dad's fun.' This meant that Flora was not fun. And this was probably true. One parent must remain sane, after all. It would have served both Hilary and Edward right if Flora had suddenly blossomed into a knife thrower or a writer of villanelles which she declaimed at midnight in the market square. The choir mistress, having conceived a grand passion for the organist and being driven mad by his rejection, had done that very thing. See where it gets you, though, Flora wanted to say today to the mournful graveside crowd and Hilary's sobbing back view. See where the Fun gets you. Broken, burnt and blooming well drowned. But wisely she did not. Deaths in families pretty well always produced bad feeling. No sense in courting it. If Mother was being very brave, so be it. It was a lie. Mother was just being totally inadequate in the role of grieving widow. She missed Edward like she might miss a passed-on but glorious houseplant that took a great deal of effort to keep glorious. She found the analogy pleasing for if a glorious houseplant dies you can go out and get a replacement – another variety . . . one that is no trouble, needs no leaf-polishing and is quite ordinary. A spider plant perhaps, or tradescantia. That, thought Flora, is the kind of man I should have married. A man who was happy to be very, very ordinary . . .

She looked across at Pauline now. She was standing a little to the back, looking proud of her tears and doing a great deal better than the widow as Queen of Grief. After the funeral, Flora told herself, I shall probably go to pieces. Quite suddenly. So I shall need something to do. Definitely. After the funeral. So many things had been set aside for after the funeral. And now here was Giles's enthusiastically glum graveside eulogy finally, finally, slowly, slowly drawing to a close. Looking up from under her hat at the clear blue sky she willed Giles to get a move on. She *was* feeling hungry, no doubt about it. So hungry that Flora felt she could kill for a bridge roll with any filling, absolutely any filling, at all. The vicar surreptitiously consulted his list (so many people wanted to give between October 9th and March 22nd on the grounds that his ancestors had lost The American Colonies (though that might be rather a restful eccentricity for her husband to adopt if she could find a suitable reason for it) and even – God help her – Jeremy Bentham who wanted himself mummified. She decided to leave Edward if he asked for this particular bit of whimsy on the grounds that she drew the line at having his dried corpse sitting in the hall. Thank God he hadn't got started on putting the book into practice before he died or it would have been straight into the Last Will and Testament . . . And knowing the man, the wonderfully ordinary man, whose legal task it was to discharge that Last Will and Testament, he might feel obliged to carry the instructions out. Her face – she could feel it – softened – her eyes – she could feel them – went a little dewy. They always did when she contemplated that particular Mr Ordinary . . .

How she had longed to be married to someone very, very ordinary. How she had longed for a husband who did sensible things; played golf, read political memoirs or biographies, took the dog for a simple walk (i.e. not attached to a little cart so that they could garner bits of wood) watched *Panorama* and washed the car. In these last years, had she been in any way convinced God was alive and well and likely to grant her request, she would have prayed for just that. A safe, ordinary husband to match her own plain style. Flora had not the slightest illusion about her plainness. Even when walking back up the aisle with Edward, the comforting veil thrown back, she'd had a momentary temptation to hold her bridal flowers in front of her face. But everyone's eyes were actually on Edward even then, and in their years of marriage she, too, liked to look at him . . .

But this other – this normal other – she thought wistfully – was her little secret. He liked playing golf, or reading the newspaper, or sitting on the sofa with his little bald patch, his slightly pouchy eyes, his slightly paunchy belly and an abiding interest in – if not *Panorama* – then *Question Time*. Which would suit her just fine. It crossed her mind that now she was free she could do something about it. Crossed her mind, and very swiftly went out of it. Despicable thought. He was a married man. And anyway, do what?

She took a sideways look at Hilary. Pink-eyed, streaming tears, brave little profile, hankie at her nose. At least she was doing it right. Flora never seemed to get anything right. Even when Hilary was dumped by the boyfriend-before-Robin (he was running two women) Flora may have felt the hurt as if it were her own – but when she expressed surprise she was made to feel that she should have recognised such an iniquity. Edward, on the other hand, immediately said that he had never trusted the blighter at which Hilary fell into his arms and said Oh Daddy, you were so right, making Flora feel worse. Of course she cared, she cared very much, but Flora found her daughter a little daunting, a little self-satisfied and sometimes very irritating indeed. She was certainly not one to let an opportunity for drama go by if she could help it and she could even keep a coughing fit going for what seemed like eternity. That was not to say she did not care deeply – and rightly – about her father's death – of course she did. But she was also poised, very poised, to make a meal of it.

Flora turned her head away and looked about her, past the bowed heads of the mourners, to where the sun put a mellow glow on the honey-coloured sandstone of the old church. Just beyond the tower (fifteenth-century with seventeenth-century additions, Edward would wish to tell you) she could see the rise of Blowhorn Lane, which led to Lodge Cottage and beyond it she could just make out the beginning of the old stone wall. What ghosts walked hereabouts, she wondered. What have these walls seen, this church? And how fascinating is the journey of discovery when you peel back the layers of the past. Those monks – good and bad – the Catholic schemers, the Orthodox righteous and the zealous Reformers – the families with their new fortunes and their misfortunes. No different, she thought, no different at all, except for the vagaries of time.

Hilary's sobs brought Flora back to reality. Giles was giving it all he'd got and there were tears coursing down his cheeks, too. Hers seemed to be the only dry ones in the place. Rather wonderful that Edward should command so much emotion. Even as she put her arm through her daughter's and said, 'There, there, Hil, there, there . . .' she sent her mind to safer, more comforting ground where it dwelled in domesticated places. Less marble halls than the kitchen and the downstairs cloakroom back at the Lodge. Had Mrs Graves and her daughter Martha (of *droit de seigneur* fame) got on with the finger foods? Had Lucy, her neurotic cleaning person who practically genuflected at Edward and who sometimes walked into Flora so little notice did she take of her, and who insisted she was only twenty-nine but who seemed to remember The Eagles and 'Hotel California' rather perfectly and who pored over *Hello* Magazine looking for signs of facelifts and rubber breasts much as Midas might have pored over his gold – had she nipped back and managed to put the Beckhams down for a moment and place enough clean towels into the downstairs lavatory? Well – nothing Flora could do about it if she had not.

Mrs Graves and her daughter Martha were the pillars of Hurcott Ducis catering. Mrs Graves 'did' for village weddings, baptisms, funerals, eighteenths, twenty-firsts and the occasional nervous and very low-key Bar Mitzvah. The village had not yet found the need to celebrate Holi but if it came along Mrs Graves would be there, with her sleeves rolled up, staining the rice and charging for it. She was particularly appropriately named – Flora looked down into the hole in front of her again – for the job in hand today. As Mrs Graves always said, of them all she much preferred a burial. And she was a dab hand with the Funeral Baked Meats. Well, bridge rolls by any other name, prawns in aspic, little tiny sausages in sweet and sticky something or other and cream cheese and mixed dried herb roulade, sweet biscuits and fruit cake. The funeral menu might not alter but Mrs Graves had a particular face for each catering occasion. Flora had seen her performing at them all – and hanging possibilities if you included two walls in the hallway – but she did not. She simply went on putting as many as possible of the gelatinous oils and insipid watercolours away at the back of a cupboard and hanging what she must in the remotest places she could find.

Hilary swung her long blonde plait over her shoulder and stepped up on to the little podium, and Flora was inwardly sighing. Hilary was going to be brave. Pride came into the equation now and nudged irritation out of the way. Whatever else you could or could not say about their daughter, she was both confident and clever. And still beautiful. Flora blinked away the stunning possibility that between them she and Edward might have got something right, and watched as Hilary straightened her back, swung her plait once more, presented a tear-stained and agonised face to the world (as is her prerogative, Flora reminded herself), and then, as her daughter began with the words 'My father was one of the last true Renaissance Eccentrics . . .' Flora immediately remembered who the fool was who had bought him that book.

Hilary kept her eyes on the coffin while she spoke and it did look remarkably and movingly like a scene from Greek tragedy. How soothing these rituals are, thought Flora. And even she felt her eyes grow damp to think of that eternal rest in the damp, dark tomb. Until she remembered it was already occupied.

The ceremonials went on. And on. Edward, in the way of Men of Destiny, apparently, had set down his funeral arrangements in minute detail. And they were adhered to faithfully. Only in one respect were his wishes departed from – which was when Flora, instead of giving the final eulogy as designated in the order of things, read from a poem. It was much easier to speak another's words than her own. Hers were a confused mixture of affection and loathing, acceptance and irritation, sadness and excitement and panic and relief at the prospect of a new day dawning. And the wait had been so long. Before Giles and

Hilary there had been Foot's rather grand reading of Sir Randolph's testimonial and Myra (from the library) and Betty (from the post office stores) speaking together about what a lovely, lovely man he was, always so polite and gracious and never a cross word, so now there was precious little left to say.

Hilary stood down and kept her chin up. She nodded to Flora as she passed her much as the Queen might nod at a grandee on Armistice Day. Flora then walked to the front and stood there for a moment before saying quietly that she felt Edward, as a man of erudition, would want something literary in the last resort. The words 'last resort' were, she realised, wholly inappropriate, but they had the useful effect of setting Hilary off, who set off Pauline Pike who was standing at the back but had moved forward (Flora forbade her from videoing the proceedings – firmly, but kindly) and within the jumble of sounds pursuant to that, the deceased's widow in the appropriately rippling shawl, began:

> The Winter being over,
> In order comes the Spring,
> Which doth green herbs discover,
> And cause the birds to sing.
> The night also expired,
> Then comes the morning bright,
> Which is so much desired
> By all who love the light.
> This may learn
> Them that mourn,
> To put their grief to flight:
> The Spring succeedeth Winter,
> And day must follow night.
> He therefore that sustaineth
> Affliction or distress,
> Which every member paineth,
> And findeth no release:
> Let such therefore despair not,

And therefore must have end.
They that faint
With complaint
Therefore are to blame;
They add to their afflictions,
And amplify the same.

(At this point she raised her voice as Hilary's was, indeed, adding to her afflictions and amplifying the same.)

But those that are contented,
However things do fall,
Much anguish is prevented,
And they soon freed from all.
They finish all their labours
With much felicity,
Their joy in trouble savours
Of perfect piety,
Cheerfulness
Doth express
A settled pious mind,
Which is not prone to grudging,
From murmuring refined.

Flora folded the piece of paper, looked up, and smiled at the gathering. Most of whom smiled back, though some looked quietly cautious. Fortunately for Flora, poetry is not something that the British middle classes feel confident of criticising or they might have realised that the message contained was mixed, to say the least, and not altogether suitable for a grieving widow, Spring following Winter and Day following Night and so forth. Nor was the title one she could share: 'A song to excite Spiritual Joy'. But its author was an obscure female poet, An Collins, and Flora was an obscure widow, and if it sounded wrong it felt right. No one noticed. Instead there were some bowed heads, a few nodding sagely, and fleeting, knowing expressions of immense understanding exchanged. Hilary, fortunately, was so absorbed by her own response that it was unlikely she had heard anything beyond the rhythm of the piece. She and Pauline Pike seemed to be in direct grieving rivalry – with Pauline just having the edge in the highness of her notes.

Flora smiled decently at the gathering, bent her knees (which creaked in suitable *memento mori*) and delicately dropped the copy of *Great British Eccentrics* on to the top of the coffin. At least he would have something to read in that fine and private place.

Thus, over an hour after they first assembled, the mourners departed the perfect lawns and gently drunken gravestones of St Lawrence's to take sustenance from whatever Mrs Graves had concocted. As they made their slow way back to the house, Flora's heart plunged a little. She knew she should have taken greater care with the catering arrangements and not abandoned it entirely to Hurcott Ducis' finest. At least Mrs Dalloway had gone to get the ruddy flowers herself. It would be entirely her fault if Mrs Graves had had a brainstorm and scattered the house with shocking salmon-pink begonias and the guests were offered pickled eggs and rollmops instead of the usual roulade and bridge rolls. During the consultation Flora simply waved a hand and said, 'Whatever you think appropriate, Mrs Graves. After all, you've been to a greater number of funerals than I have – and seen a greater number of people into their graves than I could ever hope to do or ever will . . .' Then – unfortunately – she had tinkled a merry laugh and added, 'Why, you could do Funeral Feasts on *Mastermind*.'

Mrs Graves then opened her mouth, closed it, and appeared to ponder the absolute truth of this while at the same time realising that the statement was wholly improper. If Mrs Graves still felt aggrieved that there had been no enjoyable batting to and fro of ideas, let alone true tearfulness, her perfect revenge might lie in the provision of wildly inappropriate food. Village people could behave very strangely, Flora had found. Very strangely.

As Flora skirted her way around the grave she hoped that if the catering was oddly scattered with pickled herring and the like, the guests would perceive it to be a mistake made from profound grief and not from a complete lack of interest in what they ate. At least Giles was doing the drink. She wondered what grape variety would go with a pickled egg if the occasion arose and decided that if everyone looked upon their platefuls with creeping horror, she would tell the assembled that these were particular favourites of Edward's. Oh yes, he liked nothing more than a rollmop and a pair of pickled eggs, my husband . . . Such, she thought, are the madnesses that attend the banalities of committal.

Matthew Arnold was quite right. How she had longed to end her funeral oration with:

Spare me the whispering, crowded room,
The friends who come, and gape, and go;
The ceremonious air of gloom –
All which makes death a hideous show!

Thank heavens it was all over.

All around her was the light and air of April promise. Oh for something cheerful to happen. Or something extraordinary. Something that would push her back into the real world after this sombre piece of theatre. Charles Hammick, one of the guns, was guiding Theresa Hammick carefully around the edge of the grave. How wonderful it would be if one of them fell in. Or both. That, at least, would be *something*. If Dilly Davies had been here she might well have done – given her proclivities – but she was not – nor was Ewan Davies her husband. They were having their usual spring three-weeks break – apart as usual. Dilly was put on a cruise liner bound for – well – she never knew or seemed to care where and came back looking lovelier than ever in her bronzage – and Ewan was bound for his beloved Ireland and the salmon. An ordinary, quiet, wholly understandable pastime from which he returned looking pinker and slightly plumper – and even more ordinary. All three of which Flora thought suited him. Suited him very well. And if Dilly *had* fallen into the open grave it would have suited Flora very well, too. Very well indeed. She sighed. If only . . .

Hilary had her arm through Flora's and put her head on Flora's shoulder thereby banishing any further thoughts of graveside fun. 'Well, I thought that was just lovely,' she said, and kissed the top of Hilary's heaving head.

'Did you like my speech?'

'It was the high spot, Hil, the high spot.' Hilary nodded into Flora's chest. 'I thought it was pretty good. What Dad would have wanted.' Flora nodded back and off they went. Nobody fell into the hole and still Flora had not cried.

As they walked the short distance to The Lodge Flora mused that all this was what came of having had separate bedrooms for the last four years. *Liberate Your Marriage* the pundits suggested. The theory was that each marital moment was desired because one had to ask for it. Since at that point in the Chapman household marital moments were a bit on the wane anyway, Edward pointed the notion out in the newspaper and they thought it might be a good idea. Flora enjoyed some strange and amusing visions, which she kept to herself, of Edward appearing at her bedroom door wearing a paisley dressing gown and a wicked leer, possibly toting a thin moustache – which persuaded her that the experiment might have its fun side. Edward remained in the bedroom at the front and she moved to the larger of the two guest bedrooms at the back. She cast a hopeful eye at Hilary's room – but they still pretended she might come home one day. Edward hopeful, Flora praying not. Children grew up and left home so that adults who had been forced to act like adults while their children were living at home, could revert to childhood themselves, was what she thought. Apart from a parent like Edward, of course, who had never quite grown up in the first place. Perhaps that was why Hilary liked him so much.

Flora made her new bedroom comfortable – which was perhaps the wrong way of looking at it given it was supposed to encourage something altogether more hotblooded. She painted it pale peach and installed pretty blinds. It looked perfectly reasonable. But then – in a sudden flush of potentially hot-blooded expectations – she went mad and a ordered a fluffy white carpet, the kind of carpet favoured by ageing Hollywood *grande-dames*. Hormones were such a useful excuse for any lively behaviour in a mother of a certain age. Flora deflected any further criticism from Hilary by looking her firmly in the eye and beginning a sentence that seemed likely to involve sex and her parents – at which point Hilary turned on the coffee grinder, and that was that.

Flora and Edward went through the Lancelot and Guinevere motions at first, both of them trying to be full of sexy longing, then they tried sexy fun – (though no paisley cravat nor seductive leer nor moustache appeared) – and flirtatious dalliance with each other. It was, Flora thought, bowel-freezingly embarrassing and must – surely – have had Edward diving into his pillow in silent laughter just as she did. She tried to overcome the humour of it and – despite its being shepherd's pie and peas or spaghetti bolognaise – to sashay past him at meal times. She tried wearing musky scent (a winner, apparently, if your marriage is jaded for it apparently reproduces the female aroma though Flora could not recognise her own which was more, to put it kindly, of the sea) and he tried to show her a good time – but the reality was that gradually, gradually all marital moments in the bedroom ceased and his insomnia and her chattering and laughing in her sleep, were left to disturb no one. If they did surprise themselves with the odd foray into conjugality, it was on the sofa downstairs and rather friendly and innocuous and tended, oddly, to happen during *Planet Earth* or when *Climbing the Eiger* was over. The sofa and the sitting room were obviously still seen as joint territory. No more of that, either. Didn't women crumble away to dust without a regular seeing to? Hope not, she thought, as they reached the front door.

The first person to come forward and greet Flora was Lucy Stevens, with *her* pink nose from crying. Lucy adored Edward and spoke of him to Flora as the father she never had. Lucy helped her off with her shawl saying, 'Haven't seen this before and I'll bet you're glad that's over,' all in the same breath of apparent solicitude. This gesture would have been very nice if – as usual – Lucy Stevens had not paused to check the garment's label, give the fabric the once over and feel the material before shaking her head and hanging it in the lobby cupboard. With Lucy Stevens as a cleaner, Flora was constantly giving her head a little shake too, as if to dislodge a particularly confusing piece of behaviour. She did so now as she walked towards the sitting room. Lucy must go. At the doorway she took a deep breath, turned, and set her face in as sombre mode as she could to receive her well-wishers.

Mrs Graves and her daughter attended on the guests with wonderfully solemn faces. Mrs Graves kept her bun-shaped hat on, presumably as a sign of respect, and Flora found herself wondering if there was anything in the world so comforting as the sight of a woman of any age between fifty and a hundred, wearing a slightly stretched dark cardigan, floppy navy trousers and an indoor hat – and handing round a tray of mixed drinks including a very brown-looking sherry of her own choosing (over which she had fought with Giles and won, Mrs Graves being something of an expert on sherry and Functions as she put it).

There was not, Flora decided. Right now it was the most comforting sight in the Universe. As was the same image but attached to a younger version of same – of the daughter Martha – following on, also in cardigan and trousers but with a perky black beret on the back of her head and a tray of rigid bridge rolls containing tinned salmon and a very extraordinarily textured slice of cucumber.

It was pointed out to Flora many years ago by Mrs Graves that in her Mrs Beeton Book it said that hats should always be worn unless the occasion was informal like family tea. Like so many things in this microcosmic village it was absorbed as verity and not considered worthy of comment.

As she looked about her at the respectful post-funerary assembled, she wondered what they would say if she told them in her funeral words that Edward called her Bun Face – and that she always felt hurt when he did. Even after thirty years it still hurt. She would have liked to tell them that it was one hell of a relief not to have to suffer that any more . . . But she warned herself to do no such thing . . . Dignity is all, she seemed to hear a voice saying, dignity and docility is the way forward – it has been so for millennia and no doubt would continue so for ever.

*

Even sorting through Edward's desk during the days that followed his funeral was more wearying than sorrowing. His paperwork was in more order than several apple pies, and if she hoped to find a little mystery there was none. Most of the creative stuff she had seen before – the 'Jottings of a Country Gent' and his poetry. 'Ah! Sweet Hurcott on Auburn nothing hath . . .' and other equally queasy stuff. But when she found the beginning chapters and notes of the History of Hurcott her curiosity got the better of her. There it lay in its neat buff folder. She sat in his leather chair, feet up on the disgusting elephant's foot he insisted on keeping for the purpose (Well – it's dead now, been dead a good long while, no point getting het up about the rights and wrongs of it) and read the opening lines of The History of Hurcott Ducis.

'Let us begin at the beginning,' he wrote, 'and with Lodge Cottage. Lodge Cottage, in the pretty village of Hurcott Ducis, is the home of the writer'. Which writer? she wondered. And then realised he meant himself. She itched to find a pencil and cross out 'Let us begin at the beginning' and 'the writer' and substitute 'my' – but what was the point? Instead she went on reading and it was as if Edward, at his worst, was there in the room.

'The writer has ascertained that the current dwelling is sited on what was once the gatehouse, or something akin to that function, to the Priory of St Athanasius, Athanasius being one of four great Greek doctors of the church . . .' Edward then wrote most fully on the subject of the four Greek doctors . . . Oh how often Flora had wished the *Encyclopaedia Britannica* to hell, and Oh the pretence that they had bought it for Hilary's use.

Flora liked digging around things and the surprise of discovery. She was happy to be humble with people who knew more than her and she liked mysteries. Edward did not very much care for anyone knowing more than he did . . . She remembered Giles's face stern with suppressed emotion, standing at the graveside and saying the exact opposite. 'He was a man of great achievements and great modesty.' Flora swallowed hard and went back to the History. It was safest.

'The writer,' wrote Edward, 'has discovered that some of the old Priory's stones were used in various ways – some to build the church of St Lawrence in the Village and some to rebuild parts of the outlying walls to the Priory, now a Manor and renamed Hurcott Hall . . .

'The gatehouse was considerably refurbished and adapted into a residence to house the estate overseer (from where this writer now writes). The whole might well have stayed in the family had not Thomas Hurcott been heard to say some treasonable things in 1539 about the King of England . . . In consequence Thomas was executed and his family turned out. The Crown reclaimed the estate, including the modernised gatehouse, and it became part of the divorce settlement given to Henry's fourth wife, Anne of Cleves, sometimes known rather amusingly as the Flanders Mare on account of her exceeding ugliness . . .'

On reading that, Flora remembered Aunt Helen's words, 'Very plain . . . Big boned . . . Never married again.' So Edward went to his death thinking it was perfectly acceptable to find the term 'Flanders Mare' amusing. Mind you, he had also gone to his death thinking it was perfectly all right to call his wife

Bun Face. Insults down the ages, she thought, how little has changed.

'After her divorce Anne of Cleves stayed occasionally at Hurcott Hall and was said to be fond of it in winter months because it was a warm building. This was on account of the brick and the angling of the windows which . . .'

There followed a long and technical description about why the Hall might be warmer than many. Flora skipped it and read on. 'Anne of Cleves also enjoyed her Palace at Richmond, her Castle at Hever and her manor at Bletchingley. At first Richmond, Bletchingley and Hurcott were said to be her most frequently used homes but later she used Dartford which Henry VIII developed into a much more modern and convenient home in 1541, and which was also endowed to Anne of Cleves. Hurcott gradually fell out of favour as Dartford had no Great Hall and could not, therefore, be opened for Banqueting and was therefore, with her reduced income, a much cheaper option . . .'

He then went on to write in some detail about the decline in the Tudor economy which suffered severe inflation (quite a lot of statistics here) during the second half of the century. Flora thought there might be similarities between herself and Anne of Cleves for apparently the ex-Queen's allowance was cut once her ex-husband Henry died – and Flora was aware that she would miss, paltry though it was, Edward's Heron 'shilling'. But Anne sounded practical and sensible, at least.

It was oddly comforting, as if Edward were still in the room – though he would not have countenanced her quietly reading through the pages. An idea began to sprout. Edward had left behind a good many notes and a pile of expensive-looking books. Widows had done things like this down the ages. They took their deceased husband's raw *magnum opus* and made something of it. She couldn't think of an example, but then, they might not all have been acknowledged. Flora found herself smiling again at the thought. She could be very methodical, and imaginative. And, if she applied herself, so she daydreamed, why – then – when it was done she might be hailed, after all, as the brilliant, clever Flora Chapman whom nobody had quite realised was so scintillatingly talented. A very nice little fantasy. It might even make Hilary sit up and take notice. That would be *very* nice.

Among all Edward's dry-as-dust listings about Hurcott was mention of a date-carved stone set in the remains of the original estate boundary walls. This was the wall, much added to and improved and rebuilt where necessary which now made the boundary of the new estate of houses behind Lodge Cottage. Flora had no idea that such a stone even existed. Perhaps he had made it up? But Edward would never do such a thing – as with the crossword, so with his facts, he was a stickler for truth. Flora was sure that if he wrote that there was a stone then a stone there must be.

Well, he obviously found the existence of such an artefact about as dull as he found Flora – for he made no further attempt to explain or conjecture or locate it. Nor did he try to explain the singular fact that the stone was carved with the date of 1557 but had, judging by the style of it and according to a highly respected nineteenth-century antiquarian, been carved perhaps forty years or more later. And there Edward left it, wanting to get on to the next bit – the pattern of the drainage and old field system – rather than dwell and linger over such a fascinating little nugget.

Lying back against Edward's old leather chair and chewing her pencil end, she thought how odd it was that Anne of Cleves – who was vaguely involved in their marriage beginnings – was now raising her head at the end of it. One does not look for signs, Flora told herself firmly, but sometimes they happen and sometimes they bring an odd kind of comfort. Flora began to think of Anne almost as an old friend, or at least an ally. A Flanders Mare and a Bun Face. Certainly if she and Flora sat together across a bottle of Chardonnay they would have quite a lot to talk about. 'After Anne of Cleves's death in 1557 the lands and outbuildings, together with the main house, were returned to the Hurcott family, whose Catholic views were acceptable again now that Mary I – Bloody Mary – was on the throne of England. Thomas Capel was steward. That cruel Queen died in the following year and the house and lands were once more given in long lease to good Protestants, the Bryans. Whereupon the Capels wisely converted. The Bryans held it until 1595 when the last of the family died and the lease passed back to the Crown. It was said that Queen Elizabeth I had a fondness for the place and visited it in her last years, but there is no confirmation of this and she was something of an age by then and it is highly unlikely she would make such a journey . . .'

How typical of Edward, thought Flora, to add that bit about Elizabeth and her age. He always referred to the no longer young women of the village as the Old Ladies, as if they were in shawls, rocking chairs and the last stages of dotage. Not that he did so to their faces, of course. Even Edward was not that silly, which is why they all loved him and why Flora sometimes thought she would go off pop if she didn't tell them how he insulted them behind their backs. She never did. Bun-faces were born to be kind. But had Edward been sitting here now Flora would have pointed out to him that the Old Queen had a lively reputation for keeping the young men at court dancing to her tune long after her teeth and her hair had fallen out. For all Edward knew, Elizabeth was happy and energetic well into her sixties – playing the *femme fatale* and living it up. Oh yes – if he were in the room with her – she looked around hurriedly but he was not – she most definitely would have pointed this out . . . How brave she was now that he was no longer here. Being bereaved was a little like the morning after the night's party before when you think of all the things you might have said.

'The original gatehouse was razed to the ground in 1709 and a new lodge built in the manner of Wren. I am indebted to Mr Joseph Farrell and his history of some of the buildings in and around Hurcott Ducis (price £1.20p and available in St

Lawrence's) for some of this detailed information.' Flora smiled at this careful acknowledgement. 'Some of' was highly significant. If there was one other person who took himself more seriously than Edward, it was Mr Joseph Farrell – although nowadays he must be over ninety. Mr Joseph Farrell would brook no nonsense when it came to being acknowledged in even such a humble history as Edward's. Joe Farrell had moved away now, but he had his spies, no doubt.

Edward concluded his chapter on the history and environs of his own house with 'Thus it is that the outer wall of the estate is the only remaining feature of what was once the grand and noble Priory of St Athanasius – a wall that is a reminder of the long and chequered history of both the great estate and the present writer's own humble home of Lodge Cottage.' It was then that Flora, about to turn the page, felt unwonted expectation and fervently hoped that her deceased husband had not yielded to the urge to quote 'Ozymandias'. Oh please God no, she thought. She turned the page. He had. Pound to a penny. There it was. Yet again. Edward could adapt 'Ozymandias' for any occasion and had once declaimed a couple of its lines to Hilary's geography teacher when proof was produced that Hilary, far from being persecuted with detentions by same, had not given in any homework for over a month and showed little aptitude for the subject. Edward raised a finger and fixed the mild-countenanced Mr Frobisher with gimlet eye and said 'I met a traveller from an antique land/Who said: Two vast and trunkless legs of stone/Stand in the desert . . .' Which came as a great surprise to Mr Frobisher who was not a great one for English literature. Nor, really, was Edward, but it was something Flora had once quoted to him in the early days and he liked the ringing tone of it. He learned it off by heart. How she wished he had not.

The chosen lines this time were 'Look on my works, ye Mighty, and despair!' Which Flora had thought herself as she flicked through more of the pages. '. . . In 1787 a wing was added to the rebuilt Lodge and another one proposed – but never built . . . There was a Tudor knot garden, restored by American owners in 1899, to the front of the Hall but this was destroyed during the Great War to make way for ambulances. The Lodge, now half its original size, survived throughout and was sold several times during that century, coming into the Chapman family in 1986. They have owned it ever since.'

Then there was a pencilled note in Edward's handwriting at the end saying 'Pauline – Royal and Transatlantic connections. Must expand.' Which made Flora smile. She scratched out the name Pauline, closed up the file, and took herself off for a solitary walk to think things through. It would certainly be an interesting way to pass her time, to complete the History. And she could do it – Oh perish the thought – without any interference from Edward.

Up Blowhorn Lane, past the church and the duck pond she walked, letting the place touch her with its sense of the past. A Queen of England walked here once – even if it was one known mostly for her lack of attractions. Perhaps two Queens of England, if the suggestion about Elizabeth visiting the place was based on a truth. Flora tried to imagine Henry's rejected Queen here, now. My Lady of Cleves – big, bony and horselike – striding through the meadow, or by the old cottages, her skirt brushing the edge of the pond and with a silly little scrap of a dog jumping at her hem. That was what history did for you if you let it – it allowed you to feel the warm breath of the past. A little electric thrill passed up and down her spine. Now that really was something to look forward to. The History of Hurcott would be just the right lifeline to see her through.

She turned back towards Lodge Cottage. Her spine was straighter, her lips drawn more firmly into resolution. But first – first – came the matter of Edward's own historical artefacts. His personal belongings. The touching, tormenting residue of a life now gone. Those must be dealt with before Flora could begin on anything else at all. Those, and the question of her insidious Little Treasure.

2

A Surprise Involving Pink Lips

Lucy Stevens had neither husband, brother, father nor boyfriend and her sons were nine and six years old. Nevertheless she was – as she so inappropriately put it - drop-dead positive that she could make use of Edward's clothes and bits and pieces if Mrs Chapman did not want to keep them. Mrs Chapman did not want to keep them but neither did she want Lucy Stevens to inherit them. Lucy Stevens, throughout her few years as Flora's Little Treasure, had shown herself to be a warmly appreciative person of any items that came her way. She never actually acquired anything before it was given, but Lucy was always right there at Flora's elbow before Flora properly had the thought. Flora imagined that the inside of Lucy's house would be a snapshot of her own entitled *The Way We Were*. Over the years the removal of goods had evolved quite effortlessly into something of an unspoken power struggle.

There was no logic to this at all, of course. There was no reason why Flora should not feel grateful that her old kitchen stools found such a willing home, nor that her glorious revelation about doing away with the downstairs nets had been so keenly applauded and gratefully received. But it irked, it irked. Edward just waved his hand and said, 'Oh, let the girl have the –' whatever it might be. 'She has so little.' But Flora reckoned she had a darn sight more than anybody knew of, if their own depletions over the years resided in No. 2 Cherry Tree Crescent.

The time had come for Flora to dig in her heels. Flora was

determined. Lucy had irritated the knickers off her these last few days, draping herself over Edward's desk, dusting in Edward's bedroom, and looking longingly into the distance with a 'He'd want me to have . . .' look on her face. The irritating thing was that he probably *would* want her to have. But there could be no place in Lucy Stevens's life for Edward's personal effects and clothing, none at all. Nor did Flora want to see anyone else, including Lucy if she had a mind to, wear a man's tweed jacket and sports gear that had once been her husband's. There was something goosebumpy about the possibility. Quite how she would go about such a challenge she did not know, but she vowed that Lucy Stevens should not have one stitch, nay one microstitch of Edward's wardrobe. It was a battle that Flora was determined to win. And she hoped to lose her Little Treasure in the process; a tremendous double achievement. *Multum in parvo.*

The disposal of Edward's belongings was the tough bit of widowhood, Flora was told lugubriously by almost everyone. Maybe it would be tough – emotionally challenging – she'd feel better about herself if it were – though really doing the deed so quickly could as easily reflect heartlessness. Between her Little Treasure and Hilary was between a rock and a hard place. Lucy volunteered to help, with menaces, and if Flora did not act swiftly she would also have Hilary there weeping all over the place and clutching various old jumpers to her chest as if it were Edward's living flesh. And Flora needed, in the psychobabble of the day, to be private and move on. From past experience this would not be easy – or possible – with her daughter in tow.

Three or four years previously when there was an urgent call to help earthquake victims she had made the mistake of asking Hilary to help sort through all her old infants' clothes and toys (much to Lucy's chagrin). Hilary fell upon anything and everything and clutched moth-eaten rabbits and small, faded pairs of tiny dungarees to her chest as if they were shields against the devil. At first it was touching. After an hour of it and nothing yet in the charity pile, it became quite tedious. Especially since Flora remembered how hard it had been to get Hilary to dress *in* the bally things when she was small. If Flora's memory served her right, the dungarees in question were Hilary's most loathed and fought-over garment. In the end *Mother* put her foot right in it by suggesting Hilary take them all away and keep them for her own children when they came along. Hilary went into even more of a fit over this. 'But this is my ho-o-oo-me,' she wailed. 'They belong here.'

Irritation got the better of Flora and she said, too late, a touch crisply, 'It may be your home, Hilary, but it is not a storage depot.'

At which point Hilary straightened her back and said, 'I'll ask Dad.' Which went straight back to childhood.

At which point Flora raised a telling finger and said, 'It has nothing whatsoever to do with your father.'

And – yes – they were off.

Once Hilary returned home the repacked boxes were removed from the loft and discreetly taken to the collection centre. Never to be mentioned again. Which is what Flora should have done in the first place.

This time Flora wanted to sort everything out in peace and tranquillity. She therefore told Hilary, after the funeral, that Lucy was booked to help, that Lucy needed the money because she had two small children to support and surely it was better that Hilary get back to work. Unfortunately, Lucy overheard this conversation and there were a few meaningful glances exchanged which meant, like it or not, that once Hilary had departed, Lucy would be there to help. And help herself, presumably. How it irked. Flora knew that for her own self-esteem something must be done.

Funeral over. History of Hurcott pushed to the back of a drawer. Mother concentrating on collapsed Hilary for the next several days. All made easier by knowing that the buff file was hidden away and waiting. It was her private engagement and made everything, including poor Hilary's grief, seemed easier to bear. Then – disaster. On the day before she went home Hilary suddenly sat bolt upright on the sofa as if the idea of tears had never entered her head, took her mother's hands in her own, looked her mother in the eye, and said, 'Shall we get Dad's will?' Then she rolled on to her back, stared at the grubby cream ceiling, flung her forearm to her head – a heroine *à la* Holman Hunt and said, 'I suppose this place will have to be sold. My home. My dear, dear home. I can't bear it.'

'Well I haven't got a copy,' said Flora firmly. Which was true. 'But I doubt it will come to that. Selling the house.'

Hilary then sat up and with mysterious ease moved from Holman Hunt to a George Grosz Fraulein in less than a second and said sharply. 'Well I don't think there was any money left to speak of, was there?'

From the way she spoke it seemed that Hilary was a young woman with expectations and the occasion of those presumed expectations had arrived.

'We can't do anything,' Flora said gently, though her heart beat rather hard and fast, 'Nothing at all until Ewan returns from his holiday. Your father lodged the will with him.' This was equivocation at its most helpful. Flora knew exactly what was in the will but she truly, honestly, hand on heart, did not have a copy in the house.

'Are you sure Dad didn't leave a copy with you?'

'No, dear,' said Flora sadly and truthfully. 'He never included me in anything if he could possibly help it.'

Almost at that point a tear fell. If only it had. If only she could show Hilary that she, too, grieved. But she was like a watched child on a potty – the more she was watched and waited for – the more she could not oblige and crack up. 'It hasn't quite hit me, yet,' she said forlornly and hoped this would do.

Once Flora put Hilary on the train she seemed to breathe out for the first time since it all began. Alone now she felt quite calm, quite sensible and over the next few days it became perfectly clear that her lack of cracking up was a blessing. There was so much to do in connection with bereavement. It did not end with the cards to funeral guests, *which* funeral guests, what clothes to wear and food – no – After The Funeral came the deluge with letters to answer, banks to deal with, telephone calls, his email, her email, kind words in the street – 'Oh such a lovely man, Oh such a distinguished member of the community, Oh how we will all miss his charm and gaiety . . .'

After a day or two of this Flora felt she'd been married to a cross between John F. Kennedy, Father Christmas and a selection of film stars combining all the manly virtues from Errol Flynn and Sean Connery. But she smiled her thanks and went on her way. It was never a dull moment being a widow and it was all entirely surreal. Like taking part in a drama or a farce. When a cheery-voiced stranger, for example, telephoned to talk to Edward – she found herself delivering the message 'Edward died two weeks ago' with all the ringing firmness of Vivian Leigh wanting to go to Tara. And when Sir Randolph came tottering up her garden path accompanied by Foot, she very nearly flung wide her door and curtsied. It was true enough, death had its funny moments.

Sir Randolph was now in his eighties. He reached the doorway, held on to one side of it with an ancient knotted hand and with the other reached out and pinched her cheek. 'Pretty little thing,' he said. 'Very pretty little thing.' But since, on entering the sitting room, he walked straight into the chair she offered and then, on feeling it all over needed guidance to place himself therein, she realised that he wasn't exactly in fizzing ocular shape and that she could take no crumb of comfort from his pinchings. Flora waited. She assumed this was the moment when whatever financial settlement was due would be discussed. After years of service it was not an unrealistic expectation. It might if large enough, thought Flora, help Hilary over the worst.

Foot stood at the old man's side but did not engage his eyes with Flora's. In all respects, Foot was not there. Sir Randolph put out his hand, palm upwards, and Foot took from his pocket a shiny object. Foot then handed it to Flora. It was a rather nice old-fashioned silver whistle. She looked at it, then she looked at Sir Randolph. 'Well, go on,' he said peevishly. 'Blow it. He's never going to get sent on his way across the Lethe if we don't pipe him aboard.' At which point the non-existent Foot also took a whistle, very similar in size and shape, out of his own pocket and put it to his lips.

Very solemnly both he and Flora blew. The noise was deafening and entirely unmelodious. Sir Randolph smiled a happy smile. 'There you are now,' he said with satisfaction. 'Priests and vicars no good. No good at all. Need a bit of action. Haven't got the lung power myself. But you'll do. You'll do.' Flora, completely at a loss, stood and waited as the old man stared with sightless eyes into whatever it was he saw. 'Y'know I remember him as a young man coming to me – good-looking boy. Shall miss him, shall miss him . . . Good company, he was. And now no more.'

He then rose from the chair with Foot's help. Told Flora to keep the whistle as a memento of Edward's good service over the years, and departed. It was not until the car had driven away that she realised it was probably the meanest bit of severance pay ever paid to man – she also realised how much Edward would have loved it. Sir Randolph could not have conducted himself in a more pleasing way for her husband. There is no sanity surrounding death, she thought again, and nodded to herself, each behaves in the way he or she wants, and each is different and strange to the other. In the last great mystery there were no rules. Well – except one – that a widow should grieve. Failed.

Hilary, having returned to her Robin, waited to hear when Ewan Davies could see them about the will. Flora knew she must keep a grip so she agreed to allow herself one (and only one) glass of wine each evening to be drunk while contemplating the potentialities and interesting possibilities of the solo life. There were moments, of course, in the days following Edward's death when she made four pieces of toast instead of two and when she bought two bits of fish instead of one, and when someone cracked a joke on the radio and she turned to share it – but they were fleeting in their pain. You rarely got a new life thrown at you when you were still hale and hearty but old enough to be a little wise – and she hoped she was up to embracing it. Day to day she dealt with the minutiae and looked forward to the time when the decks were cleared, the path was swept, the sheet was clean, and she could concentrate on the Hurcott History.

Meanwhile she must make use of this calm before the storm. Once the lovely, ordinary Ewan Davies of Messrs Davies and Davies was back from his very normal holiday, and the will was read, Hilary would be hopping. If it were not for the fact that he was Flora's idea of the perfect Mr Ordinary, Mr Ewan Davies, as opposed to Mr Angus Davies, who had been their solicitor and friend for over twenty years, could stay abroad for as long as he wanted. You could be quite sure, if The Will did not suit The Daughter (and it would not), it would be seen as Flora's fault. But maybe, like champions of old (she had been reading *An Age of Chivalry*, one of the many unopened books in Edward's study), Ewan would defend her. As their solicitor and friend his behaviour over the years had been exemplary but she always felt that his sympathies lay more with her. Or maybe that was wishful thinking. He was her fantasy man. Ewan Davies would never invest his life savings in a Steak 'n' Wine hostelry in an English village, or go up in a balloon without due care. He didn't even tread on the cracks in the pavement if he could help it. She loved that about him. It never occurred to her, over the years, that one day she would be free and in theory able to make the fantasy of his charming ordinariness real. Except for his wife of course. She tucked the thought away along with the History of Hurcott and bided her time.

To take her mind off it all she returned to the question of Edward's defunct wardrobe. Get that sorted out and the Little Treasure despatched and she could begin to feel in control of her life.

A certain licence was appropriate in the solving of the power struggle over Edward's clothes if Flora was to get a grip on her otherwise spinning personal universe. She would dispense with her deceased partner's effects in a way she thought fitting and she would send them where they could do some good. Lucy should not have them. From the depths of her hidden bits, Flora brought out the truth and looked at it for a moment. In other words – because Lucy had been so bloody stuck on Edward and so unstuck on her – Flora was going to get a bit of her own back. Uncommendable. Yet at the same time she would give – as the Good Book told her – to Charity. Let St Peter at the Pearly Gates work out the morality of that when the time came. Flora planned a neat little bit of gentle revenge in which Lucy would be left confused, very confused, as confused perhaps as Flora had so often been by her. This, oh dear, was going to be fun.

A charity shop was the very thing. She drove to the nearby market town in which there were two such places, sited opposite each other, rather oddly, and she chose the first she came to, the Oxfam shop . . . In the Oxfam shop they shook their heads at what Flora proposed and said they couldn't possibly – which, given what she asked of them was perfectly reasonable – so she crossed the market square and entered the Hospice shop where they nodded and agreed to her request enthusiastically. In this town Oxfam was obviously the dignified Great Aunt to the Hospice's nervously willing Poor Companion. Good. Once the highly specific arrangements were made – odd as they were – she said to the shop's helping women 'synchronise your watches' – a phrase she had long yearned to say – and drove home – striding purposefully up her path. Those who knew her situation saw this purposefulness and wondered at it. Those who had been married for many years saw this new purposefulness and not only wondered at it – they envied it – but only in private. Out loud they all said 'How brave she is,' and went on their ways.

Pausing only to collect yet more post-funeral commiserations from the mat in the hall, Flora closed the door behind her and started to hum a tune as she went up the stairs.

The following day Lucy arrived clutching several empty black plastic sacks to her small bosom and with a defiant look about her. Flora said nothing until they were upstairs in Edward's bedroom. Then, very matter-of-factly, she said, 'We'll go through the trunk first, then the chest of drawers and sort things into piles on the bed. Then we'll go through the wardrobe starting with the shoes and working upwards. The cupboard in the corner will be last – that's got the hats and sticks and bags and boots and stuff like that.' It sounded so reasonable, so sensible. And so they began.

Flora had already tipped out the contents of the top two drawers of Edward's dressing chest and removed all of its vulnerable-looking socks and underwear which she sorted into several bags. It was the day before the recycling collection of glass, tin and cloth and her box was already full and spilling over. Since the Green Guards touched nothing that was remotely outside the plastic container, she had to think again. There was nothing else for it and so last night, by moonlight, she tiptoed towards the pond and put a small bag of underwear and socks into some of the other boxes so properly lining the route, fixing their lids down with forceful determination since she did not want the sight of a fox dragging Edward's vests and pants across the lane in the early hours. Hurcott Ducis' foxes had a habit of nosing over-stuffed containers open and investigating any plastic bags they found. It seemed to be the vulpine equivalent of a good night out. If the neighbours see me, she thought, they will only think it is a mad aspect of widowhood and close their curtains and their minds to it. One thing she could say for her deceased husband, he had fought, and won, the campaign to not have surveillance in their bins. She had laughed at the time, now she was truly grateful.

It was a strange feeling, this orderly disposal – it was almost like putting bits of Edward inside everyone's recycling boxes – it had never occurred to her until now how personal underwear could be. The whole exercise took it out of her and left her feeling quite weak. But at least it was not Lucy. No one, apart from a wife, husband or long-term lover, should riffle through a dead person's underwear, even if it is clean and folded. Even for a deceased's spouse – the very woman who bought it all in the first place – the act contains an air of betrayal.

Only very much later, with her one glass of wine, as she sat by the window in the lamplight and reviewed the day and evening just passed did the enormity of what she had done hit her. This, after all, might be grief. It was certainly not normal. And nor would the following day be normal. In fact, nothing looked like it would be normal for quite a while. If ever. Now it was time for the rest.

The two women faced each other across the bed. They had worked efficiently and harmoniously and speedily. Each type of garment was folded and piled neatly upon the counterpane. The black sacks were safely stowed on Flora's side of the room but they were still empty. With luck the confrontation would never take place – if the Hospice's ladies were true to their word.

'Shoes next,' said Flora.

And Lucy immediately knelt on the floor to go through the boxes and loose items with a definitely proprietorial air. 'Pretty worn out,' said Flora.

'Oh, not really,' said Lucy.

They stared at each other and it was quite clear what they were thinking. They began to fill the sacks. Eventually Flora, her heart beating with inappropriate excitement, looked at her watch again and said, 'Will you make us a cup of coffee now? I think we deserve it. There are chocolate biscuits in the pantry.'

Reluctantly Lucy stood up. She eyed the remaining few piles on the bed, the shoes on the floor, the now filled array of bags and cases leaning against the wall – with the eye of one who covets all she sees. But she was being paid to do a job and this included making hot drinks. She nodded, gave the room one last lingering look, and went downstairs. Almost immediately Flora heard a car coming slowly along Blowhorn Lane. She went to the window. Yes. Right on time. There they were. She shoved the few remaining items into the empty bags, and waited.

The car was very bright green and very small and shiny. A Good Woman's car. She opened the window. After the Lodge's two battered wooden gates were negotiated, renegotiated and tried once more for luck, the car passed through the enormous gap very gingerly and parked on the drive by the front door. Out stepped two ladies with almost identically white hair and haircuts – fringed straight across the forehead and short and straight at the sides. They were also wearing beige skirts and pastel tops – one the colour politely known as pistachio and the other very pink. On their feet they wore flat shoes in brown, though one of them wore daringly dark stockings. Hospice shops in bigger towns might be serviced by more glamorous-looking women, but in this area of rural rectitude those who served were comfortingly, warmly, homely.

The ladies looked about them – at the house, at the garden, at the parking arrangement – and then, as if satisfied with all they saw, they began to walk towards the front door. At which point Flora called out in a theatrical whisper, 'Wait, wait there. Hallo. Thanks for coming so promptly.'

They looked up, much startled.

'I can't come down,' she continued, deciding there was no reason she could think of for not coming down and therefore not offering one. The two ladies stood with their hands on their hips staring up with puzzled expressions.

'But it's all right,' called Flora in a stage whisper, 'Wait there.' She quickly finished putting the sorted piles into bags, tied them all securely, and began dropping them out of the window. With great success.

'Right-ho,' said one of the ladies, 'I get it.' And they both began stowing them in the car.

Flora had put *Hello* Magazine on the kitchen table. Because of this she knew that Lucy would take a long, long time to prepare their coffee and return with it. 'This is the last one,' she called to the waiting women below. The final bag containing an assortment of sticks and boots and odds and sods thudded on to the gravel just as Flora heard the rattle of mugs and spoons on a tray and Lucy coming up the stairs. She waved at the ladies who waved back and called out cheery thank-yous. Those who stand in charge of a charity shop must accept the world as it is and not as they would like it to be. If a woman wishes to play Rapunzel and let down her black plastic bags, who were they . . .

'Must go,' she said. And closed the window. The timing could not have been better. When Lucy pushed open the bedroom door and re-entered the room, she saw Flora pulling out drawers and checking they were empty – and a bed and floor and a series of surfaces that were also – empty.

Lucy's face was what Flora's Aunt Helen (now deceased) would call A Picture. It reminded Flora of Rembrandt's series of etchings depicting emotions. Back in the days when she had visited art galleries (plain young women always had time on their hands which was not always a bad thing) Rembrandt's love of silly finery and posing had touched her and these studies of human response made her laugh. Now here was Lucy living it. Rembrandt could not have drawn better a woman in the throes of utter surprise and confusion and loss as Lucy presented when she re-entered the room. Happily the coffee mugs and the biscuits were on a tray which Flora took from her as she stood there and stared.

'Where's it all gone?' she asked.

'To charity,' said Flora firmly. 'They came and collected it all while you were in the kitchen.' She was very close to laughter – nervous of course. She controlled it.

Bemused and with a little squeak of amazement Lucy crossed to the open drawers and felt in them as if they might reveal a magical trick – then she ran her hands over the rucks and indentations of the counterpane where once had lain good-quality clothing. Flora sipped from her mug, nibbled her biscuit, continued to suppress her laughter, and waited. Shaking her head Lucy opened the wardrobe and felt about in it. Empty. Except. As she fluttered her hand about in the darkest corner there was the sound of plastic being rumpled. She pulled out a long black bag decorated with a drycleaner's motif. It contained – Flora suddenly remembered - Edward's dress suit – not worn since he went to the Game Fair up at Grantham. She smiled remembering that she had asked why he could possibly want his dress suit for country pursuits and he became quite uppish with her and told her that they didn't spend the whole three days up to their necks in muck and bullets nowadays – that there were some perfectly civilised evenings arranged. Gourmet stuff. Wind quartets. That sort of thing. Quite different from the way of Game Fairs in the early days of their marriage. 'They need to be,' she replied.

When she was first married Game Fairs were rough-and-ready jaunts and after the first couple of visits she never went again. When you've seen one brace of dead pheasants you've seen them all, was how she put it, and the joys of Falconry and Ferrets held little charm. On both occasions she attended Grantham it rained and the plumbing facilities in those early days were, to put it kindly, a little less than adequate. Some years on Edward argued that this had all changed and that Fairs were now recognised as big business, with sponsors, and facilities and – well – wind quartets. But by that time she was a planet removed from fancying it and much more inclined to look forward to a few days in the house on her own. Edward was already becoming very, very exhausting. He never asked her again after the first few years and agreed that it was, largely, a man's pursuit. So to see him packing posh gear was strange. Flora had considered going with him this time but, as he'd said, they hadn't booked her in and it was too late now. 'Next year, perhaps?' she had said. And he'd agreed. Well, so much for that.

Of course she had taken the dress suit to the cleaner's afterwards. Flora undid the first few inches of the zipper on the plastic bag and checked. Yes, there it was, Edward's cleaned dress suit. A sorry reminder, really, rather than a poignant one. Like all men, he looked wonderful when he wore it – even better than usual as everyone liked to tell her – and there were times – yes there were – when she looked at him and her heart did strange things and she loved him all over again and they had danced or laughed or did the party chit-chat and felt happy and unremarkable in their coupledom. But not for a long time. How was it that their united happiness just seemed to fade away rather than be lost to too much arguing and fighting and – latterly – indifference? How was it that two bodies which knew each other so intimately could turn their backs so cheerfully on sharing their nights? Too late now and best forgotten. She realised that she was grieving for her marriage more than for Edward.

Lucy was looking at the plastic bag, hope replacing her expression of fear and amazement. Flora longed to waggle her fingers and say Hey Presto but managed to contain herself. Whatever was being said of her, or not, in Hurcott Ducis, she did not want to add to it. Of course she must give the dress suit to Lucy. No way out of that. At least the rest of the stuff had escaped her acquisitive little clutches. A mollified Lucy went home with the black plastic bag flapping in the breeze. Had Flora any idea of what such a gift would bring in its wake – she would have thought twice, thrice about gifting it.

Odd behaviour, mine, thought Flora. She remembered the newly bereaved retired doctor's wife, Stephanie Blount, a woman renowned for her mild temperament and capable lap, who had behaved immaculately up to and including Dr Blount's cremation, and who suddenly began behaving in an entirely uncharacteristic way by becoming rude and aggressive and foul-mouthed to people who came to condole. 'If one more person squeezes my sodding hand and says they know how I feel I shall do a bloody murder,' was what she reportedly said.

Now Flora could believe it. So yes, it helped to remember that even the best of bereaved could behave strangely. Woebegone empathisers did not bring succour. He was dead. He was gone. He would never come back. She would find compensations. She would find other things to do. That History, or even some slovenly idleness. Love, with her features, must be out of the question. But she would not do Good Works – which, she remembered, was the second suggestion made to the doctor's widow and resulted in her not only pushing the vicar's wife in the pond but holding her down while using several loud words of the Anglo-Saxon variety.

Flora's sympathy at the time lay with the vicar's wife, the straightforward Mrs Bernice Oakes, committed spouse of the slightly vague Reverend Arthur Oakes who, after she clambered out of the pond with immaculate dignity, despite weeds and other unmentionable stuff adhering to her bony shoulders, forgave her assailant with great good grace. Now, Flora found her sympathies were more with the widow Blount. There was something altogether infuriating about the way everyone talked either in hushes and whispers – or loudly and heartily. It made one consider taking up the trumpet as a life-enhancing option. Between her husband and her daughter Good Works was what Flora felt she had done for most of her adult life. Now there were other possibilities.

Ewan wrote to say that he would be back in the office on Thursday. It surprised her that he did not come to Edward's funeral but she decided that he was too discreet to make the grand gesture of cancelling his holiday. His letter of condolence was lovely as was his request that Flora name a charity of her choice for his donation. She longed to write back and suggest the Great British Eccentrics Society, of which Edward was member number one in a field of one, but it would worry Ewan. Humour was not his strong point where the proprieties of life were concerned. She liked that about him, too. You could make a throwaway remark to Ewan – something along the lines of – Oh, it doesn't matter if they haven't asked me to their party – and he would wrinkle that balding brow of his and look concerned and think about what he could do instead of taking the easy way out and saying something such as More Fool Them and going on his way. Flora knew this because she had once said that very thing to him about Betty Gregg's Post Office Party when Edward was away and he had discreetly, and kindly, sorted it out.

The appointment made was for Thursday late afternoon which was perfect. It meant that Hilary could arrive in good time for lunch and she could also – with a bit of luck – get back to Cambridge on the same day, too. With all Edward's clothes gone and this final deed over, Flora would be able to feel the corset was definitely off for good. She was not looking forward to the reading of the will and could imagine the Lady Bracknell of a scene as Ewan spelled out the truth of it. She braced herself accordingly, and rang Hilary.

'Excellent,' she said. 'Be good to get it all sorted.'

'Yes,' said her mother faintly. 'Though I wouldn't get your hopes up too high . . .' But she was talking to a dialling tone.

That evening, at dusk when the April showers had cleared – Tuesday, a night to remember – Flora had a sudden desire to see if she could find this carved stone that was supposed to be in the boundary wall. She put on her wellington boots, took the torch, and plodded through the wet hinterland between where their garden and paddock ended and the boundary wall divided it from the new houses. There was a long line of hawthorns and elder and, from the middle of June the most wonderful pink dog roses marking the end of their civilised world and the beginning of the new buildings, and nothing was touched by electric mower, hedger or strimmer. It was very shaded and nearly always damp and tonight the trees were dripping with moisture. No one was likely to see her as she roamed around.

It was not an easy task in the half light, even with a full-blooded torch, as the mosses and lichens needed rubbing away and each of the older stones was bumpy and irregular enough to require careful checking. She was about halfway through the first corner when the evening finally turned to night. A sudden vision of returning home to a glass of something cheering came to mind. She had all the time in the world now and need never race through anything ever again. She placed a large stone at the point where she had stopped and felt pleased with herself. Clever Flora, she said as she made her way home. She cast off her mucky boots, which made dirty marks on the kitchen floor when they landed, and she decided that she would tell Lucy, very soon, perhaps tomorrow, that she no longer needed a cleaner. That she could no longer afford a cleaner. Well, she couldn't. She would give Lucy her severance pay and that would be that. It was not an interview that she relished but once it was over – Freedom.

Just as she was pouring out her one glass of wine – she still allowed herself only one a night – into a very large glass she had found at the back of one of the cupboards – or possibly 'hunted high and low for' was nearer the mark – preparatory to putting her feet up to watch the news , there was a ring at the doorbell. Very reluctantly she put down her glass, opened the door, and found a strangely countenanced Little Treasure on the doorstep. She looked unusually nervous but was bold enough to step determinedly into the hallway. She was wearing full make-up, which somehow did not bode well.

'Lucy,' said Flora, surprised. 'Come in'. Her heart sank. 'Is everything all right?'

Lucy stood there with an air of importance, a disturbing sense of having grown a couple of inches.

'Oh yes,' she said. 'Everything's fine.' She walked confidently into the kitchen. The Little Treasure saw the very large torch on the kitchen table and the discarded wellingtons. 'Problem?' She asked.

'Oh no,' said Flora, 'I was just looking for something in the garden.'

'Lost something?'

'No – nothing like that'.

Lucy was prepared to wait.

Flora gave in. 'Well, I was just looking for a special stone. In the far wall. Something historical apparently.'

They both blinked at each other, waiting. If Lucy has come to have another go at me about Edward's clothes, Flora thought, I shall be very terse. 'Anyway – you didn't come to discuss – er – stones,' said Flora.

But then, surprisingly, Lucy said, 'Oh I know about that stone with the date on it. It's supposed to be something to do with that king who had all the wives – and one of them lived here or something.'

'Yes,' said Flora forgetting her sinking heart. 'Have you seen it?'

'No – but old Mr Farrell came in to the school and gave a talk on local history. Edward –' and here she paused – 'talked about it. He said it was in the old wall somewhere.' She laughed, but not very nicely. 'The King divorced his wife because she looked like a horse or something and then dumped her down here. Was she local then?'

'No', Flora snapped. 'She was German. She came from Flanders which was part of Germany.' Flora could feel herself reddening which didn't help her temper. There was something very unpleasant about the easy way Lucy spoke so cruelly. Flora could imagine it being said about her, *Shame it had to be the husband who died first – such a good-looking man and she's – well – she's a bit –* 'Anyway, Lucy – you didn't come here to talk about Tudor history . . .?'

Lucy raised an eyebrow at Flora – a trick Flora did not know her Little Treasure could spring – and said with a smile – 'No. And sorry to come so late but –' She placed a large brown envelope on the table between the bottle of wine and the torch. 'I thought I should return this.'

She pointed to the envelope. 'I found it pinned to the suit.' Her eyes were gleaming oddly. If Flora had not known her better she might have considered the light in them malevolent. 'The dress suit,' Lucy added. 'It's a note from the cleaners.'

'Thank you,' she said, puzzled. 'About a stain, probably.'

They both stared at the envelope. Lucy made no move to go. As if to be helpful she said, 'Mum's looking after the boys.'

'Oh good.'

'Aren't you going to open it?'

Lucy moved nearer.

'It'll keep,' said Flora, putting the envelope down next to the glass of wine. Suddenly and quite desperately, she wanted her drink, her private ritual. She remembered her manners. 'Would you like a drink, Lucy?' she said as she picked up the glass.

'I think there's something inside it,' said Lucy.

'Really?' said Flora holding it up to the light. 'Seems all right.' She gave Lucy a look reminiscent of her time in the infant class. It always worked there.

'No – I mean in the envelope. Another envelope.'

Flora looked. There was. On the front of the outer envelope, the one with the drycleaners' logo, was written 'Found in pocket and returned.' She took out the second envelope. On the front of it in small, much flourished handwriting, was the word 'Edward'. Flora opened it. Lucy came closer, holding her breath. She was looking not at the envelope and its contents but at Flora's face.

Flora read the note, also written in the small, much flourished handwriting. It said:

Darling Edward
By the time you read this our weekend will be just a happy memory. Three beautiful, beautiful days. It was wonderful. You were brilliant at the shooting and I shall keep the sweet little posy pot by my bed to remind me of you. I'm so glad you liked the yellow jumper. All my own work. Next time, Monsieur, it will be Paree!
Here's a kiss.
P x

And there was – a pink kiss – the perfect lip imprint. Baby-pink lipstick. Now where had Flora seen such a colour before?

'Goodness,' said Flora. She was thinking on her feet, and nearly off them. So that was where the yellow sweater came from. When he wore it for the first time Flora told him he looked as if he had been dipped in custard. And he agreed. The pink kisser had obviously been given a quite different impression. Honestly, husbands!

If the watching Lucy held her breath for much longer she would expire. Which, Flora felt, would be no bad thing. She looked her Little Treasure straight in her questioning little eye. 'Ah,' she said, with saccharine sincerity, 'Edward used to call me his Poppet.' She waited for Lucy to burst out laughing but Lucy did not. She just went on looking at Flora intently, though with just a trace of disappointment. 'I'd quite forgotten,' said Flora gaily, 'That he'd left that silly note in the pocket.' She put down the untouched glass and made a move out of the kitchen. 'Thank you so much,' she said. 'Thank you for bringing it back'. By now she had reached the front door which she opened and held open widely and pointedly. 'But you shouldn't have bothered.'

Lucy hesitated. Flora stood her ground. She clenched her teeth in what must have been a very strange apology of a smile. Beyond the door the evening was dark and mild with a peppering of stars. A beautiful late April night. Oddly she seemed to hear the tune of 'April in Paris' floating over the hawthorn hedge and rippling through the Nellie Moser. For the first time since Edward's death she felt the beginning of tears. 'Poppet,' she said harshly to the hawthorn hedge, and nodded at its very sharp thorns. 'My Poppet,' she said loudly to the rustling new leaves of the Nellie. Then she turned towards the messenger and said 'Poppet', very firmly, and 'Thank you, Lucy,' and 'Goodbye.'

Off into the night went Lucy Stevens, her backward glance saying she was still unconvinced. As, indeed, she should be. Flora, feeling as if all the air had escaped from her, closed the door and looked down at the note again. Her hands trembled. 'By the time you read this . . .' But he never had, had he? Of course not. Whoever P was she did not know that old-fashioned husbands seldom took things to the drycleaners if there was a wife about. Which made her think that whoever P was, she was unmarried and probably young. If only the wife in question had remembered to check the pockets first, she thought. Flora wondered in a detached way what she might have said to him when confronted with the silly note but she would never know. How clever of him to wriggle out of a situation like this. She looked up at the mild night and the stars. Then she looked down at the ground. Yet again he had dropped her in it without a care in the world (quite literally) himself.

As if the will and Hilary's likely reaction to it were not enough to be going on with – now there was *this*. Whatever *this* might be. Or who.

Poppet, indeed. I'll Poppet him, she thought.

Wishful thinking.

3

Hilary Gets a Shock

The meeting with Ewan Davies, thought Flora, reminded her vaguely of similar scenes in Jane Austen where money and marriage and inheritance were concerned: Fanny and John Dashwood came to mind as eager-eyed Hilary leaned forward in her seat in certain expectation while Flora sat as upright as if she had a whale's rib stuck up her back. Even Ewan, Flora saw (for with tenderness she noticed such things) was strained, which meant that with his experience of life, death and wills he, too, knew that Hilary would take the news badly. Ewan sat on the opposite side of his desk in a dark suit, with a dark, sober face. One thing was certain, Hilary, who was listening intently, was not amused.

While the solicitor spoke Flora daydreamed. His face was sun- or possibly wind-tanned, the little bald bit on the top of his head was the same, though paler, and his nose was a deep almost-mahogany, as were his hands. She quite forgot herself. 'I'll bet you've been playing golf,' she said, sitting upright suddenly and laughing. 'Not fishing at all.'

'Both,' he said politely.

'You're a real sports fiend, Ewan, aren't you?' She smiled at him fondly. Edward only enjoyed rugby and Eton fives and tolerated village cricket.

Since the solicitor was in the process of explaining that the total value of Edward's assets, including the house, was minimal and that everything was put in Flora's name to avoid the – er – consequences of some of Edward's investments, it was a strange interjection on Flora's part. Ewan hesitated, coughed, and looking surprised and torn between ordinary human exchange, smiled fleetingly before going on to describe the rules of probate and other legalities.

'*Mum,*' said the scowling Hilary in a voice of such disgust that Flora blushed violently. 'How could you? In the middle of all this?'

Flora didn't know. Ewan leaned across his desk and patted Hilary's hand and said , 'People behave in all sorts of ways at times like these. It's nothing to get upset about. I see it often.'

For which Flora could have kissed him and Hilary backed off.

'Now,' said Ewan, looking more relaxed, 'I'll go over the whys and wherefores of everything I think you'll need to know and then, when I've finished, you can ask me whatever you like.' And he began. Eurotunnel, the Far East, an Abercrombie UK Pension, Giles's restaurant. Disasters all. Lodge Cottage was safe in Flora's name, so was a small annuity and not a lot else. It was enough. Flora had battled hard to persuade Edward to move from their tied house on the Estate to a home of their own. In the end she had only achieved the move by asking his father to plead for her. Her father-in-law simply said, 'Stop dreaming, Edward, and Just Do It.' And It was done.

Lodge Cottage was affordable because it backed on to land where they were building the new housing complex (the new constructions were made from a curious pale grey mock stone which never grew lichen and looked forever young and whose design was wickedly mean and pinched). Edward fought valiantly, and won, to have the access road moved so that they would not have streams of what he called Yobs-in-Four-by-Fours crunching past their door at all hours. After that both sides left each other alone. The shrubbery, the old stone wall and their paddock kept them separate and at peace. Three and a half bedrooms were quite enough, and a garden of less than half an acre was perfectly adequate. She was no dedicated country wife, nor horticulturalist, and Lodge Cottage required only the minimum of care. Which was now Lucy's undoing. Apart from the question of affording her, Flora could put her hand on her heart and say, 'I do not need you any more.' And how her heart lifted when she finally spoke the words. I am a manageable woman living in a manageable house, Flora thought – and didn't mind the idea one bit.

What was left of the house by the time all the previous owners had picked at it was a good, solid mid-eighteenth-century building with a pretty garden which still had its original nineteenth-century iron railings to the front, good wooden gates, and a roughcast old stone wall around the rest of the plot. Sometimes noises carried from the new houses but not often – the paddock saw to that. It was dear Ewan who helped them to hold on to the scrap of land when the Edward and Giles fiasco threatened it. She loved the paddock and the way it separated her from the sparkling new little boxes and sometimes she just wanted to go out and roll in it like a cat establishing its territory. Lodge Cottage – for all its smallness – had charm and the charm was enhanced by its being lopped off and asymmetrical rather than a perfect little classical villa. It was like a sweet-faced dog that has only three legs and has learned to look cute to make up for its shortcomings.

There was one great practical reason for their buying in Hurcott Ducis. It still had a railway station. It was remarkable that Dr Beeching had left a railway station intact here, but rumour suggested that there was a certain lady of Hurcott who knew a little more than was good for the axe-wielding locophobe and that she it was who insisted on the station remaining. Some said this was his mother, some said it was his aunt, others said it was someone of an altogether different kind of close relationship. Whatever the reason – there it was – a functioning railway station – a lifeline. Hence, very likely, its gradual expansion into something approaching a small country town. But its core was still village. Everyone was entirely interested in everyone else's business and what they didn't know they made up. All in all, Hurcott Ducis was the perfect place in which to live, widowed or not, and whatever Hilary might say, following the outcome of the reading of the will, that is where Flora intended to stay.

When Ewan had finished and leaned back and removed his spectacles and relaxed a little and smiled, Hilary gripped the edge of his desk.

'Is that it?' she asked.

'It is,' said Ewan.

'So what happened to the money?'

Ewan kept his smile and said, 'I've just explained. Your father made some very unwise decisions.'

'He was far too clever to do that,' said Hilary. 'I know my father. And he was clever.'

Ewan looked at Flora, who looked back at him pleadingly. Ewan coughed. Flora looked at him even more pleadingly. Flora imagined, very hard indeed, the image of a puppy on the front of a particularly sentimental birthday card, and tried thought transference. Ewan sighed. And explained to Hilary all over again – in gentle terms – how her father had been somewhat feckless. He reiterated that it was nobody's fault but Edward's, and that the word fault was too harsh. 'Of course your mother did try to dissuade him –' he crinkled his eyes at Hilary – 'but you know what your father was like. Dynamic.'

There was a short pause and then: 'Poor Dad,' she said eventually. 'He must just have got sidetracked.' Hilary gave her mother a sideways look. The solicitor faced the daughter and the daughter faced the solicitor and it was the daughter who blinked.

'Your father was always – a little – over-enthusiastic – in his choices, Hilary. And I think if he were here now he would put his hand up. He was extremely glad that the house was in your mother's name.'

Flora was fairly sure, now, that she could love Ewan. Loyal support breeds all kinds of affection. How very easy it is, she thought, when someone shows they like you, to dare to like them back. There was something about the serious, soft way he spoke to Hilary that gave her the feeling she had a champion. She looked at him fondly – his little bald patch, his slightly crumpled features, his pinky brown suntan which she was sure would only touch the bits of him that poked out of a shirt – the way he placed his hands flat on the desk in front of him just-so – no – he would never choose to go up in a basket or wish to be associated with a Great British Eccentric. He was also – and perhaps this was why he was such a nice person – a man of sorrow and acquainted with grief – in the guise of his beautiful bibulous wife – and Flora would very much like to . . . Hilary turned to her mother and said angrily, 'So what do I do now?'

'I think,' said Flora trying to sound nonchalant and cheerful and putting away the fond image of Ewan sitting with his very ordinary slightly balding head on her lap in the sun-drenched, daisy-filled paddock, 'that you'll have to wait until I pop my clogs.' She gave Ewan a grateful smile and shrugged and said to Hilary, 'These things happen.' But she knew that would not be the end of it. Nor was it. Hilary squared her shoulders and said, 'Why can't you sell the house?'

It always amazed her that Edward chose the name Hilary for their daughter. Hilary – the Lenten term at Oxbridge – Lent – a time for meditation, consideration, offering up the spirit and forgetting the cravings of the flesh . . . 'After all,' she added, with the heedlessness of youth, 'you don't need all that space now.'

Ewan sucked in his breath but Flora was there before him. 'If I did that,' she said, with what she hoped was a bland smile, 'then I would have to come and live with you. It's a possibility.' Who would blink first this time?

Ewan did. His face no longer wore the calm professional benign expression but a look of absolute horror. Plainly what he wanted to say to Flora was, 'Have you gone stark, staring mad?' Wisely he did not. Instead he brought firm, professional, fiscal order to the proceedings. 'It is a very bad time for property,' he said. 'And I would not recommend it. Indeed – in the light of my responsibilities towards you both – I would positively discourage such a move. I have seen too many parents and children end up in a bad way when such schemes have been undertaken.' Flora very nearly kissed him. Hilary, it was clear, very nearly brained him.

'Such as?' asked Hilary.

'Oh – parents who sign over their houses to their children to avoid inheritance tax and then the child marries someone who has no conscience – the result is often disastrous and miserable.'

'Well Robin is very nice. He wouldn't do anything like that.'

'All the same, Hilary,' said Ewan, 'I cannot, as your executor, agree with you.'

And Flora thought that it wasn't – really – Robin she was worried about. She and Hilary needed time. Time to what? Time to bond, she supposed.

That night Flora stood at the open doorway of Edward's empty room. She had something to say to this husband of hers. Lucy, in perhaps her last act of admiration for her deceased employer, had re-made the bed after their clothes-sorting with a smoothness and exactitude that approached the military. This increased Flora's impatience but the bare room was so empty, so spiritually empty, that she thought this conversation would probably be like so many other conversations she could remember with her husband – without impact and scarcely listened to. Nevertheless she told him that she knew about his affair – or one-night – or one-Game-Fair – stand, or whatever it was, and that she did not mind the hands-on nature of the activity so much as she found it hard to forgive him the deceit. And that she was going to have to tickle up this Pink Lips person and deal with her so that, with a bit of luck, the disturbance she felt would go away and she could just get on with her life. And leave him to get on with his death.

Dear Edward, she thought, suddenly, what an endlessly surprising man – she would never have thought him capable of keeping such an adventure a secret. I'll bet, she thought, he's giving them a run for their money right now whether it's Satan's or St Peter's lot. She went over to the window. Lucy had drawn the curtains to signify mourning. Flora pulled them right back to let in the bright moonlight, and left the room. In a month or two or three she would probably get around to decorating it – lilac maybe, or apple-blossom pink. But perhaps not quite yet. As she passed the washing basket on the landing she spoke to it. 'And I'll deal with what you're hiding, later.'

After a day or two, when the heated telephone calls between them, interspersed with tears, had died away and Hilary was still cross but resigned, Ewan called at Lodge Cottage to see Flora. Although she had sent him a card thanking him – as delicately as possible – for all he had done – she had not expected him to call. He was her first truly welcome visitor since Edward's funeral and she was quite inappropriately pleased and found herself patting her hair.

Ewan always surprised her when he wasn't in his office uniform of dark suit and unremarkable tie and sensible, solemn face. Today he was on his way back from playing golf and wore a bright blue shirt and yellow trousers with a paler blue-green jacket. A very odd combination. The shirt's top button was undone which managed to look shockingly saucy. He was about her age, she supposed, and had a strange way with colours. Perhaps it showed a hidden wildness. The yellow trousers were terrible, absolutely terrible, an outrageous example of the uniform of the professional class of countryman at rest. If they were married she would soon have them off him. The misplaced thought made her smile. Poppet indeed. The discovery had certainly added a little grit to her oyster.

'Those trousers,' she said, 'are very – bright.'

He laughed. 'So I'm told. Can't see it myself. But it means the spotter plane can spot us when we get stuck in the rough looking for a ball.' He looked down at them quite unrepentantly.

'You go in for bright colours when you're not at work, Ewan, don't you?'

'Do I?' He said, pleased. 'What a noticing sort of a person you are, Flora.'

The visit had the immediate effect of putting a bit of a kick into her step. Recently the post included brochures from A Seniors' Singles Club (they must scour the obituaries for business – how clever – the name of the deceased's grieving wife or husband was always mentioned); a flyer from a company offering 'Frail, Disabled and Partially-Disabled Holidays' which she took very personally; a gardening magazine offering gadgets for the weak and feeble. She also read a piece in the local paper headlined '10 Years Old and Still Going Strong. Congratulations to the Over Seventies' Fetish Club' – to which article she found her eyes strangely drawn . . . Ewan's arrival dispensed with these various assaults on her younger id. One did not have to be twenty to feel secret little trills of pleasure. Presumably one felt them when one was Frail, Disabled or Partially-Disabled, too, but she was none of those things nor, she reaffirmed, was she likely to be for a while – putting her knees to one side. She must stay fit and well. If Hilary was going to be her carer they needed to move on to balmier emotional climbs first.

They sat in the garden with their coffee. Flora was thinking about how happy she felt. Ewan looked the back of the house up and down. 'You know,' he said, 'there are some very old foundations here – you can see the line of them at the base of this wall.' He went over and bent down and ran his fingers over the raised surfaces – she watched his hand tracing the contours, it was a nice hand, and she found herself again imagining them both sitting on the sofa and watching *Question Time* or *Panorama* with a mug of cocoa . . .

'Flora?'

'Sorry?' she said. 'I was thinking about something else.'

He said again, 'I should think a lot of interesting people have lived here over the years.'

'They have.' She told him about Edward's history and that she thought she might finish it. He nodded. 'Good to take your mind off things,' he said. And then a light of something came into his eyes – sad, perhaps, or merely regretful? 'Boredom can be a destructive little demon . . .'

With one hand he balanced his mug of coffee on his slight pot belly and with the other he tapped at some sorry dried-up-looking daffodils that poked their heads out in front of the old garden wall. Flora saw them through his eyes and felt a little ashamed. She really ought to do something with the garden. Ewan looked so at ease here. Perhaps she could persuade him to help? Begin the pottering together even if he still had a wife. The gardening implements for the weak and feeble returned to haunt her. She shook herself. Absurd. It was one thing to invite a married man into your bed – and quite another to invite him to help you with the gardening. That really was a step too inti-mate . . . 'I'd like to know more about Anne of Cleves,' she said, getting her mind back to something sensible. 'She was given the original estate in 1540 apparently – when Henry VIII divorced her. Which means –'

Ewan nodded comfortably. 'Oh yes,' he said. 'Her.'

He made such a delightfully restful picture of a man relaxing in a garden. How fond of him she was . . .

'Married Henry VIII, didn't she? Number three, was it, or number four? She was the plain one. The German girl? The Flemish Mare?' He said this last with a little laugh. He obvi-ously found the sobriquet amusing and was still smiling about it as he continued sipping his coffee.

Flora had been looking at him with dewy eyes and feeling pleasant tender feelings. As soon as he said those words the softness surrounding him vanished. She remembered her Aunt – and Edward – and then even Lucy saying much the same – *Lucy* – how easy it was to sum up the whole of a personality in a word like ugly or plain. She said sharply, 'What a way to go down in history.'

'Yes,' he said contentedly.

'Have you ever seen a picture of her?' she asked.

'I don't think so. There probably isn't one if she was as bad as all that.' He laughed again, obviously pleased at the wit. Flora stiffened and remained silent.

He was still looking indulgently at nothing in particular and Flora remembered her childhood when she had cut herself out of a number of family photographs because Rosie was so pretty – she was about eleven or twelve when the light dawned – and although as far as she could remember nobody had ever said anything – she just suddenly knew. She was plain. A little flame of a painful memory began inside her and she stood up. Her body language might have warned him for she put her hands on her hips and stood with feet apart. She could not be more obvious about wanting him to go. 'Well,' she said, 'I suppose if I'm going to get on with it I'd better get on. Research to do. Pictures to find. As you say, a lot of interesting people to get through. Pretty and plain, handsome and ugly – all grist to the mill.'

He stood up, more obedient than surprised at her sudden change of tone. 'Good,' he said. 'I'm glad you're busy.' She wished she had been a little less abrupt. He put his mug on the table with pedantic exactitude – moving it with his fingers until he aligned it just so – Oh dear, she thought, that kind of thing could become irritating – and his face became professional – which at least saved him from a scolding. Flora nearly told him what it was like to be called plain Jane and no nonsense – throughout childhood, throughout school, and Bun Face throughout her marriage and how she had every sympathy with the blind and the wheelchair-bound *et al* who constantly battled against being thought a little vacant. Being plain belonged in the same camp. Of course there was a faction that said 'she's no beauty therefore she must be very bright' but this was not Edward's view of things. Flora did not look romantic enough to be an enjoyable wife for him. Hilary with her long blonde hair and blue eyes and Holman Hunt dramatic gesturing was fine, acceptable in every respect – Hilary's mother, alas, had a serious design fault – one which Edward, very kindly, pretended to overlook. And now, here was Ewan, hardly Adonis, banging on about Anne of Cleves being as unattractive as a raw-boned horse. And finding it funny.

Flora's chin came out a little further. A glimmering of recognition flitted across Ewan's face. Cautious now, and backing away slightly he said, 'I just wanted to remind you not to consider selling the house. I know Hilary wants you to but it is your only asset.'

You can say that again, thought Flora sourly.

Then he relaxed and looked about him. 'And it's a lovely little place. Hard to match. And you shouldn't do anything to upset your equilibrium just yet. You've been through quite enough.' She relaxed a little. It wasn't Ewan's fault that he was the victim of historical prejudice. And he was kind to her, always had been, no matter what he privately thought of her features. She resumed her smile and said, a touch stiffly, 'Thanks for your help. I always value it.'

He looked relieved. 'Don't be bullied. That's my advice.' He tapped at the drooping heads of the very sorry-looking daffodils again. 'Yes. That's my advice. And today it's free.' He gave her a very formal, slightly disapproving look – and then laughed. 'And if you ever need a bit of help,' he said, 'I'm quite good at gardens, too. But I'd probably charge for that.'

Oh, she thought, so taken aback that she forgot to pursue the offer, so he *would* like to get his hands dirty with her. This was the point at which she should sidle up and look into his eyes and ask something skittish – what he would like as payment for instance – or how together they could have a good old go at cross pollination. But faint heart and the words 'Flemish Mare' proved a barrier. If he could laugh at Anne of Cleves he could just as easily laugh in her face, too. She was aware of the legend that all men were out for a bit of the other if it was remotely on offer, but in all her thirty years and more of marriage no one, no one at all, had ever so much as winked in her direction. Well, apart from Sir Randolph and he had only done so once he'd lost most of his sight. This did not breed confidence now.

They both laughed, a little uneasily, and she said, just to compound the current hopelessness of her state of mind. 'I don't think I'm ready for gardening.' She said it weakly. 'That history project will be enough for me to be going on with. And anyway, I'm no gardener. As you see.' She waved her arm in the direction of the wildly overgrown bushes of drying forsythia and jasmine and other unidentifiable explosions of greenery. 'I might even pay Wally Binder to come in and give it a tidy.' Now that was a symbol of her newfound status. A financial decision made all by herself. 'If he's not too expensive,' she added, out of deference to her husband who would be spinning in his dually occupied grave.

Ewan nodded and said a little wistfully, 'It's a good idea. I always wished that Dilly had an interest –' he faltered, she did not speak – seldom was his wife ever mentioned – 'I'd have liked her to join The Players with me but . . .' And then he stopped and the moment passed. 'But you could join . . .' He gave her an encouraging smile. Flora was torn between saying yes to please him, and knowing she would never, ever, dare to tread the boards. Or want to. 'Oh, I couldn't act for a toffee,' she said.

He turned to go. 'Ah well – just a thought. It would have been nice to have you in the group.' And he gave a little resigned flap of his arms and set off into the house.

Flora was aware that she had thrown away an opportunity by being absolutely honest and vowed to become wilier. Too late for now, though. In any case if she *had* hurled herself at him with a winning smile and a garden hoe he would probably have put it down to the weirdness of grief – and patted her on her plain little head and continued turning the sod. Or run a mile. Anyway, as he said, there was always Dilly.

'Shame,' she said, 'that Dilly won't join.' And was about to ask And how *is* Dilly – when she realised that this would be a little tricky to answer. The same? Worse? A little better today?

In her darker moments good sense gave way to fantasy and the idea of marrying someone like Ewan rather than a changeling eccentric like Edward seemed all that a woman could need. Roses, roses all the way. But it was never like that, was it? Or seldom. It certainly had not been roses, roses all the way for Dilly Davies. And something must have caused it. Ewan never, ever spoke about the fact that Dilly *drank*. Hard not to know it with the number of times she made it so obvious. Most recently Dilly was taken in by the police drunk in charge of a horse. Very drunk – facing the wrong way as a matter of fact with her snood caught under her chin. Funny if you were not related to her, not funny for a local solicitor. It even made the national press, in a small paragraph, so funny did the world find it. Edward laughed over the story until Flora asked him how he would feel if it had been her. He stopped laughing, it was true, but managed to make her feel serially dull by saying, 'But you wouldn't do anything like that – you're just not capable.' Which immediately had her contemplating something outrageous with a bottle of gin and a sheep – except she could not think what – which very probably compounded Edward's view of her. It didn't help when he patted her arm and said he preferred her that way, sober. Flora Sobersides. It was enough to make you frolic in the village pond naked. Dilly had done that, too.

It was unfathomable to Flora. Dilly was a startlingly beautiful woman. Fair-skinned, eyes blue as night, honey-haired, rose-lipped, white-teethed, small-waisted, slight-hipped, long unblemished legs. All that she had, and still she ended up weeping into her mascara in a police cell while the baying hounds of the Ducis Vale *Mercury* pounded on the desk sergeant's window.

Suddenly, looking out at the garden and the early May sunshine, with the daffodils struggling for air and the grass needing to be mowed and the weeds showing every satisfaction with their being left entirely alone – suddenly she had a wonderful feeling of safety and pleasure. Perhaps it was the very pressure of being beautiful that made things so difficult? For much of the time – if you were without ego – you could pass through the world quietly and comfortably. The effect of beauty was something Flora would never know, that was for sure. 'I wonder,' she said out loud, 'how Anne of Cleves felt knowing she was being compared to a horse?'

Ewan shrugged from the doorway. 'It was different then.'

Was it? she wondered. Well, of course it wasn't. What he meant was that women shut up then. Expected it even. She looked at him in his silly trousers with his little bald spot and his rounded belly and she wondered what it would be like to lie naked with him. 'What a very silly thing to say, Ewan,' she said. And then drifted off for a moment visualising herself stripped to her vulnerable nakedness and him saying, 'You look too much like a horse, my dear . . .'

'Flora?' Ewan was speaking.

She mentally put her clothes back on. 'Yes', she said happily, 'you're right. I'm not going to sell the house. I'm going to enjoy all this peace and calm and – contentment.' Ewan's face adopted a slight shadow of doubt so she quickly added, 'And get over my sadness in a quiet and easy fashion. How wise you are, Ewan, how wise you are.'

He stood on the top step looking down at her and seemed gratified. Why should she care how Dilly was? Much more relevant to ask Ewan how he was. Selfishness was an enjoyable commodity. One of the things she had learned was that you were excused niceness fatigues if you were plain. No one really noticed either way, though on the whole Flora found being nice easiest. But in her widowhood, for the time being, she was allowed to be whatever she wanted. Why mention his – or anyone's – wife? Why be good? He seemed to be reluctant to go. She set aside the Flemish Mare entirely. If he was reluctant to go – well then. She started humming 'I love Paris in the springtime' as she followed him indoors. 'You know,' he said, 'despite what you say, you might think about joining The Players. Something to do, after all.' She wondered, hopefully, if the renewed suggestion might be to do with her singing until he added – 'You could sew for us . . .' Thus reminding her never to get her hopes up about anything. He smiled. 'They're quite good.'

No they weren't. Flora had seen only one of their productions many years ago. *The Constant Wife* with Bernice Oakes as the formidable Mrs Culver – and it was dire. They might be capable of better things but it was hard to tell given the kind of plays they put on. Very dated thrillers and comedies of manners from between the wars in which men wore blazers and flannels and were called things like Cedric (how much it said for the conservatism of village life that the local men jumped at the chance of donning a striped jacket and a boater) and in which women wore startlingly bright lipstick, bodiced frocks and a mass of costume jewellery. Ewan was not in The Players in those days – but their repertoire now was much the same. *Merrily We Roll Along* was the most recent. When she and Edward saw the poster they both said, 'There'll be nothing merry about it.'

'Shame,' said Ewan. 'You'd have been a breath of fresh air.'

He had no idea how saying such things touched her heart.

Emboldened she looked at the clock. It was nearly twelve – why not? Might help to loosen them both up a bit. She offered Ewan a glass of wine. Too late she realised that she could not have done anything more wrong. He jumped away from her as if scalded. 'Too early for me,' he said loudly. 'Far too early.' He backed away into the kitchen units and might just as well have been waving garlic and crucifixes at her. Of course – how could she have been so thoughtless? 'Oh me too,' she said, 'Usually.' But he did not look entirely convinced and she was quite sure that she looked the very picture of a guilty soak. What she wanted to say – which shocked her very much – was – 'Forget the wine then. How about a trip to Paris instead?'

That evening, just before dusk, when she felt sure no one would see her she put on her still mucky wellingtons, took her torch just in case, and set off for the old stone wall. Picking up where she had left off – so cleverly marked with the big sarsen – she ran her hands along each course of stones and then went back to the start and tried again, setting her sights lower all the time. It became obsessive. I will not go back indoors until I have found this stone, she told herself, and prayed that it was not an elaborate hoax on either Edward's or Mr Farrell's part. She badly wanted to find the stone. Since the day's conversation with Ewan she was even keener. She could ask him back to see it.

And then, just as she was giving up, just as the earth took on that sudden stillness which says the day's creatures are retired and the night's creatures have yet to emerge – she found it. Right down low it was, almost at knee level, hidden by lichen and tussocky grass – but quite discernible even in the half-light. Just as it was described, with a raised decorative edging surrounding the date 1557, the initials A and C surmounted by a crown – and on either side a swan and a coronet which Flora knew from her notes was the Cleves crest. Feeling more pleased than she imagined she would, she set the big stone to mark the place and with her wellingtons making satisfying sucking noises, and the thrush and blackbird making their last chorus of calls of the evening, she returned home. Now that was *something*, that was. Good.

After careful thought Flora sent Hilary a letter which touched, briefly, on the lack of material inheritance but which, rather cleverly Flora thought, reminded Hilary of the spiritual legacy her father had left her. All the happy memories and the fun. That night, when Hilary rang, Flora expected it to be difficult but no. Hilary just said that the letter was sweet and that she and Robin thought that her mother needed her and that she could get compassionate leave and she was coming down to stay . . . 'I could do with a week or two off myself, actually.'

Flora's heart – unmaternally – sank. 'That would be lovely later,' she said, 'But I'm just getting used to being on my own and – well – getting into the rhythm of it –' Hilary was understandably frosty. 'What do you mean, rhythm?'

And then Flora lied. 'I've just asked your Aunt Rosie not to come – she was all set to come back from Japan and I said no. Now if you come she'll get all offended and you know how . . .' She did not even sound convincing to herself. Rosie never took offence at anything, which came, Flora supposed, from a misspent life. But she panicked. She was just getting used to being on her own, just getting used to her freedom or the possibilities of it – and now this. And then she had a brilliant idea.

'Well – the other thing is that I'm so involved in your father's history of Hurcott and it's taking up so much time. And I do want to finish it for him.'

'Dad's last great work,' said Hilary, fondly.

'Oh yes,' said Flora smoothly, 'in fact, I was out at the old wall tonight following up on something he wrote and I found the Cleves datestone just where he said.'

Hilary snuffled. 'He was so brilliant . . .' Her snuffles became louder.

'Yes he was,' said Flora, 'and we must never forget that. And I want to do his –' she took a deep breath – 'History great justice – and I'll need to concentrate for the next week or two so would you mind . . . .?'

Hilary wavered, 'We-ell . . . I could help, couldn't I?'

Flora rushed on with another brainwave, 'And I'll tell you what you could do for me since you're in London – you could go to the Calligraphy and Wordiform Society in Bloomsbury and ask about the carved lettering. I'll send you a tracing. I need to know – as your father says – how previous historians date it to late sixteenth century when it so clearly says 1557.'

There was a hint – just a hint – of respect in Hilary's voice as she agreed. 'You are being thorough,' she said. 'Dad would be pleased. You're just sort of tidying it all up. Aren't you?'

Flora squeaked rather than spoke a 'Yes.' Though she would've loved to yell 'No.'

'*Edward Chapman's History of Hurcott with Particular*

Reference to the Anne of Cleves Datestone . . . It'll be just great. The village will have a person of importance to commemorate. We ought to talk about his headstone, you know.'

Flora said quickly, putting Hilary's infuriating title to the back of her mind, 'A year, the vicar said, before we can erect it. In the meantime – that carving date. Let me know as soon as you can. Oh – and I hope my letter was helpful. I'm sorry about the will. I know it was a disappointment.'

'Oh well – Robin says that we're fine at the moment and Ewan was right – we may as well wait until later.'

'Hmm,' said Flora. 'Makes sense I suppose. And we'll talk about the headstone once I've finished all this paperwork and – um – tidying up.'

When she put down the phone she poured herself a very large glass of Edward's more expensive red wine. 'Cheers, Anne of Cleves,' she said, 'wherever you are.' For now she could invite Ewan to Lodge Cottage again because she had found the stone. She slept very well.

Gradually, over the days that followed, she corrected Edward's dreadful prose. She used some of the history books piled in his study and they were most enlightening; factual but enlightening. It seemed that Anne of Cleves was really Anna of Cleves and Flora decided to call her that. It sounded right. And there was some useful information about the how and the why of Anna's arrival in England to be Queen. It was cheering to accomplish something of a cranial nature before getting on with the domestic side of things. Cleaning and washing and hoovering were put in their place by the information and ideas floating around in her head. One of the ideas lodged there and so – checking that it was not the middle of the night – she telephoned Rosie in Tokyo. Following that she made a phone call to the travel agent in town. Both of which conversations were satisfactory. Then, feeling perfectly content, she set off across the paddock towards Anna's stone, humming *The Ride of the Valkyries* – for there was no one to tell her to stop – to make her tracing.

Perhaps Anna walked this very route, she thought. Perhaps she walked it when it was a properly laid-out garden, maybe a herb garden with evening scents to soothe Anna's bruised, rejected heart. After all, you couldn't have a more public dumping than the King of England's. If she were anything like Flora it would be that public humiliation she would find so hurtful. No wonder she was said to enjoy her country manors and estates in the years that followed her divorce; the Tudor Court, like Hurcott or any small community, would be full of prying eyes and gossiping tongues, though Edward was right and she did seem to like Richmond Palace too. Any scandal involving royalty would be discussed with ardent delight – nothing new under the sun – and would probably be quick to lay the blame on Anna rather than the King. Spin now, spin then, thought Flora sourly. Like the good folk of Hurcott Ducis thinking that if one of the Chapmans had to go, pity it was not the dull female half. Well – if she got this History right, maybe the surviving female half could show them her other side. It would be no good looking for admiration or sup-port if she told them about Edward and Pink Lips. The village might pity her – but they would not be surprised – quite the reverse – and probably it would only enhance his reputation as a dashing lad. No, she would have to deal with that little aber-ration in private. And she would.

Earlier that day she had finally dealt with the contents of the laundry basket. The one place in the house that still contained a little bit of Edward's personality. There, beneath the feminine bits and pieces of Flora's, was his custard-yellow jumper. She remembered Ewan admiring it tremendously when they met up somewhere or other and Edward was wearing it. So – rather than take it all the way to the charity shop – Flora washed it (lovingly, by hand) dried it, and pressed it. Then she parcelled it up and put a note for Ewan inside saying that she knew he liked it and hoped he could use it. She would deliver it tomorrow when she also had another fish to fry.

She knelt – not entirely comfortably given her knees – on the

4

Pond Cottage Brings a Suitable Enlightenment

Either Flora was the changeling of the family or her sister Rosie was, for they could not be more different. Rosie was born both with the looks and the ability to make a good marriage. They overheard their mother saying this to their father and pondered for days on what a good marriage might be. Rosie was three years Flora's senior and led in places where Flora could not hope to follow. For over ten years Rosie was personal assistant – in every way – to the owner of a cosmetics company with many an unsuitable flirtation along the road. That really did take Flora's breath away – to have an affair within an affair was – well – shocking. Beautifully, beautifully shocking.

When Rosie's boss sold the company to a Frankfurt-based consortium and took a less onerous role in the business, to everyone's surprise, they married. 'Now she'll pay for her pleasures,' was the way most proper folk saw the situation, including their mother who, though by now in a hospital bed from which she would never return, still showed a sense of righteousness. This was obviously not the good marriage envisaged. But Flora knew that Rosie would not pay. Rosie was a woman destined to be paid. No children for Rosie, no husband with a sensible job or any of that settling down in one place nonsense. They travelled about the world – doing a little business, having pleasures, and bringing a whiff of exoticism into Flora and Edward's lives if they made a rare visit. Rosie telephoned from Japan when Edward's funeral took place. She was sympathetic, apologetic, practical. 'Can't get back,' she said. 'Wouldn't be much good if I could. I'll come as soon as I can. Just let me know if there's anything you want.' Flora understood. Rosie's saving grace was generosity. She would give you the coat off her back, as Flora once said, and it would be quality. When Rosie said anything you want, she meant it. And Flora was going to take her up on the offer.

Edward, she was delighted to think, would not only be rotating in his grave at the idea of her employing Wally Binder but he would be now be spinning out of control about the next thing Flora had in mind. It was the phrase 'Next time Paree . . .' as written by Pink Lips that rankled. If it had been 'Next time Bognor Regis' or 'Next time Felixstowe' she would not have taken it so hard. But Paree . . .?

Rosie owned a Parisian apartment, her original little love nest, where it was not unknown for Rosie to take one of her illicit amours when Harald was safely out of the picture. It was scarcely used now. The place might have the taint of wicked unchastity about it but – frankly – if there was the taint of anything wicked going, Flora was up for it. It would be an interesting challenge, going to Paris alone, and now she had an excellent reason. Research. *Next time Paree*, indeed. She hoped, yet again, that wherever Edward had come to rest, up or down or stuck in Limbo, that if there was a consciousness within his spirit and they allowed him to eat breakfast he was rotten well wincing into the cornflakes.

Rosie was delighted. 'That's the girl,' she said. 'And when I come back we'll think about your love life. You'll need another man sometime and I'll help you choose one.' The implication, and quite right in Flora's opinion, was that she was not very capable of choosing one on her own.

'Thanks,' she said. 'Now – about the key . . .'

The conversation with Hilary that followed was exactly what Flora feared and expected. Difficult.

For Hilary said, with some astonishment, 'Paris? Alone? Then I'll come too.'

'No,' said Flora firmly.

'Why ever not?'

'Because I need to grieve alone,' said Flora. 'Come with me next time. That would be nice. I'm sending you the tracing.'

'Why Paris?'

'Why not?'

For all the best travel there is a focus for the traveller even if it is only a double bed in a discreet little hotel. Flora's focus was the discovery that the marriage portrait of Anna of Cleves was owned by the Louvre. For some reason this portrait of a long-dead Queen of England by Hans Holbein, the portrait that Henry VIII commissioned and with which, when he received it, he fell in love, now hung in the greatest Parisian art museum. Flora would go to the Louvre and see this woman, this Flanders Mare, for herself. There was another portrait, a miniature, housed in London at the Victoria and Albert Museum, but Flora did not want to see it yet. She wanted to do what Henry had done – she wanted to see the portrait he saw of Anna for the first time and make her judgement according-ly. The miniature portrait was given to Henry by Holbein some time later, apparently, though taken from the same initial sit-ting. But by then he had made up his mind. It was in London, it was easily accessible, and it must wait.

Now for the one final thing she must do that morning before setting out. Flora put on the most dramatic-looking of her black widow's weeds – so much easier it was to be in mourn-ing – and walked the short distance to Pond Cottage. On the way she posted the envelope to her daughter and called in at Little Beeches where she put a parcel and a note inside Ewan and Dilly's front porch. She walked on, pleased to have done something nice for him. In the note she said that she would be away for a little while and looked forward to telling him why when she got back. She wrote down her mobile number, just in case. Braveheart. Then on she marched, her black weeds flying out before her.

By now it was seven o'clock in the morning, clear and fresh, with birds twittering away and the sun glinting through clouds and God should have been in His Heaven and all right with the world but the Browning moment was somewhat diluted by her mission. She felt caught between the three states of merry widow, grieving bereaved and cuckolded wife. As if she had stepped into the wrong play. One thing to suffer the guilt of not suffering enough about an unimpeachable husband, quite another to discover his incontrovertibly peachable fidelity without the possibility of *habeus corpus* and confrontation.

There were many things about Edward that Flora would not have found particularly surprising – that he had a gambling addiction, that he secretly collected rude postcards, that he fiddled his tax expenses perhaps – but never in a million years would she have believed him to be a Lothario. Even a very low-key Lothario. Indeed, signs of his Lotharioism had never entered her head. She took comfort in the same way many a wife has taken comfort, and probably many a wronged husband, too. She blamed the other party. Having seen her own sister in action and seen what success a determined woman can have, Flora decided that it must be the same in Edward's case. One day Edward was probably sitting innocently on a stile contemplating his navel when the two-bit floozy with the very pink lipstick came upon him and stole his honour away. This might be telescoping events a little but – largely – it must have been like that. If it was not, then Flora was – well – naïve was the kinder word but fool was more fitting. And Flora did not wish to think herself a fool. For over thirty years she had lived with Edward so she did know him, she did. No Lothario he. Whereas she whom she suspected of seducing her husband might not look exactly like a siren but . . . Flora preferred the comfort of the fantasy. Despite suggesting she pull herself together she was not entirely resigned to someone pinkly pouting their way into her – she accepted – unusual marriage. Bitch in the Manger this may be, she thought, but whatever the illogic, she needed to know more about the origins and unfolding story of Edward and Pink Lips.

Pond Cottage was one of a dozen or so small – now *bijou* – dwellings on the outer edge of what had once been the manorial lands and which, before that, were the lands of the local priory. As she passed Duck Cottage, three doors up from her destination, she felt a little pang and shook her head and pursed her lips. That was the Dobsons' – she missed Mary badly – especially now – but the cottage was let for two years – alas not to a nice couple of Hindus, or a jolly couple of Rastafarians – but to a pair of crisp-suited bankers who certainly wouldn't frighten the horses. Mary and Geoff were still in Canada and not due back for months. 'Come on out,' they wrote shortly after they left, and then Mary rang suggesting it. But they were staying in a fairly primitive place in the Laurentians, researching Iroquois and Algonquin histories and Edward and Geoffrey did not get on very well. They'd get on better now, she thought wryly, and walked on.

The row of cottages looked very pretty in the morning light. They were near the centre of the village and would have been troubled by traffic and parking and dog-walking gawpers had they not had wonderfully long front and back gardens which gave them their privacy. When the dear Dobsons first bought theirs it was, like most of them, nearly falling down but the whole row was renovated and extended, each one now a sweetly desirable little place. The cottages faced the pond and leant against each other in a strange perspective that would have suited Alfred Wallis very well. When she first saw them Flora remembered Crabbe and his Village Life – 'I paint the Cot, as Truth will paint it, and as Bards will not . . .' It could not have been an idyllic life for the original tenants. Far from it. They were built very many years ago – centuries – to house the local landowner's labourers, so it was said, and probably stood on the site of much earlier dwellings of the kind that sprang up around monastic walls. In the Farrell history he stated – more in hope than certainty – that the pond dated from Priory days when it would be stocked with carp and other such voracious scavengers – which made the name of the owner of

Pond Cottage considerably more amusing than it already was.

As Flora walked up the path of the bijou little dwelling that had once been so humble, she thought how extraordinary it was that a modest piece of history like this base cottage should be owned by a woman who liked video cameras, Chris de Burgh, and bloody posy pots. And other people's husbands. She rapped on the wooden front door with her knuckles, which really hurt and improved the mood no end, but she was quite unable to use the knocker which was wrought in the shape of a fish – and then she waited. Her black shirt flapped around her calves and her black jacket billowed around her and she could see from her shadow that she did not look very friendly. Indeed, she looked quite scary which was better than docile and plain, anyway.

It was rather unfair to call so early, Flora happily realised, as the door opened slowly and not very wide and Pauline Pike peeked out looking like a mouse caught stealing cheese. She blinked at the sunshine, then at her visitor, after which her eyes opened very wide. There was a momentary silence while her mouth moved into gear, and then she said very brightly, 'Flora. It's a bit early isn't it? Do you want to come in?' The door did not open much wider; the question was rhetorical.

'Thanks,' said Flora, and pushed the door slightly. Pauline stepped backwards into the narrow hallway which seemed dark after all that sunshine, and Flora followed her. They were toe to toe. It was a little like doing the tango as they moved their way slowly towards the kitchen.

Once in the kitchen, which was small and perfectly arranged with little corn dollies on little shelving units and dangling bits and pieces of strangely rural craft matter dotted around the room, Flora saw that Pauline was in her nightgown, a Victorian affair with many a flounce and ruffle and she was making little birdlike movements with her pretty little hands as she plucked at the ruffles. Flora found herself wondering – quite unperturbed – if Edward liked that sort of thing. Very feminine, it was, exuding purity. Absurd, really. If Pauline Pike had reached the middle of her thirties (at a kind guess) as a virgin, Flora would eat her tights. Dangerous such a nightie was, with that long ruffled hem on those steep stairs in the corner of that kitchen especially if one lived alone . . . For one short, sinister moment she dwelled on this – and then moved on. Those steep stairs in the corner of the kitchen, she knew from the Dobsons' place, led up to the tiny landing with its one bedroom and the bathroom. Pauline was staring at her. Flora said, 'May I use the – ?' And pointed ceilingwards. Pauline looked more cheerful. Presumably she thought that this was the reason for the visit. Flora was caught short on her early morning stroll. Older woman, weak bladder.

'Of course,' said Pauline, relaxing. 'How *are* you, dear?'

It was the *dear* that did it. 'Bearing up,' said Flora stiffly as she ascended the stairs.

'Would you like a coffee?' Pauline trilled after her. 'Or something herbal? I've got redbush.'

Have you, by gosh, thought Flora, grim-lipped. It would have been more honest to say that she'd quite like a gin and tonic despite the hour but the news of this would go all round the village and by the time it got back to her she would be yet another certified alcoholic. That's if Ewan hadn't told everyone about her already. 'Thank you,' Flora called crisply from the landing, 'Coffee please.' And then, with steely determination, she pushed open the door of Pauline's bedroom. It was small and the window was tiny and it looked more like the room of a child. There was the little bedside table with its litter of tissues, clock, magazines, lamp and handcreams – and right in the middle of all the clutter sat – a posy pot. She picked it up. Very sweet, it was, she could see that. White china with very bright pink roses. Pink seemed to be a preponderant colour in this little game. She looked at the unmade bed. Crumpled linen, pink candy stripe. A small double bed. Intimate space for two, luxurious for one. She closed the door.

Before going back down stairs she went into the rose-budded bathroom and flushed the lavatory. Clever, she told herself. Clever. On the back of the door was a thin sliver of pale orange silk that billowed and let out a flowery scent as she pulled the door closed. Welcome to the house of seduction, she told herself, though the corn dollies and dangling macramé scarcely qualified.

Back downstairs she sat at Pauline Pike's small and perfect pine table, on a sweet little wooden chair with a heart cut out of its middle back panel. The last time Flora saw such a chair it was in an impossibly saccharine illustration for the interior furnishings of Heidi and Old Grandfather's alm hut. Until now it was one of her favourite childhood books. That might change.

Now, how to conduct a conversation with your dead husband's lover, the existence of whom may have come as a surprise but whose function in your dead husband's life did not actually threaten your own relationship with him? She could not quite think how to approach the situation – possibly she should think of Edward and herself as brother and sister and apply the same criteria to the situation as a sister might. There would, at worst, be a sense of betrayal because your brother had not told you about his lover, but in many ways it would not be your business how he conducted that side of his life. She was about to apply this criterion and see how it fitted when a further thought came to her – a blinding realisation – a Damascene moment of shocking intensity as realisation dawned . . . Oh, she thought, Oh my good *God* – she had been cheated. No – *really* cheated. For she suddenly and startlingly realised that she had lived that most seductive of things, that most seductive of things that people like Vadim and Bardot, Sartre and de Beauvoir put their names to – she had been living in an Open Marriage. The infuriating aspect of which was that she had not known she was living in one at the time or she might have made better use of it.

'Well, well,' she said, before she could stop the thought. 'If I'd only known.' Pauline had her back to her and was fiddling with the kettle and jug. 'What?' she asked, not looking round.

Flora felt oddly cheered having reached this point of understanding, more like a woman of the world, more like someone
a bit sinful. 'Oh nothing, I just thought of something quite
amusing.' Pauline turned and carried the mugs to the table.
'It's good that you can laugh a little,' said Pauline as she set
their drinks down. She looked dramatic and pale and there
were shadows beneath her eyes. She also still looked like a
nervous mouse, pink eyes and all – though quite a pretty one
in a small-featured way. Flora felt a little sorry for her. Pauline
pushed a very dainty flowered mug towards her, along with a
decorative, dimity sugar bowl. It crossed Flora's mind to wonder how her husband could possibly have changed his colours
so much as to be able to spend happy times in this daft and
prissy environment.

Pauline sat down opposite her. 'Is it getting any easier?' she
asked. There was something other than grief in the question –
a sense – perhaps – of tight-lipped annoyance. Flora had the
distinct feeling that the Pink Pike was asking herself why it
couldn't be Flora and not Edward . . .

'It hasn't been as devastating as I expected,' said Flora carefully. 'Though obviously more than thirty years of marriage
does not go lightly. I expect the glooms will descend but widowhood is quite a busy business, really. Not much time for
grief.'

'Really?' said Pauline sadly. 'That's good.'

'It'll be more difficult for you,' said Flora kindly.

Pauline nodded. And then realised. She looked up at Flora.
Flora took the sweet little posy pot from her pocket and put it
on the perfectly pristine pine table between them. Well, obviously, at that point, the floodgates opened.

Later when Flora had mopped away at Pauline for what she
felt was quite enough time for a cuckolded wife to administer
to the cuckolder, and when fresh coffee had been produced,
Flora said, 'Was he sitting on a stile minding his own business
when you seduced him?' Pink-eyed Pauline blinked – and then
a little of what Flora's mother might call Backbone appeared

to surface in her. 'Oh no,' she said. 'Nothing like that. I was worshipping nature in the back garden – *au naturelle* – and didn't hear him ring the doorbell and he fought his way through the briars behind the house – you know I've left them so I won't be seen from the rear when I – nature worship –' (Flora longed to tell her that with that tiny bottom it scarcely mattered if she was seen rearwise or not – but refrained – it would be too hard to remove the sense of envy). Like a prince and Sleeping Beauty, Flora thought, and she could see it would go straight to Edward's romantic heart. 'And I had quite forgotten that he was coming to see me with the petition about Tommy Leggatt. You remember Tommy Leggatt.'

Flora nodded that she did indeed.

'Tommy Leggatt, exactly. Well – suddenly – there he was.'

'*Tommy Leggatt?*'

'No, Edward,' Pauline Pike gave a little tinkling laugh which – when added to the smallness of her rear – was not to be borne.

'Tommy Leggatt has been dead for two years or more,' said Flora incredulously.

'Two almost to the day, actually.'

This did make Flora swallow hard. Blind as a bloody bat, she'd been. Was it any wonder Edward no longer pranced into her bedroom in provocative garments. He was prancing elsewhere. All that protective delicacy regarding the separate sleeping arrangements was unnecessary. He must have welcomed it with open arms. But who could blame him?' She looked at Pauline and she had to admit two fundamentally unpleasant things. Pauline was prettier than her and she was younger. The fact that she was probably not half so intelligent mattered not. When did it ever? The woman quite obviously adored him. Or made a good fist of seeming to.

Pauline, nervously spooning away at the sugar and letting it trickle back into the darling, dainty flower-covered sugar pot – went on, 'The petition was about letting Tommy Leggatt continue to live in his cottage despite the fact he was ill. We managed over two hundred signatures. Edward and I were out every night . . . And then he went and died.'

'Edward had a way of doing unexpected things,' said Flora.

'No, I mean Tommy. Tommy died.'

'Well, I know he died. I went to the wake. So what did Edward do, then?'

Pauline sounded surprised. As well she might. 'He organised the funeral.'

'Well I know he organised the funeral because I helped.'

Pauline blinked.

'Yes. I chose that bit from Wordsworth . . . *There is a comfort in the strength of love . . .*'

Pauline's eyes were disturbingly glassy again.

'From "Michael",' said Flora shortly. 'I've always liked it.'

'Oh, I thought he chose it.' Pauline looked sad.

'He never opened a poetry book in his life. Unless I did it for him.'

The Pike backbone was resurrected. 'He read it beautifully, Edward.'

'Yes, yes,' said Flora. 'And I expect wherever Tommy was he thoroughly enjoyed the attention. But what did Edward do then?'

'Well – he spoke to the vicar and he organised the –'

'No – I mean when he came into your back garden and found you – *au naturelle* –'

'Well, he apologised. I said it was all right, and we had a cup of tea. And then he said he would help me collect signatures that night, if I liked. And he did – and well –'

Flora remembered it differently. 'He said you asked him.'

Pauline's eyes welled up again, she shook her head and dripped on to the table until Flora absentmindedly wiped at it with a tea towel.

'When you had the cup of tea together were you still *au naturelle?*'

'No,' said Pauline with dignity. 'I put on my robe. Immediately. But it was no good. Once he'd seen me naked he couldn't think – he said later – about anything else.'

The robe in question was presumably the sliver of orange silk Flora saw in the bathroom.

'I expect it kept slipping off all over the place,' said Flora conversationally.

'Well yes it did,' said Pauline confidentially. 'It's silk.'

'It would be.'

Pauline sniffed delicately. 'I'd always thought of Edward as a little distracted, somehow. Even though he was married. And then poor old Tommy Leggatt was the alibi for what had to be. Maybe God sent him.'

The woman was obviously touched. 'Hmm,' said Flora. 'I doubt it. God doesn't take kindly to adulterers. Do you often sunbathe starkers and not hear the doorbell when you are expecting distracted men?'

Pauline lifted her nose into the air like little lap dog. 'I can't help it,' she said, 'If love happens.'

Flora remembered her sister saying something very similar. Quite often. She longed to reply with something tart, something along the lines of love doesn't just happen, it gets helped on its way – nurtured – quite often by a well-placed flash of a nipple – which is what she should have said to Rosie maybe. But she kept her counsel. She was not sure if this conversation was helping her or not, but it seemed to be helping Pauline – and it was strangely fascinating. Irresistible, in fact.

'Did it happen here?' Flora gestured with her hands to indicate the cottage.

Pauline mistook the gesture and looked shocked. 'In the kitchen? Certainly not.' Then she went conspiratorial again with an amused little smile – 'Well, not at first.'

'Oh,' said Flora, a bit of her spine reasserting itself now. 'He used to like taking me over the kitchen sink when we were first married. Or the fridge. When we got one.'

That was cheap, she knew. The sugar scattered and Pauline put the spoon down with a clatter. Then the two women eyed each other. 'Does anyone know?' Flora asked. Pauline shook her head. 'Then let's leave it like that, shall we?' Conversation over. Or nearly. 'As a matter of fact, Pauline, the only thing that makes me cross about it all is that I wasn't told. If I had been I might have had a stab at a bit of extra-marital myself – I had someone in mind you know.'

This bit of hubris was silly but she could not stop herself.

'Really?' said Pauline. The implication being that it was most unlikely.

'Yes, really.'

'Who?'

And the next bit of hubris was even sillier. 'Oh – someone we all know. A nice man. A good man. A saint of a man really, thinking of what he has to bear with his own wife. A man of standing in the village. A professional man who –' And then she stopped. Pauline was looking a little too interested. The aspect of sugared mouse around the eyeballs had given way to straightforward interest, even slyness. Enough was enough. 'Anyway – that's my business. As this –' She indicated the posy pot – 'is yours. And good luck.'

It was not said nicely, nor received nicely. Flora wished she could retake the high moral ground but she could not. 'Well, I hope you made each other very happy,' she said, with dignity. But the hand of friendship was gone. Pauline Pike looked distinctly nettled. Bad mistake.

Flora stood up. 'Well – I just wanted to sort that out. No more needs to be said.' She pushed the dear little posy pot further towards Pauline. 'Sorry the two of you never made it to Paris. I'm going, though. Today. But at least you've got this to remember him by.'

Pauline then picked up the pot and cradled it to her pert little bosom. Flora felt a bit sick at the sight. She walked up the narrow hallway to the front door with Pauline following. At the open door she turned and asked, 'What do you think of Anna of Cleves, by the way?'

'Who?' said Pauline.

That was satisfactory. It confirmed that Flora was, indeed,

much more knowledgeable than the little Pink Pike.

Halfway up the path and breathing spring's good air again, feeling the sun on her skin and all's well with the world, Pauline called out after her, 'You haven't seen the video yet, have you?'

Flora stopped. 'Not yet.'

Pauline was smiling, a genuinely happy smile. She really must be quite simple. 'The first bit is ever so lovely,' she said. 'It's only in the second part where it gets bad.'

And she closed the door.

5

Gay Paree

Since Edward had lost so much money on the project, First Class on Eurostar seemed a justifiable way to travel. Putting a bit of money back into the family's pockets, so to speak. Flora negotiated a luxurious deal which included a romantic champagne breakfast. The young woman on the other end of the telephone was perfectly fine until Flora said that she was travelling solo. There then followed an interestingly uncomprehending conversation, viz. the young woman on the other end of the line could not quite get her delicate cerebral matter around the suggestion that Flora would still like the champagne and strawberries and as much of the romance as they could supply. No laughter at this. Not even a giggle. Just a nervous twittering and a request to repeat, several times, that Flora – solo – did – actually and incontrovertibly – require all the trimmings. 'I think,' said Flora, 'it will be very nice to have the strawberries and champagne all to myself.' She could almost hear the young woman fall to the floor. She waited politely until the young woman spoke. 'Right,' she said cautiously. Flora was brisk. 'Now – would you like my credit card number?'

Once *in situ* she sipped her champagne and thought how embarrassed she and Edward would be were they together here, now. They wouldn't even be able to laugh at themselves. Only lovers and those who care about the sparkle in their partner's eye would enjoy such a piece of nonsense. It was, she thought, a very great pity that Edward went and died or Edward and his little Pink Pike might have been extremely happy together. If she'd been told she could have pursued her own yearnings, perhaps fruitfully. The whole business had shaken her, definitely shaken her. Her mind kept wandering back to the ruffled nightdress. Flora had never worn ruffles in her life. She fingered her throat as if she might find some there – but no – she wore a simple, ordinary, round-necked top. No mystery. Even as a widow she was safe, comfortable and bloody dull. How little she knew about Edward's needs. And how little, presumably, he knew about hers. How little *she* knew about hers. What children they were.

But later she laughed to imagine Edward's face discovering the little Pink Pike *au naturelle* among the briars. The Chivalric fantasy – yes indeed – it would wholly enchant him otherwise how could he overcome those corn dollies and crafty mobiles and bloody ruffles? She raised her glass and saluted the clever little Pike. At least she knew what she wanted – and got it. Even if it was Flora's husband.

The waiter hovered. She realised she was smiling and that she had drunk half the bottle of champagne. No woman, even if fluent in French, should drink more than half a bottle of champagne at one sitting if she is about to arrive in Gay Paree *sans* husband. Apart from anything of an indecorous nature that might take place, there were those cobbles. The area around Rosie's apartment was full of them. If one went down, one might never get up again. With regret she offered the rest of the bottle to the pimply young waiter who – though he clearly found her odd to be sitting alone and smiling – served her kindly. 'Oh, I like beer,' he said.

'Give it to your mother,' said Flora, gesturing cheerfully at the bottle. 'I expect she'd like it?'

'Thank you,' he said, sadly. 'She'll be pleased. She doesn't go out much. They're divorced.'

Flora made the right noise. Sympathetic, enquiring.

'I wish she would go out, to be honest. She's not best on her own, though. Not like you.'

'Oh, me –' said Flora smiling broadly. 'I'm a widow. Still getting used to it.' Her voice was too chirpy, the smile too broad, she knew. If it looked odd it must have sounded even odder. The waiter moved away, smiling uncertainly, which was understandable.

Staring at her dark reflection in the speeding window she thought about children and what insidious bullies they were even in this enlightened age. Every single bit of parental behaviour was up for scrutiny: Hilary wanted her bereaved mother to wear black and do a Queen Victoria, and this young waiter wanted his dumped mother to go out all-night clubbing. The answer was very simple. Follow your heart. And lie. At least while the post-bra-burning generation tried to work out what it wanted from its mothers.

Later as she looked out at the streets and the people and the Napoleonic grandeur of the city, Gay Paree, she lost a little of her confidence in the whole exercise. At least if Edward were in the cab with her he'd be worrying about the fare, or looking in his guidebook, or wondering if you could feasibly abseil the Eiffel Tower – but here she sat, hands folded neatly in her lap, eyes wide to all around her, wondering what – apart from making the acquaintance of Holbein's portrait of Queen Anna – she was going to do with herself for the next few solo days. It seemed there was a difference between being on your own when you were not really, and being truly alone. The confidence gap. Well, she would just have to learn to overcome it. And lovely Paris was as good a place as any for the attempt.

That evening, at sundown, from Rosie's small upstairs windows she looked down on those Parisian cobbles, up at the sky. Below her the people went in and out of the *boulangerie* and above her sat the higgledy-piggledy, ancient rooflines, glowing in the dying light with the shadows of imposing new buildings beyond. For the first time being alone meant something because, banal as it seemed, no one had telephoned to see that she had arrived safely. Hilary would not think of it, but Edward always rang. It was ritual. And once he had rung her the visit would properly begin. When asked why he rang,

Edward said that he just wanted to know that she had arrived safely. Now Flora wondered, more to the point, if he had rung to see if she was safely where she was supposed to be and out of the way. Oh what a stain spreads with infidelity. She was rather glad she had never been tempted to try it. It was some small consolation to feel that she had behaved honourably. An Open Marriage, she thought, and never, ever realised it. Who was she trying to fool? Honour was no consolation at all. She wished, with all her heart, that she had attempted the seduction of Ewan Davies. Yes, she did. And when she got back she just might. Gay Paree and the residual champagne talking, obviously. Or maybe not.

The next morning she sat at a familiar café table with her coffee and her croissant and her notes about Henry and Anna and Holbein and felt a great deal better. She had a purpose which justified her presence. She pictured herself, a woman in sensible black and dark green, greyish hair, unremarkable shape, specs on the end of her nose and deep into her papers. What Parisian would give her a second look?

Reading about Henry's fourth queen made her a little sad. The essential story was baldly unromantic. It seemed that Anna of Cleves was no fairytale princess.

This foreign Queen's feelings were not spared in her short-lived marriage to Henry VIII and the ensuing process to be rid of her. Henry and his advisers made it quite clear, and very publicly, that the Princess of Cleves was considered ugly, dull, devoid of any courtly skills and personally repugnant to the King. It was the King's only attempt at an arranged, dynastic marriage and he was quite uncompromising in his displeasure. Political expediency meant that the lady could not be sent back to Cleves and so she continued to live in England, with the status of Sister to the King, First Lady at Court after the Queen and his heirs, Aunt to his children, until her death in 1557. She never married again.

Well, thought Flora crisply, there are worse things than remaining single.

The owner of the café came over and shook her hand. He had heard from her sister, he told her, about her unfortunate loss (sounded like an umbrella on a bus, she very nearly put up her hand to say, Oh it's nothing) . . . She thanked him and said she was here to try to forget all about it. He nodded and agreed that that was good, very good. But when he asked where her sister was and she told him that Rosie was in Japan, he looked very anxious. How like Rosie not to say, 'I'm ringing from Tokyo' as if it were just down the road . . . This was not good, he told her, Japan. He called his wife. This is not good, she agreed. They spoke above her head as if she were a child and they immediately decided that he must escort her to some places that afternoon, she must not struggle around on her own, he would be her companion. Flora straightened her shoulders and said that she could not possibly allow him to do such a thing, it was kind, it was generous, it was thoughtful – but she would prefer – if they would understand – to be on her own.

In the widowed state it seemed impossible to offend anyone – what the widow wants the widow must have. In this case, if it was solitude, so be it. They looked both relieved and understanding. She was left alone to read through her pages and all that happened was that her bill was withheld – and that was kind and acceptable. She thanked them and tucked her papers back into her bag. What was the point of all the theories and descriptions – culled, she supposed, from a handful of art luminaries – without seeing the real thing? The Louvre was no more than twenty minutes' walk away, the weather was fine, and the world – or at any rate this little bit of it – belonged to her for the day. She would investigate the portrait of Anna of Cleves and then she would have *steak-frites* while she also digested what she had seen. Accordingly she set off.

Back in Hurcott Ducis Pauline Pike, who had not been out of Pond Cottage for twenty-four hours being now enraged and mortified as well as sad and mourning her lover, decided to dry her eyes and face the world. She had not enjoyed the interview with Flora Chapman. Her idea of Flora was a dull woman with none of the flirtatious skills and prettiness that would make her any kind of superior – yet in that interview Pauline had not felt – quite – on top. Edward had told her that Flora would not mind very much about them, but she had rather liked to think that she would. Frankly it was a bit insulting to think that their affair was not important enough to hide so she chose not to believe him. She was wrong. And that, Pauline Pike found, was very definitely galling. 'We are not exactly star-crossed lovers, my sweet,' Edward once joked. But Pauline liked to think that they were. He was so poetic, Edward. Star-crossed lovers was a lovely way to talk about what they had been up to. Edward was so unhappy, so very unhappy, when he first came into her life – though he denied it of course – and she liked believing that because of her he had died happy.

Pauline, meanwhile, had pity on herself. Poor Pauline, she thought. Poor, poor Pauline, knowing now that Flora knew. She wondered, despite Flora's suggestion of discretion, how many others knew, too, and rather hoped they did. It would give her a bit of status – or what she called oomph. Pity for herself cheered her up enough to go out to town, now that it was Saturday, and do a little bit of shopping on her little feet. The bank had been very understanding when she said that a dear friend had died and she somehow could not shake off the sorrow but she would probably go back on Monday.

In truth the other young women at the bank gave knowing nods and winks after Pauline's call, while the young man at the bank looked at the knowing nods and winks in puzzlement. When Andy Cooper finally asked June Pepper – who – like Andy – lived in Hurcott Ducis, 'Why are you going all girlie like that?' June Pepper – who rather hoped to get married to a bank manager one day and who thought Andy might make the grade – told him. 'It's no *dear friend*,' she whispered, tickling his ear with her soft breath as she did so. 'It's that Mrs

Chapman's husband. From Lodge Cottage. They were an item. And then he died.'

Andy Cooper longed to ask if it was the wife who had killed him (he read a lot of Patricia Highsmith). He had a feeling that he remembered the man bouncing out of a balloon in the sky and it seemed possible that it was the wife up there with him who had bounced him out. But Andy did not ask June about this. If there was one thing he was aware of besides her warm breath in his ear and her not insubstantial breasts coming quite close – it was that she could run rings round him. Rings. 'Well,' he said, which seemed safe.

'Yes,' said June. 'And what's more – nobody knows.'

Pauline Pike walked delicately over the cobbles of the ancient market square. She was on her way to the greengrocer's shop to buy lemons and ginger root to perk herself up and try to overcome the heartache. Pauline's next-door neighbour, Gideon Wells, who had a way of throwing his arms around and wearing pastels that did not altogether smack of masculinity, said as she left home that morning that Pauline had the very thing to help her growing in her own borders at Pond Cottage, little pansy faces (he said this quite unselfconsciously, she noted) called Heartsease. But she did not trust the information. Frankly, having seen death so closely and so recently she did not fancy poisoning herself. Well, not unless she meant it, at any rate. Probably, she thought, Flora Chapman would like that, like her to put an end to it all so that the secret remained safe. Bad enough, it was, that her lover should die (and on film) but that his wife had to go and come round to Pond Cottage fiddling with her posy pot and making her feel small and wicked and dirty was shameless, really. A wife like that – separate bedrooms – should hide away for her carelessness and not go stalking the one woman who had managed to give her suffering husband so much pleasure in his last years. That is how Pauline Pike saw it and that is how she settled it in her head as she made her dainty, grieving way over the cobbles.

Flora Chapman was in Paris, not she, and that hurt. In fact, it made her see red. Having a married lover was quite a challenge and she had expected some kind of reward for it but no – nothing – gone, gone, gone. And then the woman – whom she and Edward giggled over calling Bun-Face – had the cheek to say that she had a lover anyway. Or the possibility. She did not deserve one, she did not, she did not. And Pauline Pike, who worried away at the information as if it were an itchy scab, did. Who could the saint of a professional man with the wife be?

She muttered gone, gone, gone to the cobbled street as she bent her head and wended her way and she remembered how Edward had described the streets of Paris – cobbled like these – and a melancholy stole over Pauline's little heart at the thought that she would never, now, visit that place of romance with her beloved, ever. It was no comfort, absolutely no comfort, to know that neither would widow Chapman. She might be in Paris now, but she was in Paris alone. Pauline had never quite believed that Edward's wife could take or leave him. In Pauline's experience, wives always bothered about their husbands once Pauline was about. If Flora Chapman did not then she'd be the first. Usually one word on the subject of divorce and they were either off back to their wives or their indifferent wives suddenly turned tiger. Edward had taken the issue of the mention of divorce several steps further and gone to meet his Maker. Pauline wept again. Rage, frustration, righteousness coursed through her veins. She was a woman wronged and with no way of revenging it. She, alone, was left to suffer in secret without the decency of neighbourly comfort in her loss. Who, she wondered, again, was Flora's heart's desire? Who was a man of standing and suffering in his marriage? Who?

As she tottered towards the Naked Banana Pauline experienced a sudden warm moment of memory. The morning, not so long ago, that Eddy had arrived at her place when he should have been checking some fencing damage up at Pope Deeping. When he saw her he was like a young boy again. All energetic and carefree and – well – desperate. Desperation in a man was always good. He was wearing the yellow jumper she had knitted him – three ply – took ages especially as it must be knitted in secret from him – and he looked – as she said – Oh my . . . They sat side by side on the settee and he announced his grand plan – they would go away to the Game Fair together. They would have three days and two nights together and he would hold her arm in public and all that sort of thing she craved. It was the happiest time of her life, bar none, that Game Fair. Edward wore that yellow jumper every day with a nice checked tie and he looked so squire-like in every way that whenever possible she dropped him a curtsy. How he laughed. She was smiling as she thought of it, that yellow jumper, for he had loved it, loved the fact that it was her little hands that had made it for him – his wife was probably useless at that sort of thing though Edward did say she could sew . . .

Still smiling, she looked up from the street and her little tapping feet that dealt with the cobbles so delicately and saw – Oh, but it couldn't, it couldn't – another man – or was it Edward himself – walking along with his hands in his pockets, a cheerful air about him and for all the world looking just as Edward had looked at the Game Fair – checked shirt, yellow jumper (she could recognise the extra deep ribbing), checked cap and all. Her eyes, never her strongest feature, went blurry. He seemed to be smiling at her as he strode onwards. She put her hand up – gave a tentative little wave – got into a tremendous visionary muddle – and fainted.

It was a secret no longer, Pauline Pike's secret love. She, being scooped up by the owner of the Naked Banana and dragged seemingly lifeless into his shop, came to and firmly told all. By then Ewan Davies had melted away. It was such a relief to tell people – and also it stopped them from thinking she was mad. Eventually, the knowledge would find its way into the bank where Andy Cooper would be astonished to hear it all over again from Becky Quinn whose mother ran the riding school. And later from Arnold Wilkes, High Class Butcher.

And even later still from his own mother, Molly. Whence, for she did his cleaning, it found its way that very day into the household of Ewan Davies via the somewhat muddled recounting of Dilly. But Ewan, who was attending a golf club meeting that morning and had stopped in town to pick something up from the office when the ghastliness happened – on returning home late (managed to get a round in as well) got the gist and shook his head and said to himself that it was no wonder Flora had started to drink and how odd it was that Edward's *inamorata* had fainted at his feet. Him of all people. Well, life was odd, and he should know. Poor Flora. He knew a thing or two about public humiliation. He must do what he could. He told Dilly they were going out for a drink and she, delighted, staggered off to put her coat on.

'First decent thing you've suggested for years,' she said as they walked towards the Priory Arms.

He raised his chin and refused to take the bait. This was no time for marital pain. His friend – and client – Flora needed his help.

As he feared, the Priory Arms was agog with the news. He bought Dilly and himself one drink each and talked to a few people at the bar. So did Dilly. When he finally got her home he made several phone calls to other people in the village. He would do what he could. At least being away for a few days might see Flora over the worst. Dilly, meanwhile, sprawled beautifully in the sitting room, said that he was showing more life that night than he had for many a year. In her *déshabillé* and quite untouchable she then fell happily asleep on the sofa.

In the flat above the Naked Banana the saviour of Pauline Pike sat sipping tea. 'It was that solicitor was wearing it,' he said to his wife. 'She thought it was a ghost but I told her – it was no ghost – it was the solicitor. And you know what she said then?'

His wife, also sipping tea, said that she did *not*.

'She said – all smiling again and smoothing down her hair like a cat that had the cream – she said, Well, he looked very nice in it, don't you think? – Not like a saint of a man at all.'

These, then, are the events that unfolded in Hurcott Ducis on the day that Flora Chapman made her way towards the portrait of Anna of Cleves.

PART TWO

6

Meeting a Reject

On her way to the Louvre Flora read Wilfred Clement's extracted 1958 lecture on the Northern tradition in portraiture: *Holbein, the English Face and the Anna portrait*. The art critic obviously admired both the picture and the painter. Flora thought that Holbein sounded interestingly masculine for an artist – creative sensitivity was presumably not required to be displayed at Henry VIII's Court – and she wondered – a little wistfully – how he might have painted her.

Hans Holbein was born in 1497 in Augsburg, a thriving, important part of what is today called Germany. It was a good place for a painter to begin his trade. He was six years younger than his greatest patron, Henry VIII, but like the King he was a man of two sides – the sensitive artist and the man who liked to ride and wrestle and live well. Both had broken noses from their love of sport, both were ambitious and brilliant; Henry liked Holbein as a man and revered him as an artist. He came to the Tudor Court on various occasions and for various periods of time between the years 1526 and his death in 1543. He was a man who could turn his hand to anything – from designing gold or silver cups and jewellery to creating arbours for masques – but his greatest achievement, the work for which Henry and his court and the world thereafter held him in the highest esteem, was his portrait painting. He had the eyes and skills of a genius and used both as no artist had done before.

Certain portrait painters breathe life into their work. They create the speaking likeness, the likeness that is called, in old parlance, 'very lively', meaning lifelike. Holbein's Anna of Cleves portrait was called exactly this by one of Henry's visiting Envoys, Sir Nicholas Wootton, at the Court of Cleves. The Envoy was well trusted and well-placed to make the remark having seen the lady in question. But a lively portrait is not simply a clever illusory likeness captured in paint or pencil, it is a portrait that has captured the indefinable essence of the subject's human qualities – where the artist's eye and the artist's understanding of psychology combine in a likeness that is only a moment away – a breath – from stepping out from the frame. When – if – they do step out – the viewer is sure that he or she will know them.

Portraiture became an integral part of the Northern European Tradition but Holbein broke the ground for those who came later. Rembrandt might now be considered the master, and Holbein would certainly have credited him with that status, but Holbein led the way. Portraiture was the acceptable Reformist focus in those times of religious and political turbulence after the Reformation. Gone were the Catholic images of saints, and Madonnas – instead came the art of the 'lively' portrait, the speaking likeness, man and woman here on earth and the image of royalty as modern day icons. These, after the Reformation, were the only safe ways forward for the artist from Augsburg.

What Rembrandt, less than a hundred years later, took to its ultimate morality in his last portraits, Holbein begins in his body of work. When Rembrandt, in his last self portraits, puts a fancy hat on his old head and paints himself not as grand or modish any more but an old man who shows you that vanity counts, in the end, for nothing, it follows on from Holbein. Less knowingly, more innocently, this is what Holbein does when he paints Anna in her jewellery and her overwhelming Brabantine cap with its gaudy tassel. A bonnet Rembrandt would certainly have envied. It emphasises rather than hides the human qualities and vulnerabilities of its wearer.

Holbein, during his years at the English court – for the very first time in portraiture – and following the new way of man at the centre of the universe – plucked out the human being from the courtly veneer of those subjects who commissioned him. Those first subjects were unselfconscious, curious and a little unsure, perhaps, of what a personal portrait meant. He captured this moment of change in his Tudor portraits. There is not one who does not reveal his or her nature – sometimes for the very things they chose to be painted in and sometimes – as with Anna – despite their trappings – and they confronted Holbein with an openness that would never occur again. It is that, I believe, that we see in the Anna portrait.

Rembrandt and Velasquez, Goya and Titian – Masters – but in portraiture Holbein was the first Master. It is perhaps the only laurel that Henry VIII deserves, that he recognised and passionately supported Holbein's genius. Even a tyrant can pay homage to artistic greatness. Holbein did not flatter his sitters, king or commoner. He painted portraits with understanding – with an affinity perhaps. His was not the dispassionate, painterly eye of Velasquez nor the wistful, jaundiced eye of the great Goya but the eye that breathed life – quirks and all – with a dedication to truth.

Why, then, did Henry fall in love with the portrait and despise the flesh and blood woman?

When Holbein painted Anna of Cleves he knew her kind. She came from the same background and traditions as him and was as far removed from the coquetry of the French court as he was himself. He painted her with sleepy eyelids – unawakened – facing frontally as if to meet the challenge of the new life ahead. He painted her with dignity and with seriousness and there is also courage in her stance. In modern portrait jargon, Holbein 'got' her. Unawakened but willing is the human – and the erotic – summa brevis of the portrait. Henry would have read the erotic message without concerning himself with why the lady was so unawakened and willing. Her complete lack of coquetry, enticing mannerisms, well learned little seductions, the stuff on which Henry feasted in his love life, were all missing from the portrait. As, indeed, was something else . . .

While Holbein cannot tell a painterly lie – he can present his subject in the most attractive way possible. He therefore posed Anna without a hint of a turn to the face both as an expression of her character – and because it showed her at her best – and this was, after all, a portrait designed to be an advertisement. Holbein chose, therefore, not to draw attention to a part of her anatomy that might be unattractive. If Holbein turned her sideways – as he did the portrait of Christina of Milan – also a potential bride of Henry's – even slightly – it would be unavoidable for him to paint Anna of Cleves' long nose. Other contemporary portraits extant painted of the Lady by her own court artist, Barthel Bruyn, show that there is underpainting – the nose has been shortened. Holbein's pose for the princess deals with the physical flaw brilliantly and honestly. It is interesting that Lucas Cranach, much admired in England as on the Continent, pleaded illness when asked to paint the princess. Perhaps it seemed easier to pass the commission to his pupil who might have fewer qualms, if qualms were called for. Henry chose to ignore the Barthel Bruyn picture and to send his own painter to Cleves. He might, in retrospect, have wished he had not. Holbein – painting the truth but choosing the good truth – posed his subject accordingly. He gave Anna a little help.

Now – Holbein liked noses. He was not a man to flinch from noses. Look at any of his portraits and he draws or paints his noses generously and lovingly – in his self-portrait hanging in the Uffizi he shows his own nose, broken like Henry's, to be a considerable presence – but he clearly felt that Anna's nose was a nose that was best not celebrated in paint. Face her frontally and the problem is solved. He is *not disguising the nose, merely avoiding it. Holbein's entirely honourable method achieved the same result. One can comfortably say that he knew how much Cromwell, his paymaster after the King, wanted this match and while he would not sacrifice truth for painted lies, where he could accommodate, he did so.*

In the end his court painter gave Henry a portrait that told him all he needed to know about the young woman with whom he contemplated marriage. This is no sophisticated, fashionable young woman who will fascinate away his hours with her skills and wiles – at least not yet – but Henry ignored Holbein's truth. In his rush to assuage his mortification at being rejected by several eligible European ladies, Christina of Denmark and Marie of Guise particularly, Henry ignored the character in Anna's portrait and concentrated on its surface charms. The Tudor Court with all its aggression and uncouth masculinity was no place to be a King without a wife. A feminine hand was needed. Henry, most definitely, wanted to be wed.

In the end it mattered little what he was told in letters from envoys and what Holbein painted into the portrait so discreetly. Anna of Cleves was found to be lovely enough. Henry was in no mood to be gainsaid. If the portrait of Anna of Cleves were to be cleaned and restored it would show how its sumptuousness and its colour would dazzle any hopeful King. Even now, dulled by the patina of time, it has a glow and richness about it. Holbein at his most seductive indeed.

So the mystery of Henry and Anna and the success of the portrait and rejection of the real thing is partly to do with the King's own psychological state at the time of the painting's arrival, and partly to do with Holbein's eye for a cunning pose and his painter's way with surfaces. Anna of Cleves, five hundred years on, is still exactly what he painted, a dignified young woman quietly waiting for the world to open to her and love her.

At the museum Flora enquired where the portrait hung and followed the signs. The place was waiting for the onslaughts of the day for it had not yet filled with people. It was in that hour before tour groups and school outings made rendezvous and the few visitors were not hurrying themselves. Flora, by contrast, almost raced along, turning this way and that, ignoring enticing works as she sped past, up in lifts, down again, sideways, trotting through rooms of paintings which she scarcely noticed. As if Fate herself were in charge of her. Looking back, a long time later, she was surprised to remember how little she felt as she crossed the threshold of that most famous of art museums. It would change her life, that visit. Bells might ring, sirens might sound, but they did not – nothing broke the low notes of whispered conversations, nor disturbed the gravity of the place as she made her early way through the galleries.

How strange it was, Flora thought, to be rushing towards an unknown painting, in a foreign gallery, with a heart beating so fast from excitement. Very strange. It was only a portrait after all. But there was her heart again, missing a beat. She was practically palpitating by the time she arrived at the small side room. She read the information card fixed to the wall first. It was to the point.

ANNA OF CLEVES BY HANS HOLBEIN THE YOUNGER (1497–1543)

Anna of Cleves was Henry VIII's fourth wife. This was the betrothal portrait painted in the summer of 1539 when she was not quite twenty-four. She was a great disappointment to the King when she arrived in England in January 1540 and he divorced her after six months to marry Catherine Howard. She remained in England for the next seventeen years and died, after a short illness, in 1557 at Chelsea, London.

Then, at last, she stepped back and looked.

The portrait hung against a wall of dusty green silk – set between two much smaller contemporary portraits of men in flamboyant sixteenth-century dress. Flora had the room entirely to herself. She stood about two feet away from the picture and gazed. It was almost as if she was staring into a mirror so exactly still and similar were their poses. But of course the woman in the picture was young. Flora looked at her and she looked back at Flora. Neither blinked. Well, thought Flora, there is plug ugly and there is not very attractive and there is plain, and the young woman whom she saw in the painting was certainly none of these. The Brabantine bonnet Anna wore took her hair straight off her face, left her forehead entirely bare, and meant that there was nothing between the viewer and the subject's face which was a very nice oval. Flora liked the young woman at once.

There was a small bench in the middle of the room. Flora sat down, facing the portrait. She could see that Henry's approving eyes had not lied. The young woman – though overdressed by any standards – had a tawny rather than creamy complexion (though Flora thought this might just be the patina of age) and a sweet and appealing face and she was glad that she had avoided looking at reproductions of the portrait; it was striking to see it, to see her, for the first time and in the flesh – well – so to speak – and for Flora to see why Henry chose her. Maybe she was only halfway fair, maybe Holbein did spice her up, but there was no real sign of it in the painting. None at all. Those sleepy, slanting eyelids looked out in unsophisticated simplicity and were, to Flora's mind, beautiful, while the Princess's expression was genuine and guileless.

Flora stepped nearer. Holbein had painted a glow about Anna that gave her a hint of magic. Maybe he was not quite as honourable as history suggested. Maybe he knew that the marriage was a *fait accompli* and that Henry would see what he wanted to see no matter how he painted her. According to Scarisbrick, Henry loved a gay and lively court, and Henry knew that the way to a gay and lively court was to have a queen to guide it. This woman was not yet that queen but one in the making, willing to learn. The outward facing pose says that she is willing and at the same time Holbein puts in as much as he dare about her naïvety. Maybe the pose was also helpful if the story of her long nose was true. The serendipity of art, Flora decided.

There were other stories – such a mythology existed around this one beautiful painting – the most convoluted of which was that Anna's gown contained a hidden message about her intellectual drawbacks. It suggested that the jewelled banding on Anna's skirt being bigger on the left than on the right – said to translate for those who understood it as a pun on the courtly French for 'trait à gauche, pas à droit' – or – 'très gauche, pas adroite' – in other words the subject was not skilled in the manners and accomplishments of the English court – was Holbein's message to the King. Flora could only think that if this big hint were true and if it were the way of the court to read such puns in those days, then Henry would recognise it and act accordingly. It seemed to Flora that for a painter to say such a thing about a potential Queen of England to the tyrannical King was – to put it mildly – dangerous. And anyway Henry already knew that Anna was unsophisticated. His envoy, Sir Nicholas Wootton, accompanying Holbein to Cleves wrote to the King saying, 'She can read and write her own language but of French or Latin or other language she knows none, nor can she sing or play an instrument for it is considered undignified and shallow for German Ladies to do so . . .' And you couldn't be clearer than that, thought Anna. So Holbein's message was unnecessary. All he needed to do was paint what he saw. It was Sir Nicholas Wootton's job to write what he saw and he had done so. Wootton said she was fair and it was Holbein's job to make a true portrait of her. Would Holbein do otherwise? Given what Flora had read about him she did not think so. She looked hard at the portrait. The portrait looked serenely back. Almost ready to speak, it seemed.

It was then that something touched Flora's heart about the painted face. She stood up and went nearer, holding up her hands to block out the richness of Anna's embroidered cap, the opulence of Anna's jewels and the golden gorgeousness of her ornaments so that she saw only the unadorned features. When she did this, the face looked back at her with a simple openness, confronting the world with absolute honesty. When Flora removed her hands and let the face take its place within the gold and rich rose velvet of the painted gown the expression remained quite certain in its calm determination. Here I am, it said. This is me.

Anna's waist was dainty and neat, her crossed hands elegant, which belied her being called large, bony and masculine by one sneering historian. If they ever looked at this portrait they looked without seeing. Even though the young shoulders seemed wide as an American footballer's in the padded finery of its German court dress and the bosom – which looked full – and was all but hidden by an armoury of gold and jewels – the figure could not be anything but slender. Above the face the heavily decorated cap that held and hid all Anna's hair was framed by wings of the finest gauze. Flora smiled. These silly little wings gave the portrait its only touch of levity, a lightness to counter the heaviness of everything else – though Flora read that the background colour would once have been a singing blue-green rather than the slate-like darkness accrued with age. The portrait might be as imponderable as an icon if it were not for that face which was absolutely real – so real that for a dizzy moment Flora thought she could ask it a question and it would answer. But what question?

Time passes. Flora stands back from the portrait now, her head on one side. No matter what angle she chooses, she thinks, this is the most engaging portrait she has ever seen. Or perhaps she has found it at a sympathetic time in her life. Or worse, perhaps she has never truly looked at a portrait before. In the past a portrait was merely an arrangement of colour and light and form and curiosity, brought alive by the sitter's story. Now, knowing all she knows about the painting and the princess, she looks beyond the construction of the work and its vulgar anecdote at the person, only at the person, and not at a dumped princess. This is a human being, this is a young woman who could just as easily be a friend. Anna is real. Edward would have laughed if she had said that to him. He would have leaned forward and tapped the long-dried paint, feeling himself allowed such privilege, and he would have pointed out that the girl was two-dimensional – nothing alive about her at all. Well, Edward, she thinks, sometimes enlightenment comes more easily to those who stand and look or listen. Milton was right – 'They also serve . . .' If Edward were with her now she might – and at long last – have the courage to point that out to him.

Flora moves nearer to the painting – close enough to touch it if she chose – not that she would – but the attendant says nothing. All around Anna, in other, grander rooms, there are portraits far more valuable and famous – there are Rubenses and Rembrandts, Titians and Velasquezes – trumpet calls of paintings, paintings that hit the headlines. Somewhere in the museum is the most famous portrait in the world, *La Gioconda*: the *Mona Lisa* sits behind bullet-proof, fire-resistant glass and an infra-red security system. Mobile telephones are held up to photograph that most famous smile and heads and elbows jostle to get near so much famous beauty. The *Mona Lisa* is a celebrity and like all celebrities her fame brings magpies, keen to remove a piece of her – and with the magpies comes fear. This German princess, and temporary English Queen, is left to her own devices in matters of her safety. No infra-red security for Anna. No celebrity she.

'I think,' says Flora softly, for the gallery is empty apart from the attendant, 'that Henry was mad.' She looks down at her notes and reads aloud: '" . . . She excels the Duchess as far as the golden sun doth excel the moon . . ." And the English courtier who wrote that to Henry was probably right . . . After all, he was in Cleves and he could see for himself . . . It was probably Anna's rival, the Duchess of Milan, he was talking about.' The Princess of Cleves looks out unblinkingly. Five hundred years of being dismissed, thinks Flora, *would* make you impassive. 'If you're a Flanders Mare,' she whispers, 'then I'm the Queen of Sheba.' She would like to think that – just for a glimmer of a moment – the portrait looks amused.

Perhaps the attendant is used to early visitors muttering at the paintings. In any event she does not look up. If she had Flora might have shared with her the revelation that Anna is rather comely. Flora would not mind looking half so attractive. Or even a quarter. This Anna is dignified and so quietly amenable within her painted existence that to remember what lay before her makes Flora sad. Or Anna *was* quietly contented and dignified when this was painted. For of course, when she sat for the portrait she had not suffered the huge humiliation of such a public rejection so far from home. It makes Flora shiver just to read about it. This is the young woman who came to England – perhaps full of hope, perhaps full of trepidation, certainly determined to please, expecting to be treated like a queen and instead she was treated like a cast-off bawd. Henry, cruel in his anger, even told his council of men that her very smell was obnoxious to him. That most personal and private of things between a husband and wife, her very scent, open to the sniggerings of gossiping legal scribes. Flora looks again. These were the last days of this young woman's innocence and happiness. Within six months of sitting for the painting she would be far away in a foreign land where it was dangerous to be her friend until the King showed the way. Anyone who has ever been bullied knows how that isolation feels. Flora knows just a little, a tiny bit, of what it is like to be thought second-rate and not worth bothering with. How much worse if those who would not bother were afraid for their lives?

She returns to the bench and sits there, hunched up, chin on her hands, not even seeing the painting now, but dipping into the past, caught up in the vileness of it all. How did Anna manage? How did she cope without going mad? How did she survive the stripping away of her clothes and her privacy and not retreat forever into blackness? Her breasts and belly, according to some jubilantly prurient historians, were publicly reviled by the petulant King. Her virginity denied. How – how did she survive? That is the question Flora wants to ask her. How?

She brings herself back to that face. Well – yes – the expression is docile but there is a firmness about the chin and mouth, a sense of position perhaps? After all she was a princess. And a princess with the blood of several royal houses in her veins. Henry might shake her belief in herself as a woman and a wife, but – from the way those lips are set – it seems unlikely that he would shake her faith in her royal dignity. But how he tried. What a pig of a man he was, that Most Noble Prince Henry of England. At that moment Flora hates him. She likes Anna and that is what you do in friendship if someone hurts your friend – you despise them for it. It was called loyalty and that is what Flora experiences now, a wave of loyalty for Anna and a desire – that seems perfectly natural – to want to set the record straight. Flanders Mare, indeed. At the very thought she finds herself apologising, mentally, for the disgraceful behaviour of this English king.

Even as Flora thinks this she has the strangest sense that she may have spoken the thought aloud, or that it has been taken from her mind and noted elsewhere. She stares searchingly at the portrait, and the portrait stares back at her. Its dignified sweetness seeming now to be tempered by its frankness. You could almost, thinks Flora, feeling the little tremor run up and down her spine, you could almost believe that the painted face contains a glimmering of life. It is as if it – she – wants to speak, as if her demure calm is about to be broken by an overwhelming desire to say something to the woman who observes her.

Flora feels odd, alone, although there are people all around her now – gradually filling up the gallery – and despite her sense of unease she is held there, waiting for something to happen. What that might be she cannot possibly dare put into rational thoughts. Just a something. It is absurd, ridiculous, frightening. It is alive.

Words echo in her head, long buried lines of Eliot's, 'Oh, do not ask, "What is it?" / Let us go and make our visit. / In the room the women come and go / Talking of Michelangelo . . .' And in a way they are, those visitors, for they are looking as Flora has looked so often, not into the paintings hung there but around them. Checking the catalogue notes or squinting at the information cards on the walls – less at who is portrayed, but how and why. And then they hurry on to find easier comfort in the better-known painters, the more familiar images, the big stars like da Vinci, Raphael, Titian's *Man with a Glove*. But here in the celebrity B camp Flora knows that something has happened between her and the painting of Anna of Cleves – a connection, a bond. Perhaps all portraits are capable of this if you spend time with them, she thinks. Flora looks at the other portraits in the room. They seem uncommunicative by comparison. No – Anna is unique.

The other visitors' chattering moves on, leaving silence. The direct look from the painted face, the light in the eyes, the mouth set as if to draw breath, it all seems real. *A speaking likeness.* The picture, the young woman, wants to speak. In the rooms beyond the people come and go . . . But there is a life here, a princess protagonist, a dark fairy tale, perhaps, or a story of good triumphing over evil, something to be spoken of after centuries of silence. Flora's bun-like smile and overweening husband is a but a pinprick, a mouse-bite. She leans towards the painting, as if to see it breathe, hear it speak. It is almost, almost there – almost alive in Flora's head – and then – the moment is broken.

A voice – clipped, English, confident – is speaking in English. Very firmly in English. Flora is suddenly aware of a scuffling and a nudging of people crowding around the picture now, pushing at her to move, which she does. It is a group of perhaps eight or ten adults none of whom will see fifty again – and the voice that addresses them slices through the benign breathing warmth like a cut of ice. Flora blinks, stands to one side to let the scufflers and the nudgers form their semicircle, looks across the heads and shoulders of the assembly and sees that the portrait is merely surface once more – that what seemed about to happen has not happened. Flora, irritated at the disturbance, waits, and because she can do little else, she listens. After all, she is of an age, too, as they say, and she could fit into this group very well. Except, she adds to herself hastily, except that her black and bottle-green clothes are dramatic if unstylish and she would never, ever be seen, dead or alive, in beige. Nor, she reckons, smiling up at the portrait, would Anna.

Miss Penelope Murdoch is not stylish and will never see fifty again either, nor sixty, and she therefore knows a thing or two about a lot of things. She is a clever woman, an art historian by training, and has no truck with the way Braque once dismissed her profession (for she is determined that it is a profession) as being as relevant to painters as ornithologists are to birds. Miss Murdoch is a Brown Guide in charge of a very small collection of Works of Art back home in Blighty. She refers to England as Blighty, as her father, in the fag-end of the colonial service, did once. She, too, might have been in the colonial service had there still been Colonies in the old-fashioned way – as it is she went among art history students at a good-quality Ladies' College and – providing she is not asked to pronounce on the visual and historical value of art works made after nineteen-fifty – or thereabouts – and containing nothing comfortably recognisable – she's your girl. And she loves her art history. She especially loves it when those gathered about her know nothing. This group is called 'English Art Abroad' and – although the artist was German – Holbein was the man who shaped the face of the English court when it was at its most tumultuous.

Miss Murdoch begins by saying that Holbein is a good taker of likenesses but that she does not feel, as some do, that he is a genius. This portrait of Anne of Cleves, for example, if it were not for its ornamental qualities, would be very dull. Flora feels herself colour with indignation at this and casts a quick, apologetic glance at the portrait. This, too, seems to reflect a little more pinkness on its oval cheeks and who, thinks Flora, caring nothing for the silliness of the thought, can blame her?

Miss Murdoch, who wears her Guide's badge so proudly and has with her a sheaf of notes, must know so much about so many things that she may find it very tiring making up her own mind about art. That is the best Flora Chapman can think about such thoughtlessness.

Miss Penelope Murdoch now speaks and Mrs Flora Chapman, who is not of Miss Murdoch's party, nor trained as an art historian, sidles up to the group and listens. It is as if some careless acquaintance passes comments on a friend. 'Anne of Cleves was Henry VIII's fourth wife. But they were married only briefly. She came from Flanders – now northern Germany – and was a Lutheran. Necessary as Henry had broken away from the Pope. Henry was enchanted by the portraits Holbein painted of his new Lutheran Queen – this three-quarters one to scale and another, a miniature, which is in the Victoria and Albert Museum in London and is exquisite but which cannot have been a true portrait by very reason of its subject's reasonable looks.' Miss Murdoch pauses and gives a theatrical turn towards the portrait as if to emphasise her point. Flora manages – just – to hold back. 'When it was received by Henry it was described as "very lively" – this means lifelike – by those who had seen both the Princess in the flesh and the Princess on the vellum. Vellum is calfskin. Both portraits were painted on vellum and the larger – this – was later transferred to board. Calfskin, due to its porous nature, has a surface that is particularly good at holding colour.'

The group look slightly squeamish at this but Miss Murdoch, who is at her most confident when discussing technicalities, does not notice. Miss Murdoch likes this kind of information because it is factual. Miss Murdoch and Edward

Chapman would have got on very well.

There are more facts for the group. The miniature in London, apparently, has a rich mid-blue background and it is likely that the background in this portrait was also once either a rich mid-greeny blue or kingfisher and it is time that has turned it etc etc. Why they used the colour Miss Murdoch simply *does* not know if it was so unstable . . . Flora, half amused, half astonished, thinks Miss Murdoch could as easily be discussing an inferior brand of polish. This is the first time she has had anything to do with a group art visit and it is not the engaging exercise she imagined.

Miss Murdoch, having made it clear that Holbein was a nuisance for using a colour that changed so radically, continued her tale of the pictures' journeys. 'So then – the portraits arrived – the big one first the miniature later – and Henry was enchanted with his new Lutheran Queen – remember that Henry had broken with the Pope and Rome and was now Excommunicate – so her Lutheran status was important. The prospective bridegroom's enchantment quickly evaporated when Henry saw the portrait's subject in the flesh . . . She was rejected and Cromwell eventually lost his head.'

How much rested on physical beauty then, as now, Flora thought sourly. A man could die of it. Something of a miracle that Anna did not die, also, considering Henry's past methods of removal. Anna, she thought, must have very scared indeed.

Miss Murdoch seemed rather jubilant on the subject of Anna's looks: 'As other portraits of the Queen by her court painter Barthel Bruyn – notably at St John's College, Oxford, clearly show – had Holbein painted her at any other angle except facing straight ahead, it would show her long chin and even longer nose. No beauty she, not at all.'

Miss Murdoch said this last with such consummate satisfaction that Flora nearly spoke up. Takes one to know one, she thought rudely.

Flora had her back to the portrait almost protectively and she felt a warmth, a definite warmth, all around her, which might be her own blood pumping with indignation, or a heating duct. Then, from behind her, she heard a very slight noise that might be an intake of breath – but when she looked around she saw no one except the unblinking, sweetly docile, face. Imagination, she decided. Or perhaps she made the noise herself. People do that sort of thing when they get older, she thought gloomily.

Flora wondered whether this was because the painter got it wrong in the first place, or whether it was to flatter the sitter. Anna did not look like the kind of young woman who needed to be flattered. Flora did not warm to this guide person. Her tone had a definite air of the celebratory about it, as if she loved to dwell on physical imperfections. It should also be said, thought Flora sharply, that Miss Murdoch's own nose was no slouch.

Flora now scowled. One thing a plain woman can do is to scowl marvellously well and most alarmingly. Scowling, she felt, sometimes made her more interesting. At least Miss Murdoch would see the deep disapproval on one of her spectators' faces, even if that spectator was an interloper. 'It is Holbein's most frontal composition and made as sumptuous as possible in order to detract from the very plain face of the sitter . . .'

Flora scowled more deeply. How dare the woman? Miss Murdoch paused and peered very positively at the portrait again. It was a pause and a peer designed as a flourish. Did the painting wince? It had every right to do so. Then again - Flora thought she heard a soft hissing noise but she could neither swear to it nor find the source. Whatever the reason, the sound seemed entirely appropriate. Like the breath of history. 'So, in painting the dress asymmetrically, Holbein sent the strongest message that he could to the King regarding Anne's dullness, ineptitude and complete lack of suitability . . .' She spoke this last with such emphasis that it would be a brave man or woman who denied its Absolute Truth.

Flora was that woman. She turned towards the speaker and

surprisingly found herself saying, 'Well – if that were so and Hans Holbein was known for putting hidden messages into his paintings for his clients – which sounds very far-fetched to me, if not downright dangerous for the painter – then the King must have been pretty dim himself not to notice . . . I mean, how come a twentieth-century eye – twenty-first century eye even, can tell all this and yet a sixteenth-century eye – one that was familiar with that sort of thing – couldn't?' She gave an enjoyably dismissive wave of her hand and added, 'I suggest it's flim-flam. All flim-flam.'

All eyes turned towards her. Miss Murdoch blinked. The group shifted and muttered nervously. Behind her Flora was quite, quite sure she heard an approving exhalation of breath. As if someone had heard and was utterly satisfied with the statement. Nonsense, of course. But nice nonsense. It made her feel that she did not stand here alone.

Miss Murdoch gave Flora what could be called A Killing Look – and continued. 'Now – to prove my point – if you stand away to look at the portrait you can see that Holbein has painted her attire in such a way that one forgets, when look-ing, to see the face as a separate entity. But if you do look at the face you will see that it is far from pretty and certainly not beautiful – in fact – it is plain and wholly expressionless. He has made the perfect iconesque painting which shows nothing of the sitter in human terms. Henry VIII fell, I am quite sure, for the glorious richness of the portrait, the jewels and the gold, and forgot that he was looking for a wife and compan-ion. The trick of the icon – to read the pattern and not the indi-vidual parts – Holbein transformed plain, dull Anne into a beauty. When Henry saw her in the flesh for what she really was – he called her his *Flanders Mare*.'

Her group made a suitable sound expressing shock. Flora said loudly, 'Oh how I loathe that expression . . .' Miss Murdoch tutted but continued her gallop to the end. 'It also seems that the lady was so repugnant that the usually red-blooded Henry could not – er – perform as a bridegroom should.' She gave a roguish little grin at the group who all looked slightly nervous and Flora shook her head several times and let out a little grunt of disapproval. Miss Murdoch ignored it and said, 'Well, whatever we think, the rejected Queen was soon pensioned off and left to her own devices. It says much for Henry's admiration of his court painter, Holbein, that he went on working for the King until his death four years after completing this portrait.' Miss Murdoch appeared to rub her hands together as if to say *that* was *that*. She looked very self-satisfied.

'You are quite wrong, I think,' said a commanding voice which Flora surprisingly found to be hers. 'Firstly I think you will find that there is some question over whether the marriage was consummated or not – Henry's desire for a divorce making it more likely he conveniently forgot. And as for the Queen's physical attributes – why – if you look again you will see that the face is far from plain. I reiterate – I think you are quite wrong . . .'

Silence. Then Miss Murdoch squared her shoulders and said, with icy politeness, 'Oh. And are you in – er – a position . . .?'

Flora stood firm. 'Well – my name is Flora Chapman and Anna of Cleves once owned the house I live in – or at least the site – or the foundations – or . . .'

Miss Murdoch raised a quelling eyebrow. 'Really?' she said. 'And you think it gives you authority?'

'Yes,' said Flora, wishing she had never got started. She was about to add, in a more conciliatory tone, that she spoke as any observant member of the public might speak but the words faltered. Something then seemed to give her a shove in the back and it was as if a great hindering lump had been removed from her throat. She said, with extraordinary confidence, almost laughing now, 'Well, I speak as that, but I also . . .'

'Yes?' said Miss Murdoch. 'You also speak as . . .?'

Flora said, to her surprise, 'I speak as her sister. After all, someone has to speak up for her – I mean – she can't exactly

speak up for herself – now can she . . .?' There was that pleasant warmth again, like the breath of approval.

Flora had never seen eyes genuinely pop before. Miss
Murdoch's certainly bulged at this. 'Well,' she added, 'less
histrionically I suppose, I speak as a woman who doesn't take
kindly to hearing bad things said about another woman. Sister
in that way.' The blankness in the group's eyes told her that
these were not people who ever scudded down to Women
Against Greenham with blankets and flasks of tea.

This did not altogether enlighten the eyes of the group or its
formidable leader. They remained silent and unflinching
though their eyes had returned to their sockets. 'Sometimes,'
said Flora, sticking out her chin and turning her gaze back to
the portrait, 'experts forget to link their eyes with their hearts.'

As Flora stared again at that painted face it stared back at
her. Flora could almost read her thoughts. 'You know,' she
said, 'if Anna of Cleves is to be known as the Flanders Mare,
then you can say without fear or favour that she is a very fine
piece of horseflesh.' Flora studied Miss Murdoch's badge.
Then looked into Miss Murdoch's eyes. 'Well, Miss
Murdoch?' She was pleased to see that some of the group
returned to the portrait with a kinder look.

Flora might, she considered afterwards, be going mad. But it
seemed, as she stared, that the portrait breathed. Caught in
paint before her was a much maligned woman. And she, Flora,
empathised. That was all. Anna of Cleves looked out of the
frame as a young woman with something to say. After five
hundred years of such calumnies, if she didn't have something
to say it would be very surprising. So, thought Flora, let her
say it. And if she can't, then let Flora say it for her.

Yes – there – no doubt about it – the face of the portrait
smiled.

Just at that moment – at that very split second when Flora
thinks she could reach out and take the young woman's be-
ringed hand – she sees something out of the corner of her eye.

The group also turns, Miss Murdoch turns – Flora has the strangest sensation of fright – for coming through the door are what you might expect to see if you *had* gone suddenly mad – coming through the door are two men in white coats. They are wearing sinister white gloves and one of them carries, rolled beneath his white-coated arm, what Flora – for one incredible moment – thinks must be the straitjacket. The two men are smiling which is even more sinister. They move the beige crowd away, they move Miss Murdoch away, they advance towards Flora – and – well – her knees nearly crumple – maybe Anna felt like this when they told her of the King's loathing – but then the men also move Flora away. What they have come for – is the painting.

This is where her fluent French helps. Once she has recovered herself she asks the men who are busy taking the portrait down and tucking it up in rudimentary packaging so that they can carry it away without damage, why they are doing so. The face on the portrait may even look a little startled as Flora sees it disappear under a soft and heavy grey cloth wrap. They laugh – the men in white – they recognise that even though she speaks their language she speaks it with an English accent. They tell her, between guffaws as they make the portrait secure enough to go down to the storeroom, that the painting is to go to England. Yes, it is to go to England and be part of a bigger exhibition of this and other portraits. But this portrait, they tell her, and they say it with the pride of Frenchmen, this portrait will be the jewel in the show.

And with that, they hoist Anna of Cleves, gripped tight at the corners, shrouded in soft grey cloth with her edges protected, away down the gallery and out of the door. The attendant gives them no more than a nod as the men pass by. And then it is all over. Flora looks at Miss Murdoch, the group stare amazed at the blank on the wall. 'Well,' says Miss Murdoch with high good humour, 'we managed our talk *just* in time.' She casts a not very nice little smile in Flora's direction. 'And they've taken your *sister* away. For cleaning, I expect.'

7

Setting Out and Arriving

Well, well. Modern times. Why mock when a woman calls another woman sister? We called each other sister and it was a form of endearment, of support, of closeness. Why laugh? A sister would, surely, defend another sister from a scornful tongue and hurtful sayings. If the woman in grey wishes to speak so unkindly about me, as many before her have spoken, then it seems to be a very wonderful thing that someone – like a good sister – should defend me. There have been enough degradations, enough unkindnesses, enough speculations about my honour since I first set foot in England, now let there be some credit.

Do those who make these unjust assertions and speculations think I have no need for truth because I am made of paint? Truth is never unwelcome and now that I am to return to England it is as good a time as any to speak out. I hope, Flora Chapman, that we do meet again. I might have need of you. It is not a happy memory, my previous arrival. Not an occasion on which to look back fondly. If this time my portrait is as badly received as I was then, it will bring no shame on me but on those who will not look, those who still prefer mockery to enlightenment. All the same, Flora Chapman – England again . . .

When Hans Holbein came to paint me I had no idea that he was considered a genius and that through his painting I would capture the King's heart. I was not at all worldly and had, until then, been my mother's companion and helper. If I could not play the lute and dance and construct poetry I did at least have a disposition to be a good wife and a good mother. The requirement for queenliness I already had, the rest would follow. Certainly I had no misgivings, nor did my family. How could we know that such perversity and cruelty existed within a Royal Prince? In Cleves I lived a life that was – thank God – free from the cruelties of religious intolerance. I was a happy young woman, brought up formally, and quite content to stay with my mother at the Court of Cleves. But the Envoys from England, looking for marriage with me or my sister Amelia, changed everything. I was the elder, twenty-three years old, the portrait was painted, and I was chosen. Perhaps I should have been better informed about the English court before I set out on that journey – I might have understood better what was to come. But none of that was spoken about, all was assumed. Princesses of Cleves were not expected to ask questions about their marriages. My older sister Sibylla, Duchess of Saxony, was a renowned beauty and much celebrated and I had no fears it would be different for me. Henry was described to me as a most noble prince and I had no cause to doubt that. I would manage my marriage quite as well as Sibylla.

There had been one previous attempt to wed me to a suitable husband, the son of the Duke of Lorraine. I was eleven at the time and he was two years my junior. It was a good match but nothing came of it and, in the way of these ironies, many years later, after Henry's proposal was refused by the sixteen-year-old widowed (sixteen, Flora, and twice married to old men) Christina of Denmark, Duchess of Milan, so that he chose me instead, the then Duke of Lorraine, my one-time betrothed, married her – Henry's first choice. These things both amuse and give pause for thought. The circle of suitable spouses for Royal Houses was always small. Particularly for a King whose wives seemed to die quite regularly.

Once the King had made up his mind I was sent for at once. Oh, Flora, I should have guessed that Henry's thoughtlessness to have me travel during the winter was a sign – but then I saw it only as exciting, even romantic. The impatient and imperative King of England would have his way and my entourage assembled in the worst months possible for such a long journey. But my head was high and my heart was happy. I set out regally, a Princess of Cleves, with an escort of three hundred men and women, all richly attired, and I had such gowns made for me that I could only gasp at the sight of them – and gold and jewels, too. My brother William spared nothing for the honour of Cleves and it is both wrong and arrogant to suggest our court was coarse or boorish or impoverished. My royal blood was kin with the Grand Court of Burgundy and as such our heredity was greater and infinitely more noble than the upstart Tudors. It is true that the Duchy of Cleves in which I grew up was sober and formal compared with the French and English courts, but boorish? Never.

So much fool's nonsense has been invented over the centuries about my state of mind and heart at the time I left Cleves. There have been suggestions that I was already in love with someone else in Cleves and never wanted to go to England – this was portrayed in a film called *The Private Life of Henry VIII* – in 1933 and I have known people stand in front of my portrait and declare it a true story. Where such an idea came from is a mystery. As far as I know there is nothing in my life to warrant such an invention. There was no chaster court than Cleves. The possibility of any kind of dalliance, even innocent, was too remote to contemplate. The very idea that I left a lover behind is absurd.

Then there was a book, *My Lady of Cleves*, and that is even more absurd. It suggests that I had an affair with the King's painter, Hans Holbein, which is why he painted me to look more beautiful than I really was – an apologia for my apparent plainness this was – by suggesting that it was beauty in the eye of the loving beholder rather than in the flesh that he painted. Flora, you were quite right, I am straightforward, guileless and as if I could possibly hide – or want – something so intrinsically dangerous – and beneath me – as an affair with the King's Painter. Even had I been goose enough to be attracted to him,

Hans Holbein was much too ambitious in the matters of Henry's court to have anything to do with such a madness. Heads rolled, men were quartered and had their bowels burnt before them for a great deal less. Besides – the very idea that I – a Daughter of Cleves – could stoop so low – and with a mere painter from Augsburg, even if that painter was Hans Holbein – is impossible.

The truth, Flora, is simple. I came to England a virgin, pure in body and mind. Of course I did. But I was neither slow-witted nor ignorant, though it was useful in those dark first days of my arrival to be thought incapable of understanding much of the English language and incapable of understanding what was happening all around me. A little more good sense and a little less arrogance might have told my new acquaintances that a princess of royal blood would hardly remain idle in learning the language of her new home nor would she be stupid. Many a woman, it seems to me, has survived by holding her tongue and looking meekly downwards. Besides which, for the duration of the journey to England Henry sent a Mrs Gilmyn to be my female escort and educator in the English tongue and Tudor courtly ways. She was not idle.

The simple fact is that Hans Holbein painted a good likeness of me, a true likeness. Others said as much. I saw the portrait for the first time when I came to England and it was truthful. When Henry's envoys came to Cleves they met a quiet, dutiful young woman, eyes modestly downcast, good at her needle, able to read her Bible in German, swathed in demure Brabantine fashions and beloved by her mother. A young princess who was happy in her family – certainly a young woman who would prefer amenability over controversy. They would, with all that I have endured, find me very different now. Indeed, even within six months of arriving in England, and with the humiliating divorce behind me, I was no longer the modest, trusting young woman who first stepped on to English soil. I was alert and – to be truthful once the settlement was made and I was safe – I was excited again. I blossomed.

Nearly five hundred years of surviving fashion in art, which moves in and out like breathing, serving fashion in all things, has taught me much about the world. I have lived through half a millennium of eavesdropping and most of what I have heard about myself, about Hans Holbein, about this portrait, about Henry and the whole Tudor and Cleves business – is invention. May we please, on the occasion of this second visit to England Flora, make this right?

So then, without any doubts about Henry's affection or his character, I set off for England. And, Oh that first journey when I still was wide-eyed and willing was more exciting than anything I ever knew – or expected to know. It was both romantic and a little dangerous for although I remained a Catholic – I was educated to read the Bible in my own language and I believed that others should be free to do so – I came from a religiously reformist court and my brother the Duke was a Lutheran and no friend to the Emperor. I remained true to the Old Faith and was a Catholic on the day I died. Henry, too, remained a Catholic all his life. The English Religious Revolution effected the overthrow of the rule of the Pope, not the overthrow of the Catholic faith. We were in harmony on such matters at least.

We travelled throughout late autumn and into the dead of winter and even though we took the direct route it was still arduous in both its length and in the pomp and ceremony that heralded every stopping place. Given the upheaval of the times it was not without its dangers. We might have our progress barred as we travelled towards the sea – barred at the very least – if not attacked – on the long, landlocked journey to the coast. But the Queen of Hungary, the Catholic Emperor's Regent, in her sisterly way, gave us safe passage across the shortest route and we chose to trust her word. The alternative was longer and harder and Henry, I was told, was hourly more eager to be my bridegroom. You may imagine the thrill I experienced at such a thought. To be setting out to marry the Golden Prince of England who was eager, *eager*, Flora, to marry me? It was as if

I were Queen already. From being a quiet, respectful Daughter of Cleves, I was now a celebrated Princess. There were no restrictions, no Puritanism then, all was lavish and gorgeous and all for me. I was entertained beyond anything I had seen before, at so many towns – Antwerp, Bruges, Dunkirk – by the time we came to Calais, which was English then, and the ships that would bring me to England, it was cold, very, very cold, and I was weary – but I was also alive to it all, as eager to reach my new country as Henry was to have me there. If some of his accompanying people wrote to the King of me that I was handsome – which they did – then part of that was due to the elation I felt. I was young and naïve and in a maiden's state of nerves – full of hope and willing to please. Whatever love was, I was ready to embrace it.

I reached Calais on 11 December 1539, by now accompanied by an English as well as a Cleveian escort. It was my first connection with an English town. And the people who came out to meet me were so delighted, so warm in their welcome, it made me confident of my acceptance. They wanted a Queen and it seemed to them that I was the right mettle for it. I took them to my heart and they took me to theirs and the English nobles accompanying me were so very pleased at the fine way we all behaved. Flora, at no time then was there any mention of my not being handsome or fair. Good feelings abounded and the warmth of everyone I met made up for the exceptionally cold, raw air. They took me to their hearts and I took them to mine. With the people it was a true love-match and I dared to expect the same from the King.

And then, alas, we were prisoners of the elements. At Calais the weather, which had not been good for the whole of the journey, was worse, much worse, and we could not sail. I was feasted, entertained, made to go out and about to see various people and – despite my years – by then I was exhausted with it all. What I really wanted and succeeded in as much as possible, was to prepare myself for the English court with good Mrs Gilmyn's help. I wanted to learn the language, learn to write the language, learn the games of cards that my future husband enjoyed so much – know more about music and all the courtly elegances – poetry, even dancing – and generally become immersed in English ways for him. And I did. The Envoys accompanying me wrote of me favourably, praising me to the King. Strange, then, Flora, how such views seemed to change so completely after my meeting with Henry.

In Calais I was considered quick of mind. If I am nowadays described as dull or stupid, if it is believed that later divorce negotiations foundered on my lack of English it is conveniently forgotten that my escort, the Earl of Southampton, thought I did very well until his royal master told him to think something different. He wrote, I was told, to Henry from Calais saying that I had quickly picked up the game of Cent which His Majesty enjoyed so much and that I had 'played as pleasantly and with as good a grace and countenance as ever in all my life I saw on any noblewoman'. The Earl was not a man to mince his words if he found fault. Henry, like many a bully, had a selective memory.

In the end I was lucky that the English court decided to believe me to be such a dullard. Very soon after my arrival, I dared not be seen to be otherwise.

There were some fifty stormbound ships waiting in the harbour at Calais. Two of them, the greatest, were covered in gold and silk flags and banners while others were covered with streamers and more banners and men, hundreds of men, all cheering and waving their hats, and buffeted and wetted by the weather. It was breathtaking and designed to be so – Henry loved his navy and his ships. I responded with genuine delight and this pleased everyone. At that moment and in the following days everyone, everyone was pleased with the Princess of Cleves.

The storms kept us there for over two weeks and when they finally cleared, and the sea calmed, we sailed for England in the grandest pair of decorated ships that I had ever seen or believed possible. I felt honoured and loved and pleased to have been Mrs Gilmyn's excellent pupil.

I was – if not proficient – then able to speak more than a little English, write a little English and understand almost everything. Mrs Gilmyn not only helped me with my English speech
and English manners, she knew which were the fashionable
perfumes and all the other little pleasures and nuances that
would make the passage of my arrival and marriage the
smoother. And I was willing to do anything and everything to
make my husband happy. Sinful though these delights were
after my life in Cleves – where we had no such frivolities – I
revelled in these new forms of entertainment. I very quickly
learned to love music and to observe, if not yet participate, in
dancing. On my arrival Mrs Gilmyn faded most usefully from
all memory as my new English Ladies-in-Waiting came to take
up their duties which allowed the perceptions of me as ignorant and unsophisticated to continue unchallenged. Had she
been with me she would, most likely, have reported to her master that I knew a great deal more than they gave credit for. Nor
did I take offence when she told me, in the most genteel terms,
that perhaps my gowns and my caps would not suit the taste of
my new husband and I prepared myself to change them when
I arrived in England.

Deal to Dover, Dover to Canterbury, Canterbury to
Sittingbourne, everywhere the reception for me was a wonder,
the people crowded forward and cheered and the joy was
mutual. Those who still argue that I was provincial and awkward might care to consider how much formality and pomp
surrounded these journeyings and how regally and properly I
conducted myself. Meek and mild I may have been, but I
knew my place in the order of things and it was not a lowly
one. I was a princess of royal descent and conducted myself
accordingly. From Calais onwards I received such displays of
love from the common people that I could only love them
back. The people of England had fierce loyalties and a mind to
support what was right. They never spoke of me as raw-
boned and coarse-looking – and they came close enough to

see for themselves, believe me.

In addition to the advice of Mrs Gilmyn, I observed the English Ladies-in-Waiting sent to me, I noted what they wore, and within a short time my clothes were made in the same acceptable French fashion – square-cut and low-bodiced with the hoods made to fit away from the face and revealing the hair in the French way. The English court was not a place for modesty in dress. A month after my arrival I looked no different from any other fashionable lady of the court and Mrs Gilmyn was removed from my service. She was not alone. There were many who clung fast when my star was high – like the new Ladies-in-Waiting who came begging to serve me at the outset – and who quickly went away from me in its nadir.

After my first meeting with Henry at Rochester it was clear, by the time I reached London, that my status was changed. The Tudor Court was not an easy place for survival. I was warned of this by my own envoy, Olisleger, when we finally arrived there and the place felt so unkind and devious. It was a court riven with religious and political factions and those who led them were headstrong, ambitious, dangerous, watchful. If Henry had only been kinder I believe we would have done very well eventually. A willing woman, so I learned later, is more than half the battle. But Henry had set his teeth against the marriage at our first disastrous meeting in Rochester and nothing would change his mind . . .

Oh Flora – *Rochester* – New Year's Day 1540 – which should have been such a happy beginning and was not. I arrived there to stay in the Bishop's Palace, which was very fine, and a great relief after stopping in Sittingbourne which had only ordinary inns to care for me and my retinue. I was very, very weary by now – so weary – and the weather was miserable and cold. How long it was since I had left home – how many miles I had travelled – and I needed rest. But there was none to be had; at Rochester, on New Year's Eve, I was met by ever more noblemen and their wives with more feasts and receptions. Then came New Year's Day after which my life and my expectations changed so painfully and dramatically that each moment is carved in my memory though I only learned the truth of it all much later. Tudor gossip could never keep such a tale to itself.

Henry decided to ride in secret to Rochester to surprise me on New Year's Day though we were not to meet formally until several days later in London. He was as eager to see me, the Princess stepping out of the portrait and into his arms, as I was to see him, of whom I had only heard fine descriptions. But, Flora, if you or anyone thinks that the King of England could do anything so dashingly informal as ride to Rochester in secret to surprise his new bride – you do not understand the way of the Tudor Court and its spies. I knew he was coming – of course I did. Before he set out Henry told his first minister, Thomas Cromwell, that he was going to ride to me in secret 'to nurture love' – and since Thomas Cromwell was the champion of our marriage and wanted the alliance desperately, it is impossible that he would leave such a meeting to chance. This was Henry playing the gallant, the Knight Errant, the golden Prince of Chivalry. But I did not know the rules of the Chivalric Game – that a lady-love, because her heart is true, knows her true amour even when he arrives in disguise. We did not have Chivalric Games in Cleves – nor was Henry – in the end – a glorious gallant knight.

I was, as reported, watching bear baiting when he rode into the palace and I did indeed continue to watch the bear baiting after his arrival in my presence, but it was not want of knowledge of who he was that kept me continuing to look at the bear outside the window – it was – quite simply – shock. Where was my golden prince, my noble paramour? Henry VIII was gross, red-faced, panting and sweating, old and virtually slavering. I was speechless with disgust and horror. Had I spoken I might have wept. A lady-love might recognise her true amour but when he is a fat, monstrous brute? What does the lady-love do then? Remember, Flora, this was not like marriage in these islands now. I had never seen this betrothed of mine, nor had

anyone told me the truth about him. Henry's Envoys described
the King as most excellent and handsome and skilled in sport
and the lute and all manner of things. They spoke of him as if
he were the most delicate, the most elegant of Princes. They
said nothing about his obesity which he tried to hide with
absurdly wide padded shoulders, or his fleshy jowls, his small,
cold eyes and his wet little mouth – or his great legs one of
which was swollen and sore and made him limp. How could
they dare? To speak of the King like that was treason.

When he arrived – dressed as just another rich nobleman –
and entered the room where I waited – I was, wholly and disastrously, aghast. If my face owned any beauty it fled. I knew
this great ox with his red face and tiny mouth and slitted eyes
was the King. Of course I did. He made absurdly princely ges-
tures – he bowed his huge body down and tried to smile. But he
could not. We both faced each other as if we had seen a death.
Which in some ways we had. The truth was that we were *both*
disappointments to each other. I was taller than he liked, I was
not fair, I was not buxom nor daintily slender – and I was not
a coquette to act pleased nor a wittily spoken English girl – and
I was horrified at the sight of him which contorted my features
into nothing like the calm sweetness of the Holbein. In short I
was not like his other wives, or his dead wife Jane, nor like any
of his preferred dalliances and I was certainly not as he had
expected from the portrait. Perhaps worse than these for such
a vain man – the first look he saw on my living face – was
repugnance. How could it be otherwise? His big belly over-
hung his codpiece – a travesty of manliness. And above his
absurd wide shoulders, when he removed his feathered hat to
bow, his short cropped hair – damp from sweat – made his
head above that great body look small and absurd. He was
pouring with dampness from the ride and from his great size no
doubt. My sister's husband, the Duke of Saxony, was not handsome and he was older than Sibylla, but he was of a good shape
and size whereas this, this, was truly shocking. It is true that
Henry's voice was soft and courteous but his eyes displayed

exactly what he felt, cold anger. And, I am quite sure, mine showed repugnant fear. We both stood there, staring at each other, my bones as water at the disappointment, his too, and in that moment the potential failed. That is all. It was at that moment when our eyes met across the room and he loathed the way I looked and I loathed the way he looked – we both read it in each other's eyes. Disappointment, revulsion – these cannot be overcome. As a woman I must prepare myself to bear them for I had no choice, but as a man – and a king – Henry would not.

I do not know whom Henry called for in his heart at that moment, but I wanted to run home to my mother. And I knew I could not do that, nor ever could again. I was trapped. So I raised my chin, curtsied deep and low again, and became as charming as I knew how and returned my gaze to the bear. I was near to fainting but I knew that I must recover and be gracious, and so I was. But it did no good. I saw his face cloud over. While he could dismiss my distaste and pretend that he was the only one to make the rejection, he knew, he knew, that I felt the same. The English ladies might be clever at hiding their revulsion but I could not. How Henry of England could persuade himself that he was a desirable bridegroom – could nurture love in anybody – is only explained by his being a man who surrounded himself with fools and sycophants.

When I finally saw this portrait of mine, Flora, instead of being pleased, I wished with all my heart that the painter had done me less justice and not shown me to be beautiful enough to capture the heart of a king. Most certainly I did not look like that at Rochester, racked as I was with the horror of it all and the strain of such a long journey in such foul weather. I could have looked like the painting again, given time and love, but there was neither. Soon after this terrible first meeting I knew I should be scared for my safety. I remembered how the King could be with those who stood in his way. Heads rolled, bodies were split. He did not want me, and I did not want him – and we were both trapped. I knew how Henry behaved when he was in a trap. Of course I remembered, in my fear and confusion, his second wife, Anne Boleyn, and her end. After he left, I could picture my own head rolling in the bloodied straw. That Queen's death had been the gossip of Europe – how could the news of such an act not come, even to provincial Cleves? To slice off the head of his Queen? Anne Boleyn died only four years before my arrival and Henry, most noble Prince, was already preparing to marry Jane Seymour at the very moment the gunshot announced that the discarded Queen's head was severed. I, too, was now undesirable – and I did feel afraid. What Henry did to his enemies does not need repeating here – French sword or axe, it matters little when you are scared. I felt ashamed of my fears. I was a daughter of Cleves and should have more courage. My duty was to marry and make an alliance, and give him more heirs. That was my duty. And that, God willing, was what I knew I must do.

This, then, was the journey I made to England on that first occasion and this was its first result. I was Henry's captive and a woman – and worse, as he would see it, I was the enemy of his future happiness. I had to gather my wits – those wits that Henry's angry words told the world I did not possess. And gather them I did. It seemed wise to act as if nothing in the world had happened save that we had met, parted on good terms, and would meet again at our formal betrothal celebrations in Greenwich. Instinct guided me. God bless that, at least, Flora, for it was then that I saw the look in the eyes of those English attendants who had lived for my every whim until that moment. They also saw, and they also knew, that my star had not faded, but gone from the Universe completely and that if they wanted to keep their heads or their positions they must now avoid a young woman who was so grave a disappointment to such a ruthless King. Make no mistake, I knew, as soon as Henry and his gawping nobles left Rochester and the horses' hoofs rang out so fast away, that I was in some kind of danger. His love-nurturing gift to me was forgotten on that visit and was given to me later – beautiful sable furs. I have never looked upon a gift so sadly. Their warmth was a travesty.

Well, women are pragmatists Flora, then as now, I suppose. There was no more to be done except, as the King's betrothed, to make the final, planned part of my journey from Rochester to London, where on my arrival I would be formally greeted by my husband and endure all the long-planned rituals and festivities that had been so carefully arranged for our public wooing. To the outside world, it seemed, Henry was persuaded that we should continue as if we were truly happy to be betrothed. It was not entirely sham. I wanted – expected - to do my duty. I had recovered somewhat from that first ordeal and being active and busy was a good thing. Women are at their best being active during a crisis. But it was my first experience of my latent skills in hypocrisy. It was certainly not the first for my betrothed.

Henry was a man who liked to have a clear conscience. He liked to be able to sleep easily in his bed and to do so he needed to justify his every action – particularly if questionable – with religious acceptance, textual or intellectual force, the support of his bishops and council. I learned about this striving for public acceptance later. It was the difference, perhaps, between the honest despot and dishonest apparently law-abiding King. Henry could arrange anything, including having the Christian text bent to his will, which he did in the case of his first discard, Catherine of Aragon. He killed her, too, in his own cruel way. King Henry could call upon people of power and position to do his unpleasant, underhand work for him. Even his Archbishop was ready to bend the knee – and pay the ultimate price – dishonesty before God – if needs be. While dreadful, personal things were being said of me, and while Henry's Council worked night and day against me, to my face Henry was all charm. I was not deceived, nor was Olisleger who guided me through this dangerous time, but we were all playing the game of false piety and duplicity. When I eventually met Henry for our proper formal ceremonials he had recovered his aplomb and was as gallant as the watching world could wish. I learned later that he was at his most deadly when he was being most charming.

Very soon I understood that Henry could not chop off my head – even had he wanted to – for there was nothing treasonable in my behaviour. Even Henry could not kill a wife for the length of her nose and the colour of her eyes. But Henry was not a man to take blame or swallow a need for revenge and I was, nevertheless, one of those mistakes that took a life; Cromwell – the man who wanted the political alliance so badly and arranged it all – who had encouraged Holbein on the mission, Cromwell had his head removed instead. That it was Henry who agreed to the marriage enthusiastically, was immaterial. That Henry saw my portrait and declared his love for me on the strength of it was also immaterial. A scapegoat was required. And although logic might suggest Hans Holbein to be as much at fault – it was not convenient for Henry to lose his favourite painter. Cromwell had, however, fulfilled his role, become over-proud – and paid for it.

I know that the dynastic and fruitful possibilities of our marriage were good and Cromwell should have been spared; that politics moved on in the year following our marriage and that Henry and England were not so isolated from France and Spain – no longer needing a strong alliance with Cleves and the German States – was not Cromwell's fault. Indeed, it is perhaps a tribute to his cleverness in creating the alliance with Cleves that those two strong countries became more tractable towards Henry *after* England and Cleves were joined. It was good diplomacy. But Henry suffered from that other trait that is so poisonous – he was stubborn and he had power. I was like a much-prized and now broken toy to him and the only way to make amends for the disappointment was to be thrown away.

I can say it now, though never in my lifetime. Henry was a fool. A petulant fool. If he had not allowed his sulking to get in the way of his duty and had taken his ancestor Edward II's example – a king who cared nothing for his wife yet fathered an heir with her – he could have kept our politically astute marriage, achieved the heirs he wanted and needed and have his dynastic security. I was well enough built and young and likely to bear Henry the abundant sons he needed. But, in his perversity, just at the moment when he could have achieved everything, he acted with all the pettishness of a spoilt baby. He stamped his foot, dug in his heels, and refused to play. The very parts of me that he so shamefully described as being unpleasant to him – my hips, my breasts, my robust build – were indicators of fecundity. I am quite sure of it. I may have grown up in a formal and proper court, but there was birth happening all around me, and there were women who were married and with child – and my own sister married and gave birth so I know very well that a generous shape is best for childbirth. Queen Jane, I learned later, was built as Henry liked his women, small and delicate and fair – and childbirth killed her. I truly believe, with my hand on my painted heart, that if Henry had stayed married to me and we had made sons together, he would have been a happier man, and if he were a happier man then he would have lived longer. And in living longer he would have spared England much bloodshed and corruption.

I became close to Mary and Elizabeth during the King's life-time. Once I was safely divorced and no threat Henry encour-aged our meetings, though little Edward was kept away from court and scarcely saw any member of his family for fear of his catching some infection. I accompanied both daughters on for-mal occasions, rode in carriages with them, dined with them, danced with them – and was in every sense a valued aunt. Henry tolerated – even perhaps liked – this state of affairs and my portrait, too, was kept and respected. But after his death, with all the religious and political upheavals that followed, life became more dangerous. The religious world turned upside-down with far-reaching consequences for English politics and royalty. The scars of those religious differences never healed though Elizabeth, in her reign, showed a healthy wisdom. By saying that the way a man worshipped was according to his own conscience and that she had no mind to try to put a window in men's souls she saw off some of the worst. She, like me, learned the art of non-provocation. And she, like me, learned to live as a single woman in an age where such a phenomenon usually counted for very little.

So you see, Flora, it was because of those turbulent times that my portrait came here to France. For when another Cromwell, Oliver, sold the royal art collection the French, wise and cultivated connoisseurs, bought many of the works, including me. I was glad to go. The stories about me and the lies and inventions and personal insults persisted. No one, it seemed, remembered the Princess of Cleves who was liked and admired in those years spent in England after her divorce; no one remembered the step-aunt who had shown affection and warmth to those sad Tudor daughters. By the time I arrived in Paris, somewhere around the mid-seventeenth century, I was known to the world as The Flanders Mare. It would be fair and good if the things said about me over the centuries were redressed for there is no evidence for them. This visit back to England, which I would not have made had I a choice, will be strange, like going home, even more so than if I were to be returned to Cleves. But a home of mixed blessings. Perhaps, Flora, with the interest you have shown, perhaps we will meet there again and perhaps, this time, you might understand the truth of it, and will make the truth prevail.

8

Anna Finds a Champion

The memory of Anna's injustices at the hands of Miss Murdoch would not go away. In the days following her visit to the Louvre an enthusiastic Flora plundered the bookshops of Paris to find out more about the Queen from Cleves. The process of discovery, she thought, must be similar to the experience gardeners enjoy when they dig out the weeds – somewhere in the middle of everything she read was the rose, the simple, beautiful, unadorned rose of truth. So many different versions of what might or might not have happened when Anna arrived in England existed, both written as fiction and written as historical fact that Flora decided the way to make sense of it all was to try to get under Anna's skin and inside her mind if she could. The portrait was a good starting point. The portrait, she felt, was the only truth she had so far, and it had told her quite a lot already. If she began with that, and the way the Princess looked out at her, with judicious research she hoped to find the rose.

On the Eurostar going home Flora considered the irony of the painted Anna returning to England to be celebrated as a masterpiece. Well, England owes her that at least. It was not hard for Flora to imagine how it felt for the tired young woman to be so far from home, so publicly rejected, so frightened. The Murdoch woman made it clear that Anna still needed a champion and Flora would be just that. She had no idea how but finding out all she could seemed the best way to start. That and the application of a bit of commonsense.

As the miles rolled on and she sipped her champagne she winced in embarrassment to remember her exchange with the Guide. It was entirely Miss Murdoch's fault – if she hadn't gone on and on about Anna and Flemish Mares and being ugly and whatnot and finding it all so amusing Flora might have left it alone. But she was goaded, goaded, into using that strangely outmoded language. Sister. She had never, in all her life, thought of herself as anybody's sister except Rosie's, and rather a poor one at that. The sisterhood, whatever its form in her growing-up years, was not a place she either knew much about or entered. But there was just something in the way Miss Murdoch spoke as if the failure of the marriage, the failure of her own womanhood, was all Anna's, that made Flora seethe. It was such an old-fashioned attitude. Flora was a plain woman and as plain women go she had never been one to put her head very high above the parapet but she was glad that she had, despite the wincing, for she rather enjoyed the experience. There in the Louvre, the fanciful part of her thought, it was as if, somehow, the portrait was alive to her thoughts. The practical part of her put the sensation down to new widowhood, foreign food, over-tiredness and an unsettled brain rather than dark – or even light – forces.

Except, except . . . Was it not curious that there was the connection with Hurcott Ducis – and even with Flora's own house? Her mind returned to that room and that portrait and the feeling that the picture spoke to her, pleaded with her even, to defend it. In the Louvre this seemed perfectly acceptable. Here on Eurostar it seemed foolish, arrogant and weird. But she would like to do something. Perhaps it would connect up with Edward's history? Surprising comfort came in a phrase of her mother's – applied to anything uncertain that had to be done – 'Ah well – at least it gets you out of the house.' Metaphorically speaking Flora probably did need getting out of the house. And it could be a two-way benefit – both in discovering Anna's true history and giving Flora something that she genuinely wanted to do. A focus. Dangerously near to A

Project but it couldn't be helped. Good. It would focus the work. One of Edward's problems was that he went for the widest-ranging attempt, the heroic, and found it unachievable – whereas Flora preferred to set herself a boundary and work within it. Anna of Cleves and the Hurcott connection was simple and perfect. Out of that might come a very satisfying piece of work.

She stared into the dark window. Hilary. It's a shame that she can't share the idea with Hilary. A braver mother would just say outright that she was going to focus on one offshoot of her father's Last Great Work and pursue it because that was what interested her and that was what she felt capable of – but Flora was not a brave mother and Hilary was unlikely to be understanding. Edward was heroic, boundless in his brilliance, and Flora knew better than to try to say different. Hilary had little enough opinion of her intellectual powers at the best of times – so Flora must find a way of doing what she wanted to do and keeping Hilary happy. *Just tweaking your father's history here and there* was suitable language. In other words, she must lie. If she did a good job Hilary might bend towards her a little and not notice that the scope of the work had changed. That, she thought, raising her glass to the reflection in the window, would be nice.

As they rattled through Ashford Flora thought about Ewan – with his little bald patch and his tender bit of rounded belly – and his kind eyes – and his irritating penchant for being married. She daydreamed as the last miles clattered along. It seemed so silly – Ewan wasn't happy and she was nearer unhappy than not – you'd have thought Fate would step in and see the sense of it and do something. Dilly could hardly mind. Dilly never showed the slightest interest in her husband of an affectionate nature. In the light of her own experience Flora wondered if Dilly and Ewan still shared a bed. And then found herself blushing at the very idea of wondering such a thing. But she did wonder. In fact, she thought about it very seriously and decided that, alongside her research into Anna of Cleves, she would do a bit of research into the Davieses' sleeping arrangements. If they did share a bed, then perhaps there was no more to be said – but if they slept alone – well then . . . It might be a kindness all round. Quite where this sudden boldness of thought came from, Flora wasn't sure – something to do with finally daring to put her head above the parapet perhaps, something also to do with Anna's story reminding her that attraction for a mate is never a given and that when you were blessed with it you might as well push on and try. And then there was Paris. The apartment felt illicit, Paris felt illicit, and look where Rosie was now. Too much conscience was not good for a woman.

Men were like cars – they were absolutely lovely until they went wrong. And no doubt the same was true for women. Dilly had obviously gone very wrong. Flora had not even gone wrong once. She was a well-behaved woman and maybe it was time to change that a bit. Let others worry about the morals of the situation. She might have stood a chance if Edward the Maserati had kindly informed her about his own little affair – she might have made a bit of headway herself – seen a bit of the seamy side at the very least, though Ewan was more of a Ford Fiesta. Nevertheless the feeling of resentment was useful as it made her feel justified. I deserve it, thought Flora crossly as the train pulled into Waterloo and she gathered together her luggage. I deserve it.

In the Terminal her confidence drained with the hissing of the brakes. The image of the pink-lipped Pike swam, gills rippling, into her mind. She was not much looking forward to living in Hurcott if word got out. No one would believe that she was quite amenable to the idea but a little cross at being left out of the loop. She could hear the tongues wagging. 'Well, Flora Chapman would say that, wouldn't she? Poor thing.'

In the train travelling back to Hurcott she wondered whether she would have had the courage to proposition Ewan if she had known about Edward's little dalliance? Unlikely. He might have said yes. Also unlikely. But she *might*. And so might *he*. Edward and the Pink Pike had taken away her chance of illicit happiness by remaining illicit. Perhaps. It was hard to imagine Ewan behaving like Edward if she had cavorted *au naturelle* in front of him in the middle of the pond. But he just *might*. Flora would never know. The sadness of the missed opportunity overtook her. At least Anna of Cleves made that thrilling journey even if she suffered a spectacular rejection at the end of it. At least she had tasted excitement and glamour and had been shaken up to make a new pattern of herself. All those terrible, terrible things said of her, all that cruelty in such a cruel age. And she came through. That chin of hers in the portrait said something about that. At least Anna had ventured. Nothing ventured, thought Flora ruefully, nothing ventured . . . that's me.

To the rhythm of her feet as she marched along the platform, past the Wally Binder Little Flowerbed of Horrors, pulling her suitcase behind her, she hummed 'Greensleeves'. To think that Henry VIII was capable of writing such a beautiful song and could then chop the head off its object . . . Really Anna was saved much misery by not remaining married to such a monster. But Flora also wondered, and not entirely idly, what, if anything, Anna had put in her marriage's place. What was her life after Henry? After the first weeks and months in England how did it all change? Flora wanted to know everything, everything. What was it Flaubert said of Emma? *Bovary, c'est moi*. Well, she thought, and *Anna is me*. She gave up her ticket in a fog of anticipation.

The note in the hall read, 'Many thanks for the jumper. Please give me a ring as soon as you return. Love Ewan.'

Cor, she thought, as she dumped her bag and tottered down towards the kitchen and the telephone, this could be it – you go away for a few days and . . . He wrote the word *love*. He had certainly never used that word with her before. It was, she was sure, wonderfully significant.

By the time Flora made her telephone call to Ewan the story of 'The scandalous double life of Edward Chapman, distinguished local countryman, and the Brownie Leader who fell in love with him and now mourns in secret . . .' was splashed all over pages 1, 2 and 3 of the local paper. With photographs. Not that Flora knew anything of it, of course. But Ewan – if in no other capacity than that of her solicitor of long standing – felt something diplomatic was called for. At least the nationals hadn't taken the story. There were quite enough scandals of higher profile to thrill the buying public. He had done his best. Talked to the most prurient of the villagers, asked for discretion where he could. Putting the word Love on Flora's note was a way of expressing friendly solidarity. A hard word to write, he found.

The conversation between her solicitor and Flora was somewhat stilted as Ewan was in his office when he took the call and his secretary was sitting opposite him waiting for further instructions on the day's work. The secretary, Cora Prout, had very wide eyes and very wide ears. Ewan was therefore economical. The fewer people who knew about Flora's business, the better. Flora, who knew nothing of the secretary's ocular or aural propensities, was hurt by his off-handedness. The word Love gave her courage. To her warmly intimate 'How lovely to get your note when I got home, he merely replied, 'Ah – yes – good of you to reply. However, I am rather busy at the moment. May I telephone you later? Will you be at home or are you going out?'

To which Flora, stung, embarrassed and near to tears, said stiffly that she was not sure if she would be in (and was tempted to say that she probably would be out abseiling or visiting the over-seventies fetish club). She apologised for disturbing him and ended the conversation crisply. 'Well, Ewan – obviously it was not urgent so – goodbye . . .' Which had the unexpected effect, when she put the phone down, of making her think she was even closer to Anna than she previously knew. One minute they were saying things like 'Love or Nurturing Love' and the next . . . you never knew where you were, she thought crossly, even with a dull, old, slightly balding, slightly pot-bellied solicitor.

Back in his office, on putting down the phone and seeing his secretary's enquiringly bright eyes staring into his, Ewan found himself thinking much the same – except for the gender. He had not expected her to be quite that icy. After all, they were friends of a sort and he was only being protective. He was not looking forward to announcing Edward's misdemeanour to her. From the way she spoke to him just then she might think he had colluded. Well – there was nothing else for it – someone had to tell her – he would leave the office as early as he could. The information must be given face to face and not ducked. It would probably be shoot the messenger, he thought gloomily, and she would probably want her nice handknitted jumper back.

Badly done-by women down the centuries may as well stick together, thought Flora. With the surge of empathy for Anna of Cleves still hot in her veins she decided to follow it through at once. No nonsense, no shilly-shallying. Accordingly, without even unpacking her used underwear, and feeling quite proud of the fact that she had left it unwashed (for it suggested the creatively committed) she set off for the village library which, though small and sporadically open, was useful and efficient. But to her 'Morning, Myra,' which was usually greeted by a broad smile and a few wayward wisps of grey hair as the Myra in question bobbed up, or looked down, from a bookshelf, Flora received a sad little smile, a touch of her hand as it came to rest on the desk, and a whispered 'Hallo, dear.' She re-composed her face into its brave little widow-woman mask, and bore it. She had hoped the village would have eased off the condolences by now. She put in her request and got the sad little smile once more.

There followed a very strange series of *non sequiturs* which had Flora feeling that she might, after all, have become a little mad. Paris and talking portraits and now this. For Myra said, 'It is all absolutely ghastly for you. And we on the Parish Council feel something of blame.' Flora did not quite know how to take this statement. Tiresome. She wanted to put Edward's death behind her and get on with life. She sighed. 'Well,' she said carefully, trying to strike a midway note, 'I'm recovering slowly. Of course it came as a shock but one must accept that everyone is mortal – even dear Edward.'

'Well, we of the Parish Council do *not* accept that,' said an indignant Myra.

Frankly, Flora thought, the Parish Council might see themselves as a godlike body, but coming between a man and his death seemed to be pushing it . . . She smiled, vaguely, and said, 'Well, Myra, I have accepted it, and so, I think, must you.'

'Well, we of the Parish Council, Flora, say that it never ought to have happened and we are looking into it. It's our responsibility.'

'Is it?' By now Flora was confused and slightly offended – Ye gods, was even her own state of widowhood to be wrested from her? – 'I don't think you can really say that, Myra. After all – he chose to do it, nobody forced him. It was Edward's decision alone.'

'Oh no –' said Myra, the grey wisps falling thick and fast now, 'it takes two to tango, you know.'

Flora was momentarily speechless. *Tango?* They both stared at each other – rather nervously now.

Eventually Flora said, kindly though cautiously, 'He was inexperienced. And it was his choice.' Myra's eyes grew irritatingly wide. 'There is no one else to blame. Pauline filmed the whole thing though I haven't as yet been able to bring myself to watch the video.'

There was almost nothing left to be seen of Myra's face as the rest of her hair descended. 'Filmed it?' she whispered, pale with shock. '*Filmed it?* But that's absolutely scandalous.'

Flora said, 'Well, I think Edward asked her to.'

Myra sank down on to the desk, her large tracksuited haunch spreading out behind her. She put her head in her hands thus shedding the last of the bobby pins. 'And to think,' she said in a voice soft with the horror of it, 'and to think that we let her loose on our children. We shall all probably be sued. Sued.'

Flora looked at her watch and braced herself. 'I've only got a few minutes,' she said firmly. 'Can I –' and she produced her list. Myra regretfully shed her role of commiseration with a brave little woman, patted Flora's hand, and became a librarian once more. Except she had never been quite like this with Flora . . . with Edward, yes, she had hurled herself rapturously into any tasks he set her, but not for Flora.

Now it was all for Flora as if she were performing a task for royalty. Myra shinned up a shelf, made out all the requests for orders from the main library immediately – and hunted for anything vaguely linked to the old Manor. Nothing was too much trouble. Flora must sit and wait, no point, no point at all in both of them rushing about. If it was not there, Myra could get it – yea, even from the ends of the earth and verily. Eventually a somewhat dazed Flora took away two dusty novels of fifties vintage both with approximations of the fourth wife of Henry VIII illustrated on their front covers, both of whom seemed to sport fifties perms and a fondness for Hartnell's frocks.

As she walked on towards the High Street and the post office, feeling unnerved by the sudden kindness, she met with many a strange and sympathetic stare. Callous as it might seem she longed to say to everyone that she had moved on – a bit – and so must they. But the sympathy of passers-by is not easy to deal with. If Flora grabbed someone by the shoulder and delivered a little speech about happiness and reasonable solvency she would look even madder. Why, Myra might come and snatch these very books from her hands. So she bore it. And went on down the road towards the stores and post office still as the brave little widow-woman.

Betty Gregg, a pale and rather bloodless woman who really could have been anywhere between thirty-five and fifty with a soft spot for Animal Rights, came from behind the counter and removed her spectacles and squeezed Flora's arm with surprising enthusiasm (she was usually a bit of a tartar and would ration sets of commemorative stamps at will) and said, 'We want you to know that we are on your side in this. A terrible thing to happen. Terrible.'

Déjà vu, thought Flora, weakly. 'Well – that was Edward all over,' she said brightly. 'Forever trying out new things and paying the price.'

Betty looked even more shocked than Myra. Flora sought to calm her down. 'It was the way he was. And he did ask me first.'

'Did he?' said Betty in a slightly higher pitch.

'Oh yes,' said Flora. 'He asked if I wanted to join in.'

Betty squeaked something quite incomprehensible.

'Almost his last words to me were that I should be more like him and take a few risks . . . He may have been right.' She gave what she hoped was a suitable laugh – somewhere between sorrow and stoicism. 'But I'm not like that.'

'No, you are not, Flora. And all the better for it.' This was said with a fierceness that Flora found comforting but she did not know why. 'Ah Edward,' she said, and shrugged a playful little shrug. 'Always the adventurer.' Betty looked much as you might expect the Queen to look on hearing her Archbishop of Canterbury was a swinger. Edward had always been a particular favourite of the postmistress's, buying as many commemorative stamps as he liked. Flora decided to put the oddness aside, whatever its fount. 'Enough of all that,' she said firmly, and took a half-dozen eggs and some teabags from the shelf behind her. She put them down and looked around for a copy of the *Mercury*. Betty Gregg was draped across the pile.

'Can you add on a paper for me, please?' said Flora, squinting at the half-hidden weeklies.

Betty took on a very hunted look and did not move. Had the circumstances been different Flora would have enjoyed her evident unease – the post office was usually a place for which you needed Dutch courage – or at least a nip of something strongly caffeinated – to stiffen the sinews before entering – but she was growing irritated now. Enough was enough. Flora tried to pull a newspaper from under the postmistress who was forced to slide herself off the pile but whose hands and elbows remained on top of the front pages. 'Do you really think you should?' asked Betty. There really was no answer to that. Well, not one that sounded sane. In all her days of entering the post office Flora had never seen Betty either sit or lean on anything. 'Perhaps not,' she said in a humouring voice, and paid.

Flora left the shop with the eggs, with the teabags, without newspaper, but with the beginnings, very definitely with the beginnings, of a headache. Perhaps she would just go home and sort out her dirty washing after all. The bid for freedom from domestic constraints did not seem to be supporting the realms of liberated widowhood. Clearly the world she inhabited saw her in the continuing role of miserable widow, bereft and husbandless, tottering on the edge and therefore unable even to bear local news. By the time she arrived home Flora had seen at least half a dozen Hurcottians and the encounters had done nothing to improve her mood.

When Ewan rang, shortly after her return to Lodge Cottage and when she was on her knees in front of the washing machine, she left the call to be answered by the machine. 'You want me,' she found herself saying to an unremarkable bra, 'you come and get me.' The upshot of which was, when he arrived on her doorstep a little later, on his way home from the office, she was distant and polite with him, as he was with her. But he held his ground so she invited him in. He came in. He then stood very awkwardly in the sitting room and looked pained as he said, 'I am so sorry that it all had to happen like this . . .'

Oh not *again*. She thought. She put up her hands to stop him. 'Ewan – please – I'm fine – it happened – he's dead. I'd much rather talk about something else. I'm really in no mood to play the grieving widow for ever and I've got one or two ideas to get on with . . . Or perhaps only one now . . .'

'No, Flora –' Now he put up his hands so that they both looked like mime artists doing cat's cradle.

'No, Ewan –'

He might have asked me about Paris, she thought, or thanked me again for the jumper. She had wrapped it up so beautifully. Disappointment strengthened her resolve.

'This is what I'm going to do to take my mind off everything,' she said firmly. But before she could go on to explain, Ewan took both her hands in his. He was looking at her very oddly as he held on to her hands. Concern was it? Or kindness – or could it be – love? Stay cool, she told herself. Remember that even Ford Fiestas can be a bit racy if you put your foot down. Flora's look of coolness and, she fancied, careless determination as she looked him in the eyes changed to astonishment as there came a sudden and very terrible high-pitched grinding noise from the kitchen. Ewan released her hands. Both of them rushed to see the cause. It came from the washing machine which was now in spin cycle. Very fast spin cycle. Too fast, it seemed, for the needs of the contents. Ewan leaned forward and pressed the stop button. The machine ground to a whinnying halt. After the two-minute wait for the door to be opened – the necessary amount of time to protect small children from throwing themselves into the still rotating drum (when she bought it and they told her of this delay feature she unsuccessfully asked for a machine without this facility since she was without any such dear little endangered things) – during which the two of them stared at the porthole as if it might yield up the secret of the Universe – Ewan opened the door and peered in. Out tumbled the unedifying, twisted mass of all her underclothes and there, poking up from the centre of the drum, one end of it caught in a hole, was a half hoop of curved wire. Her underwiring. The bra was even more unremarkable now.

So there they were, she and Ewan, head to head at the door of her washing machine, he with a pair of pliers, she with a torch, looking foolish, and about as likely to persuade him that she and her life were absolutely fine as a bird with no beak. What man would ever consider embarking on an affair with a woman who could not even do her own washing successfully?

She did not mention Anna of Cleves after all. It was hardly the moment for it as she stood there with the half hoop in one hand and the well-worn item of underwear in the other, with Ewan stiltedly explaining that the newspaper had got wind of a story – almost certainly untrue – about Edward and Pauline Pike and he felt – and he hoped she would forgive him if he overstepped – he felt that he ought to warn her. The whole village knew. It was in the local paper. If it was true then it was a very unpleasant and probably (he did not sound at all convinced) very exaggerated account of the affair and he hoped she would deal with it as calmly and courageously as she had dealt with Edward's death. For a moment she hoped he might put his arms around her, or touch her, or something, but he did not. Take my hands again, she pleaded inwardly, but he stepped back, looking down, the tips of his dear ears very red.

'Ah,' she said, folding away the decrepit bra with dignity. 'That.'

She decided to wing him a bit, since he now stood well away from her on the other side of the room and showed not the slightest likelihood of reaching out and comforting her, not even to the extent of offering her a handkerchief in case she cried (she didn't). What a cold unfeeling person he was. She had been mistaken in him. He could not care less. No wonder Dilly drank. It was probably the only way she could get any fire into her life. She winged him by calmly stating that she had known about Pauline Pike all along and that she did not mind in the least. Truth has a ring about it and it was Ewan's turn to look like a fish. 'So you see,' she said, nicely but coldly, as she opened the front door for him, 'none of you really needed to worry. I have many things to occupy me now and really and truly I'm fine. Just fine. Really.' She closed the door on his confused face as it said goodbye, then leaned against the wall in the hallway, and wept. Women like her did not get their fantasies made flesh. Not even little balding, golf-playing, pot-bellied ones.

Over the next day or so Flora made sure that everyone knew that she knew about Pauline Pike and she cared not one jot how it appeared to the village. This was Edward's legacy, not hers, and she was not prepared to play the wronged and suffering widow. Undeserved sympathy, she found, was the most unpleasant offering to accept, bringing with it a sense of guilt and self-loathing. She assumed that the truth would make everything much easier but she soon discovered differently. On meeting the Vicar and Mrs Vicar in the lane – and listening to their faltering suggestion of how hard it must be for her, Flora said robustly that it was not at all, that she accepted it, that they both had their lives, she and Edward, and that the affair was part of his. Feeling rather proud of this speech, and thinking that it was about as truthful as she could get and quite a weight off her shoulders, she was taken aback completely by the Vicar giving her an awkward pat on those same shoulders, which immediately made them sag with guilt again, while Mrs Vicar held her tight into her Boots face powder and said how brave she was, how brave . . .

The only person who did not know, who must never know, was Hilary. It was a secret to be tucked away much as Flora had tucked away that video. She left Hilary alone for a while in the fear that with all this heightened awareness going on she just might blurt it out; have a touch of the Tourette's and come out with a stream of bad language and a vivid description of the Pink Pike's soppy ruffles and floating orange thing. When she was a little more in control and the disappointment of Ewan not so acute, she rang her, rapping her knuckles on the table thrice before picking up the phone, to remind herself to say nothing.

'You sound muted,' said Hilary, with only a faint trace of told-you-so. 'Was Paris disappointing after all?'

Flora did not rise. If the two of them were ever going to fill the void then rising was not helpful. Instead, when Hilary said, 'I wish I'd come with you,' Flora said – with some feeling, thinking about Ewan and using the bruising she felt, that she wished Hilary had come, too. 'Perhaps we'll have a little holiday together next year,' said Flora. To which Hilary, programmed, said dourly, 'Well I can't afford it. Now.'

'Ah well,' said Flora, risking the old parental saw, 'we'll see . . .' And then rapidly changed the subject. 'How have you been getting on?' Hilary gave Flora a short history of her feelings and they talked about Edward for a little while and Hilary had a little cry. Flora decided to grasp the nettle and said, 'I'm looking forward to getting down to your father's history. It looks very interesting.' Hilary made a noise. Flora rushed on. 'It only needs a tweak or two,' and crossed her fingers.

'Hmm' said Hilary doubtfully. 'Well, tweaking's fine but you won't run away with yourself and do something silly with it now, will you?' As if Flora was likely to get out her crayons for a good scribble. Still she did not rise. 'No – just put it in order and finish researching a few things and so forth.'

'Just collate them sort of thing?'

'That sort of thing. With a touch of focusing.'

'Just a touch?'

'Oh yes.'

'Good for you'.

'Thank you, Hilary,' she said, meekly. 'I shall be Dorothy to his Wordsworth.'

Hilary made another noise that might or might not have been approval, and Flora said she would give her daughter a ring in a few days – perhaps there would be some news from the calligraphy people – and put down the phone. Talk about walking on eggshells but at least the bonding had begun. Do anything silly – indeed – how dare she even think of saying it? On the other hand there was nothing like a bit of anger to stoke the fires of enthusiasm. I'll show you, my girl, she thought, and I'll show him, too. It was going to be a two-glass night, Ewan's Dilly or no Ewan's Dilly.

Settled, she began looking at the novels so kindly dug out for her by Myra. Both books starred Anna of Cleves as principal heroine. Each one was concerned with how Henry's love of a portrait and repulsion of the real woman could have come about. One suggested that Anna of Cleves and Holbein had an affair which is why he painted her to look so beautiful. Impossible, surely? And that Anna was persuaded to wear a blonde wig since the King favoured blondes. Unlikely, if the dignity in the portrait was anything to go by. The only basis for the story seemed to be from contemporary sixteenth-century historian, Hall, who reported that Anna had long fair hair. Wishful thinking. Anna was definitely a brunette.

The other novel, *Anne of Cleves,* suggested that Anna was given to flushing an unbecoming scarlet and scowling when she was feeling insecure. Two attributes of Flora's which made her like the author of the book even less. It was given to very few women, or men, to look attractive when they were unhappy. Even more unbelievably the author went on to say that Anna had calloused hands from doing good works and getting on down in the henhouse back in boorish Cleves so that when, surprised by Henry's unscheduled visit to Rochester, she had covered herself with a foul-smelling unguent, largely goose fat, to soften – or lighten – her chapped skin, she stank of it. This, presumably, to cover the fact that Henry told his Council that he 'liked not her smell'. Extraordinary imaginations some of these Historical Romancers had. Or was it coyness? Or pheromonal ignorance? All these theories were fascinating but Flora could not find a shred of proof. No – the truth of Anna was in the unadorned story which was quite bad enough without embroidering it.

The Cleves of the sixteenth century did not look boorish.

With its softly curving landscape – not totally flat then – and its castle with pretty crenellations and its swans – it looked a pleasant, gentle place. A landscape and climate not very different from England. Her Palace stood at the top of a hill and the air must have been fresh and wholesome. Nothing in the description of Cleves can have prepared Anna for the harshness of her journey or her unkind welcome in England.

Over the next few weeks Flora cross-referenced what she had learned in Paris, with other accounts of the Cleves Princess's fall from grace, some authenticated with contemporary documents, some by hearsay, and not once did she find reference to Anna being called the Flanders Mare. It seemed that this most famous and cruel of epitaphs was never used in Anna's lifetime but was coined much later from a Bishop Burnet's *History of My Times* at the end of the seventeenth century and was used again by Horace Walpole – a man given to disliking bluestockings – when he published his first attempt at a history of art in English in the eighteenth century. How very unpleasant, she thought, sourly, to think up such a lasting indictment.

Nowadays it would be called *spin*. For centuries Anna was an historical laughing stock simply because a turn of misogynistic phrase appealed. Bad enough the way the world was now about beauty or lack of it – but ten times worse then, it seemed. It made Flora all the more determined to rearrange this point of view. After all – as someone very eminent said – there is no such thing as history – merely biography. Emerson was it? Or Thoreau? Flora's brain was creaking. It was a very long time since she had used it in this concentrated way. She began to enjoy it. Even Ewan faded away. Slightly.

Much of what she read was almost unbearable, the viciousness of its insult beyond anything – almost – that might be said by one royal, or celebrity, of another nowadays. There was plenty of evidence of Henry's blustering, ungallant, insulting descriptions. Breasts, belly, smell, virginity – the lot. Quite enough to make a bishop blush, though not, obviously, enough to make a bishop tell his King to mend his ungodly ways and honour his wife. How interesting it was, she noted, that before Henry told the world of his dismay, everyone who met Anna praised her. And although this might be something to do with diplomacy, on the whole the praises were more believable since they were usually first hand – either from those nobles accompanying the Queen-in-waiting to England – or those who saw her at home in Cleves. But Henry stamped his foot, said, 'I like her not' and – lo – she was transformed into a brown-faced, pockmarked, frumpish, raw-boned nincompoop.

The German court dress of Anna's Paris portrait did not exactly show the Princess off to feminine advantage. Her character shone through despite the clothes rather than being enhanced by them, and the French Ambassador, Marillac, wrote that he found her old-looking and only of middling beauty. But very soon after her arrival she replaced her heavy German style with the more fashionable five-pointed French hoods that showed the face so dramatically – and low-cut gowns that bared the shoulders. She made these changes almost certainly from her own intelligent appraisals of the fashions. If Flora doubted that the Princess would change her hair colour as Hall suggested, there was nothing undignified in her changing the way she dressed and becoming fashionable at court.

If Flora recognised Anna's dignity, Henry allowed her none. As if the goose-fat and its delicate literary distillation of a much more unpleasant truth were not insult enough, the King's ungallant attestation went even further during the annulment proceedings saying that he also found his wife's body loathsome and her breasts and other parts so slack as to make him think she was no maid. He faced his fond and saintly bishops and lily-pure nobles with this unnecessary addition. So now Anna was not only ugly, dark and thick, and unpleasantly smelly in her womanly parts – she was – just to make quite sure he had kicked every available part of her – no virgin either. Which, Flora thought wryly, made Edward's occasional verbal assaults on her seem rather affectionate by comparison.

Flora looked at the reproduction of Anna's portrait again. Not possible, she decided. Not possible. Not the ugliness and certainly not the unchasteness. If the Cleves Court was as proper as described this last was quite impossible. Flora smiled at the absurdity of all of it. She could quite see why any writer of historical romances would want to turn this nonsense into fiction and want Anna to have lived and loved. To give Anna a happy past complete with lover was to be kind to her . . . Flora considered this. There were worse ways to live in Tudor times than without sex she guessed. At least it meant you didn't die from syphilis or puerperal fever. And anyway, some of the happiest men and women she had ever met were nuns and monks and jolly Catholic priests. Not all of whom were devils in their habits.

The thread of irony ran through everything. That Henry should accuse Anna of 'being no maid' and then marry Catherine Howard, the much-bedded fifth wife – his 'rose without a thorn' – against whom the princess was purity personified.

The more Flora read, the more she admired this endangered young woman who faced heaven knew what fate and survived. Not that Edward was a tyrant – but he had elements of Henry in his complete lack of respect for her or anyone else who did not entirely agree with him. Visionless, was one of his favourite words of derision. 'Edward – could you not plant quite so many trees around our boundaries . . .' '. . . Visionless, Flora, visionless.' Which is, of course, what she was once the saplings began to grow. Flora must have been the only home-owner in the whole of Hurcott Ducis who thanked Fate for sending a freak storm in 1990. Edward had not set the trees in deep enough, or staked them, and happily most of them were blown clean away. Visionaries, it seemed, need not be practical but they did need to be insensitive to the wiser suggestions of the world around them. If you were a king, of course, all the more so.

In Edward's notes on the ex-Queen and her ownership of Hurcott Ducis Manor he enjoyed using the term 'Flanders Mare' as often as he could. How enjoyable Flora found it to strike it out of the manuscript on every single occasion. She could hear him spitting out the words 'Politically Correct' which made the editing process even more enchanting. He ended the section about Anna and Hurcott Manor by stating, 'And thus Anne of Cleves, Flemish Mare, found her ill looks had served her well in the gaining of such rich estates as Richmond, Bletchingly, Hever, many manors such as Hurcott, Halifax and Dedham which must have been a great comfort to this otherwise despised and wretched woman.' Flora had pinned the postcard of Anna above her desk and looked at it now. Ill looks and wretchedness did not spring to mind. Nor, after the divorce, could she find anyone saying such things. Quite the reverse.

Then as now, Anna, like most women thrown into post-divorce circumstances, made it her first task to set up her new home and have her own front door. That it was Richmond Palace and one of the finest front doors in the whole of England made it all the more pleasing, obviously. Now that she was to be known as the King's Sister – a clever bit of legal chicanery to mollify Duke William of Cleves – her Palace door was open to her new family. Her stepdaughters, Mary and Elizabeth, of course, but also the King and his new wife. But if her door was kept open and all welcome, it was still her door and nobody else's. She could close it, whenever she liked, and be protected from all the gossip. Flora knew well enough how that felt.

Over the next week or so there was quite a lot of closing of Lodge Cottage's front door. The atmosphere surrounding her in the village changed from cool to being sticky sweet with unction. It felt as if she lived life outside of her home in a sugar bowl. Sweetness all around, ersatz as cyclamates, and little puckered looks and anxious mutterings and murmurings as people hurried on their way. Perhaps that was the only way

9

The Phantom of the Louvre

The last attendant has left the building. The London Gallery's storerooms, below ground, are in darkness now, and they are silent. The waiting portraits are all of women except for one portrait of a child. The exhibition for which they are assembled will reflect the one abiding interest Henry VIII holds for the world. His peregrinations around the nubile young women of Europe, his wives, his desire for progeny, the outcome of all his hopes. These carefully selected portraits of sixteenth-century women, including Anna of Cleves, wait to be hung and viewed by eager eyes. For all he threw a Pope over his shoulder and defied an Emperor, it is Henry's love life, his sex life that holds an endless fascination. Several of the exhibits might sniff at this continuing public prurience. And one in particular has every reason to consider that the Tudors were not all they were cracked up to be . . .

Anna, waiting quietly in her frame, thinks it is about time she took her place in Henry's misbegotten pantheon. She has never before been included in an exhibition surrounding her ex-husband though now, with Holbein's star so high, her worth as a portrait, if not yet as a wife, has been recognised.

The room is hushed. It is the hour of the spirit rather than the flesh, the hour for portraits to breathe again. Out from her frame, into this silent dimness, steps Anna of Cleves. All the way here, wrapped as she was, softly muffled as she was, coming across the sea again, she has been suffering a quiet rage. There are straws and there are the backs of camels, she thinks, having absorbed many useful colloquialisms during the five hundred years of her existence. Enough is more than enough. I have been voiceless in my frame for too long. As she wanders along the line of racked or propped or crated pictures she considers her companions.

Anna smiles to see one portrait in particular and for the moment her crossness abates. It is the magnificent Ditchley portrait of Elizabeth I. What a fine painting. Anna searches the face for a sign of the young Elizabeth she knew, a child of seven when she arrived in England and a young woman of twenty-four in the year she died. But the face is a mask and about as far removed from Holbein's human truth as stone is from flesh. The ageing Queen stands upon England, her feet firmly in Oxfordshire and pointing towards Southampton. Anna knows the gossip. If the Tudor Court practised complicated etiquette in Henry's day, how much more idiosyncratic was it in Elizabeth's. Down the years Anna was surprised to hear reports of Elizabeth's vanity with her male courtiers and the silly, indulgent behaviour she encouraged and with which she ended her days. In Anna's time Elizabeth grew from a watchful, precocious, neglected little girl into a young woman who was clever, shrewd and open to advice about maintaining her dignity and her position. She – like Anna – spent much of her time living on her wits and keeping her own counsel, a situation that Anna knew well and understood. Yet this Ditchley portrait is an example of the other Elizabeth, the latterday self-indulgent Queen who could dismiss her courtiers at whim. Sir Henry Lee who commissioned the portrait was banished for openly taking his mistress to court when his sovereign was the only spiritual mistress allowed. The portrait was commissioned, so the curators said, when Elizabeth was in her sixtieth year, as a gift from Henry Lee to thank the Queen for allowing him back. To Anna this petty behaviour was irreconcilable with the Elizabeth she knew, both as child and young woman – one who, like Anna, in her early years showed the mettle of a great survivor. Such foolish behaviour, in the end, surely made her vulnerable?

At her own wedding celebrations, when she became Queen Anna for that brief time, she made it her duty and her pleasure to be kind and affectionate to both Mary and Elizabeth, Henry's motherless daughters. And after the divorce, when all three of them led uneasy lives, the girls remained close to their Aunt Anna. Richmond Palace was a favourite Tudor residence and Anna made them welcome there. Henry, newly in love with his Catherine, allowed it.

Anna smiles and nods at the portrait – she has no quarrel with Elizabeth, though, had she lived and still had the Princess's ear, she might have suggested caution in her pursuit of beautiful, destructive young men. To remain unmarried was one thing, Anna knew the value of that, but royal indiscretion on a grand scale was quite another. Shades of her father in Elizabeth. Mary's coronation was the last occasion at which the three women were together in public. Anna remembers affectionately how, with Mary newly enthroned and happy, Anna and Elizabeth laughed and danced together and revelled in their grandest clothes and jewels. Elizabeth suppressed her love of them for the quiet, studious, fearful years of Mary's reign, but looking up at the Ditchley now, Anna smiles to see that her love of finery never really went away. As soon as Elizabeth was Queen off went the simple and the plain, on went the grand and gorgeous. Perhaps fine dressing, as it did for Anna, symbolised liberation, pride in survival and the cele-bration of pleasing herself.

Elizabeth's white, bony, high-cheeked face with its penetrat-ing dark eyes and aquiline nose is surrounded by a ruff of winged gossamer making a silvery glow and a pearly diamond light. She is every bit Gloriana. No prettier than me, thinks Anna, but how she made herself shine. She smiles up at her. Elizabeth's haughty portrait face smiles and softens. Women are not her usual friends of choice but Anna of Cleves was kind.

'You are dazzling, Elizabeth,' she says admiringly.

Elizabeth acknowledges this. 'Why yes. I made myself into a

fairytale Queen. But in you, Anna, Hans Holbein saw no reason to hide your human qualities. He caught you right.' The soft smile continues, the eyes are lit with warmth. 'I wish,' says Elizabeth, 'that you had lived longer, and into my reign, for you were always kind to me and I would have done you honour.' Anna nods. There is no reason to doubt the statement.

'But Mary was kind and honoured me. Because she was plain and rejected and lonely, she understood me from the beginning, in those first bad months she showed me great affection. We were regarded as two of a kind. Plain women. Rejects both. It was a good friendship.'

Elizabeth nods. 'We did love you. You behaved so warmly and with such dignity. And later, when it was done and you were our aunt and settled upon with money and property with your own little court and our father's beloved Richmond Palace was England a place to be happy in? Did you want to remain in England?' Elizabeth shifts her foot slightly to show a little more of the England sitting beneath her dainty heel. Anna knows that Elizabeth's happiness, by contrast, was a shifting one.

'I was – in the end – very happy. And – you must forgive me – I achieved it all without being obliged to live with and more to the point – to bed – the King your father – who disgusted me. I had his generous settlement and none of the duties. Life after the divorce was a delight.'

Elizabeth returns her face to its mask-like state and replaces her impossibly small feet in the position Marcus Gheeraerts painted them – back neatly together and standing on the heart of England. It is a dismissal. Anna ignores it.

'He was a great King,' says the daughter.

Suddenly Anna has had quite enough of diplomacy and a little bubble of rage returns. 'He was cruel, egotistical, sentimental and perverse – and he smelled,' she says firmly.

'I loved and revered him,' says Elizabeth tersely.

What the Murdoch has begun in her Anna will continue – and have done with quiet humility. Anna owes the world nothing and certainly not a well-behaved silence. 'Oh, Elizabeth, that is your prerogative. But he was unworthy of those feelings. None of us dared say these things then but I shall say them now. He was cruel to me, to you, to everyone who crossed him. He was a tyrant and –'

'And desperate for a son,' says Elizabeth, with amusement. 'A son who would be a great Tudor monarch. After all,' she smiles into her step-aunt's eyes, 'after all, only a son could ever be that.' The irony is not lost now, nor ever was lost on subsequent generations and certainly not on Anna, who smiles back. 'I would have borne him a son – or two – three maybe. Despite my repugnance. I'm certain of it.'

'So was my mother,' says Elizabeth frostily. The words hang there in the silence with the ghost of Anne Boleyn slipping between them.

'But,' says Anna, 'I was of a build for it, and not likely to miscarry being of a placid nature. Your fool father bemoaned the wideness of my belly – nature's gateway – and said he liked his women dainty and small. He dismissed my body when it could have saved him.' Her eyes, unusually, flash. 'And left me such a legacy of insults, too. He was no true prince.'

The face in the glittering picture colours beneath its mask of whiteness. 'Saved him from what?'

Anna calms a little and says, 'Cuckoldry and self-harm and the terrible blackness of his last years. And you, Elizabeth, might have had a kinder life. If I had borne sons, then you would have been free to marry where you chose. Perhaps.'

But even as she says it, Anna knows that it would not have been like that. If she had produced several sons it would not have made her stepdaughters' lives better or freer. If anything it would have made them more tightly bound, more necessary for marriage alliances. 'Or almost to marry where you chose . . .' she adds, less comfortably. But the eyes in the picture have returned to their unmoving glaze, the hands to their impossibly structured elegance; it is not a subject to be continued.

Propped alongside Elizabeth is the almost informal, slightly flirtatious portrait of a youthful Marie of Guise, the woman who married Henry's nephew James V, King of the hated rival Scotland. Marie became the mother to Mary Queen of Scots. The portrait, by Corneille de Lyon, is lively too. Both women, Elizabeth in her splendour, Marie in her sober black velvet, ignore each other and continue to look outwards. They have nothing good to say – not now nor ever will have. Marie's portrait was most likely made at the same time that Henry VIII was seeking a new wife from abroad and was contemporary with the Cleves portrait. It is high irony for Anna to be in the same place as this woman whom she often wished Henry had married instead of her. Best, particularly now, not to dwell on what might have been . . .

Anna turns away and would have followed Elizabeth and ignored the French woman who was not known for her sweet nature. Anna finds those dark, passionate vengeful French-women frightening. She always preferred the quiet life. After all, it is the way she has lived for nearly five hundred years – within the frame, hearing all, saying nothing – but Marie of Guise, sharp-eyed, swift and silent as a shadow, is by her side. The Dowager Scottish Queen places her back very firmly towards Elizabeth while she speaks directly to Anna. 'Between you both,' she seems to spit the words and the black velvet of her French hood jerks towards the pearly figure behind her, 'With your new religion and your denial of the blessed Pope, you took my daughter's, *your cousin's,* rightful place on the throne of England, as you took her life.' Her voice is cold, not hot. She looks at Anna but she addresses Elizabeth.

Throughout her existence in England Anna managed to avoid such religious confrontations – she went about her business in neutral fashion. What good would it do to stir up old hatreds? Now she holds up a calming hand, but Marie of Guise brushes it aside. 'As for you – the Cleves Princess who did not please – you came from the sinful heart of Lutheranism, the so-called new religion against the old and proper and *only* true faith. Your arrival gave Henry the alliance he needed to continue outside the True Church. You, Anna, should be ashamed for not standing up to him – for your honour if for nothing else. And you, Elizabeth –' The head jerks again but still she does not turn to look at the white-faced Queen. Elizabeth is immobile as before. 'You, the bastard usurper, went on with it all and continued the pattern. You – a bastard – ruled excommunicate rather than let the lawful heir, my daughter, my beloved Mary of Scotland, ascend the English throne. You may have reigned long but never happily – you and your young men and your cults. Forcing love. Essex made a fool of you at the end – an old woman nearly shuffled off her throne for the love of a peacock of a man thirty years her junior . . .'

Anna dares not look up at Elizabeth but she can see that those little feet are twitching, just twitching to –

'It was –' Marie snaps her fingers – 'that close to your losing your kingdom to the young dandy, Elizabeth. For your whole reign, from the very beginning, you never slept sound in your bed. You feared proper Catholic claim. And then you had my daughter murdered. And *still* you did not sleep easy. You could never see beyond a boy's pretty face and a well-turned leg. That schemer Essex was the miserable reward you got for your heretical troubles, your playacting at love. You ended your life with nothing but fear and the nightmares of a cousin's blood on your hands.'

Even now, with all the iniquities Anna has seen and heard over the centuries, such an accusation to such a great figure is very shocking. The Elizabeth she knew was not one who would easily kill a cousin. In the Ditchley Elizabeth's face does not change, nor does her stance, her feet, though twitching, still remain firmly, securely upon England.

Marie of Guise – her face returned to its hint of a smile – silent as she came – slides back towards her frame. As she moves she turns back towards Anna. 'That man,' she says, 'that so-called Gracious Prince, Henry, made a mockery of every woman he encountered – wife, Queen, daughter, sister by law and sister in blood. And had you kept the true faith, your life would have been spared the humiliation of going to uncivilised England and being made a fool of. You might have stayed at home, or married well, you might have been happy . . . You might not have remained a virgin like her – you *are* still a virgin, are you not, despite your wedding night?'

Anna shakes her head. 'I have no wish to speak of that.'

Marie of Guise, perhaps disappointed at Anna's discretion, gives her head an irritated little shake. And then she is gone, stepping into the frame, looking out with sightless, half-smiling eyes, dead to Anna's remonstrance.

Anna sighs. She thinks – or perhaps hopes – that there is the glitter of a tear in Elizabeth's eye – but she cannot be sure. What, after all, is there to say? It is true enough that this brilliant Tudor killed her cousin, killed a queen . . . Another thing that would never have happened if Henry had stayed married to Anna. Even so, to be included in a regicide by a French woman – whom she had never met before – no – bad enough to be remembered as ugly and unwanted and to have your virginity discussed – but to be considered a supporter of regicide . . . 'I become very weary of that misapprehension, Marie,' says Anna loftily. 'I was a Catholic always. But I did believe in reform. Only someone with the brain of a gull could think that the Catholic Church did not need it!'

Speaking out, she thinks, is like putting air into her lungs. For too long she has kept her counsel. That was how she survived those years in England when Henry remarried. But no longer. 'If you had sensibly married your daughter to Henry's son Edward all the bloodshed would have been avoided.' Marie does not respond. 'But no – not the Great Marie, putative Queen of Scotland – Edward was not good enough for your daughter and see where your ambition sent her. To a traitor's scaffold.'

Marie of Guise cannot stay silent. 'Edward was the son of an excommunicant. And a Protestant. My daughter died a martyr.'

'He was the heir to the throne of England. Your daughter plotted against the people's choice of sovereign. Queens and meddlers never did know the art of perspicacity, the art of compromise. Too many deaths and you still hold on to the pride of it all.'

'It is called Faith.' The portrait movs irritably. 'Faith – not opportunism.'

'Much has been done in the name of Faith. Then and now. I witnessed horrors done in the name of worship. If my step-daughter Elizabeth did one sensible thing it was to allow religion to be a private matter. How wise she was . . .'

If there were no tear in Elizabeth's eye there is now the gleam of righteousness. 'Mary had to die,' she says imperiously.

Anna turns to her. 'No, Elizabeth,' she says, as if she is still her counselling step-aunt. 'It is never justified to kill one of God's anointed. And you feared her beauty, too.'

A little mischief of a smile creeps around Anna's lips as she says this last – for Elizabeth's expression is no longer righteous – it is highly indignant. No matter how the centuries have passed, Elizabeth still demands to be the greatest star in the firmament of masculine desire.

The Duchess of Guise says piously, 'Beauty . . . Oh the vanity of earthly beauty. Mary was a beauty. Elizabeth feared that.'

Elizabeth looks as if she feared no such thing but Anna knew the stories. Mary Queen of Scots was said to enchant everyone she met, even her jailers, with her charms – and yes – even women.

'If it had not been for vanity and they had met as cousins, they might have loved each other and my daughter's neck would not have taken three ragged falls of the axe to end her life.'

'Beauty,' says Anna, 'is a burdensome commodity. It was so much easier for me to negotiate with Henry's advisers for my settlement while they considered me ugly. Whenever Henry sent his ministers to persuade me that the divorce he required was correct theologically, in law, and morally, I never objected. My way was not the way of your mother, Elizabeth, I never tried to find a piece of biblical text to counter Henry's, nor persuade him that he was wrong in any way. I hung my undesirable head, was dumb, and waited for the settlement negotiations. The less I angered Henry, the better they would be, and they were.' Anna cannot resist a little crow of triumph and Elizabeth blinks.

'Everyone thought that I was ignorant and unable to understand, but I was neither. My silence and my acceptance earned me my rewards. Yes?'

Elizabeth nods. There is a grudging look of admiration in her eyes. 'You were a clever woman,' she says.

'Yes, Elizabeth, and so were you. And like you I was popular. The people of England wanted me for their Queen. I saw it in the cheering and blessing that the welcoming crowds poured over us as we made our way towards London. At the darkest moments it gave me courage – the knowledge that the people of England loved me – though I never boasted of it. I won many hearts on that long journey – the nobles who accompanied me also liked me very well. Until they were told to think differently.'

Anna of Cleves places her pretty hands at her stomach, a pose that has become comfortable over the half-millennium, and raises her chin. 'My settlement needed to be generous for I could not go home. The English were lucky that I was not the kind of woman to weep and wail or seek revenge. Had I demanded that my brother come and exact vengeance – well . . .'

Marie of Guise looks sceptical at this. 'Hubris, Anna. Duke William was not renowned for his resourcefulness or courage,' she says. And then stops herself. It is well-known that when Henry rejected Anna, the Duke did not rush in with his sword – nor even wave it in the air – he was too protective of his own position – but Marie shrugs her beautiful bare French shoulders. This courageous German princess has suffered enough insult. Marie returns to her frame. The eyes of the two Queens, Marie and Elizabeth, sit within their frames in icy rivalry. Both were beauties in their own way, thinks Anna, and it brought them no comfort. But that is their business. She turns her back and moves away.

This storeroom is filled with portraits of hopeful, ambitious, doomed royal women. For a moment Anna allows herself a feeling of superiority. Hers was the happy life, what was left of it; so few of these women were happy like her, a single virgin of means and content to remain unmarried. She was well aware, after Henry's marriage to Catherine Howard, that the eyes of the gossiping Tudor Court and the whispering watchful world were on her. Catherine. Now there was an ill-starred little thing. Poor Catherine, she thinks, looking about her. Not even represented here. Poor little giddy, ill-educated girl – too pretty for her own good, offered up to the ageing King and died for it; raised so high she was bound to fall. Such pawns we women were.

As if to remind herself – and perhaps to let the others hear – she says aloud,

' . . . And in those first months of my divorce I behaved with such good breeding and with such good will that it banished any notion of boorishness in my upbringing. Indeed, my delicacy and the dignity of my manner was remarked upon. It won Henry's heart, and later Catherine's. Despite the French King, Francis, hoping I would create a drama, it was his own ambassador, Marillac, who wrote to his master of the "Great Moment When Anna of Cleves Met Catherine Howard". The moment when I showed the watching world how a German princess could behave. As Marillac remarked, and with some approval, I was a different woman by then. So much for his once calling me old, of middling beauty and thin when I first arrived. My clothes were now of impeccable taste, the height of fashion, and I could match the young Queen in figure and gracefulness if not in jewels. No one could match Catherine for her jewels. Henry gave her more than he gave to any other wife.

'Our meeting, on New Year's Eve at Hampton Court, was a difficult occasion for Catherine – especially with Marillac standing by – as she was not bred to such events. But it was not at all difficult for me. Knowing how to be gracious and deferential is easy but knowing how to behave in the face of deference is not so easy. I was there as an honoured guest, to meet the Queen, I could hear the shufflings and whisperings as everyone wondered how to arrange the occasion. Henry, nervous or hopeful and, as always, reticent where there was something difficult to be done, hid. But I had planned exactly how to please and how to make the assembly squirm. I had no qualms and I abased myself. I curtsied, then fell to my knees and refused to rise when the young Queen implored me to (perhaps I felt a little fluttering of something close to revenge to see how anxious the young Queen was). When Henry showed himself from his hiding place he was very well pleased with it all, two women being deferential to each other in his name was the pleasure of such a prince. I rose up at last and we two women embraced and kissed – and then went in to dine.

'At first they placed me in an inferior position. A test, of course, and I knew it was, and made nothing of it. Later, having won the right by my acquiescence, I was raised up and sat with the royal pair where I talked and laughed with the King and Queen as gaily and as warmly as a welcome old friend. Henry seemed charmed by my grace and ease. And even more charmed when I presented him and Catherine with a beautiful white horse each, caparisoned in mauve velvet. A Princess of Cleves, indeed.

'Looking back on that New Year, I can say that it was a truly happy time, a moment of surrender that put me in command and secured my future elevated position and happiness. Later, after more friendly conversation, Henry went to bed and Catherine and I danced and talked and laughed together very easily. She was a very simple girl – not artful or particularly clever – and it was remarked that we made a pretty pair together. The world watched us closely and we were aware of it, and the world was doubtless surprised at this most difficult of transitions being so easily accomplished. I chose to be gracious and amenable. The Queen and – more importantly – the King were grateful – as indeed they should be. And I think the example of my behaviour was both marked and taken to heart by Mary and Elizabeth with whom, now elevated, I sat.

'As the King's Sister and I owned sixty-three manors, twenty-three farms, thirty-eight combined manors and advowsons, a handful of rectories – The Palace of Richmond, the Castle of Hever, Bletchingley – and many other places. I had an income of six hundred pounds a year. Which you will credit was a noble result. As for poor Catherine? Was she happy? The question is rhetorical. She was happy until she was unhappy. While she had the love of the King, and the secret love of his gentleman of the bedchamber, Thomas Culpeper, she was probably happier than she had ever been in her life. But she died on the scaffold without a head, without her jewels, and without a sign of parental kindness. Silly little foolish thing, starved of love and dead by the executioner's axe after less than two years. Buried by the side of her beheaded cousin Boleyn – victims of a dangerous husband who would have beauty and youth at any cost – and who happened to be a king. So whose was the triumph? Beauty's? Or cordial content?

'By putting myself beneath Henry's heel he had raised me up. You will scarcely find a breath of scandal adhering to my name, nor bad words said about me in the years that followed the divorce. There are not many of rank from those days who can say the same, nor now either. The French might hint that I liked my wine too well, but it was not taken seriously. I liked wine, of course I did, and I came to know a little about what was good and what was not, and I bought it in quantities. But I kept a good table for my guests. Cookery amused me, too. But mainly I was happy and contented and that is the heart of it, wine or not. I think none of these ladies here in these frames can say that.' She looks about her, that determined chin raised, the eyes resolute. 'In the end,' says Anna, 'it was my fate to be called Not Fair and to live. When Catherine, Henry's rose without a thorn, fell, I held my breath like the rest of the watching world. I knew that interest would light on me again. I could do nothing to avoid it and so I returned to Richmond Palace (I was staying at one of my other estates when Catherine was pronounced guilty of treason) and I continued with the pattern of my days and I waited.

'Gossips and mischief makers suggested that I returned to Richmond to be near the court because I expected Henry to annul our divorce and take me back. Well – perhaps that was a reasonable assumption. But I tell you – despite a fleeting sense of pride in the matter – I hoped he would not. He and I were warmer by then. Henry visited me after Catherine went to the tower and this set tongues wagging for we were reported as making cheerful company together – as much as Henry could after such unhappiness. But he very properly brought others from his court with him so that there was no possibility of scandal. Elizabeth and Mary were shocked, too, by the events and my only role, if I had any role at all, was my usual one of aunt, sister and friend.

'Well, the King could be very, very charming when he chose, delightful company, with a good mind and a capacity for amiability. But he could also be the darkness and the devil. Would I want to be a Queen renewed? Consider the question rationally. Would any woman – once so humiliated and now wealthy in her own right in those times – wish to become the wife of such a man? I was rich, I took domestic orders from no man or woman, I had no involvement with the day-to-day dangers of the court and I dictated my pleasurable days. I could cook all day if I chose, and I sometimes did. I was particularly interested in good ways to present fish, for we had any number of fish days, and I enjoyed my experiments (so did the visiting King). This was hardly a situation that I would give away for the possibility of wearing a crown and sharing a bed with a gross, half-rotting husband who showed a penchant for cutting off his wives' heads. I enjoyed a life of interesting days and merry company. I was liked by many, loved by some and accorded a great dignity by my association with the King. Third in rank when I did attend court was quite good enough for me. I had been victim once to the perversities of the Tudor Court – and that was more than enough. Besides, after Catherine, Henry was truly broken. He spoke of himself as one who has been young and is now old . . . A very terrible admission for Henry. And when he took up with his sixth and last wife, Katherine Parr, the Widow Latimer, he was marrying a nurse, not a wife. Of the two of us, I am reported as saying that I was the more beautiful – and it is true that I said it. Others said it too – but I think – by then – Henry had learned the folly of falling for a pair of tempting eyes. Had Henry chosen to marry me again after Catherine Howard I would not have been able to deny him – therefore it was best to seem to be willing – but I did not want it and I could never care for him after such foolishness and cruelty . . . In the end he married wisely. 'Of necessity he married the Widow Parr' says Bishop Burnet in his history. Though I would scarcely trust everything that historiographer says since in the same volume he coins the name for me of the Flanders Mare.

'I missed my own family but now I had my step-nieces, those intelligent, neglected Tudor girls, and Henry from time to time. I was a trusted part of the family. It was all quite remarkably perfect . . .'

Anna turns and looks up at the Ditchley portrait again. She wonders where Mary's portrait is but tactfully does not voice the thought out loud. Elizabeth is calm and dignified now and it is best kept that way – she has a temper – and matched her father for it – and there has been quite enough upset between the sisters over the years.

'When Henry died and Edward came to the throne, with Protector Seymour, my fortunes were less happy but I continued to live well (to the despair of my comptroller who considered me a spendthrift and capricious) – and beyond my means – and my religious practices were pragmatic. Tudor England suffered a terrible economic plague in the years immediately after Henry but I had no pleasure in making economies. Why should I? As if I had not paid for my frivolities, and handsomely. I liked dresses, I liked sport and I liked all merriments. The world was always keen to keep a single, rich woman in check. I loved my life, and lived it to the full, and was remarked for it. Well, good.'

Suddenly and much louder, Anna says with amusement to the pictures all around her, 'Save me, oh save me from curtsying to ageing powerful men who choose youthful gee-gaws to strut and hobble about with. What fools they are.' From further down the storeroom comes another voice which is vaguely familiar to Anna. 'Amen to that,' it says, with extraordinary fervour. And there is the gentle rustling as if someone is settling the folds of a silk gown. This, thinks Anna, will be Christina of Denmark. Brighter by far than Catherine Howard, though just as young, who refused Henry because she only had one neck. Had she two, it seemed she might accept. Her wit would not have lasted her long in the Tudor bedroom.

Anna follows the sound of the rustling along the dusty footway through storage space – and there she is. The Duchess of Milan, fresh as when she was painted five hundred years ago. Holbein's works, such as still exist, have survived well and this has been cleaned to show it in all its lusciousness. No wonder Henry desired her. Anna feels something of a frump with her dulled paintwork and her sludgy background. If only Henry had wooed this smiling, dimpled girl properly then she, like Marie of Guise, could have saved Anna from leaving Cleves and she would never have known either such great pain or such great happiness. Impossible to know how she feels about this now.

From behind Christina's portrait peeps Jane Seymour, Queen of England. Anna hides a smile. This is not the usual way for Jane Seymour to be displayed. Anna saw this portrait often enough when she was at the English court, for Henry worshipped it and deified its subject. Jane's picture is, perhaps, Hans Holbein's best portrait lesson in how to be Henry's Queen. She shows quiet humility, the paleness of a medieval icon, the fabulous jewels designed for her by Holbein and a chaste mouth worthy of the mother of Henry's only surviving son. Yes, thinks Anna, peeping is the right word for Jane Seymour. She was that kind of woman. Why take a good full look when a little eye-lashed peep would do?

But Anna thought privately that Jane was no Madonna. Surely there is something quite sinister in the way she colluded in her cousin Boleyn's death? Jane was willing to marry Henry as soon as the gun was fired at the tower to say that her head was cut from her neck. So far as Anna was aware, no one who dared speak of Queen Jane in anything but glowing terms could find a reason for Henry's choosing her. The French Ambassador Marillac, acknowledged that she was a pale, unrobust, un-beautiful little thing. How Henry ever fell for her really was a mystery unless it was that she differed exactly and in every particular from the coal-eyed, white-skinned, wide-mouthed, brilliant-minded Boleyn. That little pursed mouth of Jane's, the semi-praying hands, the small body and fair skin – English to her marrow. Holbein gave her to the world as he saw her, as she no doubt truly behaved, and Henry loved the picture. It was the pair to Holbein's majestic portrait of the King. Her small presence made Henry's all the more dramatic.

Anna considers the differences between her and Jane. Light to dark colouring, of course, but in temperament, at least originally, they were much the same. The docility that Henry was said to love is there, so different from the flashing eyes and fireworks of the Boleyn woman. Why, she wonders, do husbands want fire in a woman's belly until they are wed and then damp embers ever after? And what is the virtue of docility, what did that say about Henry's true confidence in himself, what does it ever say when docility is required in a marriage? And what came of all this sweet docility? Henry's best Queen dead in childbed little more than a year after her marriage and the son dead long before manhood, the country torn apart.

There is a chill in the air for all those deaths. Anna moves on. Childbirth. Something that Anna was tacitly forbidden once Henry annulled their marriage – for who would marry the divorced wife of unpredictable Henry? He might change his mind, he might take umbrage that one with whom he had shared a bed so disastrously should be seen to share one successfully elsewhere. If she had given birth to a son Henry's mortification would be complete and public. No man would risk that – nor would Anna. Marriage was forbidden her. And after Henry's death? Why, it was not something she needed. And there was – if a disappointment – also a relief in all this. Anna knew, as all women knew, that childbirth was a dangerous occupation. In Henry's case, of course, it could be just as dangerous to be his Queen and barren of boys.

Anna considers herself lucky. She was godmother to many, she was loved and welcomed, or in Edward's case respected, by all three of her royal stepchildren – she had her orphanages – and she could live her life – within her own estates – exactly as she chose as the times grew more dangerous. After Edward, while the foundations of the Tudors rocked, Anna made her recipes and tasted her wines in safety, away from London. Good sense kept her quiet and domesticated while little Jane Grey – bright star of humanist intellect – was put up for a nine day's Queen. Many wept for her as her ambitious parents denied their daughter any last kind word on her way to the scaffold. Anna continued living quietly at her estates during those days of turbulence, fearing the worst, until Mary was safely on the throne. Little Jane Grey – the brave words she spoke from the scaffold melted the hardest of Catholic hearts. To preserve those tormented Tudors, Mary would say that the execution had to be done, as her sister would say many years later with the Scottish Queen. Who would want to bring a child into a world so bloody?

Anna could justifiably wonder how such a royal line had the

gall to call her own Cleves uncivilised. It was not dancing and French hoods that made a court honourable, it was something altogether deeper and lacking in England during Anna's life-time. Even Henry's will was perjured after his death so that the Reformists held power, which was never Henry's wish. Such upheaval there was on the death of Henry that it frightened them all. To be a Catholic was no longer acceptable and while Anna had learned to be pragmatic in her dealings with the world, and its spies, of whom there were many, her friend, the Lady Mary, Edward's heir should he die childless was under most savage surveillance. And young Elizabeth, too, had to watch her every step. Both those daughters, whom Anna came to know well as their step-aunt, were remarkable in that they lived and died with huge admiration and love for this cruel, perverse father of theirs. All children were taught to respect their parents in those days, but the feelings both Elizabeth and Mary had for the King were profound and genuine. Another mark of the man – that he could be charming and witty and amusing – and great – and could leave you with affection for him even after he had whipped you.

So – whenever a goose-wit such as Miss Murdoch stands in front of her portrait and prognosticates about her dullness and her lack of intelligence, Anna longs to point out that by the time the New Year celebrations of 1541 were over she was mistress of the art of Dealing With Tudors and had learned, with the greatest of pleasure, how to please herself. Something that Marillac commented on when he wrote to the French King saying how well and handsome Anna became during the succeeding years. It would be so good if those truths could stand in place of all the continuing calumnies.

Anna returns to her frame and its gilded security. This gallery of wronged and redoubtable women is as frustrating as it is upsetting. Anna knows – with all due modesty – that she was cleverer than many. And happier than most. But this is not what will be said of her. She will always be the Flanders Mare and the ugly German reject. That Murdoch woman speaks for

10

The World's a Stage

Flora kept her head down and did her research. By the beginning of June the village of Hurcott Ducis regretfully put aside the dashing death of the local steward and his love for the Brownie leader for other more pressing events. The summer season was a busy one in the village. It began and ended, as always, with the summer production by The Players and Ewan was once again in the thick of it.

It did not take long for Flora to thaw. She wanted his company and was too sensible to hold a grudge for long. She put her irritation at his crassness about Anna of Cleves to one side on the grounds that some of the best historians in the land had attributed unpleasant epithets to her. Ewan could be excused. He was a good and loyal friend and you gave those up at your peril. So, as they stood silently and awkwardly by the duck pond one evening she asked him to come and call whenever he felt like it, that she would welcome him, that she wanted to talk about Edward's history, and show him the stone, and she waited.

By the middle of June Pauline had lost much of her cachet as the heartbroken lover. Her moment of glory was fading now as the village moved on with its life. She was barred from the Brownies but she went with Brown Owl – who was kind – and Brown Owl's husband (who was a steam train enthusiast and safe from women's charms) to see the late summer production of *French Without Tears*. *French Without Tears* was a play about getting your man and it made Pauline cry. Until that moment she had no idea how much she wanted some masculinity in her life again. There was just something so wonderful about seeing her pretty, feminine ruffles snuggled up to a pair of thorn-pulled corduroys. As for Edward's widow – well – you could never convince Pauline Pike that she suffered at all but she kept the thought to herself. It would not do for people to think her unworthy. Frankly, Pauline found Flora's new High Moral Ground unfair, and meant to do something about it. It was quite unacceptable that she should now be the wronged, unhappy wife. A man of status, and in the village, with a difficult wife? It was not hard to guess whom Flora's hidden love might be.

Flora, out of loyalty to Ewan and nothing else, also went to see *French Without Tears*. As she walked towards the village hall, past the pond with its ducks settling down for the evening, past the Priory Arms whose glowing windows looked tempting in the half light the timeless, seasonal nature of the scene made her wonder about the days when Anna came to Hurcott Ducis. Was it much different then? In the summer there would have been mummers and masques and visiting troupes, there would have been maypoles and children's games, and the church – and the people – high-ups and low-downs – would be the same. Different size, different clothes, different expectations – but in their hearts just the same with their loves and hates and secrets and hopes . . . little and big wickednesses and answering kindnesses. Just as Flora kept her counsel about her true feelings in her widowhood out of a sense of propriety as well as self-protection, she had no doubt that Anna kept her counsel about her feelings for Henry after her divorce, too. Stepping into the porch of the village hall, Flora tried to imagine what it would be like for Anna, if she were alive again, to return to England – she would be back by now – stored and waiting – about to be shown as a work of art and not a dumped princess. As she took her seat, Flora remembered again the dreadful Miss Murdoch. How very good it would be, she thought, as the lights dimmed, to bring that woman to heel.

As the slightly shabby curtains parted – well. There was Ewan, wearing a toupee, still looking his age but playing a young buck of a teacher. Flora longed to leap on to the stage and drag him away from the humiliation. Be ordinary, she wanted to whisper, do not feel you have to shine at anything. Remember, she sent the message silently. They also serve who only stand and wait. He was in nearly every scene and she could not take her eyes off him. If they did waver, just for a moment, and she was brought into reality, she was reminded that The Players could be very bad, and they were. Something about the sets was extraordinarily familiar, but she kept her eyes and her thoughts on Ewan. It was the only way to survive.

A few seats up from her sat Pauline Pike, whose eyes never left the stage. For some reason this made Flora feel uncomfortable. Ewan – she realised grudgingly – rather suited a toupee – and he moved with surprising agility – leaping about and stretching out on sofas with tremendously engaging style and delivering some of the archaic lines with masculine gusto. All that golf, she supposed. He was, she was sure, quite the best of them, even though she was biased. Flora looked about her but Dilly was nowhere to be seen. How unsupportive, she thought, trying not to smile. On stage Betty from the post office attempted to do elegant things with a long cigarette holder and a maid came in and dropped a tray. Flora returned her gaze to the safety of Ewan. She could not bear, even, to look at the costumes. It took someone who knew how to sew to see how flimsy they were. But she would resist the role of seamstress for the time being. She had other, much more important, things to be getting on with.

When it was over and they had clapped and clapped and Ewan seemed to look directly at her as he bowed (which he could not do because the lights were dazzling – she knew this really) Flora left her seat feeling very happy. She wasn't quite ready yet to stop the flutter Ewan's presence caused her (though if he continued to wear the toupee she might get there considerably quicker) but maybe the flutter was enough? And then, with a smile that she just could not stop, she saw Lucy across the crowded porch. Lucy. Here? Flora dared to nod to her one-time cleaner and she nodded back but that was all. Now they were as remote from each other as were the Hebrides. Why, Lucy did not even notice that Flora was wearing a new swirling blue skirt, or if she did she disguised her interest.

It was turning to dusk. As she walked home from the village hall the deepening blue sky was star-filled, the air was balmy and Flora had the feeling that – if the world was a stage – then Hurcott Ducis was her world – and she had just seen into the very heart of it. Here was her community and here she was, walking back to Lodge Cottage all alone and safe feeling and quite unafraid. Anna would have felt the same down here . . . Though it was unlikely that she shared Flora's other thoughts which were that she had a tin of hot chocolate in the cupboard and a packet of shortbread that needed application and sometimes such things were enough. Would Anna have known chocolate? Unlikely. How sad. But she would presumably have known other dainties to enjoy alone. It was absolutely true, the hearts and hearts' desires of people did not change down the centuries. All the trappings did, and the politics, the rules, the language even – but not the central beat of the human pulse. For Flora that was what lifted history out of dry dullness – the human connection – and it was what Edward chose to ignore. Flora worried, occasionally, that she had just simply gone barking mad in the Louvre – what was she on about with portraits whispering to her and messages coming out of the paintwork across the centuries? But now she knew that it was a perfectly sane reaction – a desire to connect and respond. The big difficulty for Flora was how to connect herself back.

Behind her she heard the pitter-patter of little feet. It was Pauline Pike who had left her companions to hurry to Flora's side. Flora knew it was Pauline before seeing her. Odd emotions went through her, but mostly she felt irritation. This was not helped when Pauline, slightly breathless, caught up with her and said, 'I wondered how you were getting along,' as if Flora were a geriatric after an operation.

Flora was still suffering the gauntlet of pitying kindness. Only yesterday the long-time widowed Stephanie Blount, now restored to good works and no bad language, stopped her on her way to the library for a chat. 'I remember how hard it was,' she said, standing there looking youthful and pretty for her sixty-odd years – 'when I suddenly realised that it was for ever. I'd been out into the garden for the first time since winter and dug a bed over and was pleased with the result – then I came in and Gerald wasn't there – no one was there to say Well Done, or to admire my achievement. That's one of the hardest things, isn't it?' She went on, 'Learning to praise yourself instead of having someone there to do it for you?'

All Flora could think – and a tear came into her eye (which was a suitable reaction after all) was that it always had been like that for her – Edward never once told her she had done something well or prettily or cleverly . . . She had not even been given the space to be a good mother, a good parent. It was after that little encounter with Stephanie that Flora telephoned Hilary and gave her a – marvellously convincing – update on her father's history. She had thrown most of it away but she said only that it was coming along well – fair enough and a sensible equivocation – and Hilary was pleased. *Carpe diem*, thought Flora, for she had an immense maternal bridge to build. 'Oh yes,' she added brightly before Hilary put down the phone, 'It's shaping up just fine and we'll be all the further on when you get the information back from those Wordiform people.'

'I'll be on to them tomorrow,' said Hilary in a voice Flora knew well. Flora suddenly felt rather sorry for those Wordiform people.

She was almost at the pond when Pauline Pike caught up with her and Pauline Pike was not looking at her with kindness. She was looking at Flora with – if anything – resentment stamped upon that little daisy face. Flora had a very dreadful desire to knock her petals off. What was it about this woman that made Flora, usually so mild, feel so pugnacious?

'And I wondered how you were getting along, too,' said Flora sweetly.

Pauline shrugged. 'Oh I have good days and bad days', she said, 'But I'm getting along. There is a life to be lived, after all.'

Flora said that she was very glad to hear it.

'Yes,' said the little Pink Pike cheerily. 'And I've just decided to join The Players. So that'll give me something to do. People to meet. You know. Take myself out of myself.'

Flora's heart, for some odd reason, contracted. 'Really?' she said, 'The Players. What a good idea.'

'Yes. And you? How are *you* getting by without him?'

How tempted she was to say, 'Brilliantly well, thanks.' She missed it by a whisker. Instead she also shrugged and said, 'Oh you know – this and that.'

'I don't see you out and about much. I thought you might still be in mourning.'

They both looked at the fabric of Flora's shirt, brighter even than the skirt. It was an old Jacquard print – she'd made it herself years ago – highly coloured. One thing about her looks and colouring was that whatever shades and tones she wore they never improved anything much. Flora said nothing, just gave an attempt at a brave widow's smile and wished the Pike would go away. She did not.

'They said in the post office that you were finishing off that history of Edward's. The one we worked so hard on together.'

'Yes,' said Flora, 'I am.'

The post office? How on earth did the post office know that?

'I could take it on for you. I did so much of the research anyway. Though I never got round to finding out about the royal and transatlantic connections.'

'Oh?' said Flora noncommittally.

'That queen. The one who lived here?' She had the annoying

habit of making every statement a question. No wonder Flora found herself becoming violent.

'Anna of Cleves,' said Flora, shortly.

'Was that her name?'

'It was.'

'You've been finding out about her, too?'

'Yes,' said Flora, not wishing to share her. 'Well, she came here from time to time.'

'Well, I know that.'

As they walked Pauline pulled a handful of honeysuckle from an overhanging bush. It was a casual gesture but reminded her of Edward. If he found a rare plant he took it home to 'nurse' it.

Pauline waited and then said, 'How long ago did she live here?'

'Oh,' said Flora, 'long ago. About five hundred years.' She did not want to discuss Anna with the little Pink Pike. For some reason it seemed beneath her dignity.

'We discovered that she lived in a big house round here.' Pauline looked about her vaguely as if expecting a Tudor queen to pop out of the shrubbery at any moment. 'And that she was divorced for being too ugly. That's as far as we got.' Having delivered this she looked very smug and infinitely more slappable.

There was a short and weighty pause. Flora breathed in deep and said happily, 'Yes. That is what they say. That she was far too unattractive to be married to a king . . .' She wanted to steer the conversation away from Anna so she added, vaguely, 'It needs a lot of research.'

'Surely not,' said Pauline Pike as another blossom fell to the floor.

Flora kept her smile. 'Anna of Cleves was replaced by a very silly girl called Catherine. Who had her head chopped off. I'm enjoying the research very much.'

She smiled even more broadly, in fact, she positively beamed goodwill and approachability while Pauline stood in the dusky shadows and gave her a very penetrating look. There was a short silence while Flora held on to the beaming and tried not to feel jealous of Pauline's dimity little figure, her very short summer dress with its skimpy straps and lemony flutterings. And her overfull pink pout. She looked, Flora could see, quite irresistible if you liked mousy little faces and not much in the way of limbs. After the petal-knocking Flora had a very dreadful desire to reprise the doctor's wife and push the little pink person into the pond. But a mature woman can control herself. Just. Perhaps, like Anna, she should just curtsy low instead?

'I don't really need any help, thanks. I find it seems to bring me nearer to Edward.'

Pauline's face was in shadow but Flora was sure she read something there. 'Really?' she said. 'I shouldn't have thought that . . .'

'Better be getting on,' Flora said quickly, 'Got a lot more reading to do before I start writing it all up.'

'Wait,' said Pauline.

She waited.

'I wondered,' said the pink lips, while the eyes above had a suspiciously glassy sheen. 'I wondered if I could have something to remember Edward by. A keepsake of some sort.'

'You've got the posy pot,' snapped Flora. Too late, it was out before she could control it. Was any wife to be treated thus? That the object of her husband's deceit should stop her by the village pond and say – in full view of the sleeping ducks thereon – that she wanted a memento of their shameful dealings? Since Pauline did not know quite how much Flora did not mourn for Edward, it was a bit thick. Over thirty-five years together after all.

'There's a sweet little painting of a cat I bought him. I wondered if you would mind . . .?'

So that was where the horrible thing came from. Flora almost said, Take it, take it – for God's sake take it. But she controlled herself. Power is in property. Anna knew that. Anyway it cleared up one mystery, for Flora had thought it was the oddest of choices for Edward to hang in his study and assumed it was a gift from his eccentric employer. Nothing was ever said. The cat was white and fluffy and managed to look as if it had not only consumed the entire EEC cream lake, but could disembowel a cow with one swipe of its paw. 'Well – it's all in probate for the time being,' said Flora.

'I thought it might be,' said Pauline, with an irritating hint of slyness. 'When's that likely to be over?'

Flora smiled in condescension. 'Your guess is as good as mine. These things can go on for years'. Flora shrugged. 'My hands are tied,' she said happily.

'Your solicitor's in The Players isn't he? I need a solicitor in any case. I could ask him about it.'

Flora could not stop herself from flinching.

Pauline could not stop herself from noticing. Ah-ha.

'He's very busy,' said Flora, too quickly.

'Perhaps I'll bribe him,' she said. 'Take him a pot of my quince and crab-apple. See if that will persuade him.' She gave Flora a happy little smile.

'Don't be silly,' said Flora. 'He wouldn't discuss his client's affairs with you. Have the cat if you want it.'

But it seemed Pauline was quite taken with the idea of visiting the solicitor. 'You gave him Edward's yellow jumper, didn't you?' There was ice beneath the sweetness.

Flora nodded and shrugged. 'Well it was no use to me.'

Pauline looked at her with unblinking distaste. 'Not yellow, no, definitely not yellow.'

Flora said nothing. It felt as if the Pike had won.

'Well,' said Pauline eventually, as if she had made up her mind to something, 'I thought it suited him, poor man. And I bet he doesn't get many home comforts with that dreadful drunk of a wife of his. I'll make an appointment.'

Quince and crab-apple indeed. Something not altogether pleasant popped into Flora's mind. She had read that one of the ladies at court gave Henry just such a gift to smooth the path of her young girl relative into Queen Anna's service.

Extraordinary, given his track record with them, that a Queen's ladies-in-waiting were chosen by Henry. With such terrible consequences. Much as Flora might imagine that she would like to see the Pink Pike's head roll – the image of any pretty young head lying sightless and bloodied in the straw was not a good one. On the other hand, neither was it a good one to imagine Pauline sitting opposite Ewan in that intimate little office of his with her little head on one side in that tempting daisy way of hers a-woggling her jam at him . . .

Flora leaned towards her and said confidingly. 'He's not a jam man, Pauline. The way to Ewan's heart, if you really want to persuade him of anything, is to give him a bottle of good whisky.'

'I thought it was his wife who drank.'

'Exactly,' said Flora. 'They both do. Like fishes. I was amazed myself.' She felt as if someone had walked over her grave. But the lie was necessary. Forgive me, Ewan, she said to herself. There was just something far too determined about the Pike. Dainty as a daisy she might be, but she had iron in her little pink soul. 'Irish whiskey is best. Goodnight, Pauline,' she said, and moved briskly away, keeping her hands, those hands that that itched to shove a pink person pondwards, firmly in their pockets.

The sound of Pauline's clattering heels died into the distance, the dusk gathered more deeply, the sky was full of stars and the beauty of it all made the encounter so much the worse. 'Pox take the woman,' she said to the silent ducks. 'Pox take her. Or she'll be in The Players before you could say ninepence.'

Flora had reached a point in the History where she had to apply herself to the datestone. She still had no idea why the dates did not match. Everything she had learned about the portrait, everything she had read about Anna, must hold a clue. If only Hilary would come back to her and say that the carvings were of the same date as Anna's death, then it would be straightforward. A memorial. Simple as that. If not Flora must concentrate harder. Which was all very well but she was no longer the late-night student, she was very much the early-to-bed retired teacher. A world of difference. A world. Why, she could almost hear her brain creak. And she so wanted Ewan to visit and be amazed at all her discoveries. That was the happy plan. She had everything she needed to know about Anna from the portrait. *Lively.* She couldn't be wrong about the things the portrait said to her. She, despite Henry, was loved by all. Mary, Elizabeth, her household, her friends. Nothing in the painting said differently. The portrait was the visible truth of all she had discovered about Anna.

Back in the cottage she thought how simple it seemed in Paris. Here in Hurcott Ducis she realised that the personal was not quite enough. She must go deeper, underpin what she wrote with what she knew; like an iceberg it would be, keeping most of itself hidden but informing everything.

Well, she had made a promise to Anna in the Louvre and she wanted to fulfil it. Trouble was – she felt very, very sleepy. Again. But it was still early, the Hurcott Ducis Players not being known for candle burning, and certainly it was too early to go to bed. Flora was in that state where the spirit may be willing but the flesh is weak and wishes to go on holiday – and where the flesh in most cases wins hands down with a packed suitcase. It did so now. So she did what many a researcher both great and insignificant does when they are stuck. She yawned while contemplating how to catch the Muse by surprising Her. Almost invariably, the Muse has seen it all before – and also yawns.

Out of the Parisian experience, names of royal women flew around in her head. Marie of Guise and her daughter Mary Queen of Scots; Mary Tudor; Elizabeth Tudor; Jane Seymour . . . The characters surrounding Anna and who contributed to her arrival and stay in England. Flora had looked up the forthcoming exhibition's website so she had a list. Lists were good and comforting things. They spoke from the page of important things to do, of things already half done. Fascinating. This would keep her awake for hours.

Within minutes Flora was dozing on the couch next to a pile of unopened books and her pen ceased to make its slight noise of action across the paper. Softly, as if not to waken the sleeper, the paper made a delicate shushing noise as it slid to the floor. Followed, with equally harmonious auditory effect, by the pen slipping slowly from her hands to join it. The only noises to be heard in the house after this were the sounds of Flora's even breathing and the ticking of the grandfather clock, the latter of which had a distinctly frosty edge given that its mistress was asleep and the time being a mere twenty-five minutes past nine o'clock. The last image Flora took in was a postcard of the portrait of Anna. Not a very good reproduction but Flora found it useful – a constant reminder of the young woman who seemed to speak to her from down the years. There were several such images pinned around the house, in strategic places. Wherever she goes, there is Anna. Alas, right now it is a lullaby in paint.

As her sleepy eyes close the portrait looks even more like an icon in its miniature state. Flora sometimes needs to avoid the desire to pray to it. If not plead for guidance. Tick, tick, tick goes the clock. And by the time it bongs the half-hour, its owner is – gone. It is at times like this that those whom we long to conjure may – if we are lucky – come a-calling.

Flora dreams of portraits. Of course she does. She dreams of standing in a room full of portraits; good ones, bad ones, dusty ones, glowing ones, and she does not know what to do, where to look, what to say. They stare down at her from the walls, mute and blank and she, too, feels mute and blank. Anna is there and she has a story but Flora doesn't know how to tell it ... And then into the room marches Miss Murdoch, striding up to the portrait of Anna, sneering at it defiantly, and Flora takes courage. She berates Miss Murdoch for her blindness, for her inaccuracies, for her lack of humanity. Miss Murdoch stands back in fear and amazement. It is a heart-warming scene, as only scenes in dreams that are going well can be heartening. Flora rises to the dreamed of challenge, and wins.

Bong, goes the clock.

Bong.

The Thawing of Hilary and the Quivering of the Little Pink Pike's Gills

The remaining three conundrums to be dealt with by Flora, and in no particular order, were the accurate dating of the Anna stone, whether or not she should let Hilary see the Pink Pike's video, and did the Davieses share a bedroom. Each of which was as exercising as the other.

She rang Hilary and arranged to take her for lunch in London. Nicely neutral ground for both of them and Hilary could show off her Calligraphy and Wordiform research. Flora could then also judge the state of things so far as the video was concerned and, anyway, it would be a little stepping stone for the two of them. Moving on and moving closer, she hoped.

Thinking so much about portraits gave her an idea. Before she left for London Flora sorted through the photo albums and picked out some nice pictures of Edward and a few snapshots of their lives that she thought Hilary might want. It was interesting and not a little saddening to look at them – after deconstructing Anna's portrait Flora thought she could never look at any face in any picture without trying to find its soul. The family photos were much as anyone else's might be on the surface – faces bright with hope when they first came to Hurcott. Standing close together in the garden, in a field and near the pond. Then pictures of the two of them with Hilary – all very usual and ordinary – but very quickly Flora saw that she stood away from father and daughter, sometimes behind the cuddling pair, sometimes not there at all. It was nobody's fault but her own. You did not get to your sixth decade without knowing that looking around for someone to blame for your actions was futile. Flora could, should, have done something about it, and she hadn't. That was how it was – a maternal disappearing act. She let it happen instead of keeping herself in the picture.

How dull she probably seemed. Any child was bound to be excited by fun and games and wholly irresponsible behaviour (would Flora ever forget coming home to find the tree-house that Edward had just thrown up, half hanging out of the oak tree, and Hilary with a bandage round her elbow looking pale but determined not to show fear? No – she never would). She had a photograph of the three of them, taken when Hilary was about seven and on a borrowed pony, enlarged. It was the best she could do. The others she slipped in an envelope to give to her. Flora had no further use for them – but she kept all the early photos of Hilary as a babe in arms. Then she had needed her mother – it was when she learned to walk that she upped and walked away.

As she waited on the station for the 11.05 wearing her navy skirt and jacket and white silk shirt – safe again she thought a little miserably (how long it took her to choose the right mark of respect so as not to offend Hilary and which she now realised was just plain dull) – she mused on her widow's loss. Here it was, at this very place, that she had stepped off the train into a whole new world of strangeness and surprises. Having a heart of stone being the least of them, really. It seemed, suddenly, that since Edward's death the world was full of grieving widows – heightened consciousness she supposed unless there had been an outbreak of dying husbands – these widows were all very proper – bemoaning their fate in newspapers, in glossy magazines (with photographs), on the radio, on the television (nicely made up and with hair arranged) and in books. She had been cheated out of the one full, centre-stage role she could play as a wife. Being a good widow. No wonder the Victorians made such an event of mourning – it was, like the marriage ceremony itself, the funeral and after, the validation of everything to do with love. Ecclesiastes even said something along the lines of it being better to go into a house of mourning than a house of feasting. It felt as if she was the only woman in the world to be such a fraud and she took some comfort in remembering how Anna had also had to pretend her way through much of her existence where Henry was concerned. It was unlikely they were the only two in the world, but all the same Flora felt very isolated.

It occurred to her as she walked up and down the platform that this was what it must have been like for men who loved men and women who loved women in the dark old days. Isolation and a general sense of unease, fear at the pretence, the cold shivers at being found out, always lying about your feelings. The only difference was that she didn't have anywhere to go at night – the grounds of the Brompton Oratory for example, or dimly lit clubs, or cruising in Midland parks – to mix with other stony-hearted wives and fall on each other's necks and admit that yes, yes, yes – I am feeling reasonably cheerful and not really mourning my dead husband very much at all. Oh I miss him, but . . . No. She could trust no one with the secret. She must keep it to herself. It was not even the subject of a sisterly telephone conversation, her sister being, like the rest of the world, convinced Flora was a true widow in every respect and accordingly sympathetic. Why, Rosie, not having heard from Flora for a while, even suggested she really would come back early if required. How vile I am, Flora thought. It wouldn't be long before Rosie was counselling Flora about getting another man into her life and then Flora would have the burden of keeping quiet about Ewan, too. Were you ever grown-up enough to tell the truth to the world and hang the consequence? Probably not. Was she ever going to be grown-up enough to speak the truth? Even just tell Ewan what she felt for him? Probably not. The little Pink Pike would have swum her way in by now if Flora knew anything about it. She might even be doing it at this very moment. Oh, she thought as she boarded the train, Oh I should have been braver. Or cleverer. Or both.

Atonement. She could atone to herself for some of this deceit by being truthful about the History of Hurcott. A small thing, she thought wryly, but mine own, and I will claim it as such. Not just to Ewan, but to everyone. I will write the story of Hurcott with the story of Anna and I will take full credit for it – and Edward can just go on whizzing. And Hilary, too. She swallowed hard at this last thought but faint heart never gained high moral ground. Hilary, when the time came, would just have to lump it. With luck they would have built enough bridges by then for her to accept that her mother was someone in her own right. She then had a very satisfactory mental picture of Hilary looking proud and happy. This was closely followed by a mental picture of Ewan being amazed by her brilliant erudition. It probably wasn't the *au naturelle* and orange silk way of getting close to someone you liked, but it would have to be Flora's.

A plain woman, she told herself firmly as the little white houses and fields became grey brick and arterial roads and the train started to slow for London, a plain woman has little to lose from setting out her stall early. So say the wise – unless they are in denial and would have it that there is no such thing as a plain woman which clearly, Flora thought, there *is*. The plain woman stallholder in this case, however, felt that she might never recover from having the potential purchaser metamorphosing into a slightly balding Winged Mercury. Although he was no oil painting himself, since when had that ever stopped a rejection? She had only to think of Anna and Henry to shudder at the prospect. But she had to do something and what else was there? Who is the third who walks always beside you? I will show you fear in a handful of dust. Or in your facial anomalies. Exactly.

Oddly enough she was beginning to look – for Flora – quite blooming. She noticed it this morning when she was getting herself ready. Not beautiful, nor pretty, not even handsome, but alive to the world somehow. A bit too noticeable, perhaps, for a lunch with Hilary. She put on quite a lot of pale foundation and was tempted to rub a bit of darkness under her eyes (she didn't) but still the light shone out of her. How right the Caliphs and the Crusaders were to lock up their wives – it seemed that nothing bred bloom on a female cheek quite like a bit of freedom. All in all, despite being a little nervous about lunch with her daughter, she thought she had never felt quite so ready for life and she stepped off the train full of good intentions.

When she arrived at the restaurant and despite the pale foundation, Hilary noticed it straight away.

'I thought you'd look rough,' she said, less accusing than admiring, which was nice. 'But you look very well.'

Flora immediately put it down to alcoholic flush. 'I'm probably drinking a little too much,' she said. Hilary was not surprised and accepted the suggestion. 'Ah,' she said knowingly, as if she expected little else.

'It helps me sleep,' added Flora. Something prodded her, a little demon's triton was it, to go on. 'I sleep very well – have a lot of very nice dreams actually.'

'Mourning takes us all differently,' said Hilary primly, and Flora thought – You can say that again.

'Oh, it'll all settle down eventually,' Flora said firmly. 'But more importantly, how are you?' She reached over and gave her daughter's cheek a little stroke. Hilary moved her head to one side like a kitten – but then thought better of it and sat up straight again. Still, it was a start. 'We've just got to be strong,' she said.

'I know.' Flora sipped her water and tried to look the part. 'It gets better slowly,' she added in a small voice.

Hilary just nodded. 'At least you've got something tangible of his to keep you going . . .' A silent tear escaped her eye and trickled slowly down to fall with a little silent splash on to the tablecloth, making Flora feel ten times worse. Hilary wiped her finger beneath her eye.

'What's that?' asked Flora, softly.

'Dad's creative legacy. The *History*.'

She sounded, Flora thought, exactly like Edward. It was almost unbearable seeing her so miserable and to feel so unmoved herself.

'Yes,' said Flora nodding into her water. 'At least I have that.'

'The History of Hurcott,' said Hilary, smiling now. 'The place where I grew up. Its highways and byways, its ponds and streams, its fields and –'

'Yes,' said Flora carefully, wishing to deflect the creeping sentimentality. 'Though much of the work is to do with Anna of Cleves, actually, rather than the village itself.' As she said it she wondered if, like her favoured subject, her nose was getting longer. 'He seems to have been quite taken with her, your father.'

Hilary blinked. 'Was he?'

Flora nodded. 'I think he must have admired her very much.'

Yes, there went the nose, right into the water glass.

Hilary looked nonplussed. 'I thought he said she was a bit of an old boot.'

There went Flora's conscience, right out of the restaurant door. 'Did he indeed?' she said, gripping the water glass very tightly. 'Well, he must have changed his mind when he found out about her.' Any more of this and her nose would be following her conscience out into the street.

'Well, then – whatever he wanted. At least you're getting down to it while it's still fresh.'

'Mmm,' said Flora noncommittally. Since it was historical and went back at least seven hundred years, the idea of Edward's history being fresh was an odd one. It was at times like these that she realised how wide was the gap between them. Any normal mother would be able to point this out – probably with a smile – without risking the Third World War – any normal daughter might laugh at the silliness of what she said. That was the trouble, neither of them ever had the time to be silly enough.

'I do think of it as Dad's creative legacy you know – it'll be something to show his grandchildren.'

Flora paused, glass to lip, wishing the wine would arrive. And waited. That would be the perfect solution. If Hilary was now pregnant then she could be a wonderful grandmother, shine in the role, be a wonderful mother of a pregnant daughter, shine in that role, too. 'Oh?' she said, as a question.

'When they come,' added Hilary, pinkening a little.

Flora removed the fine image of herself as a mixture of Florence Nightingale and Penelope Leach and tried not to contemplate Hilary and Robin's sex life. 'It'll be hard to get anywhere near the perfection he'd want – but it will be so totally worth it in the end.' Whereupon Hilary's eyes filled up again.

At last the wine arrived. *So totally worth it?* She really does believe that, thought Flora. And how much she cares, she thought with envy, as she leaned over and squeezed her daughter's shoulder and dabbed at her eyes with the napkin (they were always your baby, she realised, presumably until you became theirs) and gave her a glass of burgundy to sip.

'Look,' she said, just as she used to say to her when she needed to take her mind off something nasty, 'I've brought you some photos. And I've had this one enlarged . . . We were so happy that day.' She held it up for Hilary to see. 'Remember?' she said. And they spent some nice time looking through the pictures.

'We should meet up like this more often,' Flora said when the photographs were put away. 'I never thought of it before but now that I'm on my own –'

Mistake.

Oh mistake.

Hilary broke into loud sobs which Flora could not help but think were more self-indulgent than involuntary, a thought which made her feel twice as bad about her own shortcomings. No video for Hilary yet, that was for sure. But a mother's instinct is usually right. Flora saw, as she somehow knew she would, a gleam of satisfaction in Hilary's eyes as first the waitress, then the people at the next table, came over and asked what was wrong. Flora told them in hushed tones, and they left, but the light had been shone upon them and for the rest of the meal they were the stars of the restaurant starring in their own little melodrama called *A Widow and her Daughter Being Brave.*

The grieving did not, she was impressed to see, affect Hilary's appetite, which meant that Flora could have a good old tuck-in too. It was the right kind of menu for it. She chose this place because Hilary (and Edward) could not resist solid British food and because, at the Laughing Lion, so she was told by Ewan, that was what you got. It was the sort of place that solicitors went to, she thought as she looked about her, with its plain and no-nonsense white napery and dark beams. She imagined herself sitting here with Ewan. An old-fashioned chop house wasn't exactly the right place to get your blood racing but she had a feeling he would like it here, that he would feel safe. Mmm, she thought, perhaps that was why he would like it? She settled down to her meal and enjoyed the foolishness of wondering if he had ever sat at this same table.

Watching Hilary make her slow and determined way through the thick white onion soup and the thick meat-pink roast lamb, she had no doubt at all that Hilary was well on her way to recovery.

'How's Robin?' she asked.

Hilary recomposed herself. 'Oh – he's bearing up, too. But I think it's hard for him seeing me in such a state.'

'It must be,' said Flora, with feeling. 'Pudding?'

They parted on affectionate terms. Hilary thanked Flora for the photographs and said that she would come down when she could but that just at the moment she was throwing herself into her work and they were decorating. 'I know I said I'd come and stay but – it's got to be done.'

'Of course. That's fine,' said Flora, trying not to sound pleased.

Hilary and Robin were always decorating. It took the place of going on holiday or so it seemed. She even apologised for not yet having word from the calligraphy people. Flora was surprised but it seemed that despite Hilary's taking them to task, the research was slow and painstaking and could not be hurried. So there certainly must be something wrong with the dates – which was both intriguing and daunting as Flora had not the slightest helpful theory. 'I expect they are just being thorough,' said Flora. 'I'm in the same position myself.'

Hilary kissed her cheek, looked at her critically and said, 'You know, we should start wearing brighter colours now. Dad liked them and – well – we have to begin somewhere. Maybe when we have our celebration of his life you can put on something a bit happier?'

Flora said, 'Absolutely. A celebration of his life.'

'We could mark the publication of the History with a party for him,' said Hilary.

Publication? Party? Yes, absolutely, Edward to a T. 'Well – let's get it finished first shall we?' Flora had not told Hilary about the Anna portrait coming to England, nor that the exhibition opened soon. Mean of her. But she had other plans.

Bright colours was an amusing thought. And after all, she had been given permission. So Flora dared to venture into her favourite shop again and buy a cherry-red silk and quite silly suit before catching the 5.22 back to Hurcott. And she hung it in her wardrobe like a luscious, tempting sin. It had been a good day. She'd talked about Anna's prominence in the scheme of things and Hilary had accepted it which was a major hurdle over, and she had made up her mind that the video was not for showing – two important items ticked off. She felt on top of the world. She yawned. In one's sixth decade, she thought smiling, bed becomes like a good old friend.

By her bedside was a pile of photocopied pages from various sources relating to the Cleves divorce. On top of the pile was a copy of the letter that Anna wrote to Henry VIII when Henry's Council informed her that her marriage was null and void. Flora picked it up and reading it made her smile. In future, if ever Flora felt guilty about her own dissembling, she had merely to read this letter. It was an extraordinary bit of placatory nonsense – flattery was not in it, and – apparently – it went down very well with its recipient. Wise Anna. There was nothing she could not learn from the dumped Queen about the art of saying one thing while being another.

It may please your majesty to know that, though this case must needs be most hard and sorrowful unto me, for the great love I bear to your most noble person, yet having more regard to God and his truth than to any worldly affection . . . I acknowledge myself to accept and approve, wholly and entirely putting myself, for my state and condition, to your highness' goodness and pleasure . . . Yet it will please you to take me for one of your humble servants, and so determine of me, as I may sometimes have the fruition of your noble presence; which as I shall esteem for a great benefit . . . And that your highness will take me for your sister for which I most humbly thank you accordingly . . . Your Majesty's most humble sister and servant – Anna the Daughter of Cleve.

No wonder Henry gave her an extra palace, several more manors, most of Cromwell's silver, a place at his table and the odd Crown jewel if she could write like that. Well, of course someone else, her Olisleger probably, helped, but there was something purely Anna about the way it was done. Humble, to the point, exactly what Henry wanted to hear – but just with that little flourish at the end, *Daughter of Cleves*, to remind him, to remind herself, who she was in her heart of hearts. Henry's breast (if it could be found beneath his stomach) must have swelled with pride while Anna kept hers hidden. He probably pitied her profoundly for having such a jewel as himself taken away from her. He had a strongly sentimental streak and it would have touched him to the quick when he read it. Chink, chink – Flora could almost hear another chest of gold fall into Anna's coffers. The proof of the syllabub was in the eating. Anna ate extremely well as a consequence and – as was reported – she bloomed – miraculously becoming – it was said – beautiful again. She lived royally and happily and untrammelled by politics. And all she had to do was pretend to miss the monster. *That I may sometimes have the fruition of your noble presence* . . . Now that really was outrageous. Even for the rhetoric of the time. How could he fail to respond? How could he believe it? But he did. Perhaps if Flora had coloured the separate bedrooms idea like that she and Edward might have had a love-in after all.

In his office, at the serving of mid-morning coffee, which he seemed to need more than ever nowadays since Dilly had started going on about learning to fly a helicopter again, Ewan prepared to meet his new client with mixed feelings. On the one hand she was a young woman who might need his assistance, on the other hand she was the young woman who had deceived Flora and ensnared (for so he assumed it) his friend Edward Chapman. She might have information that was relevant to the Chapmans so he must see her. He was not sure how to approach the interview at all – or rather – he knew how to approach it, which was with absolute professionalism – it was whether he could do it without showing his distaste. He was prepared to dislike Miss Pauline Pike very much indeed.

Thinking this, he was quite unready for the shock – his cup midway from saucer to lips – when the door was opened by his secretary, the kindly, and very Christian, Cora Prout, and a veritable vision walked in. Kindly and very Christian Cora Prout did not approve of Miss Pike, he could tell by the disappearance of her lips, and he could also see why. Ewan did not think he had seen quite so much cleavage up close since he was a nursling. Indeed, Miss Pike seemed to be mostly made up of cleavage, with a pair of bright pink lips above and a quantity of bare knee below, the latter being just about as prominent as the first after the young lady was seated. This was not the way Miss Pike presented herself in her Brownie days. In her Brownie days Miss Pike, though always well turned out, had about her a fresh, country girl look. Now Miss Pike seemed to be a fresh young woman of a quite different kind.

'Thank you for seeing me,' she said.

To which he very nearly replied, No, no – thank you for showing yourself to me. But he merely folded his hands on the desk, leaned forward on his forearms (a pose which he felt was encouraging without being too friendly) and said, 'How can I help?'

He rather wished he had not done so as Miss Pike also then leaned on the desk and rested on her forearms and the effect upon him was quite the reverse of encouraging and quietly friendly. The effect made him want to run as far away as possible – or not – or both.

'Well, first,' she said, looking him in the eye with a boldness that he might even call brazen. 'I wanted to say how much I'm looking forward to acting with you.' She put her head on one side and half-closed her eyes and smiled a smile that was both enigmatic and compelling. 'You know I've applied to join The Players.'

'Yes,' he said.

'You were so wonderful in *French Without Tears*.' She leaned a little closer across the desk.

He cleared his throat. He leaned back. 'Thank you. Now – what can I do for you?'

'You were a real inspiration. Hope. After Edward. You know?'

He found himself nodding sympathetically. This cannot be right, he told himself, though he went on nodding.

Pauline fixed him with her eyes and her cleavage and shook her little head and said, 'How could something that felt so right be so wrong?'

Ewan had to take firm control or he would be agreeing with her. 'There was always the matter of Flora,' he said, wishing he had not. This was all very unprofessional. '*Mrs* Chapman.'

Pauline cast down her gaze and was the very picture of contrition – and who knew what might have happened had Cora

Prout, knocking perfunctorily, not entered at that very moment.

'I thought the young lady,' Cora Prout knew how to make the word lady sound like harlot, 'might want a cup of something?'

Miss Pike looked at her little diamanté watch. 'Well . . . considering the time,' She looked at his coffee cup with desire in her eyes.

'Ah yes,' he said, 'so sorry. Coffee or tea?'

Coffee was brought and the door was closed again, something that Ewan regretted. Pauline said playfully, 'Do you know, I could do with a real drink actually . . .' And she produced from her little yellow handbag, a smooth silver flask and waggled it at him. 'How about you? It's the very best Irish whiskey. Rather nice to have a splash with the coffee. Begorrah.'

Cora Prout told Valerie in the chemist's shop later that afternoon that she did not know whether to laugh or cry at the sight of her Mr Davies. 'A fish could have made more sense of himself,' was how she put it to Valerie. 'He didn't know where to look.' She shook her head and gave a grim smile over the pharmaceuticals counter. 'Mind you – she was flaunting everything she'd got. Didn't get her anywhere though – five minutes later she was out of the office with her cheeks all red and her eyes all damp and that little flask of hers tucked back where it belonged. When I went back in he was mopping his face with his hankie and as red as the rose in his buttonhole.'

Valerie tutted. 'I wonder what she wanted,' she said, hopefully.

Cora Prout lowered her voice. 'Nothing of a legal take in those clothes, surely, I said to Mr Davies. And he said that he had recommended she speak to his brother next time who was better at that sort of thing.'

'Very wise,' said Valerie.

'Yes. And if it doesn't have four legs and a wet nose Mr Angus Davies just isn't interested. Pity Mr Chapman didn't say the same and send her on her way. Fancy choosing *her*.'

'Oh, *he* was too nice. She chose him, I'll bet.'

Both women went into a little reverie for a fraction and then Cora Prout said, 'As if Mr Ewan doesn't have enough of that behaviour with Mrs Davies. A bottle of aspirin, please. All that chest . . . I ask you. *She* won't be popping up on his Christmas list, I can tell you that. Not with little silver whatnots of whisky floating about. I heard him telephoning Giles Baldwin after she'd gone. Something about The Players – but I couldn't *quite* hear.'

'Pity,' said Valerie. 'Did you want those aspirin?'

'Not really,' said Cora. And back to the office she went.

*

It did not take very long to track down Miss Penelope Murdoch, Brown Guides being available online. If Flora said so herself she had made very good progress with Anna and her portrait and with luck the datestone information would come in any day now and that would move it all along nicely. When she had finished typing it up she would get it bound into a beautiful copy for Hilary and Hilary could then decide to do whatever she liked with it. Publish and be damned. But it would have Flora's name on the title page, in quite as large letters as Edward's. Truth would out at last.

The exhibition of portraits opened in London soon and that is where Flora and Anna and Miss Penelope Murdoch would have their Philippi. With, Flora hoped, Ewan as witness. The plan was for him to be astonished and fall to his knees with admiration as she revealed how brilliantly she – not Edward – had accumulated, researched and made sense of all the information surrounding Anna of Cleves and the Hurcott connection. And if he didn't fall to his knees then any other degree of display would be acceptable. Except having her hand shaken which, in her gloomier moments, she thought might be the case. Just once, she thought, just once, I am going to shine.

Quite where that left Hilary and her dreams of her father's rather broader-based Grand Work Flora had not quite settled, but Hilary was not going to be in this scene – in this scene there was only to be Miss Murdoch, Ewan, Flora and – of course – Anna herself.

Hilary rang to say that at last she had full and final confirmation that the carving of the stone was no earlier than the very late 1590s – probably 1598 or 99 and definitely not before that date. The Calligraphy and Wordiform Society made a very thorough job of the research and they could say, absolutely firmly, that they were right. They had no idea why it was carved beyond the fact that it had all the hallmarks of a datestone to mark a death. And they, too, confirmed that the carved devices were those of the Duchy of Cleves.

'Which we knew anyway,' said Flora, half to herself. So there was no respite from the mystery after all. The stone was placed there forty years after Anna's death but with the date 1557.

'They also confirmed that it's an expensive job. Classy. So it was done by someone of rank. Or at least, someone with money and a knowledge of the arts, and Italian art in particular.'

'Well, thanks, Hilary, that's confirmed that the date is still a difficulty anyway. Now to try to find out why. I've drawn a complete blank so far.'

'I'd keep reading your way through Dad's stuff,' said Hilary with complete confidence. 'I'm sure he will have found the reason for its being there . . .'

'Mmm,' said Flora a little queasily. 'Possibly.'

'Oh certainly,' said Hilary, and rang off.

That afternoon she sat in the garden looking out over the sunny paddock and sipped her tea and ruminated on what she knew. And largely that was negative. Hardly anyone who knew Anna in her lifetime in England would be alive forty years on, unless they were a child when she arrived. Something bounced around in Flora's head – to do with Henry's daughters. Mary had buried Anna with all due pomp and her tomb was still there in its position of honour by the high altar at Westminster Abbey. Grand enough. But that was on her death in 1557 – so what was the connection with something happening so much later? Elizabeth was on the throne by then – and she probably would have a memory of Anna – but why would she do such a thing? Elizabeth was old then, very old. Something must fit but for the life of her Flora could not think what. More reading was required. She settled herself with a book about the last years of Elizabeth's reign. There might be something in there to stir the feeble brain cells.

Later, her reading having tailed off in the balmy air and golden light, Flora rang Ewan at his office, judging that he would soon be leaving, and suggested that he call in to Lodge Cottage on the way home.

'Hilary has had the carving properly dated,' she said. 'And I'm no further forward in knowing why it's there. Come and see if you can throw any light on the mystery.' It was as good an excuse as any. And flattering, of course.

Even before he stepped over the threshold Flora was offering him some elderflower cordial, several times and very loudly, so loudly that he actually winced. Women, he felt, could invade you from all sorts of angles with the most simple of enquiries about drinks when they put their minds to it. He was still astonished about the silver flask. Women had such small livers, after all. Apart, it seemed, from Dilly.

'What I could actually do with,' he said, as he sat down in the garden in the shade of the old stone wall, 'is a cup of tea. Cora Prout seems to have something against leaving a tea-bag in for longer than it takes to take it out again. I mean, I know I'm careful about stimulants but I don't mind the odd shot of caffeine.'

Flora made it strong enough to stand a spoon up. She was beginning to make a list of things that Ewan liked and a strong cup of tea was now included. How manly. How ordinary.

'I continue to thank you for that yellow sweater, by the way.

229

Very nice and bright. Cheers me up.'

'I thought it matched those startling trousers of yours.'

'Oh really?' He laughed. 'Does it?' He laughed again. 'Did you make . . .?'

'It's handknitted,' said Flora. Equivocation was easy if you were plain – people expected you to be truthful.

'You're a woman of many talents, then, Flora.' There was a certain amused air of admiration about the statement. She put aside the uncomfortable idea of taking pleasure in being complimented on *knitting* of all things, and the even more uncomfortable idea that she couldn't actually *knit*, and smiled in a curtsying sort of way.

'Actually,' she said, truth being sensible wherever possible, 'I'm much better at sewing and embroidery.'

'And you still won't join The Players?'

'I'll get this history project finished first. Then let's see.'

'At least,' he said, 'I've given Pauline Pike her marching orders. Or rather Giles, as membership secretary will do so, at my suggestion. Very odd. He seemed ecstatic at the thought of telling her himself. Wouldn't take no for an answer. "I'll do it and glad to," he said. So if you do join you won't find her there to embarrass you.'

Loyalty. How precious it was. Maybe more precious than love?

Flora breathed out. 'Good of Giles. And you. Thank you,' she said, and because she could not help herself for the sheer wickedness of it she said, testing him, 'I think she drinks, Pauline. Do you?'

He was still a solicitor and at first he did not rise. She waited. Eventually he said quietly, 'You might be right.' Which told her all she wanted to know.

They both sipped their tea.

'Edward and Giles liked a drink.'

'Did they?' Ewan looked anxious.

'Well – Edward liked good wine – he and Giles enjoyed showing off about it and they sometimes drank too much together – but not drink, drink – not like –'

But if he was going to open up with her, it was not today. 'That's a bit different,' he said, and looked at the very interesting ground as if it might yield up the secret history.

She kindly changed the subject.

He looked up from the very interesting ground gratefully.

'Now about this stone,' she said firmly. 'Two things interest me about the carving. One, obviously, is the date – which is definitely anachronistic.' Good to use the right word. She'd been calling it an anomaly until Hilary corrected her.

Ewan pursed his lips and nodded and looked very ponderous. 'So it's definitely an anomaly then?' he said. Which made her laugh and him look perplexed. The path to ruin was not a smooth one.

'Sorry,' she said, 'I wasn't laughing at you only – oh well – it doesn't matter – let's say it's an – um – anachronistic anomaly.' They both looked at each other and went 'Hmm'.

Flora longed to say – Your turn: It's an anachronistic anomaly and acutely anticipatory. Edward usually pulled a face if she tried anything of a witty or jocular nature and – to cite a rather tasteless cliché in the circumstances – her attempts to amuse her husband usually went down like a lead balloon.

'I do know that the date on it is the date of Anna's death – 1557 – she was only forty – but why the style of carving is a good few decades on from that hasn't been answered by anyone. There must be an answer somewhere, mustn't there?'

'Ah yes,' nodded Ewan, only half listening. 'How nice.'

Is it? thought Flora. But he looked so content that she hadn't the heart to go on trying to be intelligent about stones or dates or anything at all. Maybe she did not need to impress him. Maybe a friendly welcome was enough. If this was the way to a man's heart and his other bits, she thought, bring it on.

He sipped his tea. 'There is something very pleasant about coming here,' he said. 'Very peaceful – no tensions.'

Which implied that there was no peace and much tension at

Little Beeches. Suddenly she hoped he wouldn't say any more. Despite this being the right moment for him to shuffle his chair a bit nearer to hers and say that his wife did not understand him, Flora hoped he wouldn't. If he did, she knew that, even though she would try to avoid it, he would sink in her estimation. Loyalty was something she always longed for and never got from Edward and she always admired it.

'I sometimes feel quite useless at home,' he said to his teacup. And then he smiled at her with sad resignation. 'I probably am.'

'It's peaceful here without Edward, that's for sure,' she said, half amused.

'Oh Flora,' he said, 'I'm so sorry.'

There was the moment. All Flora had to do was lean across and place one of her hands on his, tell him that she understood and pucker up. And she might have done so – indeed – her hand began to twitch in her lap – when he said suddenly, out of nowhere, and quite jovially, 'Well, well – mysterious even from the grave this Flanders Mare, then.'

Grit teeth, no use taking umbrage again, better fight Anna's corner. 'She was actually rather beautiful, I think.'

'Really?' he said. 'How do you know?' He laughed.

'Ah,' said Flora, 'you just wait and see.'

More tea was drunk, more talk of the village and other local news was exchanged and the afternoon began to slide into evening.

'We ought to go if we're going,' said Flora. 'Before it gets too dark . . .'

They both looked out over the old paddock to the part of the wall that was visible beyond. The sun had turned it pink and gold. 'I like to think it looked just the same in Anna's time,' said Flora.

'You're a romantic,' he said, but kindly. 'Now take me to this famous stone.' And they set off.

A romantic. It was the nicest thing he could have said.

The meadow grass was uncut and high, and full of

celandines, greater and lesser, poppies, clover and daisies. Their feet made a shushing noise as they walked side by side. Flora had a longing to slip her hand through the crook of his arm, or take his hand in hers, but she managed to control it. All those years ago on that cycle ride to Hever she had mistaken the situation and forced the issue and look where it got her – married and widowed and never really being loved and just putting up with it because even that was more than she might expect with a bun for a face. So she kept her hands firmly by her sides but hoped that he might suddenly turn and clasp one – or both – of hers – and make a declaration. Oh dear, she was a romantic all right. Too many Victorian novels. They walked on and he did not clasp anything.

'The paddock looks beautiful,' he said. 'I'm glad you could keep it after all.'

'Thanks to you.'

When they reached the part of the wall and the stone Ewan took off his tie and stuffed it into his pocket and bending low he began running his hands over each section of wall, each string of uneven stonework. 'Beautiful,' he murmured. 'Weathered and coloured and softened by time.'

Flora copied him – the stones felt warm to the touch – oddly comforting. Weathered and coloured and softened by time – he could have been describing her, really. She wished, at that precise moment, that she was a course of weathered old stones that had his hands roving so affectionately over her knobbly bits. In any case she was smiling and could not stop. Well, if he didn't like the way she looked when she smiled, too bad. 'Yes, they are.' She said. 'Nice to think some old things can be called beautiful.'

He laughed too.

She knelt down – a little gingerly – next to him and pointed to the stone. 'It's here. See the carved figures – 1557 and the initials A and C intertwined and her swan below the ducal coronet of Cleves. There's been some fancy carving, too, but most of it has been covered up or worn away.'

'Marble,' said Ewan. 'Lovely veining.' It was a relief for Flora to stop crawling – the knees were now hinting at strike action – and Flora was grateful for the lovely veining which kept them in one place for at least half a minute of knee recovery time. 'Very odd place to put it isn't it?' she said eventually, with just a hint of reproach. 'Right down low. Just above knee level. That's the other mystery. Why put it there?'

Ewan stared at it for a moment or two. Then he nodded. 'It occurs to me,' he said, 'that when Dilly and I went to Egypt –'

'Oh when was that?'

'For our honeymoon,' he said, very curtly. 'Or part thereof.' He might have added, from the tone of his voice, *and that's an end of it.*

Flora thought that Ewan knew how to stop being ordinary when it counted. Egypt for a honeymoon. How wonderful. An image of rain and the Isle of Wight swam into her mind – and was swiftly let out again by the back door.

'What about Egypt and this wall, then?' she asked, as matter-of-factly as she could.

His good-natured smile returned. 'When we were going round some of the ancient places the guides pointed out that though the walls looked as if they were only a few feet high, they were originally much higher – much, much higher – and a lot of their original structure had been covered up by time or by other buildings or by making way for other buildings. In the same way, this wall must have been considerably higher when it was originally built.'

Suddenly Flora remembered Anna's letter to Henry citing 'the fruition of your noble presence which I shall esteem for a great benefit . . .' There was a lesson there. So she clasped her hands and said, 'Oh how clever of you. Of course. That will be it. The stone would have been higher once. You are wonderful.'

Ewan looked pleased.

Well, she did think it was clever.

Now he was running his hands over the surrounding stones

and nodding. 'Look,' he said.

She looked.

'See the curve.' She saw the curve.

'It's been a lodestone.'

She nodded. 'So it has.'

He smiled. 'Do you know what a lodestone is?'

She smiled back. 'Haven't a clue,' she said contentedly.

He kindly explained.

There, bent low, bathed in pink and gold light, quite hidden by the line of hawthorns and elder, she was given a little lesson in stresses and strains whilst struggling as best she could with her own kneewards version of them. It was intimate and friendly and very, very secret where they were. She shuffled a bit nearer on her knees but the knees were no soldiers of Valentine and objected quite unpleasantly – nevertheless she persisted for it crossed her mind that one day, and not too far off, there would be no more contemplation of a leg-up, or over, or whatever the terminology was because she just wouldn't be able to – get a leg up, or over – she'd be too old and dilapidated. She might never get a chance to be in such a position, albeit an uncomfortable one, with him again – why, they could be doing anything hidden away here and no one would know . . . But just as she took her courage in both knees and moved towards him – he stood up – tie trailing from pocket like a schoolboy. 'This is a very beautiful old wall,' he said. And proceeded to creep along the length of it and round its right angle, pulling at the tussocky grass and peering hopefully as each course of stones was revealed.

Flora followed as best she could. He's going at a lick for someone of his age, she thought irritably. Flora was getting very concerned now about the way her own joints were reacting to this enforced bending, the ankles weren't doing too well either. If she didn't stand up soon she might have to be helped, which would hardly be a sensual moment of delight between the two of them. She shuffled along a little further trying to concentrate on easing herself into a more comfortable position

– when he stopped. 'As I thought,' he said. 'It must once have been the top of a gateway. Look at the way these stones are laid.'

'Well that's marvellous,' she said, and stood up, hiding the creakings and her little gasp of relief with 'Brilliant, Holmes. But how does that help us with the dates?'

They both peered at the span of stones. 'It doesn't exactly,' he said. 'But it means that the date of her death was built into the old manor at some point and for some reason and in a place of some importance – where it would be seen. It would not have been cheap to do – not a whole new door or gateway.'

Flora nodded. 'There's nothing in the records of the place that I can find – nor was anything found out by Joe Farrell or Edward.'

'Well – it won't necessarily be registered anywhere. But there were bound to be other changes and improvements over the years – as it passed from hand to hand. I know all about that from conveyancing. Expansions, retractions, new boundaries, settlement . . . Not all of which will be noted – as I know to my clients' cost sometimes . . .'

'At least I'll know what I'm looking for now. A new gateway. Built –' She considered for a moment. 'Built – according to the dating of the carvings – when Elizabeth was on the throne – just before she died, in fact. Well – that's a good enough bit of detective work to start with. And it calls for a celebration.'

Elizabeth again. Her head was buzzing with all the new information. 'How about another cup of tea?'

Ewan nodded. 'Good,' he said, and undid another button of his shirt. It was a warm evening. Perfect, in fact, for anything. And back through the deepening light of evening they went. Dilly was not mentioned but as they arrived at the back of the house Flora's telephone was beeping away. Ewan patted the empty pocket of his jacket, tutted, and then looked at his watch. He made an odd swallowing sound. It was past seven o'clock. 'I've left my phone at the office,' he said, surprised.

'Where did the time go?' He looked at Flora as if she might have the answer and it was to her credit that she did not say how it flew when you were having fun.

'That'll be Hilary,' she said as she put the kettle on. 'I'll call her back. She's so interested in all this.'

He looked relieved. Flora checked the number. It was the Beeches. Oh, have another gin, she thought crossly, and pressed the wipe button.

She felt so pleased with it all that Flora took courage and decided to have a glass of wine instead of tea. 'I hope you don't think it's too early,' she said cheerfully. At least her knees had settled down again. Age was creeping and she just wasn't ready for it. She had read recently that red wine could be bad for joints – it was among the pointers to better health in one of those leaflets that make you feel quite ill while waiting at the doctor's surgery. It seemed that red wine was extremely good for the heart – which was really unfair since there was nothing wrong with hers. Red wine and knees and heightened arthritic acidity – was this all that loomed ahead in her empty nest? Or might she be standing at the threshold of the beginning of a whole new way of life? She turned to say something – anything – that might tempt him to look at her stall. It was on the tip of her tongue – and then Ewan said, 'And how is Hilary?' And it was gone.

'Bearing up is the term for it, I think,' she said, half relieved.
'It'll take a while. They were very close, her and Edward.'

'My darling daddy,' said Flora with a touch more heightened arthritic acidity than she should.

But he was shading his eyes and looking out at the paddock. 'It's a lovely spot here,' he said. 'I'm glad you didn't sell up and move in with her.' He said it innocently enough but there was every indication that he knew perfectly well what was going on.

'I love it here far too much,' she said. 'And you must come and visit whenever you like.' Which was as much as she dared say. She poured her glass of wine and put it on the table beside the teacup and saucer. It was nice to see two things set on the table again, comforting.

While she stood in the kitchen dreamily waiting for the water to boil for his tea and thinking that if she tried very hard she could just about imagine what life might have been had she married someone like Ewan – that this coming together, this perfect harmony reached at the end of a beautiful day, might be a normal experience – he leaned against the doorway and watched the sun finally fading away to a pale pinkish purple glow and looked as much at ease as she felt. So she plucked up courage and said, 'There's an exhibition opening in London and the Louvre portrait of Anna of Cleves has come back to England – along with a lot of contemporary portraits – royal women in the sixteenth century – turbulent times – all that – some by the same painter who painted her, Hans Holbein. And it did cross my mind that we could go and see it . . . With her Hurcott connection and everything.'

'You and Hilary?' he said politely, still staring at the darkening sky. 'That'll be nice.'

'No – well yes – I suppose – but she's very busy at the moment and I thought you and I could go. If you were interested. I've done so much research on her and she is fascinating, quite fascinating . . . And I'd like it.' Suddenly it sounded very lame . . . *I'd like it*. Hardly enticing. She found herself crossing her fingers and squeezing her eyes shut as she spoke. 'Just a thought,' she said. 'You'll be busy. But I just thought . . .'

Squeeze, squeeze, squeeze.

'Good idea,' he said enthusiastically. 'I've always been interested in local history – partly what I do I suppose. But of course Edward being Edward really got stuck into it. He was tremendously dedicated to things like that. Ahead of his time, really. I never seemed to get interested in anything very much. Except golf. And fish.'

Flora turned her back and added to the eyes tight shut her worst possible face-pulling – and that, she knew, was saying something. It helped her frustration a little as she slopped boiling water into the pot. Edward. Hrmph.

Ewan, still lost in gazing at the deepening sky, went on. 'And now, suddenly, people seem to have woken up to the fact their history is important. Everyone wants to find out about the past or their ancestors. As if by doing that it will help to make sense of the present.'

'I think what's remarkable is that it shows us that we're all basically still just the same. I've always thought that was history's real value.'

'Have you?' he said. He sounded slightly surprised. Maybe he, too, thought that Flora having an idea of her own was a *rara avis*.

'Yes I have,' she said, louder than she meant to sound, and began stirring the tea. She had used her prettiest Spode pot. *Rara avis* indeed. She'd show him. 'I've been interested in history for years – and years.' Even louder. 'It was me who introduced Edward to it, really.' She threw the teaspoon down with a clatter.

Ewan blinked and looked a little nervous. 'Well,' he said gently, 'that's lucky then, Flora. No reason why all your hard work shouldn't be enjoyed by the whole village. We can all get involved. It might be good for our collective soul. As you say – a reminder of just how small and inconsequential we are – Kings and Princes and labourers alike are but fleeting. All golden lads and lasses must like chimney sweepers come to dust.'

'It'll need time to brew,' said Flora, mollified.

'Nice pot,' he said.

'Thank you.'

'If I know anything about Edward,' said Ewan, running his finger down the door lintel and scrutinising its paintwork, 'it will be along the lines of Out of Chaos, Flora, you have brought forth Order . . . Get into a muddle, sometimes, those whacky geniuses.' He looked at her and smiled with just enough collusion to make her forgive him.

She turned away from him and began pouring milk into the cup. 'And you'd really like to go and see the portrait?'

239

'I think it's a great idea.'

Released from gurning and eye-squeezing and finger crossing and feelings of frustration, Flora nearly fell over with pleasure. How extraordinarily nice, she thought. I have made a suggestion and he does not – like Edward – snort with derision. 'So you'll definitely come?'

'Definitely. I think my artistic soul's ready for an overhaul. You know what they say about lawyers.' He laughed a little sadly and Flora longed to say that his soul didn't need it at all.

She poured his tea. Nice and dark. And returned the teapot to the bench. Then, absentmindedly she handed him the glass of red wine. Absentmindedly he took it. And sipped it. She picked up the teacup and said thoughtfully, 'It just seems to me that Anna of Cleves was much maligned and if – through looking at the history of the village – we can do something about correcting that historical opinion, then we should.'

He said, 'We can all go on a visit to the exhibition and pay homage . . . United in something more important than wheelie bins for once.'

Oh no – thought Flora – Oh no . . .

She had a sudden, awful image of the whole community of Hurcott Ducis coming up to London on a charabanc and crowding her out in her moment of triumph. Foot would be yawning, the Reverend Arthur pontificating, Myra and Betty vying for statement space . . . She'd be lost in the opinionated stampede, for who would expect her, Flora, to have anything much to say?

The brain can go woolly with shock, or it can sharpen. Desperation is a wonderful mentor, Flora discovered. 'Do you know,' she said, 'what I'd really like to do?'

'No,' he said.

He was smelling the wine now, cradling the glass in his hand, rubbing the ball of his thumb on its curved underbelly.

I'll bet you don't, she thought sadly, looking with longing at that caressing thumb.

Out loud she said, 'Well – before anyone else from Hurcott

goes up to see the portrait, I'd like to go on my own – well – with you if you will – just to be able to see it quietly again. I've become so involved over these weeks that it feels as if I'll be going to see a friend – and I wouldn't want to overwhelm her.'

It was possibly the silliest speech she had ever made but it came from the heart. Ewan's eyes glowed with sympathy and understanding. 'Absolutely,' he said, 'and then we can tell the village all about the exhibition afterwards and they can organise it for themselves . . .'

'Oh yes,' said Flora, her heart thumping near to a faint. 'It's on for ages, the show. I could give a little talk about it all beforehand – in the village hall. Tell them about the stone and everything to do with Anna.'

Stop there, she told herself, as the words *over* and *egging* and *pudding* came to mind, stop there.

'Yes,' he said, sipping, smelling, savouring and letting his thumb rove where it would. 'It would be good to do something here. We don't do very much as a village any more – well I suppose we're nearer the size of a small town – but this puts a bit of collective heart back into things.' He laughed. 'Sir Randolph will probably claim her as one of his ancestors and try to pinch the stone – or get Foot to dig it out. But we can make such a song and dance about group ownership that he wouldn't dare touch it.'

'Well – we'll just have to emphasise what a survivor she was and how this stone represents that and must be kept where everyone can see it. A lesson for all our lives. Those were hard times to survive well in. The whole century was full of dissent and friction. All the Tudors were kept on their toes.' Survivor, thought Flora, and a very little tinkling bell began a-tinkling.

'I find the Hurcott connection with Anna really touching. She came here when things got more dangerous than usual in English politics – and all the religious struggles. She'd be made safe at Hurcott – out of the way, overlooked, could worship as she chose, dress as she liked, do whatever she wanted and no one would be there to rebuke her. The villagers would leave her alone and the gentry who came to visit would be the sensible, unambitious types, happy to be away from the court with nothing on their minds to cause her anxiety. She was liked, you know. People enjoyed being in her company. Even her stepdaughters, who were at daggers drawn between themselves, loved her and visited her together. Maybe even here. I can imagine everyone loving the peace and quiet and fun and simple pleasures of Anna's household . . . She was famously a good cook and sport –'

'Sounds like my kind of woman,' said Ewan playfully.

'And enjoyed her wines . . .'

He did not flinch.

'Quite similar to myself, in fact.' Flora took the glass from his hand and sipped.

Now, of course, was the other moment. Fate had sent two. Flora could not make it clearer than this – short of pointing to herself and saying Take Me. Just how long could a silence linger before it became pregnant? Ewan looked at the glass, and then at her. 'Wasn't this supposed to be yours?' he said.

She handed it back. 'We can share it.' She moved nearer. He looked at his watch. 'Good Lord,' he said, 'is that the time? It's nearly eight.' He kept his head bent low over his wrist. But she saw that the tips of his ears were red. She took the glass and drank again and waited till their eyes met.

'What's the time now?' she asked, laughing despite herself. Ewan was more scared than she was.

He looked surprised and said, 'About one minute past. And I must go.'

'Must you?' She poured a little more wine into the glass.

'Solicitors and clients,' he said, 'very bad combination after dark.'

'And friends?'

'Perfectly acceptable,' he said, smiling with relief.

There were long shadows in the kitchen now and the walls were lit by that thick golden light of last sun before it sinks on the horizon. 'And leaves the world to darkness, and to me . . .'

she said, slipping past him out into the garden again, and sitting on a chair. She looked towards the paddock and the wall and said, 'Come and sit down and enjoy the last bit of the day. It's a time I love. Edward would never sit down for long. Always active, always on the go.'

She heard, rather than saw, him sit down next to her. Once she was sure he was settled she turned her chair to face him. He looked quite at home, quite comfortable. 'Oh, I'll sit and stare any time of the day or night,' he said. 'Especially on summer evenings like this. And with a glass of good Médoc in my hand.'

'Is it?' she said. 'I just opened a bottle from the cellar at random.'

'Château Briolet,' he said, 'and why not?'

Why not indeed, she thought, but the game was – for the moment – over.

He rolled another sip of wine over his tongue. 'Go on about our German Queen who's a bit like you.'

'Well, from what I've read her life was not quite so good after Henry died. Well, it wasn't for anyone, of course, unless they toed the Protestant line. We should remember, you know, that people really cared about their souls in those days. Whenever I go into an old church or cathedral and see how bashed about it is I have to remind myself that people did it believing it was God's will . . . We've come a long way since then, perhaps too far . . . Anyway – maybe markers, stones, were important both to break down or build up – to the rigid they represented idolatry, to the free mind they represented continuity, strength of purpose. I think that stone is a marker of Anna's qualities, her qualities that history decided were of no consequence and usefully forgotten. If I can find the connection between the late dating and the fact that the aged Elizabeth – who was her stepdaughter, then her step-niece, was on the throne – I'm sure it's the key to it all.' The bell had rung for those words and they surprised her. But it seemed the way forward.

He was looking at the beautiful sky and nodded. 'It's all a mystery really. It would be so good to believe in a happy kingdom come . . . That the soul was in good order. I mean, why are we here?' Flora wanted to say that she knew why she was, but managed not to interrupt him. 'If we knew that then we could forgive ourselves a little more for what we do on earth now.' He smiled at her.

'Oh, you – you're a good man. A very good man.'

He stood up. 'Am I?' he said.

'I think so.'

'And you are a very good woman.'

She moved towards him.

'And I must go,' he said.

'You see?' she said. 'You are a good man.'

'Not really,' he said, looking up at the sky again. 'Not really good at all.'

'Well – whatever you think. But *I* think that's exactly why we look for ancient connections. To remind ourselves that our human goodness was always in us. As well as our human badness, of course. While the world was being torn apart, Anna came down here and lived among the villagers and life continued its proper course. Do you see? And somebody, many years after she died, thought her life was good enough and worth marking with a stone. A big, heavy, indestructible reminder that someone once lived and was good. Which she was. As we can all be if we want.' Why, Flora, she thought, you sound quite intelligent, if a little soppy.

'The certainty of history mixed with the unshakeable goodness of the human spirit ruled by a benign God?' He looked into his nearly empty glass. She took it. And drained it and said, 'I'm not giving you any more, you know.'

'I should hope not.'

I'd give you Edward's entire cellar if you asked, she thought.

'Perhaps,' he said, 'the past just shows up the thinness of the way we live now. You see every aspect of the black heart of wickedness in the buying and selling of property and the making and ending of marriage, believe me. It's more than thinness, it's degeneracy. And it sets up a terrible expectation – as if you can buy goodness with plastic surgery – give yourself the face of an angel but keep the soul of a devil inside.'

'Goodness,' she said, and touched her face.

He reached out and touched her cheek.

'At least you've never even considered plastic surgery – and you certainly could have.'

'Why sir, your compliments have a very cruel back hand . . .'

He quickly took his hand away. 'I didn't mean –'

'I know,' she said. And went back indoors. She put the glass in the sink and switched on the lights. The magical hour was over. She had lost. The pretty Spode teapot sat there disapprovingly. She picked it up.

'To be beautiful and rich is not something either of us have to worry about, Flora,' he said. 'That's not an insult, it's a compliment. If you have both then you are afraid that time will remove one or the other.'

'You're right,' she said. 'Of course you are. At least we don't have to worry on either score.'

Just for a moment their eyes met across the teapot. Hers defiant and his – well – affectionate certainly – but also surprised. 'A blessing to be plain and ordinary,' she said, and laughed and just for that moment she thought she probably meant it.

Then Flora decided to do some small thing for Anna. She raised a finger at him. 'No more calling my Queen Anna the Flanders Mare then.'

'No more Flanders Mare, I promise.'

'You know,' she said, 'for all the fuss and bother they caused, Anna only ever referred to her looks once in all the mentions of her throughout her years in England. And that was after Henry had chopped off the head of her replacement, Catherine Howard. It was rumoured he would take Anna back but he didn't, and he chose a widow called Katherine Parr instead of Anna. Anna went slightly hoity-toity over it –

showed surprise at his choice – and remarked that she was the more beautiful – a fact to which several contemporary sources attested – but whether she said it out of huff at not being made Queen afterwards, or whether she said it in a moment of triumph for all the unfair things said in the past, we'll never – quite – know. But I just think it makes her seem much more human. I know I'd do the same as her – if it were true.'

If she hoped that Ewan would change his mind and immediately do a Sir Galahad and say that Flora was, indeed, beautiful he did not. Instead he leaned his bottom on the edge of the Aga and said, 'I'm looking forward to seeing this paragon. We must go soon.'

'Yes,' she said, feeling foolishly thrilled.

'But now –' He pushed himself away from the stove's comforting warmth – even on a summer's night it was seductive to the bottoms of men – less flesh on them Flora supposed – and said, 'Now I really must go –' He checked his watch, sucked in his breath, looked suitably regretful and that, at least, was a comfort. When the door closed behind him she stood in the hall for a moment and hugged herself. 'I have a date,' she said. 'A date. And the Pink Pike's head has rolled.'

Flora then leapt into the sitting room and watched his shadowy progress as he toddled off down the road, past the wheelie bins and into the distance along by the pond – the misty semi-moonlight shining on his little bald patch, his hand tapping the side of his leg. She felt that comforting tenderness for him all over again. He was the antithesis of Edward. How unfair it was that nice, kind Ewan was so enviably loyal to a wife who drank and mounted horses the wrong way round and went around being rude to people, while intolerant, brilliant, unkind Edward had a wife who never caused him a moment of serious grief in his life and he could barely praise her mashed potato. Self-pity was a very dreadful thing, she knew, but really, who better was there to feel sorry for you than yourself?

She turned from the window. At least she had arranged to go

to London with him, and alone. At least she would not have Myra and Mrs Vicar and all the others patting her shoulders with kind, unbearable sympathy. Even if their visit together was more to do with curiosity about a dead queen's facial qualities than romantic desire. It was another chance. Something had been said between them tonight – only Flora was not exactly sure what.

She returned to her researches with renewed vigour. It was a doorway, that much she now knew, and it was not a paltry expense. It was also the product of a cultivated mind. Two virgin survivors were in her investigations now – Anna and Elizabeth – and if she could only find the link, if there was a link, then perhaps it would bring with it the answer to the anomalies of the datestone. Virgins? Survivors? There might, just, be a connection there. The truth of Anna's wedding night, or the lack of it, seemed to be one of the last great mysteries surrounding her. Did they, or didn't they . . .

12

God Send Me Well To Keep

The catalogue experts spent most of the afternoon in the harshly lit storeroom. Up and down they paced musing together over snippets of information from various sources, deciding which morsels of enlightenment about which of the portraits would grace the exhibition walls and catalogue. Anna watched them. Much of their morselling was complimentary to Elizabeth, the Great Queen in her Ditchley splendour. The portrait of her sister, Mary, has mysteriously yet to arrive from the National collection whence Elizabeth came hot-foot leaving Mary behind. Anna knows she will be wondering, sourly, why yet again she has been trumped by the Whore Boleyn's daughter. Much as she tried, and much as both were fond of her, neither Elizabeth nor Mary were reconciled for long, even in Anna's lifetime.

The experts stopped in front of her portrait and ticked it off their list. They half-heartedly suggested that they might return if there is something to write beyond the well-known anecdotes of her failure to please, her plainness, her ghastly clothes, her likening to a Flanders Mare and her dull wit. 'It's a fine portrait,' mused the senior of the pair in another of his profound musings. 'Holbein could do no wrong despite the paucity of subject matter . . .' Anna, still and correct in her frame, feels humiliated all over again. The other expert, though not so expert yet, a sweet-faced young girl with perfect teeth and a double-barrelled name, straight out of the Courtauld, nodded her agreement. They have not looked thinks Anna sadly. *Paucity of subject matter* was new and the barb found its mark. As if she had not lived interestingly in those interesting Tudor times. As if she had not lived with dignity and loyalty, too, when others, better placed than her, could not manage it. She looked across at Elizabeth and Elizabeth acknowledged her with the briefest connection. Anna, firm in her frame, had the look about her of a woman who thinks that eventually – whatever the odds – her day would come.

Both Queens watched the experts pause before the portrait of Jane Seymour, now properly unwrapped and propped against the wall. Cleaned and brilliant its Holbein colours sang out. 'Exquisite,' they breathed.

Both Queens slightly pursed their lips. Jane Seymour, those pursed lips say, was no beauty. It is the painting that is beautiful.

This is what the experts always say about Anna, that it is the painting not the portrait, but in her apparently modest heart Anna thinks she is the more appealing of the two. Jane's prissy mouth and flat, pale eyes do not excite. It is Holbein's colours that thrill. And anyway, thinks Anna, allowing herself a touch of hubris, the mythology of Jane Seymour's perfect marriage was untrue. Anna learned from one of her gossiping Ladies that a short while before Jane became pregnant Henry kept himself from the Queen's presence because she spoke out too readily in defence of the Pilgrimage of Grace. Unwise lady. Henry was the King who married a woman for her wit and then spent the rest of his life attempting to quieten it. The lesson that Queen Jane learned with difficulty came easily to Anna. She never crossed the King, he admired her for it, and she survived very well. You never, she thinks, find that written about me in a catalogue. That instinct for dignified survival was something she might have passed on to Elizabeth and Mary but the Tudors were not naturally good at dignity. Too passionate, by far.

Why, wonders Anna, couldn't the catalogue experts record the words of Marillac, the French ambassador, who praised her wit and vivacity and wrote of her kindly. In those difficult years it was perhaps better to be known for one's wit than for one's beauty – though Marillac later wrote that she had both qualities. It would be nice if they acknowledged that now but no – it is always the old insults they prefer. 'I wonder,' says one of the experts, 'whether Henry really did find her so repellent that he couldn't make it with her in bed?' Anna colours. It is always that question. The wedding night. Did we or did we not consummate our marriage? Did I, or did I not, cause Henry's impotency? Was I, or was I not, left a virgin for the rest of my life? Well, certainly it was in that marriage bed that the fairy-tale wedding and all the fine trappings of the day crumbled to a stark reality. You could not have found a greater contrast between the preparations and the night.

'It was at Shooters Hill that Henry welcomed me, finally, to London. The crowds were huge, and happy, the river full of decorated craft of every size, some firing canon to welcome me, and all the courtiers were dressed in their furs and velvets. The whole display, that thing the English do with such brilliance, was perfect. I had never known any celebration like it and that it was for me was thrilling beyond measure. I looked very queenly, I think, and Henry looked almost foolish he was so weighed down with jewels. He was a hulking jewelled giant – his hat, his cloth-of-gold gown and slashed crimson coat, the collar about his thick neck – all ablaze with gemstones and gold. As if that could make him attractive. But he played the willing husband to perfection and he was impressive. In our jewels and in the January sunlight we both seemed on fire, which was the effect the court and the people wanted and which Henry's Masters of Ceremonials had arranged. Those who saw us could only be humbled by our shining majesty. We shimmered in our cloth of gold – and shivered in all that wintry cold – but the tents in which we waited, separately, to come out to meet each other were swathed with warm hangings and perfumed with heated spices. These were the last moments of being made to feel as if I were the most precious woman in the world.'

Sad it was but neither of us wished to be alone with the other.

'How this point of my story has mangled the minds of men – and women – for half a millennium. Did Henry, or did he not, consummate our marriage that night? How well it has been documented, and how cruelly, that he said he had felt my breasts and my belly and found me not to be a maid. As if he were any judge when he was fooled so easily by Queen Catherine. This I can say – that I was a true maid when I married him. Though whether I was still a maid after our marriage I do not know. Certainly Henry did not lie still and silent with me but I was in such a state of terror and repulsion at the sight of that gross body that I can remember almost nothing of what took place. Gone were the jewels and grandeur, now he was white-gowned and gross and had eaten so much and drunk so voraciously that he was red and hot as if he were in a rage and came heavily perfumed into the bed. I lay there while he lifted my nightdress and felt my body in its most intimate parts. He rubbed against me, put his hand on my belly and then below, and the shock of all this sent me numb with fear. Muttering and murmuring, he was, his mouth working on my shoulder and my neck, and there was nothing of pleasure in it for either of us I think. But he was a king and my husband, this was spoken of as a holy moment and I knew something of what was expected, which was acquiescence to what was ordained by God as good between a man and a woman. When that great leg of Henry's, with its putrid smell half hidden in the pungent scent of roses and other heavy perfumes, moved near to me, the vileness of it fairly knocked the breath from my body. How thankful I was when the rubbings and graspings and wet-mouthed wipings stopped and Henry simply kissed my forehead and said, 'Goodnight sweetheart,' and sighed and slept. "God send me well to keep" was the motto I chose as Henry's bride. It was well chosen. Nothing better could reflect what I felt that night. I yielded myself to God – and my fate. As the new Queen of England I could only hope that children would be my reward. Carved above me were the lewd and pregnant cherubs of the great bedhead to remind me of what Henry and I were expected to achieve. For all I knew, or cared that night, we had achieved it.'

'This,' says the senior of the two catalogue experts, pausing at a gap on the wall opposite Anna, 'is where the Mary Tudor portrait will hang when it arrives. We will hang it quite near Anne of Cleves – but not next to her – that would be too close.' He peers and smiles. 'Two rather frumpy women together. Not good. We will hang Mary next to her sister – tremendous contrast – Gloriana and Bloody Mary – and we'll hang Anne of Cleves opposite them both. That will show the Ditchley to perfection. It will be the one the press want to use. They always do.'

The sweet-faced assistant expert nods at her colleague's comments. The Ditchley portrait is safe ground for publicity. Elizabeth, thinks Anna, is a celebrity. But what does this modern young woman know yet? What does she bring to the pictures she sees? She knows – as Anna knows – how to read a painting. That a skull represents mortality, that a pomegranate is resurrection, a hare means lust, an owl means wisdom – and so on. She does not yet know how to look at the heart of the matter. How to look at the paint and beyond it. That way of looking takes a few more rings on the tree of life and Anna has half a millennium's worth of them.

Hearing all this banal chatter about publicity and press and beauty or not, Anna is glad that Mary has yet to arrive, for she will be Bloody Mary to the experts and Mary finds the title even more painful than Anna finds her Flanders Mare, though there is good reason for it. If she cannot remember her wedding night, she can remember that she lived through enough of the burnings and executions of those Marian times – heard about Latimer and Ridley (wept as did half of England to hear that the pious Bishop of London took nearly an hour to burn, screaming all the way to oblivion) – heard about the ordinary folk whose ignorance sent them to the stake. Anna escaped to Hever, Bletchingly, Hurcott whenever she could. It was hard to be Mary's friend during those years.

It was, thinks Anna, the wisdom and diplomacy that she learned when she arrived in England that made her choose her last public appearance to be Mary's wedding to Philip of Spain. Those Tudors would never listen. Anna knew it was not a good match and dared to suggest that a far better husband for Mary would be the Archduke Ferdinand of Austria, the Emperor's brother – but Mary declined. Philip was merely ambitious for the English throne, and not in love, and he made the poor and careless husband Anna predicted. Mary suffered rejection all over again. First from her beloved father when he married Anne Boleyn, now her husband. It was as if by burning her way through the love of the people Mary could burn her way to Philip's Catholic heart. And it was cruel. Anna lived away from it all as much as she could, in a quiet, virtually unseen, existence. It was safest, though Mary loved her. No one was truly safe in those times and Anna read the signs. She knew very well how to keep her head low, her name from the lips of spies, her character unblemished, and she was safe in her religion. One of the strongest of the bonds between her and Mary was that Anna, unlike the much spied-on and harried Elizabeth, was a true Catholic. Mary wisely never questioned her. One or two of Anna's servants were removed during Mary's reign for holding the sacraments in contempt, but Anna never suffered so much as a shadow of a stain on her name.

Much later, to add a few more insults to their reputations the plainness of these two women was considered to be the basis for their friendship. If it were not so pitiable it would be funny to Anna. As if two women would look each other over and finding each other to be unhandsome would say, 'Yes – she's got a really plain face – we can be friends because I'm plain, too.' What more foolish notion could there be? Rather, they were two high-born women, living in difficult times and fond of each other, one of whom kept the bond supple by a liberal dousing of discreet good sense.

Anna shakes her head. How little these moderns can know of being a woman of intelligence in those times, she thinks. Even Henry's kind Queen-nurse Katherine Parr nearly lost her life for being intelligent, for arguing points of theology with her apparently loving husband who very nearly took her off to the Tower for it. History might paint these women out or change them – but so it was. How, thinks Anna, the experts could possibly call me slow-witted when I learned to balance such political and religious pitfalls, and retain the affection of all, remains a mystery. Or it should. For it was not easy. I cannot say how I achieved it. Instinct and intelligence is the nearest explanation. And the very human love of simply being alive. It makes you quite amenable.

Elizabeth. So hard it was to be a friend to her. As a young woman during her sister's reign she was more watched than any princess in history. Keeping a friendship with both Mary and Elizabeth at the same time – as adults on the Tudor stage – held its dangers, Anna remembers – and when Mary began to loathe her sister and watch her for plots and suspect anyone who came into contact with her – the success of Anna's continuing friendship to both was a valuable achievement. Particularly notable to Elizabeth.

On her way back from imprisonment in the Tower and on her way to her years of imprisonment in Woodstock, Elizabeth spent a night at Richmond Palace. Anna returned it to the Crown many years before but she still had use of it. At least Elizabeth would have good memories of her times there with her step-aunt before the world turned on her. Later Anna learned that Elizabeth had talked of that night as one she spent 'doleful with fear'. The contrast must have been great. But the next morning, so the rumours flew, when she left the Palace for the barge and Woodstock, the people gathered to see her – Henry's daughter for sure – and they rang bells to celebrate her release from the Tower, and they cheered her and they showed their loyalty and their love for her so that Mary's men warned the crowds to be silent and the bell ringers were pursued.

Elizabeth could take comfort from knowing, just as Anna once took comfort, that the people were with her – that it was hard to harm one who was so loved. People power. It has saved many from the gallows. It undoubtedly saved Elizabeth, and it saved Anna from a more deprived existence. *God send me well to keep* indeed.

It is late now. The portraits have re-settled themselves. Those that have been singled out for special mention are content. Those that have been given the briefest of entries sigh and accept it as the usual way of things. What, after all can a portrait do? Except Anna, who feels peevish.

'Does no one ask why, in a time when bad words were rife, no bad word was ever written of me? Does no one ask why my tomb is in Westminster Abbey instead of somewhere half forgotten and obscure? And on the right hand of it, too? How could I be buried there if I was considered a dull woman of no importance? If the portrait owned a foot, its subject might copy its onetime royal husband and have stamped it. "Come, then, Flora Chapman," she whispers crossly to the dusty air, "and come soon."'

13

Touching Stones

Reading about Anna's wedding night made Flora think about her own. Something she had not done for years. Their bed was hardly remarkable, unlike poor Anna's where nothing was left to the imagination; a cheerfully lustful cupid and nothing small about him and another cupid with a full and pregnant belly to show exactly what was expected of Anna and how it was to be achieved. Not surprising, thought Flora, if she failed. It was not unlike offering a Tudor version of a porno movie to get an innocent girl going. After Henry's marriage to Catherine Howard this great bed was banished by Henry, and a new, more delicate bed, made by a Frenchman and decorated with pearls, replaced it. The other bed was consigned to Scotland where it remains. Perhaps the Scottish nobles still needed help? Who didn't, Flora thought, remembering. There was something of a reminder, too, in the scent of the freesias on the kitchen table . . . Her love of them remained with her, even when her love of marriage and love of husband had long gone . . .

What a gauche thing she was, too. Although she was expected to throw her bouquet for the small group of guests who waved the new Mr and Mrs Chapman off to the station – she could not bear to part with the delicate, sweet-smelling thing, and hid it in her jacket. Wrapped like a baby it was, and a bit crumpled when they finally took their seats on the train to Lymington. Flora wanted to honeymoon abroad and the Isle of Wight was the compromise. 'You go on a boat to get there,' said Edward. And so they did. Shades of what was to come.

Edward booked them into a small hotel near Cowes and purchased and packed a yachting cap. It was a vile embarrassment, that cap, for he wore it everywhere. It was one thing to hang over the rail on the jetty while watching the yachts come in and go out, but it was quite another to wear it when they went strolling about the town. It rained a lot, she remembered, which didn't help. At the end of the four days it looked like a squashed liquorice allsort perched on his head. But he enjoyed wearing it and she agreed with crossed fingers that it suited him.

She tried, now, to remember the details beyond the yachts and the horrible cap but that first night was only a very dim recollection. Rosie told her to put a towel on the bed, which she did. Only she never asked her sister why. So she could certainly remember Edward's surprise when she flung a bath towel over them both . . . Bless his heart, she thought, for he never questioned it. It was all right, the sex, as far as she remembered, and if the landlady did find the sheets a nuisance nothing was ever said. In theory Flora knew what having It meant, in practice she couldn't remember being sure. Presumably Anna was the same. She knew, yet did not know. The big difference was that Flora really liked Edward – really wanted to be married to him with all that it entailed. Whereas Anna, surely, must have been horrified at what met her when she arrived. No wonder they divorced. Rosie once said that she liked an older lover for the tenderness and gratitude and time they brought to the business, but Flora could not imagine Henry VIII having any of those qualities. And – thinking about it – Rosie was right – they were the only qualities that could make the experience of such an age gap worthwhile. Well – that or a large cheque. Thinking about it, Anna had certainly managed that . . .

*

The day after Ewan's visit, Hilary rang. With thoughts of Anna in mind, Flora was amenable. 'Well,' she said, 'I am glad you rang. I've been wanting a few words with my favourite daughter . . .'

258

And Hilary – sounding surprised – actually played the game and said – quite lightly for her – 'Only daughter, Mother. Unless there's something you're not telling me.'

And then the *History* was broached. Flora took a deep breath.

'I'm so busy with it,' she said. 'It's coming along very nicely. Though I'm still trying to find a reason for that stone. Elizabeth's the connection, I'm sure of it. Just not how.'

'Well how important is it to finishing the *History*?' asked Hilary, back to her impatient self.

'Well, Edward was markedly keen to know the truth of it . . . A lot I'd say.'

'Well, hurry up and put your thinking cap on then.' But at least it was said with a degree of kindness.

Elizabeth. At the end of all the midnight oil it seemed to Flora that she could add another long dead monarch to the pile of those she knew intimately.

Hilary said, 'Are you sure there's nothing in Dad's notes?'

'Positive.'

'It's not like him.'

'No,' said Flora. 'He wasn't one to leave any stone unturned . . .'

Would she or wouldn't she?

Hilary laughed.

Flora smiled to herself. They were moving on. 'We'll get there,' she said.

And Hilary replied that she was sure they would.

'Thank you,' said Flora meekly.

'By the way – have you asked Giles to photograph it?'

Now that was good thinking.

'Well – no,' said Flora, 'but it's a good idea. I'll do that.'

'Yes,' said Hilary with great satisfaction. 'It's all coming along amazingly well. You've been brilliant.' Hilary put down the phone. Flora sat down on the floor. There, she thought, goes that flying fairy again. Which conversation added substantially to the guilt she felt at not telling Hilary about the trip to London with Ewan. Still – what were pleasures without a little of that commodity called sin attached to them?

Flora left a message for Giles. Her days were taken up with putting all the notes and scraps of information into order – working at the open window in Edward's old office where the horrible picture of the horrible white cat looked down on her much as the Pike might wish to look given half a chance. But the view of the paddock beyond the window spurred her nicely on towards her six o'clock downing of tools and upping of corkscrew. Anna was no longer a disconnected woman from a distant time, she was a woman like any other – with the same interests then as now. She liked to live well, she liked to have fun and she loved the pleasures of Richmond Palace. It had walkways created by Henry above the beautiful, complex gardens – places for chess and dice and dominoes and cards – places for tennis and archery and bowls – and falconing – places for all manner of merry pastimes. All the things that Anna had come to love about the way the Tudors lived their privileged lives were hers. The endless new frocks and the playing of much sport was as much a part of her new life as were the more homely pleasures of cookery and gardening. With her orphanages she had the fun of children and none of the worries as well as securing her place in the Heaven to come. All in all it sounded to Flora to be a very satisfactory way to live. And kind. Not a bad epitaph. *Epitaph?* Now there was a thought.

*

The sky was pink and lilac and lemon and as beautiful as it seemed to be every evening since Ewan's last visit. She took a bucket and brush and walked across her dewy paddock, enjoying the smell of damp grass and hazy air.

When she reached the stone she ran her hands over its craggy shape until she was sure she felt the presence of its ghost or spirit. Had Anna walked here in this very place, at this very time of day? Not to see the stone, of course, but just to walk around and be free. Her little household – later on not much more than thirty in all – would be more like friends and an extended family than the grand retainers of a Queen – she probably enjoyed that warmth after the cold reception of those first months, and being able to come down here away from the prying eyes of London and its magnificent court would surely have been a relief. It was just not possible to imagine Anna being anything but happy and easy with her household and her servants though she could be just as hardnosed as the next woman in the matter of property. She took what was offered without squeamishness and much of it was dead men's – or women's – shoes as it was for most of the favoured. Henry gave her Hever Castle which she accepted with wonderful heartlessness since it was once Anne Boleyn's home and must carry some ghost of that fallen Queen. And Henry not only offered Anna Cromwell's silver after his execution, but she also had most of his furniture and furnishings, too. Tougher times then, especially in England, and no room for twitchy sentimentality.

Bletchingley was another of her dead man's shoes. It was Sir Nicholas Carew's before he was executed for treason and before that it was owned by the Duke of Buckingham who went the same way. Flora wondered if Anna ever thought about these previous owners. She ran her hand around her neck and had a little shiver at what might have been. At any rate she was shrewd enough to let Bletchingley for a handsome income from Sir Thomas Cawarden, the tenant who complained about the amount of firewood and other items she used for fuel and heating. Who, thinks Flora, does not know the modern-day equivalent of this tenant, the man whose finger ever strays towards the central heating thermostat? Truly, truly there is nothing new under the sun.

Only the gateway existed at Bletchingley now – which was a pity as Anna had stayed there often. Flora visited the place but there was no sign of another stone like Hurcott's and precious little sense of its royal owner. Flora was hoping to see the kitchens but they were long gone. It was at Bletchingley that Anna developed her passion for domestic pursuits – cookery and preserving in particular. It seems that Henry liked to dine at Anna's table, which might, Flora noted, have given him food for thought that he could have been happy with her after all. 'Kissing don't last, cookery do,' said Mrs Thomas Hardy the second. And since Flora had never proved herself a cook, and Edward had strayed, she thought this was probably true.

Anna's receipt books and accounts were full of new recipes and the excitement of finding them was borne out by huge payments to suppliers. She seemed particularly interested in ways with fish and her tastings of wine were also recorded and were endearing. In a good Catholic household it would be a point of dining pride and jealousy, the finding of new ways to serve fish, there being so many meatless days in the religious calendar. Three a week was usual for fish days and pike, eels, lampreys, carp and trout seemed to be the standard fish at her table. Given the strict need to follow the religious laws, being seen to be inventive with fish was the sign, surely, of a good hostess. Which Anna, by all reputes, was. Solace, Anna learned, must be found in the most ordinary of things. Flora thought it was a very wise lesson.

They differed on gardening for which Flora of the half-dead daffodils showed no talent and for which Anna showed much. She grew her own herbs and vegetables and fruits and she liked to hitch up her skirts and get out there and inspect them. Her Hurcott kitchen garden might even have been on this very spot. It was nice to stand by the wall in the sunlight and imagine a time long before when there were fruit trees and herbs and vegetables growing here and when news of the mistress's imminent arrival sent the overseer and his few servants into a flurry of excitement and activity. In her reading Flora had found notes of huge sums paid to gardeners in Anna's accounts, and even larger sums paid to plant suppliers and purveyors of trees, which confirmed that her gardens were another great joy in Anna's life. I will be like that now, thought

Flora. I will. What a lesson this dead queen gave her.

But of course there was also the question of love. Or at least of men in Anna's life. Were there any? Flora was thinking of her own case with Ewan, that even she, plain and unremarkable, had a secret in her heart. Did Anna? There was nothing, not so much as a hint, apart from false and silly stories about the divorced Queen being brought to bed of a child/children in the year after her marriage was ended. This caused some consternation for Henry in case it was his (so much for the virgin) but there was no truth in any of it. How amusing it would be were she to be found to be pregnant by Henry after he announced she was his sister and that he had not consummated their match. The mind, Flora laughed to herself, boggled at how Henry and his creeping advisers would have got around that. Especially if the said infant turned out to be a healthy son. No wonder Henry sent his own physician to tend to her. He reported back that it was false rumour and Henry probably downed the Tudor equivalent of a stiff whisky or two after that.

No – not a hint of a love life. How perfect that solution would be – that the stone was placed there by an illegitimate child, or an aged lover – but no – though she came to be admired for her looks and her ways, Anna, in Henry's lifetime, seems to have been quite content to remain single. Who would dare marry – or even bed – her? Particularly if she gave birth to son after son? And presumably, more to Flora's modern understanding, Henry being Henry would not wish Anna to go on being so well endowed out of the royal coffers if she married again. And who would risk marrying the King's ex-wife who had no dowry to bring? So there was nothing – not a hint of a love life anywhere for Anna nor any suggestion that she wanted one. Scandal free, she was, in an age that was always ready to pounce yet she certainly did not live the life of a nun. Clever or what?

It was mentioned that in Edward's reign, when her income was reduced, Anna said that she would like to go back to

Cleves, but she never did. England really was her home by then. Her mother was dead, her brother said to have strange fits – the Duchies were of little consequence and she was now so well ensconced here that it would have been hard to give up all her English joys. And if she could not take a lover Anna could at least indulge herself in culture. She loved music and she paid frequent sums of money to the Bassano family, Jewish musicians from Venice, who were refugees from the Spanish Inquisition. Her own little court might not be large and grand but they should have music and dancing and Anna would pay for it handsomely, too. Anna might not play herself – she never did learn – and Flora could find no mention that she sang either – but she certainly loved these talents in anyone else and dancing was a great joy in her life. She danced with her step-daughters Mary and Elizabeth, she even danced with the new Queen (Flora wondered, thinking of the little Pink Pike again, if she longed to tread on her replacement's toes). For a provincial German bumpkin she very quickly showed herself to have a natural delight in the higher arts.

Flora put her cheek against the warm stones as if to feel the pulse of the past. It would be much the same here at Hurcott, though the house and estate was smaller than Richmond, Hever or Bletchingley. Anna would travel here with her entourage and make her domestic life and her artistic life suit her needs just as happily if on a smaller scale. There would be revels and sports and feasts, and visitors – those refugees from the stresses of London and the court – and she would enjoy it all. To be happy in a place is a great gift and Anna must have been very happy here as elsewhere. There would hardly be a stone placed in the fabric of the old building if it were not so. In fact, from what Flora read, when Henry died and the boy Edward came to the throne and Anna's income was cut, Hurcott, like Bletchingley, with its lower expenses and smaller estates, would have been a sensible alternative to any of her other, larger, properties.

Even the cold, unimaginative little Edward seems to have

responded to her warmth and to have had a care for her. When he became King he wrote that he had a fondness for his Aunt Anne and strongly urged Thomas Seymour to marry her but Flora could find no comment from Anna at this suggestion. Seymour himself voted with his feet and married Katherine Parr – who was rich in her own right as well as rich as the King's widow – before – it was said with rueful imagination – the King's body was quite cold in its tomb. Anna spent what she had and she never reined in her extravagances entirely. She took too much pleasure in them to give them all up. Flora found large bills for spices and best wax candles and the very latest in kitchen equipment and soft furnishings. Anna, it seemed, would have been a natural subscriber to *House and Garden* and *Country Life* in the twentieth century. And why not? What else did she have? She could remain in the countryside and indulge in all her pleasures and fade into the sunsets, thought Flora, and be safe from the terrors of the cities.

Turning from the wall and looking back at St Lawrence's, along the winding village street, Flora thought that Anna would even have known Hurcott's church and she would probably recognise it today. Not much of the medieval carving was seriously damaged and Flora liked to think that perhaps Anna had helped preserve it, hurling herself across the pious statuary and angelic carvings to stop the blows from rough-handed Protestant vigilantes. She wondered what the vicar would say if she told him her fantasy. Go pink probably. Send for Mrs Vicar.

Well, Flora had read all she could on the subject of Anna and Tudors generally and Elizabeth and Mary in particular, now she had to let it simmer and stew so that she could – with luck – have a Eureka moment. If she did any more research she would go pop. But she had to know the answer before the trip to the exhibition and her confrontation with the Murdoch. Flora wanted to be on safe and firm ground when she took that Gorgon on. She had a little fantasy that Ewan would cheer as she bloodied Miss Murdoch's nose with her distillation of truth. If she could only distil it. There was no simple solution. Anna had no children, no living heirs in the blood sense who might want to place a stone in remembrance of her so long after her death. She was quite cut off from her Cleves descendants, and her Burgundian relatives and all of her original ladies-in-waiting had either returned to Cleves or died. Her father was dead, her mother died without seeing her again, and her sister and brother – with his new family, never seen by Anna – were all that remained in the old palace. Everything Anna knew and held dear was in England but there was not one mention, anywhere, of a special person or special cause that might have held Anna to be precious above the rest. No intimate friendships or taking in any waifs and strays from the court as some genteel persons did at the time – many wards needed guardians and many wanted places in a noble household. But all in all the only connections that Flora could find that were remarked upon and showed any continuity were those with her one-time stepdaughters and her two great friends, the Duchess of Suffolk and the Countess of Arundel – both of whom were long dead by the time the stone came to be fashioned. But Elizabeth, though feeble, was still very much alive.

Elizabeth. It always came back to her. The bell rang louder in Flora's head. Elizabeth. But why?

How she wanted to solve this. Perhaps she would make herself stay out all night until she did so. She knelt beside the stone on those creaking knees of hers and wetting the bristles proceeded to brush away the last traces of lichen and the more tenacious growths of age. Her humming became more resolute as she resisted the creeping thought that it would be nice if one could do the same to oneself with a brush and bucket. Scrub gently away the patina of the past and come fresh and shining into the new. Whatever the new might be. It was such a pleasant task as if washing the face of a friend. When she sat back deciding it was finished the late evening sun reflected on a stone that was quite clean, its lettering even more clear despite the wear and tear of age. The downbent head of the swan, and the circle of the coronet were now properly outlined and sharp – very much like the carving on Anna's grand – though now half hidden – tomb in Westminster Abbey. It was as if Anna had signed her name there.

Flora upturned the bucket and sat on it in much the same pose as Rodin's Thinker and stared. She hoped the pose would help the thought process and she tried thinking very, very hard. A datestone for one's death, but carved when Elizabeth Tudor had been on the throne for forty years. When she was old, afraid, loveless, alone. It surprised Flora to read about those last years. The Elizabethan Age was always taught as golden and glorious but when you looked at Elizabeth's long reign it was beset with difficulties, assassination attempts, false and overweening lovers, religious rebellion and Spanish assaults with such an intensifying of these in her last decade that the throne was almost lost, Elizabeth almost taken prisoner – but again – what could that possibly have to do with Anna? What could the memory of one solitary, long-dead, German queen, almost certainly a dignified virgin when she died, one who was amenable, scandal free, a quiet survivor, mean to someone in those last years of Elizabeth's reign? And since the manor and its lands were still then in the hands of the Crown there was no family in ownership to help trace any clue.

Scandal, scandal. Surviving, surviving . . . That word again. But why? But what? But who? Elizabeth, Gloriana. It had to be connected with her – but why? With the relief much sharper the stone looked much more like the carving of the ducal coronets on Anna's tomb in Westminster. Very like it in fact. When she visited the Abbey, Flora thought that the way the tomb looked was much like the way Anna was remembered now. It was once a grand piece of marble, decorated with semi-precious stones and gilding, with highly wrought carvings – but now it was stripped of all its fine decoration, made ugly by neglect and crowded out by other more recent monuments. The ducal coronets were all that was left of a once finely wrought memorial. And it did not have swans, the romantic symbol of Cleves' tradition, like this carved stone. It was almost as if someone wanted to redress this oversight of neglect and at the same time give Anna her full heraldic honour. Someone who knew about the swans, knew the story . . .

Flora stared at it all the harder. But how – if at all – were the two connected? The neglected tomb and the elegant, thoughtful stone? And then – and then – the clouds seemed to part – and illumination flowed down from the heavens to the upturned bucket and Flora's concentrating face and she was certain that she understood it at last. Revelations were not something that usually happened to Flora – when shafts of illumination were flying about she was usually absent – but sitting there in the deepening light, staring at the wall and the fresh cleaned stone as if it might speak, she suddenly had one. A Revelation. 'But of course –' she shouted to the evening sky. She stood up and the bucket overturned making a clattering rumpus that frightened the dozing birds into shrill complaint. 'Of *course* that is why the stone is there,' she said to them. 'Of *course*. It must be. It's like a crossword puzzle where you get the clue but then have to work out the question . . .' On the whole the bird community did not seem much interested in her sudden cracking of the code. Small-brained creatures, all feathers and no thoughts. Elizabeth, her feet on England, her marriage games of cat and mouse, the lovers, the ambitious lovers, the men who wished to rule her, the scandals. Elizabeth – The Tudor's greatest survivor. But only just.

Flora looked at the stone again, touched it almost reverentially. The fashionable word for it now was *footprint*. She traced its outlines, the swan, the coronet, the ornate *Anno domini 1557*, and she knew.

Picking up the bucket Flora walked home feeling happy. Feeling proud, even. And if it wasn't the last piece of the puzzle and if she was wrong – well – it would just have to do. Now that *would* be something to tell the dreadful Murdoch woman who thought Anna of so little consequence and the Ditchley and its subject so admirable. Miss Murdoch would never look at the portrait of Anna in the same way again when Flora had finished with her.

The following morning Ewan telephoned Flora from his office and they decided on a date for their visit. Ewan then drew a line through his diary page for that day and thought fondly of Flora. She wasn't letting the grass grow. She wasn't sitting around wondering where the golden life had fled. She was getting on with things. His way of getting on with things was golf. You could put a very large amount of your angst into the swing of a club and take a great deal of comfort from the crack of its head on the ball. A very great deal. He felt expansive. It was a good idea of Flora's to go to London to see the exhibition and he was looking forward to it. And since he had noticed something of a *froideur* between Hilary and her mother last time they met, he thought he would do something to help. He nodded to himself and picked up the telephone.

First he called the place where the exhibition was about to open, then he telephoned Hilary. They were of one accord – it would be a nice thing to do – and – as Hilary said – they could make it a little occasion, something to mark and celebrate her father, too. Her mother would like that.

'Exactly,' said Ewan. 'It'll be just what Flora needs. A bit of support after all her efforts. A bit of a celebration. We'll all have a nice lunch afterwards.'

'Lovely.

'She's been marvellous, your mother,' said Ewan. 'She's put a lot of effort into the job despite discovering your father's . . .' He just about stopped himself in time.

'Father's what?' asked Hilary.

'Complexities,' he answered quickly.

He could sense Hilary's smile. 'Well, he was always very wide-reaching – sometimes it was hard to keep up with him – never knew what he would do next,' she said. 'He was wonderful.'

Ewan could only agree.

It would, on the whole, be easier not to take Dilly if Hilary was going to be there too. Hilary never quite held back where Dilly's somewhat erratic behaviour was concerned and had been heard to say, 'Pull yourself together,' which was never very helpful. He was not entirely sure if Dilly would cope. He was not at all sure about anything very much where Dilly was concerned – those beautiful eyes of hers were a blank to him . . . So if the three of them had a nice lunch together it might bring mother and daughter closer and it would be a friendly thing to do for Flora. She'd suffered quite enough humiliation with that Pike woman. Unlike Dilly, he thought Flora was probably much stronger than she seemed – indeed – now he came to think about it – she appeared to be getting stronger daily. Perhaps Pauline Pike had put grit in the oyster? He tried not to remember those undoubted charms. The more helpful and supportive he could be with Flora, the easier it would be for her to forget the pain. And it had the helpful side of helping him forget his pain, too. He, of course, was still hoping for a miracle. He then rang Flora to say that he would like to take her for lunch after seeing the Holbein. His treat. She, somewhere in orbit, agreed.

The following afternoon Flora, still feeling little tingles about having a definite date with Ewan, walked across the paddock with Giles, who had brought his camera. Everything was coming together very nicely and it was a cheerful, smiling Giles who arrived, thank goodness, a return to his old self. He'd been moping around the village for weeks and had given no impromptu wine tastings at all much to the annoyance of many, including the Vicar, who always enjoyed the occasions purely, as he said, for their social effect. As Betty remarked once, *effect* was the right word. They were, as those who missed them said, very merry affairs. Over the years, although his friendship was really with Edward, he had always been friendly towards Flora in his slightly nervous, Wodehousian way and though he was clearly a man's man, and akin in his relationship with Edward to a bibular jousting companion, he was a nice person and never did that thing of switching his interest from her to one of the younger and more attractive women of the village if they were at a Hurcott gathering together. Indeed, he quite often seemed to move nearer to her, as if for protection. Poor Giles – not one of life's survivors from the school system.

This afternoon, she noticed, he looked very pleased with himself. When she asked him why he merely turned his eyes heavenwards and said that he was very glad to be doing something positive for Edward.

'Oh,' said Flora, a little wonderingly. 'Good.'

'You're looking very bright-eyed and bushy-tailed, Flora,' he said, cheerfully.

'I'll take that as a compliment, Giles,' she said.

'Do,' he said happily. 'Do.'

They walked through the back gate away from Lodge Cottage and out into the mellow evening. 'It's been a beautiful summer,' she said. 'And every evening seems to have been golden for ever.'

'Dear old Flora,' said Giles. 'Always one to look on the bright side despite everything . . .'

She took this to mean the little Pike. 'Men will be men, Giles,' she said, absolutely hating herself. But it hit the right note.

Giles, swinging his camera nervously, turned to her with a dramatic countenance. 'Oh Flora,' he said, so fervently that she quite expected him to follow it with something like *A dashed Aunt is all very well but you can't beat a Bertie*. 'What a good idea of yours to write up this history of Edward's. What a mighty brain that man had.'

She just smiled and nodded. Usefully, little more is expected, she knew, from a plain and amenable woman.

It might have been all right if Giles had ended the fulsomeness there. But he did not. 'Ah,' he continued, with equal drama, 'a last service you can do for him. His final opus. He was my friend, whence comes such another? Take your mind off all the bad things. That Pike woman. I mean, what chance did he have . . .' Flora very nearly snapped, 'Every bloody chance,' but she stopped herself. There was a tear in Giles's eye. It was absolutely intolerable this total faith in such a rat. She shook her head. Edward's history indeed! The last service she could do for him indeed . . . As if she were a handmaiden dusting shelves. Surely she could give up on the role now? Edward's notes were hardly on a par with Macaulay and Gibbon. She could not help herself. She wanted to point this out to him. Why not?

'Well, Giles, I have to say it's proving a lot more difficult than I thought.' She spoke with as much feeling as she dared . . . 'A *lot* more . . .'

Giles was still in the painful realm of the siren Pike. 'Oh that woman,' he said. And to her astonishment he took Flora into his arms. It was all rather angular and uncomfortable, added to which he nearly hugged the living daylights out of her. 'You poor dear girl,' he said, which seemed rather an over- reaction. 'But we're all here to help. I'm here, Flora. I'm here for you.'

'Good,' she said, and a little confusedly removed herself as delicately as possible. To have an experience of a passionate nature in the wrong man's arms was highly ironical and very trying.

'You know how close I was to Edward,' said Giles, 'Well – how close I was to both of you. And now that he's gone – well –'

Flora had a sudden dreadful suspicion. 'And now that he's gone – well what?'

Giles looked uncomfortable but determined. 'I should look after you. At the very least.'

'Why?' she asked, genuinely astonished.

'Well – because love takes you in strange and surprising ways, Flora. I never expected it – not after first youth and all that. But there it was.' He looked at her with large, wet eyes behind his spectacles.

Good grief, she thought. Giles is making a pass. *Giles.*

No, no. 'It's very early days,' she heard herself saying firmly. 'Far too early, Giles.' But part of her was pleased. If she was having trouble persuading herself that Ewan would even look at her twice, she could at least take heart in Giles. She was not remotely attracted to him but it always changed the goal-posts when someone declared themselves to be taken with you – you began to feel much, much fonder of them – for their good taste among other things. And – yes – it is a truth universally acknowledged that if an unexceptional man declares himself to a woman of his fancy, she will immediately start to look on him in a more favourable light and find his unexceptional qualities less of a handicap. Unless you were Elizabeth Bennett in company with Mr Collins, of course, but she was pretty – who amongst the plain of us would dare turn any offer down completely? So thought Flora.

Giles was now quite pink. 'Will you let me be here for you, Flora? It would help me enormously too.'

'What exactly do you mean by "here for you", Giles?' She moved away from him slightly in case he took her in his arms again. Giles had never known his strength and was the archetypal overgrown schoolboy. She'd still got a pair of barbecue tongs once used by him that looked as if Uri Geller had been visiting – and that was only sausages and steak.

'Well – you know,' he said, disconcertingly coy. 'Anything you might need – that you miss – now Edward is gone. Anything.'

He suddenly looked quite desperate and miserable and she felt very sorry for him. She moved a little nearer, gingerly took up one of his hands between her own. 'It is a lovely thing to say Giles and I'm touched – I really am – but no one can replace Edward. He was unique you know.' No truer word, she thought.

'I know,' said Giles, almost in tears. 'You loved him, and I loved him, and now he's gone and it feels as if life is over.'

A strange light began to break through Flora's own halo of

pride. Clouds parted and a revelation occurred. That made twice in the last few days after a lifetime without. But not a terribly flattering revelation, this.

'You *loved* him?' she said.

Giles nodded. He took his hand away from her and put it up in a gesture of humility. 'I know he didn't return it but he knew – and he was kind about it and . . .'

Well hot damn, she thought. So much for the husband she thought she knew inside out and sideways. Not only was he carrying on with the Brownie mistress but he was having declarations from gay men all round the village too. Edward might have told her about Giles at the very least. Surely he couldn't have thought it would make her feel jealous? All those years and he kept all those secrets, she thought crossly, and she could have broken out and been free. Damn her own stupidity. She put her hand on Giles's shoulder and gave it a little pat. 'It's nice to have a friend, Giles. Thank you,' she said, and keeping her distance she led him to the stone. 'Photographing this will be really helpful.' And she put her pride back in her pocket.

After they had admired it, and photographed it, and speculated about it and Giles referred to himself as being All at Sea when it came to working anything like that out – crosswords were his nightmare – she gave the stone one last pat, saying, 'Sun's over the yardarm. Glass of wine, Giles?' And they proceeded back to the house.

'What sort of a lady was she?' Giles asked.

'That,' she said, 'is what I've been attempting to find out. Clever, I think. Protective of her privacy. Resolute. Kind. Not one to make waves. Something of an anachronism in her contented single life. It's all there in the portrait, really, Giles. Holbein showed her qualities as clear as crystal. It's just that nobody seems to have bothered to look. Her eyes are sweet but her chin is determined.'

'Sounds a bit like you, Flora,' said Giles, going pink again.

'Why, thank you ,Giles,' she said feeling a little warm glow.

'Thank you very much.'

'This Hans Holbein,' said Giles as they arrived at the back door, 'German was he?'

'Yes,' said Flora. 'So was Anna of Cleves.' In they went.

'Can't be helped,' said Giles absently, putting his camera down and rubbing his hands. 'Now what'll you have?'

In my own kitchen, she thought, and he takes charge of serving the wine just because Edward isn't here. She felt a little faint at the idea of her deceased husband's commanding so much love from so many people – for all she knew he'd been necking in the bushes with Foot and sharing more than a hymn book with the Vicar's wife. It just didn't seem fair when she had been so – necessarily – good. She *definitely* needed a drink – of something strong and red.

'Sit down, Giles,' she said sweetly. 'There's a love.'

He did so.

She picked up the bottle she had opened the night before. Giles rose again and fell on it with a startled noise – half squeak, half groan. 'Edward's Margaux . . . My stars,' he said, horrified. 'You've opened this?'

She nodded. 'Yes,' she said positively. 'Yes I have.'

Later, at her desk, and feeling a little mellower, Flora began writing up her final notes, her revelation. Elizabeth and Anna. Anna and Elizabeth. The task would be a pleasure.

Clever Flora, she told herself delightedly, a few hours later, Clever, Clever Flora – and she tottered off to bed.

On the following day a bleary-eyed – perhaps there *was* a little too much Margaux – but excited Flora began the final stage of her work on the manuscript. She planned to give the whole thing to Millingtons in Welford to copy and then bind one version in calf before presenting it to Hilary. She then made a booking with Miss Penelope Murdoch for a very exclusive bit of guiding at the appointed time that she and Ewan would be visiting the exhibition. To Miss Murdoch's somewhat astonished, 'Why me?' Flora dared to say, 'Because I have heard of your exceptional knowledge of the subject.' This, she thought, was a good example of equivocation if ever she knew one. Perfect. Miss Murdoch took the bait. Once she had Miss Murdoch in front of Anna's portrait she'd soon put her right. Then the *coup de grace*, her final revelation about Anna and Elizabeth and the Hurcott Ducis stone, and – bingo – Flora would step from the shadows of restraint. Anna would be properly reinstated, Ewan would be amazed, and the two of them could glide off to lunch together and who knows what might be said across the quiet expanse of napery. It would be Flora's finest hour.

Millingtons assured Flora that for a small fee they would proofread the text before binding it and Flora thought this was a sensible expense. The very idea of Hilary taking her to task over commas and semi-colons gave her the shivers. As she arrived home from the town Flora felt that in the nicest possible way she was fulfilling her vow made in Paris and finally laying Anna's unkind reputation to rest. She also tried, and failed, to convince herself the exercise was entirely altruistic.

14

The Winner's Tale

Anna has a few more things to say to the assembled portraits before the exhibition opens. She has heard the secrets of the great and the ignoble as well as the grand and the good and she has learned about more wars, more political upheavals, more greed, more betrayal than anyone might wish. Over the years she has listened to other queens with stories to tell. Marie-Antoinette who never shuts up about the betrayals of the common people and who vows she never said, 'Let them eat cake' – and if Anna thinks 'Flanders Mare' is bad she should see that disgraceful sketch by Jacques David of Marie in her tumbrel. Louis would have had his head off his shoulders for it if he had not already lost his own. Queen Victoria is another one – with her endless diatribe on the recent (comparatively) granting of votes for women. When she begins on 'this mad, wicked Folly of "Women's Rights", with all its attendant horrors on which her poor, feeble sex is bent . . . feminists ought to get a good *whipping*,' it's probably best to nod off. Anna has listened to them all and now it is her turn.

'When my Ladies of the bedchamber asked me each morning after the wedding if all was as it should be – I told them that it was – that the King kissed me goodnight and he kissed me farewell in the morning and called me Sweetheart. They said this would not do. I smiled and smiled and said no more. Let them worry and fret if they wanted. Quite soon Henry gave up our bed for Catherine's. From then I was left alone nightly with that great carved bedhead and I knew why. I expected Henry to return to do his marital duty with me but he never did. It was then that I realised my marriage was over and that I needed to be even more careful and wise.

'From early spring onwards he dined and slept with Catherine only. I was left at Whitehall Palace, alone with my Ladies, who said nothing directly to me but gossiped among themselves from which I gathered enough. I could do nothing but sit and wait. Sit and wait. Contempt when you are on your way downwards is very easy to judge and a good way to behave is to smile and appear to notice nothing. I had quick ears and my days with Mrs Gilmyn did not go unused. It was a useful state of affairs for my negotiations.

'I knew, of course, that most of my own Ladies from Cleves would be sent home a few weeks after the wedding, and so they were. Feeling as isolated as I did those departures were particularly cruel. I was allowed to keep a very few of my women and they – with Olisleger – were my only allies in those first strange months. If you have lived through that fear and without friends, my fine portraits, you can live through anything. There was much unpleasant teasing about my Ladies' plainness and the gowns they wore but, for myself, what Mrs Gilmyn began, I completed. A month after my arrival I looked no different from any other lady of the court. Henry was a king without any sense of duty and self-sacrifice, two of the qualities that make a great monarch. Had he tried harder then I believe we would have made do very well eventually. A willing woman, so I heard later, is more than half the battle.

'The word Divorce was first mentioned in May and by then I knew the cause of the King's absence was Catherine Howard. By then Olisleger knew too and we had many a delicate discussion between ourselves on what was best for my safety. At first I assumed Henry would dally with Catherine but remain married to me (as did most men of rank) but he was ever that foot-stamping child and he would not compromise. He did not consider anything but the path he wanted to take, he was not one to bend beneath any yoke nor could anyone make him do so. He wanted a divorce, he conveniently forgot his past experience with Catherine's cousin Anne, and he would have one.

'I believe Olisleger argued against such a plan with Henry's advisers, but Henry was unshakeable. Divorce was the only outcome he would countenance – he would marry his Catherine – poor dazzled girl – and it meant hard negotiations on my behalf. There was one moment when I betrayed how much I understood – it was at the beginning of the negotiations and the King's representatives were a little less than kindly in the way they presented me with the situation – this was when I thought of necks weeping blood and my own body cast off in the streaming red straw. So I broke down. Just once. And fainted. It was a weak, unseemly moment and I am not proud of it. They were foolish enough to overlook the fact that, far from being without English, I understood them very well indeed and grasped the whole history of Henry's marriages to behave in such a frightened fashion. Blind men, they were and frightened of Henry. And they thought me dumb. So why should I not play them well in the negotiations and get the best settlement a sister of a king could wish for. Jewels and money and property may not mend a heart, but it makes the pain so much less, and there is nothing like the coolness of pearls at your neck to soothe your anger. This is a constant.

'So, ladies, as most of you have done in your lifetimes, I lived two lives during this part of my life and I managed very well. The apparent quiet acceptance of women down the ages has shown itself to be one of the best ways to survive when you have no rights, nor real influence. Perhaps even when you do. Hold your fire and keep your powder dry is the soldier's maxim, and it was mine in those early days. Well might it be said of me several hundred years later that I was "blessed with a happy insensibility of temper, large, bony and masculine and highly unlikely to appeal to a voluptuary of nearly fifty . . ." But Mr Hume, the writer, can never have looked at my portrait. At the waist which is small, Mr Hume? And my hands which are soft and pretty and small? Mr Hume was no objective observer and can be dismissed where my physical attributes are concerned. Mr Hume was an arrogant, ignorant failure of an historian who accused Cleves of being "a coarse, boorish, petty German state". He knew nothing: "A happy insensibility of character" is more the description of him than me. Happy insensibility be damned, I would not be the first queen who has dithered and equivocated herself out of a difficult situation, would I, Elizabeth?'

If there is an intake of breath from Elizabeth, Anna pays it no heed. After all, it is time now for truths and she said it kindly enough. 'And so Henry's people and my people negotiated. And I smiled, and smiled, and curtsied, and curtsied – and signed, and signed. After I wrote the letter to my brother as Henry demanded I knew that I could never go home again for the shame of it. They chose those words, I copied them only. It said that Henry had been kind and loving to me. Why not write that? What good could possibly come from my saying anything else? Was I to write to my brother that he said I was no maid, that I was slack bodied, that I was dull to the point of idiocy? No – I allowed the more acceptable terms set down in that letter and did their bidding. I was Anna, daughter of Cleves, but I now belonged to England. Very well, I should have the best life possible in my adopted land and for that I was required to be docile. The shame was not mine but Henry's and his hypocritical advisers. My signature on that letter pleased Henry very much. He had won.

'But the other letter I wrote to Henry was in my own words and as pretty a form of deceit as you will see; that it satisfied Henry's conceit so well – after five hundred years still makes me smile. But that letter, amenable, willing, was my carriage to freedom and security for my lifetime. Henry thought he had tempered my stubbornness – you will note my chin in this portrait – Holbein could ignore a nose but not the set of a determined chin – and Henry was always a man who liked to win. I wrote about our divorce which I humbly accepted and that I hoped to have the fruition of his most noble presence sometimes . . . Which he liked very much. I thanked him for taking me as his sister but I signed it Anna, the Daughter of Cleves. I was told Henry wept to read it. I think *he* truly believed that I was sorrowful and that I had a broken heart from losing him to another love. After the divorce he even wrote to Sir John Wallop – a nice man, one of the first negotiators for my hand, whom I liked and respected – saying of my state of mind that "when she first knew of the necessity of divorce she was troubled and perplexed in consequence of the great love and affection which she seemed to have only to our person . . ." It is difficult not to smile, even now, for I was ahead of them all.

'Of course I knew that my letters home would be read by spies. Spies were everywhere in Tudor England. So I willingly wrote to my brother of my great love for Henry. It did not matter one jot to be seen as heartbroken. I even sent my wedding ring – the ring that held the words *God send me well to keep* – back to Henry on the night of the day in which my acceptance of that generous divorce settlement was signed and sealed. I asked him to break it into pieces as a thing which I knew held no force or value . . . Which action was a truth that served both ways – not only was Henry free of me for ever, but I was free of him. Six hundred pounds a year and my plate and jewels and dresses – the houses, the palaces and the rental incomes – and the goodwill of Henry and his people. A fair exchange in the end. Yes, the blinding vanity of Henry was astonishing. But vanity goes with tyranny and tyrants love to dress the part, love a mirror. And those who would say that I should have been stronger with Henry and his Council should first look at my settlement and the life I led afterwards. Most remarkably, in a court so jealous of position, no one complained or made difficulties when I took my place as fourth lady at court.

'Which is why, more than a year later, when the crooked-tongued Chapuys, the King of Court Gossip, wrote to his Spanish master that after Catherine's downfall I returned to Richmond to be near the King so that he would take me back as his wife, he was wrong. It is true that I came to be near him

– but as his friend and his appointed sister. It was the right thing to do. Margaret, Henry's last surviving sister of the blood, had died just a month before. I was his family and he was a broken man. It was also the right thing to be seen to do which was important. But we repelled each other as lovers. No sons would be made by us – the spark for that business was dead. I had seen enough between him and Catherine to know that we would never share one whit of what they shared, even if, in the end, it was so destructive.

'Most of the tales that were spread abroad by Chapuys were designed to please the Emperor and at home they were not taken seriously. He said that Henry would never take me back because I was too old to be Queen of England and too fond of wine. I was less than two years older than when I arrived, Signor Chapuys, and no one else seems to suggest that I indulged in excesses. Marillac was certain, as he told the French King, that Henry would take me back because I had "conducted myself very wisely in my affliction and was more beautiful than I was before, and more regretted and commiserated than Queen Catherine of Aragon." Whatever the middling truth there was a great deal of gossip about Henry and me and Catherine over the few months that separated Catherine's imprisonment from her execution – rumours of my bearing a child – either by the King or by someone else – and of my wish to be Queen again. My brother and Olisleger began negotiations but nothing serious came of it and that, I think, satisfied both of us.

'Of course, had Henry wanted me for his wife I could not refuse. But instead Henry and I held good company together and that was enough. I was a generous hostess whose small court was well-fed and well entertained – certainly the King liked to visit me and he came to Richmond in those dark days – his appetite at my table, not my bed, was huge – as indeed by now was he. My experiments with fish made me particularly good to visit at Lent or on the meatless days. Being a good Catholic did not mean keeping a dull table – perhaps that was why Chapuys thought I loved excess.

'The years after this and before Henry's death were my happiest time in England. All dangers were past and my settlement was secure and so I emerged, to the great surprise of the court, like a gorgeous butterfly – wearing the brightest of frocks, the prettiest of jewelled hoods, the daintiest of slippers and surrounding myself with music and dancing and cards and players and all kinds of entertainments. I loved Richmond. The Palace had good hunting in the park and good access to the river and Henry's other palaces – where I was often invited. I kept my counsel. Who knows whose head I saw on my Richmond bowling green as I sent a ball down the line to crack the skull of the jack – but never a breath of ill-temper came to the court. Always, always, it was My Lady of Cleves is most charming and gracious. Marillac, I think, knew, for he commented quite openly about my conduct – and wrote to his French Master that "Madame de Cleves, far from appearing disconsolate, is more joyous than ever and wears new dresses every day . . . and passes her time in diverse recreations and much sport."

'All the things I came to love about the way the Tudors lived their privileged lives were mine. Mary and Elizabeth were allowed to visit me, and I them, and we enjoyed our times together. Particularly at Richmond. With me they lost their watchful, anxious air for there was nothing that I needed from them except good company and the pleasures of life.

'My star shone high and no one called me plain or dull or evil-smelling ever again. I was curtsied to with proper accord, and when the men bowed and straightened they had an appraising look in their eyes. Not that I went further than flirtation. I was the King's sister, I knew his mind and weaknesses – and he would never tolerate it if I took pleasure in another man's bed. It was of little concern to me. What you have never had you never miss and many of those courtier husbands were devoured by ambition and mistrust. I was above it all, and the happier for it. My life was my own. How many of you women, so beautiful in your frames, can say the same? Elizabeth, you were bound by the heavy weight of the crown; Mary, by the oppression of your Spanish husband and terrible religious strife; Christina, by one, two, three marriages; Jane, by early death, and so on it goes. But I was single, free and independent. All I had to do was curtsy and smile. It was easy enough.'

15

Confrontations and Considerations

Flora, having had two sleepless nights trying to calm herself down before the trip to London, gave up, gave in to every-thing, and became happily and uncharacteristically neurotic. She jumped every time the telephone rang and ran out into Blowhorn Lane whenever a dog barked or a delivery van slewed by. But Miss Murdoch was booked, the history was being bound, Ewan was coming to meet Anna with her, and that was that. The action was on. Virtue must shape itself to the Deed. Anna was the reason, but hope sprang eternal.

It was gratifying, if slightly annoying, the way the whole vil-lage acted suddenly as if the stone were personally theirs. Gossip – and from who knows where – declared the stone to be found before Flora was ready for it. A hasty meeting was called in the village hall to decide what was best done with such a prize. 'I think,' she said to Ewan before the meeting, 'that we should keep quiet about our little trip until we have seen the portrait and can think a little more exactly about what we should recommend for the stone and its safety . . .' To which he, dear ordinary, honest man, agreed.

The Parish Council was sure that something should be done – as it could not, it simply could not, just be left there. Well, why not, was what Flora thought, but she kept quiet being rather afraid of the assembled getting wind of the visit to London and tagging along. Horrible thought. Ewan – as puta-tive village elder – was often called upon to make decisions. In the old days it was Sir Randolph but he had happily slid into his dotage by now and though Foot was a doughty champion for him and the old ways, time had moved on. Ewan ceded the responsibility to Flora, and put her on the platform, which just showed the sensitivity of the man.

Myra thought the stone should be taken out and put into a display case in the library. When asked why she said because the library – though small – was the seat of learning and where all the history books resided. 'No,' said Flora. 'It needs to be seen all the time and you're only open fourteen hours a week.' Mrs Vicar then said the church would be more appropriate, given that Anna represented the break with Popish ways – which just showed how much interest Mrs Vicar had actually taken in the Princess of Cleves. The Reverend Arthur, who said the church was at the heart of the village and who ought to know better about the Protestant/Catholic question regarding Anna, said he was forced to agree, which Flora thought was probably very true. Mrs Vicar could be redoubtable. 'Anna of Cleves was a Catholic,' said Flora stoutly. 'So I'm afraid not.' That shut them up.

Giles, whose house and wine shop were next to the post office, stood united with Betty (who lived above the post office): the stone could be a feature on their joint frontage, it being the first place any tourists would see on entering the village. They both kept repeating the word Heritage, like a mantra. Flora wondered how on earth Giles would manage with a tourist influx when he was iffy about Germans, let alone any other more exotic race or culture that might descend on Hurcott Ducis. And Betty, under different conditions, would almost certainly have signed a petition for Anna to be sent home. Who needs another foreigner living on our taxes?

Foot read out a suggestion from Sir Randolph that he would take command of it and that it should undoubtedly be a part of the Heron estate. But since, as Flora pointed out, Heron Hall was built a good hundred years after Anna's death – there was nothing to support his claim. Except, she guessed, a nice little tax break for him if he let the public in to see it once every fifty years or so.

Pauline Pike had placed herself in the front row next to Ewan. She was determined to rally despite being turned down by The Players and was convinced that it was only a matter of time before they saw the error of their ways. She spoke up, brazen as brass Flora thought, and said – through a fluttering of her eyelashes which – surely – set up a positive draught – that she thought it ought to be put wherever a person of standing in the village thought most appropriate. Persons of standing were not, it seemed, minor persons such as widows who had done the literary donkeywork.

Flora looked down at Pauline from the platform and wondered, for a halcyon moment, why they had stopped the ancient and charming Early Modern practice of ducking adulteresses. Pauline was as close as she could be to Ewan without actually sitting on him and her little knees, so exposed, were crossed and facing him in an attitude that anyone knowing anything about the psychology of desire would recognise immediately as Come and Get Me. Fortunately Ewan did not seem to be a man who read popular science publications or woman's magazines and appeared to be (though slightly pink at Pauline's flattering words) unaware of, or unwilling to recognise, the offer. His knees, such lovely loyalty, were turned away from hers.

'I mean,' said Pauline, moving even more dangerously around in her seat so that a little push (as Flora put it to herself) would see her on the floor, 'the solicitor amongst us.' Still in that lovely dream world, she was, where only she among women was the chosen one. Flora had seen it earlier in the bar where Pauline had stood very close to Ewan before the meeting began and loudly and clearly ordered a bitter lemon. She, pink lips just so, smiled at him now but he – oh joy – was looking up at Flora with warm and unblinking interest.

The solicitor amongst them, and the woman who found the stone amongst them, both said in unison that the Anna stone should stay exactly where it was. 'What is more,' said Flora, 'we – Ewan and I – will arrange for a little posse of people to check on it and if anyone tries to tamper with it – well – it will be the worse for them.' Foot coughed, looked disappointed, and mentally put his chisel away.

Pauline looked up at the solicitor with her shining eyes and knees. The next production at The Players was to be something called *She Stoops To Conquer* – so she had read in *The Hurcottian* – and that sounded just the right kind of play. Pauline knew all about stooping and conquering as she would tell the wine man, Giles, and she would very soon be able to twist him round her little finger. She was sure of it.

The meeting broke up in accord. The stone would stay where it was. And a photocopied facsimile of *The History of Hurcott Ducis with Special Reference to the Anna of Cleves Stone* would be lodged with the library and with the church – and with any other village institution which felt the need. In the past it would have been Edward standing up there telling them what to do. Yet Flora told them what to do with such conviction and authority that many of them blinked.

'But *why*?' asked several of the assembled, slightly irritably, 'was the stone placed there at all?'

'That,' said Flora, as she stepped down from the stage, 'is the question. And I will answer it in due course.'

They blinked again, and were silent. The meeting was unquestionably closed.

Phew, she thought as she stepped down from the stage. The visit and the lunch were still intact. Good. Together, just as planned, Flora and Anna would rise from their respective ashes.

'I'm so looking forward to tomorrow,' she said to Ewan as they parted at the door of the Village Hall.

'So am I,' he said, and was surprised to find how true that was. 'And I've got a nice little surprise for you, too.'

Flora went pink with pleasure. And thanked her stars that it was dark now, blushing not being her most appealing condition. 'How exciting,' she said, and found herself clasping her hands in a definite copy of the Little Pink Pike's carry-on.

'What?'

'Well – if I told you then it wouldn't be a surprise, now would it?' Irrefutable logic that had her practically running all the way home to Lodge Cottage thinking that the sooner she got into bed the sooner it would be morning. Like Christmas, it was. Just like Christmas. Perhaps he'd booked an hotel? Unlikely but why not make imaginative hay while the sun shone?

The following morning she walked down to the Davieses' home early. She was far too excited to sleep longer than day-break and although Ewan had said he would collect her and they could go to the station together, she had a good – well – bad – reason. It was about time, Flora told herself, that she investigated the true situation regarding Dilly and Ewan's sleeping arrangements. This morning would be the perfect opportunity to find out the truth. She donned the cherry-red silk and then wept over its unsuitability. 'You cannot make a pig's handbag out of a sow's trotter,' she told herself feebly. And wished that the blinding skirt covered her knees. She set off with chin up and a distinct sense of queasiness. The morning was a nice one, though slightly overcast and cool. This coolness was the kindest thing nature could provide. She would arrive at the Davieses' looking calm and the right colour, instead of agitated and cherry-red all over and dripping with unwonted dew.

*

In her small apartment over the mews at the slightly crumbling home of her employer, Miss Murdoch puts on her sensible shoes (no good limping around galleries) and her plain, grey, square-cut suit. To her lapel she attaches her credentials as guide – she likes to wear the badge when she is travelling to an event – she likes the accord granted her when people notice it. Sometimes someone will strike up a conversation in the train and ask her about a particular item of jewellery, or clothing, or a painting that they have seen or a place visited and she prides herself on being able to recall it and pass on some facts.

Last week, for example, on her way to Hardwick Hall

(alabaster and blackstone chimneypiece and door surrounds, classical devices and motifs in the High Great Chamber from engravings by Crispin van der Passe) a woman leaned across the carriage and said, 'Oh – you are a guide – I wish we'd had you with us when we were at Coventry Cathedral – it was so moving, so touching that the Dean's first journey abroad after the war was to Dresden. Can you tell us about that?' And Miss Murdoch who was just a little hazy on the subject of reconciliation and Coventry and any notion of I Forgive, easily smoothed the path towards the more useful information about how the modern building is aligned at right angles to the medieval church, and gave them the exact size and weight of Jacob Epstein's St Michael and the Devil.

It is rare for Miss Murdoch to be invited to address a private group of visitors – usually the bookings are made through Claygate and Pall, the agency, and from specific groups – but this booking is highly focused and very private indeed. Only two people. Miss Murdoch hopes they are not too demanding. You only need one so-called expert and you are up a gum tree. She has been asked to concentrate on the portrait of Anne of Cleves, Henry VIII's fourth wife, which, given that there are so many wonderful portraits in the exhibition – the Ditchley Elizabeth being the obvious choice (what Miss Murdoch does not know about *that* could be fitted on a postage stamp) – she was rather surprised – perhaps disappointed even, to have such a dull picture and dull story to relate.

She closes the door, nods a gracious nod to the passing gardener who avoids her eye, as he has done ever since she attempted to persuade him to plant an Edwardian herb garden in the *proper* manner, as seen at Knebworth, and gets on her bicycle. She will cycle to the station which is six miles away – good thinking time. A confident, straightforward woman, Miss Murdoch, who – she assures herself now as she pedals the springing, green lanes – knows a thing or two. Or three. Or four. She will try to manoeuvre these people away from their fixation with Anne of Cleves and on to Elizabeth. Or if not

Elizabeth then Jane Seymour will do at a pinch. They are both glamorous with many little bits and pieces to fill the time. Anne of Cleves has little glamour and having seen the portrait so recently in Paris Miss Murdoch is very much afraid that she will have little to say that is flattering. The Flanders Mare. Oh dear. And cycling away, she smiles with fortitude at the prospect ahead.

*

Flora, arriving at the Davieses' front door, felt even more garish and odd. The cherry-red long-line silk jacket and just above knee-length ruffle-hem skirt (which is what the label proudly proclaimed it to be) is wrong. It seemed so right in the shop and passable against the fluffy white carpet of the bedroom – the one vulgarity overwhelming the other – but now it felt remarkably as if she really was a cherry, overripe and all ready for picking. If she wanted to make a statement to the world about grieving being over, she could not have chosen a better outfit. If she wanted to make a statement to the world about having lost her sartorial marbles she could not have chosen a better outfit. Why, even the morning sunshine bounced off it as if shocked by her brazenness. Well, it was far too late to change. She hung her head and rang the bell.

Ewan opened the door. Flora instantly felt better about her own ensemble. She had forgotten his somewhat dashing – not to say startling – approach to casual dressing. He wore a seersucker suit in the palest of lemon stripes and a deep fuchsia-pink shirt. Together, Flora thought despondently, they looked like a bowl of fruit and custard. He wore his outfit without shame, however, and looked very pleased with himself. He invited her in and she stepped over the threshold.

'You look marvellous, marvellous, Flora,' he said and seemed to mean it.

'Thank you,' she said. 'And so do you.' They stood there for a moment staring at each other and until Flora said, 'I've come early because . . .' But he was not at all bothered. 'I'm just on the phone. Client.' He looked at his watch. 'Good – plenty of time to get the train. Shouldn't take a tick to deal with this.' He pointed to the telephone which was in his hand. 'Make yourself comfortable in the sitting room . . .' And he pushed open the panelled door to the small square room off the hall.

Flora always liked this room on the few occasions she had been in it. There was something very cosy about it – probably – she thought now as she looked at the wide fireplace with its ashes, the wooden mantelpiece with a jumble of pipes and papers, and the faded, higgledy-piggledy carpets and rugs aligned with the squashy leather sofa – probably because, even though it is overwhelmingly masculine, it is also loved.

'Dilly is –' he said. And then spoke into the telephone without finishing the sentence, merely pointing at the ceiling. 'I'll just get the papers,' he said to the caller and hurried off with apologetic gesturings down the passageway calling, 'Flora's here!' When he was out of sight Flora sighed. How could Dilly let him dress like that? And where is she?

Then, as if in answer to her sleuthing prayers there was a little *coo-ee* from the upstairs landing, and when Flora arrived at the bottom of the stairs, there were a pair of dark and beautiful blue eyes and a tousle of blonde, wavy hair, peeking over the banister. 'Come up,' whispered Dilly. 'Come up and have a drink before you go. You'll need it if you're doing probate.'

Flora put on a brave smile since it was nine-fifteen in the morning. 'Lovely,' she said. Hurrah, she thought, for Ewan has told an adulterer's lie. Probate, indeed. And them off to London for a visit and a lunch and a surprise. It put a spring in her step, despite the cherry-red flummery, and up she went.

The beautiful eyes continued to look down on her with great amusement as Flora mounted the stairs. She stared into them as if mesmerised. At least she would soon know what the state of their marriage was vis-à-vis its sleeping arrangements. Looked at, even from this angle, it seemed highly unlikely that one able to look delectable at this hour of the morning, at any hour really, could be cast off and made to sleep solo. Despite being dressed in white silk pyjamas and a carelessly open dressing gown, Dilly looked immaculate. Like one of those film stars who have been at it all night on the screen yet wake the next morning looking gorgeous and perfect and who send whole rows of women filmgoers out into the night deeply depressed. Flora felt doubly irritated at the white silk. If she could be a dypsomaniac and look so elegant, why was Ewan allowed to wear such silly colours on his days off? And sometimes even the most shocking ties on his days on. It was going to be quite embarrassing being on the train with him. Passing over the fact that she herself was not in the best of hues for a woman of a certain age, Flora's irritation deepened.

'You look marvellous,' said Flora faintly. Dilly just looked her up and down once, not unkindly, and said, 'Have a drink. You'll feel better then,' and she took her into a bedroom.

It probably was a bedroom at some point but now it resembled a cross between a wine bar, a piece of art of the unmade-bed variety and a village stall at the moment the doors close on a jumble sale. The bed, what Flora could see of it beneath magazines, brochures, clothes, paperback books and telephone wires, was made for a solo occupant – with the pillows in the middle and with only one, vaguely discernible, bedside table and lamp. Flora could distinguish no signs of masculinity of the striped-pyjamas variety. She breathed out.

'Will you have gin?' asked Dilly.

'Do you know,' said Flora faintly, 'I do believe I will.'

*

Miss Murdoch is on the platform. She has with her the catalogue from the exhibition and on its cover is the Ditchley portrait of Queen Elizabeth I. What a beauty, she thinks again. She turns to the illustration of the Anne of Cleves portrait and sighs. The portrait – which momentarily looked quite sweet – looks – as she has always remembered it – rather sour. Then she flicks the page on to Marie of Guise. There's a bit of bright-eyed glamour about her. All that French wit and style. Pity the Queen of Scots isn't in the exhibition, too, for Miss Murdoch can talk for a lifetime about her. And here is Jane Seymour – so important – and Christina of Denmark – lovely girl . . . Miss Murdoch sighs and returns to the Anne of Cleves page. Now, she thinks, the painting looks downright sullen.

*

Flora wondered as she sipped her gin and tonic and sat on the edge of what might have been the bed – she wondered when too much drink caught up with beauty? For Dilly still looked – if a little pink round the edges – lovely. Certainly lovely for a woman who was but a few years short of her half-century. That occasional blinking was tenderly touching somehow, the complexion warm but not florid, the mouth as curved and full as putto's bottom as it hovered above the rim of her glass. The only detraction was the blankness of expression. Flora leaned towards her. She did not quite know what she was going to do until she had done it – but she reached out and took Dilly's glass and placing it on what might or might not be the bedside table, and said, 'Why do you do it, Dilly? You are so beautiful. Why?'

Dilly stretched out her lovely white hand, with its extraordinarily perfect nails, and picked up the glass again. 'Well, Flora dear,' she said, 'I'll tell you.' And the answer, when it came, like so many answers to great mysteries, was surprisingly banal.

*

Miss Murdoch is now on the train. A man and a woman notice her Brown Badge. 'We had one of you in Petworth,' says the man.

'That furniture would take some polishing,' says the woman. 'Do you know the place?' Miss Murdoch nods. 'I know everywhere, nearly,' she says firmly. Set of painted rococo stools, c. 1760, made for the Marble Hall, thinks Miss Murdoch. Norman and Whittle rococo giltwood pier glasses and four-panelled mirror, also about 1760, in the Square Dining Room as well as a companion pair of giltwood console tables with green marble tops. Polishing indeed. Out loud she says, 'Much of the cabinet work is japanned and there is a great deal of black lacquer which would require no polishing.'

'It'd take a good deal of dusting, all the same,' says the woman with satisfaction.

'Fair point,' says the man.

'Chapel is most interesting,' says Miss Murdoch. 'Part of the original medieval manor built around 1309.'

'With wedge-shaped walls to compensate for the new build,' says the man.

Miss Murdoch gives him a gracious smile and opens her catalogue once more.

*

Flora was still turning it over in her dazed head, for Dilly's fate, as she put it, was smelted in the crucible of her husband's very ordinariness. Over the gin Dilly told Flora that she married Ewan thinking he was wild and exotic. Flora stares at Dilly wondering if she has *always* drunk. You could not, really, get a man who was further from that description. You really could not.

'I was beautiful,' said Dilly simply. 'And I expected to have a boyfriend who was exotic and wild to match. And Ewan drove a pink E-type Jaguar which seemed the right kind of exotic . . .'

A pink E-type . . . thought Flora. How odd. He drove a dark green Polo now.

'Well, I was eighteen,' said Dilly dreamily, leaning back and cradling her glass. 'And he was twenty-five. So mature and dangerous . . .'

Dangerous? Flora began to seriously doubt herself. Seriously. 'Dangerous Dilly?' she said out loud.

'Well – you can only judge such things by external signs and he wore outrageous clothing in the maddest of colours, and generally looked and behaved like a quite acceptable wild young man. He was always falling down and getting drunk and I thought that was wonderful and deliciously wild. And he spent money like water. As if it meant nothing to him.'

Falling down and getting drunk? Wild with money? Ewan? Well – it must be right because he certainly still wore some of the oddest colour combinations. 'Really?' said Flora.

'Really,' said Dilly.

'What happened?' asked Flora. They both knew the subtext to that.

'The joke was that he wasn't like it at all. Not really. And the reason he had an E-type and a flat in Chelsea was because he was the son of very wealthy, very indulgent and very profligate parents. A Welsh Chapel-reared father and a Scottish Presbyterian-reared mother. Can you imagine? Talk about brought up straight. Both were desperate to have a son who walked on the wild side because in their youth they had scarcely walked anywhere. They felt dull and wanted brightness, even secondary brightness. And when Angus came along he was even milder than Ewan, so it was Ewan they looked to. It was the days of swinging London and they pushed him into it . . .'

'But *pink*, Dilly . . . And wearing mad colours? Ewan?'

'Well – he's *colour-blind*, you goose. Surely you know that?'

There was an absolute silence only broken by the faint sound of Ewan talking on the telephone downstairs. Flora blinked first. Dilly began to laugh. Flora tried to be offended on Ewan's behalf (if not on her own), gave up and laughed too.

'I had no idea,' Flora said eventually, allowing Dilly to refill her glass. 'He's always struck me as – well – a sobersides.'

'He is a sobersides. It's just that he had no head for drink so that after a glass and a half of champagne he was dancing on the tables. And I got right up there and danced with him. Only it took me a little more than a glass and a half of champagne – well – a bottle and a half actually. Then.'

'Well, I suppose it would seem exciting.' Flora was remembering Edward. He had blossomed into his Dasher and Dancer mode gradually so it crept up on her, overtook her and then left her behind. 'Personally I found it very irritating in Edward. Childish actually. Wildnesses.' The gin gave her eloquence over loyalty.

Dilly was back in her own world, seeing who knew what

(Flora certainly couldn't imagine) behind those beautiful glowing eyes. 'We got married – oh how his parents liked me – the
wild young thing – and went on a long honeymoon and he
danced on the tables all across Spain and into North Africa.
And in Morocco it really didn't show up that he was colour-
blind because all the men wore bright things and Egypt was
mainly white cotton anyway. And then we came home . . . And
that was real life because he suddenly decided he wanted to do
real work. Practise as a proper solicitor. And that he didn't like
hangovers.'

'And you did?'

'Didn't get them. And I wanted parties. All I knew was that
there I was, the beauty of the family, praised for doing the right
thing and marrying well – and it was suddenly quite different.
No more parties. Silly Dilly had thrown her desirable self on to
the scrap heap of life by marrying a small country-town solicitor. Well – he wasn't a country-town solicitor then – he was a
London-town solicitor in an ambitious practice but he began
doing some jobs for nothing. Justice for all. That sort of thing.'

How honourable, thought Flora. Out loud she said, 'Well, I
suppose he could afford it with those parents and all.'

'He voted Liberal.'

'And?'

'The Davieses liked their politics like a good French steak.
Barely cooked.'

Flora tried to work out the clue, and failed. 'What?'

'Blue. And Ewan stuck to his guns.'

'Well, that's honourable.'

'Honourable, indeed. So he turned his back on the money
and they turned their backs on him for being dull and boring
and ungrateful. And the London house went, closely followed
by the Jags and the nice designer clothes and all that stuff – and
here we are . . .'

'Well,' said Flora, 'you're not exactly poor.'

Dilly sat up and ran her pretty hands through her fluffy hair.
'And we're not exactly rich. So here I am. Dilly, launched with

the expectation that an easy life was what you got in return for bestowing your beauty upon the world and choosing the perfect prince – beauty being the golden key.'

'Well it does open doors,' said Flora, wistfully.

'I was bored out of my head, darling. Bored,' she said, over the rim of her fresh glass, 'To *buggery* . . . The golden cage, darling. And that . . .' She tapped Flora's arm with her perfect nail. 'That is very hell.'

'Well, why on earth didn't you run off then?' asked Flora, with some irritation.

'Because the next one might be even worse and because – by then – I had another lover . . . One who was always the same, always available and never let me down. Ewan knew, and Ewan turned a blind eye.' She laughed. 'A colour-blind eye. Marriages are obviously made to last in the blood of the Welsh and the Scots, you see. Good people. Even those who have fallen from Grace. No pubs on Sundays for years in the one and desperate work ethic in the other . . .'

Flora could only think, She has a lover. Dilly has a lover . . . And she was thinking, What's sauce for the gilded goose can legitimately be sauce for the balding gander . . . Give that other lover a medal . . . when she realised, as Dilly caressed her glass and took another bottle of tonic water from the bottom drawer of her what was either fridge or bedside cabinet, exactly who the lover was. Someone called Gordon who always dressed in green. She held out her glass. 'I'll have another one while you're at it,' she said, all miserable again. Just for that little second or two of sheer happiness Flora thought she had won. *Colour-blind?*

Ewan called up the stairs that he was ready to go.

'Go on – run along, the pair of you. And have fun. Though quite how you'll have any with my husband and a bunch of old papers is beyond me.'

'Nice day for it,' said Ewan, as they stepped out into the morning. 'Very,' said Flora, flatly. What she wanted to ask him was why, Oh why, he stayed.

Miss Murdoch took a little time to have a snack in the cafeteria and run over her notes. The exhibition was nicely populist. All the usual suspects. Nothing difficult and no surprises. Maybe she could slip in a little extra? After all, the dress in the Ditchley was said to weigh more than seven bags of flour when it was finished and you didn't get statistics like that with the Cleves girl. It usually shocked them, that. And what a good story it was – Elizabeth – the Princess in the Tower who rose to be Queen. Miss Murdoch was always asked how such a young woman managed things so well and where she got her survival skills from; Miss Murdoch could always cite her father and the whole Tudor/Plantagenet genealogy. Then, as now, blood will out, she would tell them. She put it down to good aristocratic genes and left it at that. Catherine de Valois' groom, the seed that eventually brought forth Henry VII, had not usefully registered with her.

Flora read the paper on the train, as did Ewan. It was a comfortable, ordinary way to be together and it helped her to calm down after so many revelations. She tried, by reading the letters page, to forget the little bubble of excitement that would surface despite Dilly's somewhat pathetic tale. And she certainly tried very hard to forget that Ewan had told his wife a lie about probate . . . whatever that meant. Ah, she thought, even as she rummaged through it all in her mind, this is the female lot – to look for motives and for a complex stimulus of action that probably do not exist. Men were not so complex, perhaps, as women in such matters, or did she mean devious? Dilly had been lied to by Ewan, she guessed, because it was easier. A little white lie about probate meant – if anything – surely – that he was being protective of his wife. Since this was not a happy thought she rummaged around a little more until she managed to pull out the thought that he might have lied to protect Flora, which was much more acceptable.

How many women, she wondered, have sat chewing over

endless speculations about the behaviour of the male of the species when the male of the species is being – in his own eyes – perfectly straightforward? She returned to the *Guardian*'s letters page for comfort. There was just something about the moral high ground of New Labour that damped down all her neuroses. Ewan read the *Independent*, she noticed, with that hunger for details of the would-be lover that betokens a worrying and uncontrollable amount of interest. Already she was thinking of subtle foods and soft red wine and brandies at lunch and anything that might follow. She had a tale to tell and she would tell it and he might, he might well, look at her differently then. Brandies at lunch? She'd risk suggesting it. He must have outgrown his hangovers by now, surely. For herself she was surprised to find that the gin was sitting very happily in her system.

Ewan collected their tickets and as they came up the grand staircase to the exhibition Flora saw in the distance a familiar grey suit with a Brown Badge on its lapel, and the tilt of a firmly resolved chin. Miss Murdoch, she presumed. And behind her, dimly outlined through the glass of the dividing doors, she saw, lining the walls, the rows of portraits. Flora was ready. Miss Murdoch should see the error of her ways, Ewan should see how clever Flora could be – and the rest – she guessed – would be history. *I know why the stone was made,* she said to herself, *I know why* . . . Miss Murdoch disappeared through the doors.

It was only then, as she put her arm through Ewan's most boldly, and undid another of the buttons of her cherry-red silk, that she heard what she took to be a phantom – the voice of her daughter calling, calling, calling her. A siren song of warning, she thought, and a chill ran up her spine. She scrabbled to replace the undone button and felt her face go as crimson as her clothes. She must be dreaming, she must . . . Then Ewan looked round, called out, 'Hilary! I thought you hadn't made it.' And then turned back to Flora and said with an immense smile on his face that she had a very distinct desire to remove

– 'Flora – here you are – your surprise . . .' And up came Hilary, plaited hair gleaming, pink-eyed, damp-cheeked, but beaming. 'Hallo, Mum,' she said, and after giving her nose a good long blow into a large white tissue, she linked her arm through Flora's free one. The smile grew broader. 'Thanks, Ewan. And it almost feels as if Dad's here with us too.'

Then all three of them marched arm in arm towards Miss Murdoch and – Flora now felt – her doom. How could she say that it was all her own work if Edward was there with them in spirit, in Hilary? As they came nearer and nearer to the exhibition entrance, Flora felt the subtle foods floating away, and was left with the necessary and tantalising image of soft red wine and brandy instead. She'd be lucky if she got a cup of tea and a bun, now.

16

The Public Awaits

The portraits, hanging, waiting for the world to come and look at them and read about them and make of them what they will – whether truth or fiction, whether founded or unfounded – are used to days like this. Days when everything is ready, the late arrivals have been delivered (Katherine Parr, last again), frames polished and put in place, the catalogue scrutinised and passed, the doors about to open. The usual glittering reception for the Galleristas and Sponsors over and done with the night before. Anna and her companions are brought together thanks to the generosity of a very large bank. A corporate sponsor. The portraits may nod to each other knowingly, for corporate banks are among the best of the patrons of art exhibitions. It is as if they feel the need to clean their money of some of its connections. They provide a fine show of fashionable people at the launch reception, and it is nice for the portraits, in their turn, to have something to ogle. And usury was ever thus.

Well, the floors have been swept, the champagne glasses cleared, the smears of caviar wiped clean, it is morning and the portraits wait. The portraits with bad conscience, as Anna observes, find it hard to contemplate the past. Marie-Antoinette and Queen Victoria are not alone in their complaining. She once hung in an exhibition, *Pivots of Revolution* was it? – wrong again to call her a Lutheran – which featured both Charles I of England and Oliver Cromwell. Both of whom were beside themselves. Literally and metaphorically. And though Charles tried to remember the good days when he rode a white horse and looked tall, and Cromwell tried to remember the early days of Parliament and the Model Army when the country seemed ready to embrace everything and power had not corrupted him – they were both brought low by their more dishonourable memories. Despairing Milton was there, the good man in that group of arrogant egotists, and Charles spat to be told that he was the very model of Satan in *Paradise Lost*. Anna could only stay quiet and think that it was ever thus, the mix of politics and religion, and little had changed since her day. But at least she can say that her life, in the end, was a good one and she was happy. If it was mixed, the balance was always weighted to the good. As a single woman of rank and fortune, she had made very sure of *that*.

By the time her first Christmas arrived as the King's Sister, she had adapted very well to her new life exchanging one family for another with her step-nieces. With them there was one cardinal rule – to speak no ill of their father. Not only because to do so was treason, but even when they talked together by the light of a candle with no one near, it was not to be done. His daughters revered Henry – both as their King and their father – despite his cruel treatment of their mothers – Mary's mother taking a long time dying – and Elizabeth's taking a moment. Yet still these princesses (who must only be called Lady now that he had also pronounced them illegitimate – unkind even in this) loved and admired their King. If Anna was being hypocritical, they were not. She maintained her hypocrisy with them to the end. For lessons in hypocrisy there was no better place than the Tudor Court of sixteenth-century England.

It was wise to be an amenable ex-wife. Henry was a vindictive ex-husband. It was still talked about in her time, the stories of Mary's mother's suffering. In her last years Catherine lay ill and alone and banished from seeing her daughter for not complying with Henry's wishes for a divorce and still he was cruel. When the dying Queen asked the Spanish Ambassador to send her some old Spanish wine, old wine being good for the stomach and new wine being vicious, Henry dictated that

Catherine should be sent new wine only. Such a petty act of cruelty. The King, it seems, was disobeyed and the kinder old wine was sent to Catherine but the servant who arranged it was punished. That, thought Anna, showed the mettle of the man she might have married. But not a word of that was talked of with Mary and Elizabeth. Better that way and preserve their affection and respect. Sharp-eyed Marillac knew how discreet Anna was and wrote, in his usual shrewd way, that 'All her affairs could never make her utter a word by which it might suppose she was discontented. This I put down to the singular Grace of God. And furthermore, I hear that the Lady Anna is half as beautiful again since she left court . . .'

As she looks across at the Ditchley Portrait, glimmering in the low light, and at Mary Tudor, hanging next to it, darker, more restrained, Anna remembers how they were – Elizabeth was seven and Mary the same age as herself. Perhaps it appeased Henry's conscience to let them have affection from their new aunt, and on all formal occasions he dictated that Elizabeth and she should ride in the same carriage, and dine at the same table. Her discreet way was a good lesson for Elizabeth. Such pragmatism for the unwanted was better than provocation. Be seen to be living an ordinary life of religious propriety and simple pleasure and keep away from scandal and you will survive well enough. Did Elizabeth remember it? Anna looks across at the portrait. No, not always. Pride, as ever, goeth before a fall. Poor daughters, both.

At least the portrait of Mary I – by Hans Eworth – is not too much of a contrast with Elizabeth's pearly glories. Mary, as a newly betrothed queen shows a face that is softened by expectancy. She wears La Peregrina – the pearl that Philip of Spain gave her on their betrothal and it hangs there, like an enormous teardrop – Anna always thought that it was a sign of things to come.

On the opposite wall, a little way from Elizabeth and Mary, is a curiosity, lent from a museum in Pavia. It is a late-dated portrait supposedly of Anne Boleyn by Frans Pourbus, and the face of the young beauty is so like the young Elizabeth that you would swear to its authenticity. Yet Elizabeth poured scorn on the picture and will have nothing to do with the beautiful young woman. It is not her mother. Elizabeth may have kept her counsel about Anne Boleyn through the years but blood is thicker than water, obviously, and she has nothing to say to this imposter. The young beauty has proudly said that she is, of course, not Anne Boleyn at all but Isabella Clara Eugenia, Infanta of Spain, later Archduchess of Austria, and has *never* wished to be anyone else. In fact she has been mistaken for many famous women down the years. This cuts no ice (of which there is quite a lot floating about) because Elizabeth Tudor is no friend of the Spanish, obviously, what with the Armada and Catholic plots and all. Neither, surprisingly, is Mary her sister, though half her blood comes from Spain. You can't be treated as badly as she was by a Spanish husband and stay neutral. Elizabeth and Mary, united for once, scorn the beautiful Pourbus, whoever she is.

For Anna it is like being among the family again. And although in all her seventeen years left on earth in England, Anna never quarrelled with either sister, they had many a quarrel between themselves. Indeed, when Anna died and Mary arranged that she should be 'honourably buried according to the degree of such an estate', the two sisters were so divided that Elizabeth was a virtual prisoner. She took no part in the funeral proceedings and whether she mourned Anna or not there is none to say.

The sisters continue to ignore the unfortunate (and beautiful) Isabella who continues – most reasonably in Anna's opinion – to plead that she is also very surprised to be here as the executed English Queen considering she was painted over fifty years after Anne Boleyn's death. Isabella has also in her time, and to her indignation, been identified as Mary Queen of Scots – than which there could not be anything worse to report to either of these two proud Tudors. So she hangs there, Isabella/Anne/Mary and longs to go home . . .

Saintly Jane Seymour, still trailing her clouds of glory further down the wall, looks away from Anna and stares, rather vacantly, at her son Edward in his infancy. No bonding there. He looks out, a little king, holding his golden rattle like a tiny sceptre, and pays no heed to anyone. Holbein painted it with such tenderness. Anna remembers how much Henry loved this picture. Poor Edward – never allowed to have a normal child-hood – he has little to say to anyone, really, for he was kept too long away from childhood's chattering.

Catherine Howard is not there – for when her head left her body her portraits left the walls. Anna is rather relieved. Katherine Parr is there – and very pious and plain she looks too. Anna thinks she can hardly be blamed for suggesting that she was more lovely than the King's last wife. Fortunately by then he wanted a nurse, not a beauty, and Anna remained free.

It is time. The exhibition opens. The portraits are still and silent and whatever their thoughts and memories they remain very properly held in their paint. Anna wonders, though with-out much hope, if she will see again that Murdoch woman and the plain woman who seemed to understand her. It would be amusing, maybe a triumph, and a counter to the insults but it is unlikely . . . And then, just as Anna moves on from thoughts of Miss Murdoch to settle somewhere altogether happier – perhaps her Hurcott kitchen – just at that moment – when the lights of the exhibition space go on – she sees what might be a conjured phantom, but which – on closer inspection – is not. She sees Miss Murdoch, Yes, in that same grey suit, marching towards her, a light of determination in her eyes. Astonishing. Anna has to quickly close her mouth or the whole of Holbein's history might need to be rewritten and somebody real might see and die of it.

But Miss Murdoch turns her back on Anna and faces the Ditchley portrait. She stares up as Elizabeth returns her stare. 'Ah,' says Miss Murdoch, giving a little sigh, 'how beautiful. How brilliant. If only . . .' Then she turns to Anna. 'Ah well,' she says. 'You look a little better than I remember. Perhaps this lighting suits you.' So that Anna feels her face darken. Naturally Miss Murdoch does not notice. She stands sentinel, facing outwards, her feet apart, her hands behind her back tapping her papers together as if she is impatient to begin. But begin what, wonders Anna, feeling a little trill of hope.

From another direction comes the sound of footsteps. The public has arrived. Anna looks to the side as best she can and sees that around the corner, passing Jane Seymour and Edward, comes a little group of people, led by – the woman from Paris. It takes all of Anna's concentration not to smile. Here is my champion, she thinks to the bristling back view of the Brown Badge guide. And then she risks the briefest of smiles at Elizabeth across the way. But Elizabeth is Gloriana to her boot bows and does not respond. Apart from anything else, if she moved a muscle it would upset Miss Murdoch and Miss Murdoch, Elizabeth knows, is one of her greatest fans.

17

Brown Guide in the Ring

If Miss Murdoch recognises Flora she does not give a hint of it. Possibly this is something to do with the cherry red of her out-fit instead of the widow's black weeds of Paris. Flora is pleased. The little group gathers around Miss Murdoch and Flora reaches out and shakes her hand. 'Sorry we are a bit late – there was a queue for bag searching. And there are three of us instead of two.'

'No matter,' says Miss Murdoch graciously. She has not been paid for this little talk yet and her hirer does seem partic-ularly apologetic about the extra. 'Now – I gather,' she says to the assembled three, 'that you have a very particular reason for this little tour today – you have a very particular connection with the Princess of Cleves?'

They nod. Ewan gives Flora an encouraging look which Flora needs as she is still trying to get her head around Hilary's presence. She opens her mouth to begin but it is Hilary who says, 'Yes. My father discovered that she lived in our village. Our house is on the land where her manor used to be and he was writing a history of the village – before he died.'

They are all silent for a moment. Then Ewan says, 'There is also a dated stone of some kind that is obviously connected with her . . . .'

'My father discovered it,' says Hilary, proudly. 'It has the Cleves logo.'

Flora winces, apologises mentally to Joe Farrell for being forgotten and to Cleves for having been likened to Nike sports-wear. Flora says quickly, 'Anna of Cleves came to Hurcott from time to time after the divorce from Henry. Or at least, if she owned the manor we assume she visited it. It was certainly not recorded as being leased to anyone else.'

'But the stone is a mystery,' says Ewan. 'Dates all wrong. Made forty years after Anna of Cleves's death and no record of why. But one of us has been investigating.' He smiles at Flora and squeezes her elbow encouragingly. Until that moment Flora had no idea such a small joint contained so many nerve endings. 'Yes,' she says. Hilary nods enthusiastically. So far so good. No more standing beneath Edward's shadow. Flora will speak and she will take credit. With that decision made she takes a quick peek at Anna, half hidden by Miss Murdoch, and is pleased to see that she looks just the same. 'Shall we let our guide begin? It might be nice to know why the portrait was painted and why Anna of Cleves ended up living in England and owning Hurcott Manor and something about her life. We can save what I've got to say until later.'

The guide raises her hand. Such deference is no more than she expects. She suggests that they keep any questions they may have until she has finished her planned little talk. 'Let me have my say,' she says roguishly, 'Then you may have yours . . .' She looks at Flora and narrows her eyes slightly and a shadow of unease crosses her face. Living in the same place . . . Hmm – rings a bell. Flora gives her a big smile and hopes the cherry red will continue the camouflage. Miss Murdoch, shadow or no shadow, begins.

'First,' she says, 'though I know you want to crack on with the Cleves Queen, I think it would be sensible to set the scene.' She reads from the text in the catalogue and Flora relaxes.

'This is a small but interesting exhibition of portraits of those ladies of the sixteenth century connected to the Tudor Court, in particular King Henry VIII, after its break with Rome. It is an interesting example of the various forms and devices in which painters depicted sixteenth-century women of rank. The child Edward is included since his very existence is pivotal to the story of all these portraits . . . It is also a masterpiece . . .' Miss

Murdoch looks up. 'And in this exhibition –' she casts a swift little smile in the direction of the Ditchley Elizabeth – 'Masterpieces are rather thin on the ground.' Elizabeth rises to the occasion and Anna could swear she has grown an inch or two. She is certainly very different from the tense little girl, starved of praise, whom Anna took under her wing.

'Now,' continues Miss Murdoch, 'we will talk about the Cleves Queen – Henry's *bête noir* – quite soon but I think a little background information will be useful before we do . . .' And with that Miss Murdoch leads her little group of three away. 'You will see,' she calls over her sharp grey shoulder, 'how their histories intertwine as we progress.' Flora stays silent. She can wait. So can Anna. Miss Murdoch knows a lot of information and she wishes to show that she knows it. Let her. Ewan and Hilary are absolutely absorbed in what the woman is saying and so far there is nothing insulting in her facts. Anna's time will come. The four of them move from portrait to portrait, Miss Murdoch talking to her party as if they have no brains.

They pause at Marguerite of Valois (who, it should be said, has newly arrived from France, never been to England before, and is as surprised to be there as are Marie of Vendôme and Anne of Lorraine and the poor little Infanta) and Miss Murdoch explains that all three young French women were suggested as possible Queens for Henry VIII by Thomas Cromwell. The King suggested that his Keepers at Calais should assemble them there so that he could come and view them and was, apparently, surprised and astonished when the ladies said No. Flora found her jaw dropping when she first read about the suggestion. If ever the ego and the man were at odds it was over this – as if the French nobility would allow a capricious heretic to indulge himself in a beauty parade at their expense. It was a diplomatic death wish. 'Well,' says Miss Murdoch comfortably – 'the French wouldn't tolerate it and so they had to look elsewhere to fit the bill.'

Miss Murdoch passes on to her much preferred and more

familiar paintings of Marie of Guise and Christina of Denmark. Flora stares at Christina's dimpled smile and seemingly rustling silks. They have lit her well in this exhibition but it is the light within that is beautiful she decides, remove that and the girl herself is rather ordinary. Sixteen years old. The light within is youth and freedom and the celebration of it that Holbein has managed to paint into the shining eyes, the swirl of her mourning silks.

'I like that portrait so much,' says Flora. And then quickly adds, 'But I think I prefer his portrait of Anna.'

'As you will,' says Miss Murdoch. She is slightly, vaguely discomfited by the way Flora refers to the picture as *Anna* – there is a familiarity about it – and the word *sister* pops into her head. And then out of it again. She hurries on.

The group murmur as each story is told – Marie of Guise marrying Henry's nephew instead, Christina wishing she had but two necks. Hilary whispers to Flora, 'I thought this was going to be about Anne of Cleves and Hurcott? What's Dad's *History* got to do with any of this?'

'Patience, patience,' she whispers back, which is quite daring given Hilary's predilection towards huff. If Miss Murdoch looks cross at this whispering Flora is not afraid. 'We don't want to dwell on all the others here for too long,' she says good-naturedly. 'It is Anna of Cleves whom we have come to celebrate.'

Odd word, thinks Miss Murdoch. Out loud she says – in what she imagines is a tone of sweet irony – 'Patience, my girl.' Which makes Flora go pink with rage. This is unfortunate since it is not in the plan to be flushed. She seems to have done nothing today but change colour. The rage subsides but it leaves Flora feeling nervous. Soon she must speak out and, easy as it has seemed in the planning, the doing of it fills her, suddenly, with dread. She is, after all, only Flora. Hemingway's condemned hero might be able to spit on his way to the wall, Flora can barely swallow. It is good for me, coming out from under, she thinks, trying to believe it. Trying not to look too long at Hilary's excited eyes.

Miss Murdoch pauses at the Pourbus portrait of Isabella/Anne/Mary and says, 'Ah yes. The Boleyn Queen.' She peers closely at the paint as only an expert will do. Then she steps back. 'An excellent likeness,' she says. 'Excellent. And a fine painter, Pourbus,' she says, vaguely.

They reach the portrait of two-year-old Edward, Prince of Wales. Miss Murdoch says, 'It is a fine portrait, one of Holbein's best in which he exaggerates the boy's likeness to his father and uses copious red and the gold to represent enduring royal grandeur. It pleased his father enormously.' At which, and quite unannounced, Hilary lets out a howl of anguish. Flora immediately puts her arm around her daughter while feeling – oh dear – intense irritation *again*. Confusing emotions. Miss Murdoch's reaction is open-mouthed amazement. Ewan just stares at Hilary in astonishment – admiration almost – at the loudness of it. There is always one, thinks Miss Murdoch, there is always one – not quite as bad as this but I've had them eating rubber bands and singing 'Portrait of My Love' before now. But the girl's howl was remarkably loud and remarkably unselfconscious – a dimension beyond Miss Murdoch's usual experience. The guide gives her a penetrating look and sees that tears are coursing down the girl's cheeks. Inevitably where three or more are gathered together there is always a fruitcake in attendance for the specific purpose of driving everybody else nuts. Miss Murdoch goes, *tsk tsk*. It is as much as she dares while yet being unpaid. Fortunately the attendants who are deep in conversation about canteen matters, have noticed nothing.

Flora gives the whispered explanation concerning Hilary and the mention of a father, and keeps her arm around her daughter; Hilary's head is on her chest (dampening the cherry redness) and Flora pats her plaited head and says, 'There, there,' just as she always imagined she would over the years. Edward was better at it, of course, as he was better at everything else. 'Come to Daddy,' he would say, holding out his big, wide arms – and send Flora a look of triumph when the little toddler did. But Edward is not here now.

'Do you want to leave?' she whispers to the top of Hilary's head. 'No,' she says.

Flora gives her a tissue, and Hilary has a tremendously good blow, a trumpet of a blow. It makes Miss Murdoch jump which cheers Flora up. Ewan gives Hilary a tentative little pat on the arm. Hilary brings up her head from the tissue, gives it a little shake, juts out her chin as if to say I will go to my death head held high – pats her eyes and – strangely daughterly thing to do – hands the damp and screwed-up tissue back to Flora who takes it automatically and hides it in her cherry-red silk where it nestles against her own, rather sweet, lace hankie.

'Do go on,' says Flora firmly.

' . . . Enormously pleased,' repeats Miss Murdoch loudly and firmly. 'The King was enormously pleased with the portrait of his son as well he might be.' Just talk over the heads of the potty people, that was her motto. 'Holbein,' she adds with sickening roguishness. 'Well, Holbein *may* have felt that he had some balance to redress after painting Anne of Cleves in so flattering a manner . . . Hans Holbein died in relative obscurity in 1543 and despite this fine portrait he was never restored to quite the same favour as before.'

Miss Murdoch scents their excitement, feels their impatience – of course she does – it is part of a guide's delight to read her audience and reel them in and out at will – it is one of the perks of meeting people who are vastly more ignorant than you – even if they do have happy families and designer mackintoshes. Miss Murdoch lowers her voice slightly. 'And if we look at the portrait we can judge for ourselves if she was quite the beauty he made her out to be . . .' Miss Murdoch gives a little shiver as if a sudden chill – or draught it feels like – has run up her spine.

Flora keeps her arm around Hilary. It's quite a nice feeling. Another stepping stone, she thinks, though she is not entirely sure to where. She gives a little sideways look at Ewan. He looks perfectly happy and interested in it all. A family man without a family. How sad. Something they could have talked about in their long and fruitful lunch together – one of those romantic lunches that begin when the sun is shining and end at dusk . . . Sometimes having a family is not all it is cracked up to be. Flora gives a little sigh and decides to think positive – if she and Hilary have begun to get closer then it is not all disappointment. Not quite. Not *all*.

Anna watches and waits. Edward. It was in his reign that her fortunes changed. Richmond was taken away from her and she spent more time away from London. Hever she liked particularly. Its knot garden – over which it was said that Henry dallied in his courting of Anne Boleyn – was one of the sweetest in all England, and the county of Kent had good orchards and farming. It was no bad thing in those days to be far away from the court, far away from politics and religious persecution and the dreadful deaths of London and the cities. She was not quite so robust as the youthful princess who travelled so far and so cheerfully in the depth of winter to come to England – she was in her early thirties now and far less carefree – so the air and the peace of the countryside did her good. Hurcott and Bletchingley, nearer to London, were also havens, and Chelsea Manor with its riverside gardens and its benign ghosts of Thomas More and Katherine Parr. The past was her blueprint. Discretion, a quiet tongue, amenability, a hint, even, of not being very bright – all helped to keep her away from suspicion.

Somehow Anna always floated above the dangers of the times and she was the only family woman of rank considered safe for both Elizabeth and Mary to consort with. More, she was the only woman of rank who had a family connection with whom they both *wanted* to associate. With Anna both sisters found some kind of peace. It is perhaps this memory that makes them seem benign now. Aunt Anna was a friend to both sisters at a time when the one was for the Catholics and the other – Elizabeth – was favoured for Edward's Reforms.

What chance did either sister have for friendship? Dead mothers at odds, religion at odds, the connecting father dead, the brother a divider – at least Anna was neutral. Even pious Edward showed remarkable fondness for her in his own way and 'hoped his dear Aunt Anna should marry again . . .' That he chose Katherine Parr's widower for her held a certain piquancy. She declined most gracefully. As did Thomas Seymour – who had his eye – silly fool – on Elizabeth and the eventual throne. But young Elizabeth grew into a sensible, cautious girl and like her Aunt Anna, she kept her own counsel.

Difficult times for them all. Anna shivers remembering how her own servants were arrested for practising the wrong kind of religion. In other households of rank if such a thing were discovered the shadow of guilt would fall upon the mistress as well as the servants – but the accepted view of amenable, unremarkable Anna kept her safe so that in those dangerous years the only difficulties Anna suffered were domestic. Why, Sir Thomas Cawarden, who became her tenant and her steward at Bletchingly, caused her the most trouble of any man. He complained at almost everything she did. He complained about how much wood she cut for her fires, he complained that she caused the park-keeper's wife too much trouble and would not put it right, he complained that she used timber to build unnecessary outbuildings – in particular a brewhouse and an inn (how could these be considered unnecessary?) – and in his turn he was always late with the rent. Never once did he thank her for all the beautiful embroideries she placed there – all the elegant hangings – the pullin and fine needlework Anna and her ladies made – the German designs she made popular in England. So much for mocking her fashions – they were quick enough to take up their needles and follow her stitchery. Instead of complaining about her extravagance Cawarden might have thanked her, too, for the fine walnut furniture and the silk and satin bedhangings and the tapestries; for the well-ordered buttery and cellar and spicery, the starching house, the bakehouse, the brewhouse (he complained of the cost of her building it but he used it, of course) and the gaming rooms and music room – and more – which surely must have pleased him. And, Anna thinks, with some pride, would it be too much for this woman in grey to mention something about these achievements instead of always dwelling on her physical attributes, or lack of them? But Miss Murdoch is not one to consider such petty things. Facts and flamboyance, thinks Anna with contempt, that is her brief.

Certainly in the last years of her life it was not all ease. There were bouts of aches and inflammations as well as fevers and certainly some of her illness was exacerbated by the lack of money. She was not the world's best balancer of books, as her chamberlain grumbled, but she was too used to having wealth to change. I deserve it, she said to herself, and she still looks back and thinks that she did. If you survive what I survived, she thinks, then you deserve good things. And I did very well. Very well indeed. What use would my life be without my pleasures? I was a good woman and loved in my time, and who can say fairer than that, Anna asks herself. How very strong the urge is to reach out from the elaborate frame and tap Miss Murdoch on the shoulder and spit in her eye.

'We should really consider Jane Seymour now,' says Miss Murdoch, regretfully. 'And the portrait of Elizabeth – the Ditchley –' She looks at Flora with an interesting combination of *hauteur* and demand but Flora – apart from envying her the ability to combine two such emotions – says, 'We really would like to go back to the Anna of Cleves portrait now. It is time.' Hilary nods. Ewan is keen, too. His hands are at his sides and he is tapping his thighs in a gesture that Flora recognises as a thinking gesture – and she wonders what he is thinking. 'Penny for them?' she says, as she turns to follow Miss Murdoch towards Anna's portrait. Ewan goes a shade pinker and says – after a little pause – that he was sorry Dilly hadn't come with them after all. 'She'd have been fascinated,' he says, looking from picture to picture as they walk along. 'Just fascinated.

Bright girl, Dilly. Bright girl.' Flora does not – quite – like the affectionate way he says it. She dons her armour and mentally gives her brain a bit of a polish. I can be bright, too, she thinks.

Bright *and* Sober. It is time to impress.

They reach the portrait and Miss Murdoch's nose has a definite wrinkle about it. 'Here she is,' she says. Wrinkling a little more. 'So this is her,' says Ewan, and he puts his head on one side and stares. Anna stares back. Flora holds her breath. A friend meeting a friend. How will they react? She says firmly, 'Spend a little time just looking. Holbein painted the whole person in his portraits . . . so look for her there.' Obediently they all stare at Anna. Who stares back at them sweet as honey. Miss Murdoch taps the back of her hand and rattles her papers with impatience again.

'Such a pity Dilly isn't here,' says Ewan regretfully. 'Such a pity.'

'Concentrate, Ewan, please,' Flora says, trying not to sound tart. She adds, more kindly, 'You'll have to describe it to her. Though quite what she'll make of this being probate . . .'

'Ah,' he says, and nods sheepishly, leaning forward now and staring hard at the painted face as if his life depended on it. Gradually he begins to scrutinise each feature, each line of the head and the body, each hinted curve of a breast and dimple on a hand. Flora watches him. Eventually he steps back and nods and nods again – for the life of him, his expression says, he can find no hint of anything that might make you consider the lady to be comparable to a foreign horse. Good, thinks Flora, we have come a long way.

'Well, Flora,' he says, with pleasure, 'Anna *is* beautiful.' Her homely face makes its homely smile and they look from Anna to each other and back again affectionately.

'So now,' says Flora, 'Anna of Cleves. A much misjudged woman I should say and –'

Hilary interrupts, 'But what have all Dad's researches into this queen and her stone and Hurcott got to do with this?'

Flora takes a breath.

So, though she does not know it, does Anna. A stone? What stone? From whom? And why?

Hilary turns to Miss Murdoch and says, 'My mother put all of my father's notes and researches in order and from them we worked together on finding out about the stone. And it was all there, all the information. It just needed a bit of ironing out.' Ironing out? thinks Flora. All that midnight oil, all that getting under the skin – feeling my way – surmising, interpreting, understanding . . .

'Ah yes,' says Flora, 'I was coming to that.'

The guide taps her fingers again and her toe begins to twitch. 'Shall I begin?' she says.

'Oh,' Flora says gratefully, 'please do.' She steps back and fixes her very beady gaze on the Brown Guide's face, ready, willing and able to wade in. Miss Murdoch starts to tell Anna's story. 'As we have seen, Anne of Cleves was the last in a long line of possible brides for Henry VIII and his only marriage of foreign alliance. It was a disaster . . .' And on she goes.

Flora listens intently. Ewan and Hilary listen intently. One or two of the other visitors to the exhibition linger. It feels as if the whole room of portraits is also listening closely. And when Flora looks up she sees the portrait of Elizabeth on the opposite wall. It's fanciful, of course, but she cannot help thinking that there is also a light of interest about the Ditchley Queen's eyes. Or is it amusement? Or even pleasure? Flora stares up at her as Miss Murdoch rattles away. Their eyes meet, the painted and the real and Anna wonders what Elizabeth would say if she were alive and the story of the stone was revealed. Would she confirm, or deny it?

Flora returns to reality. Miss Murdoch has uttered the keynote words *Flanders* and *Mare*. Flora pulls herself together. She must put this right. She can almost feel Anna's humiliation. There is even a gathering crowd around them now, all looking at the Holbein portrait with interest. It may not be the whole world but it is a beginning. 'Oh, Miss Murdoch,' she says. 'Oh, Miss Murdoch – just a minute – if you please . . .'

Miss Murdoch was extremely glad *that* was over. She graciously, in her opinion, put up with Flora's constant interruptions 'to set the record straight' including one very long apologia for the German girl consisting of all kinds of proofs that she had a brain and wisdom and elegance and a capacity for fun and kindness – and goodness knows what else the girl didn't have according to Flora's paean – Miss Murdoch had to wonder why she had been asked there in the first place. And when she had her cheque safely in her hand she would say so. So humiliating it was. And much to the amusement and even delight of the gentleman of the party and the quite large crowd of people they had attracted by now. If she did not agree Mrs Chapman just butted in. Towards the end the blonde girl looked rather sullen about it all. And who could blame her? It was scarcely the behaviour of a newly widowed mother. Miss Murdoch thinks that when she finally does get her cheque she will be off as quick as quick. There is a very strange atmosphere here and Miss Murdoch does not like it at all. Nor does she like the heat and the chill that blows in on her every so often and seemingly from nowhere.

Hilary says to her mother, 'Well, that was all a bit embarrassing – the way you kept interrupting.'

'You should never be embarrassed by the truth, Hilary,' says Flora. 'You should stand fast by your principles.'

Ewan says in a quiet voice that he thought it was extremely interesting of her to know so much – and extremely brave. He says, 'Thoroughly entertaining, Flora, and wonderfully informative. How clever you are.'

Flora says, 'Bright girl?' And he nods.

Hilary says, 'Well, Ewan, I think we should give a lot of the credit to my dad. After all, he was extremely thorough and found it all out for us.' She turns to what is now a substantial audience. 'And now,' she says proudly, 'we are going to hear my father's historical detective work about Anna of Cleves's stone.'

Here we go, thinks Flora, and she looks from Anna to the portrait of Elizabeth. Deep breath.

Miss Murdoch turns to Flora and says waspishly, 'Would it be possible to have my cheque before you begin this part of it?'

And Flora says, very firmly, 'No.'

Ewan and Hilary move nearer. They look at her expectantly. 'The stone?'

'The stone,' says Flora, 'Ah yes. The Hurcott Ducis Stone.'

Miss Murdoch whispers again that if she could be given her cheque she would just like to go.

'Not until you have heard what I have to say,' says Flora, in a voice so commanding that even Hilary stops her sniffing and Ewan, without thinking, takes his hands out of his pockets and straightens his spine. Miss Murdoch definitely feels a strange hot breath on her back – first cold, then hot – it must be the heating duct. She bridles. But the fee is the fee and she must wait.

'And now we come at last to the fascinating, the moving, story of the Anna stone.' Flora pauses. She is just about to say that these are *her* ideas based on *her* extensive researches, and that she is pretty sure that *she* is correct in her surmising when the bright eyes of Hilary look at her with affection and encouragement. Flora falters.

'Go on,' says Hilary kindly. 'Go on.'

'*I*,' Flora tries to say, '*I*,' – she wants to say but no – she cannot do it. She looks at Ewan's enquiring, kind, ordinary face and she wants to claim what is hers – but those eyes of Hilary's . . . To have come so far, to have worked so hard, all that she has said so far, all that she still has to say, must she cede it? Her moment, her stepping out from the shadows, so much effort went into all this that she cannot, she cannot let Edward take the credit. But there are those eyes of Hilary's again and for the first time they look at Flora full of pride and with almost child-like expectation. Can she crush any flowering of affection now? And all for being thought a Bright Girl?

Eventually Hilary, reverting to type, gives a little nod of

impatience and Flora yields. 'As Edward stated, there is a stone set low down in an old wall on the land that once belonged to Hurcott Hall, which was owned by Anna of Cleves among others over the centuries. The stone bears the crest of Cleves – swans and a coronet and other symbols – unmistakably Anna's – very similar to some of the carvings on her tomb in Westminster Abbey, and it is carved with the date of her death. It is definitely there to mark Anna in some way but – unlike her tomb – it was made at least forty years after she was dead and buried. But why?' They all look from Flora to the portrait so that even if Anna wanted to react to this news, she can't. She holds her breath, which is not very hard for a portrait to do, and waits. A stone, with her dates on and her beloved swans and coronet? No one looks at Elizabeth but if they did they might – just – see the set of approval about her lips. They might.

'Well – it was our clever local solicitor – following on from Edward's initial researches –' Flora makes a flouncy gesture in Ewan's direction and he goes pleasantly pink,' . . . who recognised why the placing of the stone was so low. He pointed out that it would once have been considerably higher in whatever building housed it. That meant it was made to be seen, and that it had some kind of serious relevance. But what? A stone placed there forty years or more after Anna was dead and – one would guess – long forgotten – was a true mystery. But clever Hilary . . .' And here Hilary blushes with pleasure, '. . . checked with the calligraphic society in London and they confirmed that the style of the letters carved could not have been made before 1598 at the earliest – and probably a year or two later – the fashion, even in calligraphic carving, taking a little while to travel. The style of the fancy curls on the downward strokes and the fancy curves on the upward strokes were first used in Northern Italy no earlier than 1598 – and there is no record of them existing before then . . .' Flora draws breath and allows herself a Siddons pause. She had forgotten how enjoyable teaching was when you had something interesting to say and you weren't suffocating in a snowstorm of form filling.

Miss Murdoch steps forward a little and whispers to Flora that she is feeling most dreadfully hot, or cold, or something, and if that is all, she will leave now. If Flora would kindly give her the cheque? Flora says that she will not kindly give her the cheque and that she would – particularly – like Miss Murdoch to hear what she has to say. Miss Murdoch, pink-cheeked herself now and trembling slightly, her forehead quite shiny, retreats back to the Holbein portrait and there – so strange – is that heating duct again. It almost sounds as if it is purring.

Ewan smiles so warmly at Flora that she nearly reaches out and strokes his nice, kind face. But she remembers that Dilly is also a Bright Girl – and desists. 'Well – as Hilary's information made clear – it is also very unlikely, according to the society, that the script would have been used after 1603, when James I ascended the throne. The Stuarts were no fans of the Italianate and by the end of his first year as both King of England and Scotland the style had dropped out of favour entirely. So – we are left with a very short time span for the stone's creation. Probably five years in all. Which means that it must have been made during the last years of Elizabeth Tudor's reign. And I would suggest – given that the style had to get here from Italy – that it was in the very, *very* last years.'

Now they all swing their heads to look at Elizabeth's portrait. Out she gazes, haughty, glowing like a cold pearl, but her bright eyes seem to show a bit of fire about them. 'Ah, Elizabeth,' says Miss Murdoch, as if to a favoured child.

'So,' continues Flora quickly, 'it is clear that Anna of Cleves was remembered, quite suddenly, and quite remarkably, forty years after her death and funeral. Something reminded someone, and a someone of culture and wealth, about her. A someone who remembered which were her favourite homes. But who? And why?'

'Well,' says Miss Murdoch, in for a penny, 'it can only be Elizabeth herself. Everyone else who knew the woman would be dead.'

'Miss Murdoch,' says Flora, both relieved and amazed, 'I salute your logic. I agree. I think, in her very late years, Elizabeth had good cause to remember our quiet survivor and the places in which she was most happy.'

'So all this was there in Dad's papers, yes?' says Hilary, a little uncertainly.

Flora sighs and nods. 'Yes,' she says. 'Without Edward's efforts I would never have known where and how to look.'

Hilary folds her arms and looks about her with great, smug, smiling pride. Let her, thinks Flora sadly, for after all it is Dilly who is a very Bright Girl.'

'Go on, Mum,' says Hilary. 'It's exciting.'

And so, it seems, it is. The little group of three has been swelled to a couple of dozen and now they all stare hard at Anna's portrait. If Anna were to take a furtive look, which perhaps she does, she will need to control the corners of her mouth, for on the face of Elizabeth opposite where there was once only satisfaction and approval there is now an additional emotion – a touch of chagrin. After so long at the centre of the universe, it is hard for Elizabeth to be out of the limelight when there is a decent audience – even for someone she admires. And within her painted heart there is a struggle between the proud Tudor, and her common generosity. Her affection is such that she will bear it. What will be said must be said and this is, rightly, Anna's moment. Elizabeth, therefore, remains calm, despite her part in the story of the stone being a painful one.

If Mary Tudor – who eyes her sister covertly – expects (and she does) Elizabeth to stamp her foot the moment everyone turns away from her – a trait she has inherited from her father and which she continued in her own court – then Mary Tudor is astonished – and unusually touched – to see that she does not. Once again both of them declare peace for Anna's sake.

Flora continues. Despite her own loss of standing, she can still do her duty by Anna. 'Henry VIII's fourth wife was more loved by the people than any of Henry's queens except Catherine of Aragon. And there was good reason for it. She was, until the end of her days, a woman of great kindness, open affection, warmth and vitality. She bound together these two sisters who might otherwise have known very little love or affection.'

Hilary looks just a little bit softer.

'The one, when she was Queen Mary, buried Anna. The other, much later, and when she was Queen, marked her life with carved stones. Ours at Hurcott is one of these. Elizabeth's memorial. She might have become England's greatest Queen. But she had cause to remember how she was when she and Anna first met – a little rejected shrimp of a thing – and how Anna showed her how to behave in a difficult and dangerous world. A lesson, to her pain, that she forgot.'

Elizabeth goes even paler in her frame, if possible. No one has ever referred to her – not in her hearing most certainly – as a *shrimp*.

Mary hides a smile and Anna grasps her hands together over her neat little belly just a little bit tighter. Elizabeth will never – quite – be anything but Elizabeth.

Hilary and Ewan interrupt, saying in unison, 'But the stone? The stone?'

'Ah yes,' says Flora. 'I was coming to that'.

'Oh do get on with it Mum. Dad will be turning in his grave.' And she pushes a fresh tissue into her eyes. Flora, a little sadly, proceeds, wondering if Edward is up – or down – there and milking it. Behind her she hears, does she? A swishing noise like the trailing silks – and what might be an impatient snort were it possible – but when she turns there is nothing – only the shining, sharp-eyed portrait of Elizabeth and the darker, more sober painting of her sister, neither of whom seem the least bit moved by the drama unfolding before them.

'Well,' says Flora, 'I have already explained how discreetly and cleverly Anna behaved in the years following her divorce. How she recognised that the Tudor Court and its connections were riven by greed, ideology, ambition and sleaze . . .'

'No change there, then.' says Ewan.

Hilary manages a little snort of amusement.

Miss Murdoch's thin lips trace a smile.

Even Flora laughs.

'One false step, one false move and Anna could have the religious factions down on her, or the political factions down on her – or make any one of ten other dangerous enemies. In those years the example she set for both of her – much diminished – designated illegitimate – step-nieces – was exemplary. Indeed, she did more than an aunt for she did what a mother would do – she showed them how to behave in order to survive.'

Flora turns to Miss Murdoch and says, 'In art as in life, you should be aware that no book, nor any Internet site, nor any pundit on this earth can make up for using your own eyes and brain.' She flaps a hand at the catalogue which Miss Murdoch clutches to her side. 'Why, *I* look more like a Flanders Mare than Anna.' She pauses, arm out dramatically. Unfortunately no one leaps to her defence but at least the two Japanese of the additional party burst into spontaneous applause. Kind of them. Hilary turns to them and says very slowly and loudly, 'This is my father's work. He died recently and – well – he was brilliant.' She has bright, watering eyes again and has used up all her tissues. Flora reluctantly takes her handkerchief out of her pocket, her very pretty white and lacy one, which she fantasised about fluttering at Ewan over their lunch, and she hands it to Hilary. Flora imagined herself daintily dabbing at her nose – or perhaps her eyes if she could find something sad to share with him – or happy – or anything really – and its fluttering laciness would charm him with its utter femininity. It seemed altogether more seductive than twanging a stocking top which is what Rosie always recommended. You could bet he'd run a mile and anyway, Flora wore tights. There was something comfortingly all over about them. I am not a sex bomb, she thought sadly, and I never will be.

Hilary shows no regard for the little hankie's prettiness and takes it and uses it. 'Thanks, Mum,' she whispers. Flora is braced. All or nothing now. She turns to look at Anna once more and she decides that she really can see a slight, very slight, look of interest in her expression. How comforting. 'Well, too soon the King rejects Anna of Cleves, who has been so kind to them and so friendly and who is already loved by them. Mary and Elizabeth watch fearfully – both knowing how their father can behave. They have had six short months of normality – then everything is fear and anxiety again. Anna might be in danger, even mortal danger. Mary is not so anxious about Anna's mortality as Elizabeth who is anxious with good cause. Her knowledge of the fate of her mother bites deep. Both the little girl and the young woman, the Tudor daughters – both fearful in their own way – wait to see what happens.

'Well – does Anna let them down? Does she call on her brother to come to fight and defend her and let factions wreak their worst – does she do anything either aggressive or provocative? Does she scream and shout and call upon the heavens in her name – does she even – understandable and for-givable as it might have been – bemoan and defame their father? She does not. She knows very well how to conduct her-self. And she knows that those girls love their father despite all. So instead she professes herself sad but willing if it must be – to lose such a husband. She is amenable, docile, giving, digni-fied, royal. Which suits everybody. Including her. No one is injured, in particular not the daughters of the King who can remain her friends.

'How Anna of Cleves behaves in this period becomes a great lesson for Elizabeth in later years. Even to the meeting between Anna and her replacement, Queen Catherine Howard. Even Chapuys, the Emperor's ambassador and no friend of Cleves at all, describes it with admiration thus: "The lady entered the room as if she were the most insignificant damsel about court, all the time addressing the Queen on her knees, notwithstand-ing the prayers and entreaties of the latter, who received her most kindly, showing her great favour and courtesy." We know that Henry was both relieved and charmed by such a display. And this modest, acquiescent behaviour from a woman wronged almost beyond endurance . . . Is this cleverness? Or is it stupidity? Is this the behaviour of a thick-skinned dullard or the behaviour of a highly intelligent woman who wishes to survive well? I think you know the answer and I think Elizabeth certainly did. After this moment, which so many must have wished would go badly wrong, Anna was safe. Clever? Or foolish? Which?'

They chuckle. Even Hilary chuckles. There is no question that they consider Anna anything but stupid. Miss Murdoch feels that strange sense of warmth on her back again and breaks out into a further sweat. She takes a covert look but can see nothing. It must be a very, very hidden heating duct.

'Pragmatism, dignity, modesty, wisdom – these were good lessons that carried Elizabeth through the years of being under suspicion from Mary for plotting against her. Just as Anna went to court and bowed the head and bent the knee, and was seen to do so, so did Elizabeth go dutifully to Mass, and bend the knee to her Catholic sister, so that no one could declare her heretic. Principles or pragmatism? Both if you believe what is in your heart is the truth.

'It is, I think, no coincidence that both Anna when she was finally safe and free, and Elizabeth when she was safe and free and reigning Queen, were remarked for their spectacular dresses. It was their bravado – a celebration of femininity. Only the weak or oppressed comply to a standard that is not their own in their clothing.' Here Flora smoothed the skirt of her cherry-red gown with its silly ruffles making nonsense of her knees and smiles.

Hilary says – rather weakly – which is understandable, 'Did my father write all that?'

'Not all, my love,' says Flora. 'Not *quite* all.'

Well, Edward might be strutting his stuff somewhere, but he was not here and Flora was and even if Hilary was looking a little constrained, still she was *listening to her mother*. With a certain amount of respect. And that was something. At least

Flora knew it was all her own work and that would have to do.

Miss Murdoch shuffles and looks yearningly at the exit but she has to stay. If only they would turn the heating down, she thinks, for she has never known it to be so hot in an exhibition. Surely it can't be good for the paintings? And so she waits, a little bit shinier in the forehead, a little bit damper under the arms. It is uncomfortable. Inadvertently Flora has learned another great truth – that she who holds the purse strings wields the power. 'Do please hurry up,' says Miss Murdoch. 'I have my train to catch.'

But the crowd now assembled says, *Ssh!*

'There was a time when Elizabeth forgot this lesson. When wisdom, dignity, pragmatism went out of the window, and a destructive madness entered in its place. It was the nadir of Elizabeth's personal history – in the very last year of her reign – and it was after that – I am certain – she commissioned the Hurcott Ducis stone. And others for other places, too. She turned and gestured towards the portrait of Elizabeth. 'I think it quite likely – since Hurcott Ducis was not particularly important – that Elizabeth also had memorial stones for Anna placed in each of the houses and palaces she once owned – most of which have been destroyed, or extensively rebuilt – places like Hever Castle, Richmond Palace, Bletchingley, Dartford, Penshurst, Chelsea – the changes of time will have lost them – or they were incorporated in other buildings to be found and wondered over, as we found and wondered over this one. Elizabeth – who loved all things Italianate despite her contempt for the Pope – ordered them to be carved and placed as homage. Suddenly Elizabeth had good reason to remember her stepmother and step-aunt Anna of Cleves.'

Then Ewan laughed, easing the tension. 'Flora,' he said, 'cut to the chase, will you? Why?'

And she laughed back, delighted. Who cared about her own reputation when she could polish Anna's? 'Well the fact of the matter is,' she said, in a sudden rush, 'that towards the very end of her reign Elizabeth behaved extremely stupidly for one so intelligent. She ignored the lessons of her youth, ignored her brilliant adviser Cecil and her council. She became self-indulgent, careless of the times, and deaf to reason. It nearly cost her both her life and her throne. Elizabeth became a fool for love.'

It is a brave woman who takes on a Tudor monarch even if it is a painted image and five hundred years on from her living self. Flora dares not look at the Ditchley as she adds this last for – true though she is sure it is – this is harsh criticism for this proud queen. She is about to continue when a voice interrupts and just for a dreadful moment Flora thinks the Ditchley has come to life – but it is not imperious Elizabeth, it is imperious Miss Murdoch. 'I'm sorry', she says, 'But this really is the wildest speculation. Utterly suspect, I'm afraid. I really am not convinced by any of it. Not at all.'

'I can tell you that my father would never put his name to anything suspect,' says Hilary, going pink as she steps forward. 'He was a scholar and knew more, I think, than you will ever know.'

Miss Murdoch, slightly anxious about the possibility of another wail and gout of tears, gives in and unbends. 'Well,' she says, 'Possibly it could be so. Though Elizabeth was Gloriana to her dying day.'

Flora wants to cheer. Who cares whose tale this is? Because really it is only Anna's and Elizabeth's.

'No, Miss Murdoch, Elizabeth very much was *not*. If you have done your research correctly . . .' And here Flora pauses to let the shaft sink through that iron grey suiting which it does, leaving Miss Murdoch blinking evilly. 'In those last years of her reign, when she was damn near seventy – she – foolishly – dangerously – fell in love with an ambitious, ruthless, headstrong young man whom she indulged beyond sanity, and whom she allowed herself to pretend was in love with her. There is a poem published in 1599 which was accorded to Shakespeare but which it is now known was written by Richard Barnfield. You'll know it, Miss Murdoch.' Miss

Murdoch acknowledges, with a stiff little movement of her head, that she does. '"Crabbed Age and Youth cannot live together . . ." Barnfield was known to favour panegyrics and particularly panegyrics that were a mixture of eulogy and criticism. His panegyric "Cynthia" was already addressed to Elizabeth and it is highly likely that "Crabbed Age and Youth" was written in the same vein. The whole of England knew about Elizabeth's foolishness with this young hothead Earl, and the poets and the playwrights were the chroniclers of the age. The date of the poem certainly fits – 1599 . . .'

'But fits, Mrs Chapman, with what?'

'With the date of Elizabeth's great trouble – and with the date of Anna's stone.'

'What exactly was this great trouble?' asks Ewan, gently.

'Essex plotted to take the throne and make Elizabeth his prisoner . . . Possibly to kill her.'

Flora pauses for effect and while she does so Mary, quiet on the wall, cannot, just cannot, resist taking a peek at her sister – and she sees suffering in Elizabeth's eyes now, a suffering that Mary knows well. Perhaps they were not so temperamentally unalike after all?

'The Earl of Essex believed he could take Elizabeth's throne and be loved more than her, for his braveness, his wit, his youth. He really believed the country wanted him more than Good Queen Bess. He attempted a coup and it failed.'

Now she has all of their attention. They are as still as the portraits. Miss Murdoch is relieved to find the temperature has gone back to nearly normal.

'Well, go on,' says Hilary. 'Don't stop now.'

So Flora smiles, and does so. 'Robert Devereux, Earl of Essex, nearly undid all the good of Elizabeth's reign, nearly lost her the respect and reputation of the entire Tudor Dynasty. And all because she abandoned wisdom and discretion. The dates of Devereux's betrayal coincide almost exactly with the dates of the Italianate lettering on the stone. The stone itself is made from the finest Italian marble and the lettering is beautifully crafted by a Master – it is, according to experts, unlikely to have been made by a local craftsman – and so it must represent something truly expensive – and profound. It also contains the symbol of the swans – something not accorded Anna's great tomb in Westminster. There was a romantic legend of the founder of the ducal dynasty, an eleventh-century knight who was first brought to Cleves by a boat guided by swans, so whoever commissioned the carving knew this tale and knew Anna of Cleves and her family armorial very well. It is the kind of tale Anna might have told to a child . . . And this is what I think happened . . .'

'Can you speak up,' says an eager voice from the back. And lo – it is one of the attendants. If she had time to think about it Flora's cup of happiness would probably overflow.

'After the danger was past and she was safe and Essex in the Tower Elizabeth went to Richmond Palace – a place where she had been happy – a place where – as a child – she had stayed with Anna. And she brooded on her foolishness for days, locked into her rooms. To choose Richmond was certainly significant. In old age one's mind wanders to the past for guidance and comfort. She would, of course, remember the days of Anna's ownership. And Anna was quite likely to tell her stories. Of knights and swans and all. I am sure that the date of the placing of the stones was 1601 – the year that Essex was executed. In those last years Elizabeth spent most of her time at Richmond Palace and the memory of Anna's kindness and good sense cannot have been far from her mind. The stones, I'm convinced, were made as private marks of respect – finally – for the Daughter of Cleves . . . whose funeral she did not, could not, mark nor attend, being held prisoner at Woodstock by her sister. It was Mary who buried Anna, Mary who remembered her with honour and placed her by the High Altar at the Abbey. Mary who did not include the romance of the swans. Elizabeth's memorial stones were her own, personal and final marking of this extraordinary woman.'

Flora found herself suddenly very close to tears and fumbling for her hankie –which was already damp and still held by Hilary. Hilary dabbed at her own eyes and handed the poor wet item back to Flora. For a moment Anna was Flora, Flora was Anna and their tears and Hilary's tears all mixed together. It seemed oddly appropriate. Hilary, who was looking a bit pink and watery again, took the hankie back. Ewan had a very bright-eyed look about him. Flora swallowed hard, sniffed, touched the edges of her eyes with her fingertips, and continued. 'Those of us who have fallen under the spell of someone dashing and exciting and then found them wanting will understand a little of what Elizabeth felt but it is not the purlieu of a dutiful prince when there is duty to be performed. Anna did her duty. Elizabeth forgot – for a dangerous moment – to do hers.'

'I think there can be no other explanation – the dates match, the quality suggests someone noble paying for the materials and carving, and someone very much aware of artistic fashion – and forgive me –' She looked downwards with a bashful smile, 'but then as now – I hardly think we of Hurcott Ducis, if faced with the same idea, would be able to say what the fashion in memorial materials and calligraphy might be . . .?'

Ewan shuffled and smiled a bit.

'Oh, I think my father would,' said Hilary.

Which brought Flora firmly back to earth again. She made one more dab at her eyes, and went on. 'Perhaps the ritual of having those stones made and placed helped Elizabeth in her darkest time – as some kind of retribution. I think they were placed discreetly because Elizabeth was not one, nor ever had been, to exalt another publicly (being so fragile inside herself) – apart from her father. They were Elizabeth's private testimonial to Anna and our stone, in little Hurcott Ducis, is perhaps the only surviving reminder of that bond and late recognition.'

Flora then gives a bow and has a sudden regret that Edward is not here, after all, to see her performance. Perhaps, after all, he is. It certainly feels, in quite a nice way, that Flora is being watched.

'Is that it?' asks Miss Murdoch, looking fearfully in Hilary's direction. Hilary is building up again.

'Not quite,' says Hilary, who steps forward with pink nostrils and pinkly wet cheeks so that she and Flora make something of a handsome *Pieta* – minus the body.

Hilary says, 'That stone – which my father found and researched so eruditely – is now *his* eternal memorial in the old wall of Hurcott Ducis, which he so loved and which so loved him.'

Oh no, thinks Flora. That really is too, too much. She is about to object, to give the moment – and the stone – back to Anna – when she feels that Louvre warmth again – like a breath on her back. She turns but there is only Anna's portrait. Anna looks resolute. Flora feels it. Oh let it go, she decides, let it go. Flora gives Hilary a kiss instead of speaking out, and that is that. 'Clever old Edward,' she says, to no one in particular.

Ewan and Hilary both nod.

Miss Murdoch stares up at Anna's portrait for a minute. And then looks at Flora. 'Perhaps,' she says, 'you are right. My cheque?'

Flora hands her the envelope and as she walks away she says, 'It's a very good story.'

'I'll send it to you,' calls Flora.

'Do.' And with that the Murdoch is gone.

Flora is certain that the story is too good for even Miss Murdoch to resist. Use it she will. There will be no more Flanders Mare.

'Lunch,' says Ewan.

'Shame about Dilly not joining us,' says Flora sadly, 'Such a bright girl.'

'Yes,' he says. But he looks at Flora wonderingly. A vague light of truth hovers around his brain – 'And so are you, Flora,' he says with absolute conviction. 'And so are you.'

Never, thinks Flora, take anything at face value from a woman who has studied Anna of Cleves.

She watches Ewan walking ahead. Such a nice, ordinary

man, she thinks. And still in love with his wife. That is suddenly very, very obvious. Bright bloody girl. She sighs. That is love, that is. She must, she decides, be the only woman in the world without an edge to fight. She sighs again. Hilary – usefully – mistakes the sigh and links her arm with Flora's as they walk away. Is that enough? It ought to be. But Flora looks about her as they walk past the portraits and she can't help but envy them. Even Anna made her mark in time. Now she never will. Even with the *History of Hurcott* it will be Edward's name, not hers, embossed on the cover.

As they leave she turns and takes one final look at Anna but the portrait is hidden by a horseshoe crowd of interested spectators. That, at least, is something. A small legacy from her to the most remarkable Anna. And out they go.

Later, as they collect their coats from the cloakroom she looks at herself in the mirror – not a pretty sight – and the cherry red reflects on her cherry-red cheeks and cherry-red eye-whites. She steps back, grimaces and thinks yet again that if Mankind cannot take too much reality – she has just proved to herself that Womankind bloody well has to.

And does.

At which point Hilary emerges from her cubicle to find her mother vigorously washing her hands.

'Do you want your hankie back?' she asks and holds out the damp, creased, ball of a thing. Flora looks sadly at its scrumpled lace for a moment and then says brightly, above the handdryer's roar. 'No – you keep it. That's fine.'

18

Three Queens United

My funeral, thinks Anna cheerfully, was a triumph. Mary, a Queen then and my friend, gave me pride of place to the right of the altar in Westminster Abbey. A vast, expensive shelf of marble it was, with the chamber below covered with carvings and ornate decoration and inlay and semi-precious stones. A tomb monument fit for a Queen. Mary arranged for a craftsman from Cleves to make the carvings but to her design and 'In a place fit,' she said, 'for a noble Queen'. My horses and bearers were dressed in purple and gold and I had gold and purple hangings and rich velvets to hide my coffin which was set inside the tomb.

I lived and died a Catholic. I was buried in marvellous pomp with as much finery as at my marriage. And I was mourned. My Ladies – few enough by then since my great wealth had gone – wept, my menservants broke their staves and I was laid to rest – as I had lived in my adopted country – with love and admiration – and tears of genuine sorrow. How much I had seen – and how much I lived through – and made good – and survived. It was too soon for me to die – I was only forty and still enjoying dancing and gaming and music and living well – too well perhaps?I died at Chelsea (a sweet place, with flowers and good gardens and I loved it) in the month of July. I had made my will and I died a good death.

In my will I remembered both Mary and Elizabeth (poor Elizabeth for whom there was nothing to be done and who was under close guard for fear of uprisings and who could not be there at my end even had she asked it) and I am glad to say that the will was executed by Queen Mary in proper manner, including the second best ring bequeathed to Elizabeth. I am glad now that I remembered her as she remembered me, it seems. Even in death I could unite those two irreconcilable sisters in a good and peaceful act. All in all I had a good life, and a fine burial. And those who wish can see my place of rest in the Abbey, though it is no tomb of grandeur now, and those who wish can also see me to the life in Holbein's true portraits. Despite what they have said of me his portrait and his miniature are – very lively. And in them I live on.

Once the gallery is closed Mary turns towards Elizabeth. This is not something she relishes, but speak she must. 'I should,' she says, 'have allowed you to be at Aunt Anna's funeral. I should have let you participate and have a role, and make a public sign of your mourning. That would have been fitting and I did not do it and for that I apologise to you both.'

Elizabeth looks amazed for a moment, as well she might. She is also lost for words. But she is Henry's daughter and raises her chin, looks back at her sister and eventually manages to say, quite evenly, 'Yes, so you should. But I accept it was a difficult time for you – you were unwell.'

'No,' says Mary. 'Before God I cannot claim that as excuse. I was afraid of the people seeing you and loving you more than me. And I am ashamed of that now.'

Both women go back to their proper portrait poses but it has been said, and it has been accepted.

Then Anna looks towards Elizabeth. She says, 'I am touched that you made me such noble memorials, Elizabeth. And that you remembered my swans.'

But then Mary says, in a voice softer than she has ever used to address her sister, 'As am I. This has been a revelation, Elizabeth, a revelation. I did not think you had such good grace in you. It makes me happy to know it.'

Elizabeth bridles slightly but says evenly enough. 'It was for Aunt Anna. And to thank her for her kindness to us both in those dark times of our youth.'

'A little late,' says Mary, in the way of elder sisters. 'But a happy outcome from your wilful adversity.'

The bridling increases. There is a swirl of silk and a sliding of feet and Elizabeth, trembling slightly, resumes her correct position within the Ditchley. Feet firmly on Protestant England. She looks out again, eyes blazing, and Anna puts up a restraining hand. Elizabeth, about to speak, if not spit out her words – stops herself. When she does speak it is in a considered way, as a queen. 'You, Mary, may be as happy as you choose. But the mettle was in me, always in me. My father's daughter. And you were your vindictive mother's.'

'And you, Elizabeth, may have had the mettle of your father in you – but it was your mother who proved that in the last years of your life – you were yours.'

Elizabeth is no longer white. There are high spots of colour on her glistening cheeks. Her eyes blaze, but she says nothing. Anna looks at her calmly and still she says nothing. But Mary is now in full flight. 'I was happy in my tomb in Peterborough so why, I would ask, did you take me from the quiet of my mother's resting place, and my own, and bring me to London to be re-interred so near to you? Why set me in the Abbey that once so despised my mother and myself? Why, Elizabeth, did you put me into the very *bed* of the tomb with you so that we spend the rest of our days lying with each other when we never did so in life? And my mother alone again?'

Elizabeth, still looking into Anna's calming eyes, says, 'Because it seemed right.'

'Or you were superstitious about your religious iniquities.'

Anna sighs. That is too much. Too much.

After this a terrible silence descends.

Both portraits resume their places.

Anna's restraining hand falls back into its pose of restful resignation. Oh those Tudors, she thinks. Oh those insufferable, proud, wonderfully passionate Tudors. But just for a moment they were reconciled. And that, thinks Anna warmly, is the best she can do. It always was.

19

Also Reconciled

Back in Hurcott Ducis and after several weeks of kicking several metaphorical cats, Flora has come to her senses. She decides that there is, indeed, one way of living for those who have beauty, and one way of living for those who have not, and that, on the whole, brains do not always seem to come into it for a woman – yet, if ever. The response to brains and plainness is, to say the least, still mixed, most certainly in this age of botox and celebrity.

Beautiful Dilly, as Venus-given right, still does extraordinarily embarrassing things up and down the village, and Ewan continues to mop them up. It is called true love, or it is called blind love, Flora sees, and it is not likely ever to be hers. Not with even the most ordinary of men, like Ewan, or the most extraordinary, like Edward. She will remain undiscovered.

On the other hand, there is much to be said for the peacefulness of it all, she supposes, and now that time has moved on and she no longer has to play the grieving widow, she can get on with what remains of her life with as much pleasure as she can make of it. Remembering Anna and her sports and her simple happinesses, Flora wonders if she shouldn't build a tennis court on part of the paddock (if she can get permission – she knows a good solicitor, after all) and then at least she can play with Ewan in one way, if not in another. She is certainly not going to take up golf. That is an amenable step too far. But a tennis court is possible. It is early days in her new-found affection from Hilary – very early days. Right now a tennis court might be too much levity for her daughter to accept.

They are still in negotiations about Edward's gravestone and Flora and Ewan have only just persuaded Hilary that they cannot wrest Anna's stone from its place and put it at the head of Edward's grave. Flora has suggested that the description Great British Eccentric covered the man who was Edward. And Hilary might agree. 'Great British Eccentric' fits the bill. Perfectly. The village likes it, too. Anna will stay where she is best remembered as the – now famous – Hurcott Ducis stone. At least Flora has achieved a little fame, very little, and a particle of admiration for herself. And that must be compensation enough. Despite Hilary's best efforts, much of the praise is given to Flora for all her research, though *The History of Hurcott Ducis and Its Stone* is largely attributed to Edward Chapman, naturally, and the lettering, embossed on the cover, is in the same Italianate script of Anna's stone. It was the final surrender to keep Hilary happy. The stone will remain in the wall and has a glass shield over it and a dear little fence of wrought-iron railings surrounding it, thanks to The Players' fundraising. Flora can walk over and see it at any time, and frequently does so.

And the little Pink Pike? Well, poor Pauline could not believe, simply could not believe, that she had failed to be invited to join the theatrical group – but so it was. She left the village a broken woman. Well, broken-ish. But of course she may be in a village near you. And recovering fast.

After *She Stoops to Conquer*, which Flora avoided for some reason, most likely the title, she went to see the first fundraising production. They chose the The *Voysey Inheritance* by Harley Granville Barker, which was long and tedious in her opinion, but which looked wonderful with splendid, richly furnished sets and the women in fine – quite anachronistic frocks – swirling about (Myra did not trip up once). Flora, sitting in the stalls, looked around before the curtain went up on the Voyseys with satisfaction – not a Little Pink Pike in sight.

What was in sight, however, as the curtain rose on a perfectly furnished Edwardian office, were Flora's eyebrows. For now she knows why Lucy walked away with so much of her home and wardrobe – there is Edward's old desk, there is her curved hatstand that someone has mended, and there – good grief, is her old wicker wastepaper basket. Later she gasps again to see Edward's plus-fours on Ewan's – quite shapely – legs. Lucy is their props person, it seems, having obviously proved herself exceptionally good at it. Sometimes there is an answer to life's difficulties and sometimes there is not. This is a good one. But Flora does not offer Lucy her job back. She wouldn't want it anyway – she is busy preparing the Dobsons' cottage for their imminent return. She will clean for them now, and good luck to her, thinks Flora. When Mary returns life will be as it always was.

Normal.

'What you need,' Rosie says, when she finally comes to visit her bereaved sister, 'is a man in your life.' Rosie has taken a good look about the village and says, finally, that there is only one man who comes anywhere near being possible for Flora. Giles Baldwin. Which makes Flora laugh so much that she spills a precious drop or two of Edward's prized Margaux. Perhaps Rosie isn't so clever after all, thinks Flora. But she keeps what she knows to herself.

'Don't laugh,' says Rosie. 'All you need is a little more time.' She gives her sister a knowing wink which makes Flora giggle again. 'See,' says Rosie, 'you're beginning to get over it already. All you need is a little more courage, that's all. A little more courage to have a go at things and we'll make something out of you yet.'

'Thank you, Rosie,' says Flora, most amenably. 'I'll look forward to that.'

Some time later, in the name of courage, Flora hired a balloon trip for herself. The person accompanying her on the balloon trip was fully cognisant of balloon procedure and never once, as they rose up and down over hill and dale, was there any danger of Flora following her husband into oblivion. She shed a few tears for him, of course she did, and smiled occasionally to think of all his many foolishnesses. She was glad to do so, very glad. But it was time to sail on. When the balloon reached a particularly dense thicket of woodland below, Flora waited until the balloon expert's back was turned, and threw something out of the basket. It went spiralling downwards rather prettily in the cool, blue air, its fluttering streamer crackling in the breeze.

Some weeks later a gamekeeper passing through Hopes Wood picked up all that remained of a video which was much pecked at by his perplexed pheasants. Being a tidy-minded chap he took it home with him and put it on the bonfire, for it was too spoiled to be viewed. Probably pornography, he thought regretfully, and watched it melt and burn. Probably pornography.

In Paris they lovingly unwrap the Holbein portrait and rehang her between the portraits of those two rather attractive sixteenth-century young men. Not a bad bit of positioning, she thinks amenably, for a dull-witted Flanders Mare. The attendant stands in front of her, his head on one side as if seeing her for the first time. 'There's been a lot of interest in you, just recently,' he says, 'so it's good that you are back. In fact, there has been so much interest in you that there is talk – only talk at this stage mind – that you may even be cleaned now. Then we'll see what you're really like beneath those years of neglect.'

Acknowledgements

There are always many kind and helpful people involved in the writing and editing of a book but especial thanks and acknowledgements must be made to those who added the light to the dimness of the daily routine of getting it done.

They are Jane Roberts who gave up her time to show me the Holbeins at Windsor Castle Library which was an exhilarating and inspirational experience. Carol Austin, also at Windsor, who then showed me some of the precious papers and artefacts kept there. Angela Scholar who also gave up her time to show me the Anna of Cleves portrait by Barthel Bruyn in St John's College, Oxford, which was both very kind of her and extremely helpful. Lisa Kopper of Acton Court who showed me that building's original Tudor wing and helped me get a sense of period architectural space. And dear John Guinness who kindly threw open his private archive for me and whose Norfolk home has better chimneys than Hampton Court's and echoes the sound of Tudor footsteps if you listen hard enough.

Of the many helpful books consulted I must single out Mary Saaler's *Anne of Cleves* (The Rubicon Press) which was marvellously detailed and a great guide for this book. Many, many thanks to her.

Bibliography

Barnes, Margaret Campbell, *My Lady of Cleves*, 1976,
  Macdonald and Jane's, London
Beier, A. L., *The Problem of the Poor in Tudor and Early
  Stuart England*, 1983, Methuen, London
Cloake, John, *Richmond Past*, 1991, Historical Publications
  Ltd, London
Denny, Joanna, *Katherine Howard: A Tudor Conspiracy*,
  2005, Portrait, London
Dunn, Jane, *Elizabeth and Mary: Cousins, Rivals, Queens*,
  2003, HarperCollins, London
Fraser, Antonia, *The Six Wives of Henry VIII*, 1992,
  Weidenfeld & Nicolson, London
Hamilton, Julia, *Anne of Cleves*, 1972, Sphere Books,
  London
Mauritshuis Royal Picture Gallery, *Catalogue of Royal
  Cabinet of Paintings: Hans Holbein the Younger*, The
  Hague, Netherlands
Norris, N. E. S., *A Visitor's Guide to the Anne of Cleves
  House Museum*, 6th ed., rev., 1970, Sussex Archaeological
  Society, Lewes
Roberts, Jane, *Holbein and the Court of Henry VIII*, 1993,
  National Galleries of Scotland, Edinburgh
Saaler, Mary, *Anne of Cleves*, 1995, Rubicon Press, London
Scarisbrick, J. J., *Henry VIII*, 1971, Penguin Books, London
Sim, Alison, *Food and Feast in Tudor England*, 1997, Sutton
  Publishing, Stroud
Starkey, David, *Six Wives: The Queens of Henry VIII*, new

ed., 2004, Vintage, London

—, *Monarchy: from the Middle Ages to Modernity*, 2006, HarperPress, London

Weir, Alison, *Children of England: The Heirs of King Henry VIII*, 1996, Jonathan Cape, London

—, *Henry VIII: King and Court*, 2001, Jonathan Cape, London

—, *The Six Wives of Henry VIII*, 1992, Pimlico, London

Wilson, Derek, *Hans Holbein: Portrait of an Unknown Man*, 1996, Weidenfeld & Nicolson, London

Woodward, G. W. O., *Queen Elizabeth I*, 1967, Pitkin Guides, London